The clamor of the guarding gates of the Keep redoubled. The blows of the massed hordes of the Dark merged into one continuous assault, roaring like an ear-splitting cannonade.

In the white circle of magelight stood Ingold and Gil, wizard and warrior, their hands joined on the wood of the staff that glowed with the witchlight of Ingold's magic. Then Ingold turned and mounted the steps, moving down the narrow tunnel until he reached the end. He put out his hands, touching the shaking steel of the outer gates.

Only those inches of metal separated him from the wild blood-hunger and the horror that was the Dark—separated this small remnant of humanity from the spawn of ancient, haunting evil.

Ingold's witchlight was flickering . . .
. . . fading . . .

By Barbara Hambly
Published by Ballantine Books:

THE DARWATH TRILOGY

The Time of the Dark

The Walls of Air

The Armies of Daylight

The Walls Of Air

Barbara Hambly

A Del Rey Book

BALLANTINE BOOKS • NEW YORK

A Del Rey Book
Published by Ballantine Books

Library of Congress Catalog Card Number: 82-90865

ISBN 0-345-29670-2

Manufactured in the United States of America

First Edition: March 1983
Third Printing: October 1983

Cover art by David B. Mattingly

The Reaches of the Dark

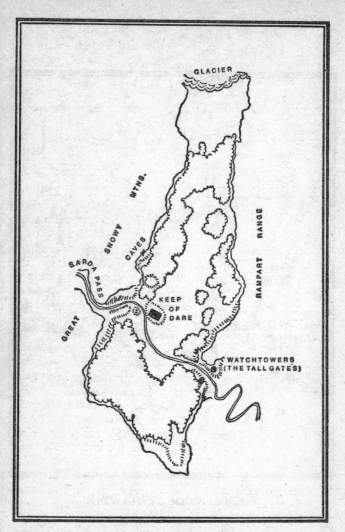

The Vale of Renweth

PROLOGUE

Gil Patterson thought her vision of the strange city was all a dream—until the wizard Ingold Inglorion appeared one night in her kitchen, seeking a place to bring the infant Prince of Dare from the ancient horror that was attacking the city of Gae.

Rudy Solis didn't believe in wizards and magic—even when he saw Ingold emerge, with an infant in his arms, beside the place where Rudy had stopped to fix his car.

But when one of the monstrous, evil Dark crossed the Void in Ingold's wake, their only escape was back with the wizard to the embattled world from which he had fled.

It was a world where magic worked within a logic of its own. And it was a world where the loathsome Dark were again ravening, after they had lain almost forgotten in underground lairs for three thousands years. Gae had fallen, and the city of Karst was jammed with refugees. The King was dead, and proud, ambitious Alwir was now Regent for the infant Prince Tir, as brother to the young Queen Minalde—or Alde, as most called her.

Then the Dark struck in massive numbers at Karst. In the fighting, Gil discovered that even a graduate student of history could become a warrior. And Rudy found himself aiding the young Queen to save her child again from the Dark.

At Ingold's urging, those who were left began the long, agonizing march toward the Keep of Renweth through trails choked with snow and buffeted by mountain winds. During that flight, dissension among the leaders was as much a danger as the trailing Dark and the White Raiders, who were coming from the plains to loot. Alwir and the fanatic lady Govannin, Bishop of the Church, were en-

1

gaged in a struggle for power. And both feared Ingold—the Bishop because all wizardry was evil in her Faith.

To Gil and Rudy, unused to the hardships of freezing cold and day-after-day marching, the trip was hard. But Gil found herself accepted as one of the Guards, the elite fighting force of Gae. And Rudy found that Alde returned his love. His joy in this was equaled only by his discovery that he could call up fire—and by Ingold's promise to teach him to be a wizard.

In the end, through the efforts of Ingold, some eight thousand people reached the monstrous, black Keep, built three thousand years before by wizardry as a defense against the previous scourge of the Dark. There, in its vast chaos of deserted aisles and chambers, they could make themselves a refuge for a time, though the perils before them were many and terrible.

Yet somehow Gil and Rudy discovered that they no longer had any desire to return across the Void to their own world.

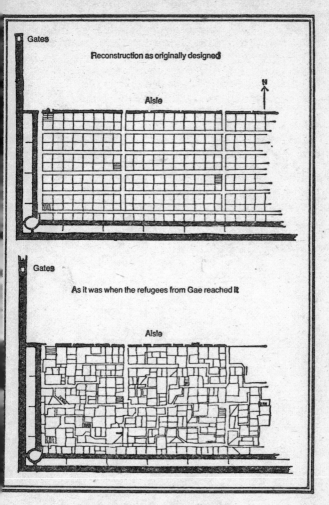

Gates

Reconstruction as originally designed

Aisle

N

Gates

As it was when the refugees from Gae reached it

Aisle

A Section of the Keep

(from Gil Patterson's maps)

CHAPTER ONE

The setting was the Shamrock Bar in San Bernardino on a rainy Saturday night. Rain drummed softly on the plate glass window, and the tawdry gleam of lights shone on the wet pavement outside. Two bearded bikers and a sleazy blonde were playing pool in the back. Rudy Solis swigged off his second beer of the evening and watched the room. There was something he had lost, something that had been taken from him, but he no longer remembered what it had been. Only a numb ache was left.

He was out of money and not nearly drunk enough yet. Behind the bar, Billie May moved back and forth along the shelf of empty glasses and bottles of beer, her reflection trailing her in the flyspecked mirror, showing her black eye make-up and the red lace of her bra at the low neck of her sweater. The mirror revealed all the usual Saturday night crowd, people Rudy had known since high school—since childhood, some of them: Peach McClain, the fattest Hell's Angel in the world, with his old lady; Crazy Red, the karate instructor; Big Bull; and the gang from the steel mill. But it was as if they were strangers. He made a gesture with one hand, and a beer bottle levitated from the shelf before the mirror and drifted across the intervening space to his hand. No one noticed. He poured the beer and drank, hardly tasting it. From the jukebox, the tinny whine of steel guitars backed a syrupy nasal voice hymning adultery. The hurt of the loss within him was unbearable.

He let go of the bottle in midair a foot above the surface of the bar and made it stay there. Still no one noticed, or no one cared, anyway. Rudy stared past it at his own reflection in the mirror—the sharp bone structure and backswept eyebrows in their frame of long, reddish-black hair. His fingers were stained with car paint and grease, and his name was tattooed across a flaming torch on his wrist. Behind him, the plate glass window had grown suddenly dark, as if all light had died outside.

He turned, chilled with a horror he could not define. No streetlights were visible outside, no sheen of neon, only darkness that seemed to press against the window, soft and living—darkness that stirred with a restless movement, as if creatures impossibly sinuous haunted its livid depths. He tried to cry out, and his voice was only a kind of feeble rattle in his throat. He tried to point, but the people in the bar ignored him, as if he were not there. A bolt of energy or power from outside struck the wall of the bar like a monster fist, caving it in amid an explosion of shattering bricks. Through the torn wall, darkness rolled like a wave.

"Rudy!" Cold hands caught his flailing wrist. "Rudy, wake up! What is it?"

He woke gasping, sweat icing him to the bone. In the darkness of the room, his wizard's sight showed him Minalde, Queen of Darwath and mother of the heir, sitting up in bed beside him, the starred silk of the counterpane gleaming around her shoulders and the fear in her wide iris-dark eyes making her seem younger than her nineteen years. The warm, still blackness of the room smelled of beeswax and of the perfume of her tumbled hair. "What was it?" she asked him again, her voice very low. "Was it a dream?"

"Yeah." Rudy lay back beside her, shivering, as if deathly cold. "Only a dream."

In the lightless barracks of the Guards on the first level, Gil Patterson woke, her dreams of quiet scholarship in another universe called California broken by an unshakable sense of impending horror. She lay on her narrow bunk for a time, listening open-eyed to the small sounds of the fortress Keep of Dare, and to the hammering of her own heart. The Keep was safe, she told herself. The one place in the world where the Dark Ones could not break in. But the terror of the dreams grew rather than diminished in her heart.

6

At last she rose, soundless as a cat. The dim yellowish glow from the banked hearth in the main guardroom threw a feeble reflection into the cell shared by the women of the day watch. It touched anonymous shoulders, shut eyes, tangled hair, the black cloaks with the simple white quatrefoil emblem of the Guards, and the hard gleam of steel. By that faint suggestion of light, she pulled on a shirt and breeches, wrapped herself in her cloak, and slipped from the room. The floor was icy to her bare feet as she made her way between the bunks in the guardroom beyond. She guessed it to be midway through the deep-night watch, the watch between midnight and morning, but time was different in the windowless Keep.

She pushed aside the curtain at the far end of that room.

Ingold the wizard was not in his so-called quarters. Actually, the wizard slept in a sort of cubbyhole that the Guards used to store part of the food supplies they'd scrounged, salvaged, and defended against all comers in the wreck of the Realm. The feeble gleam of the light from the hearth showed Gil a hollow in the sacks of grain piled in the back of the closet, a couple of moth-eaten buffalo robes, and a very grubby patchwork quilt, but no wizard. His staff was gone, too.

She moved quickly back through the guardroom, through the outer chamber used for storing weapons and casks of Blue Ruin and bathtub gin, and out into the cavernous depths of the Aisle. The great central hall of the Keep stretched nearly a thousand feet from the double gates at the west end to the dark, turreted wall of the administrative headquarters at the east. She might almost have been outside, for the featureless black walls that bounded the Aisle on either side stretched up out of sight, supporting a ceiling whose shadows had never been dispelled. Across the broad floor murmured the deep, black water channels, spanned by their tiny bridges; around her the stillness was like the great silence of the snowbound mountains outside. But instead of moon or stars, the darkness was lighted by torches that flickered on either side of the dark steel of the gates. The dim orange flame defined a small double circle on the smooth blackness of the polished floor and touched fiery echoes in bolt, brace, and locking ring.

7

Where the two halos of red flame merged, a man stood, his rough white hair fringed by the fire in a line of burning gold.

She called out softly, "Ingold!"

He turned and lifted an inquiring eyebrow. Gil pulled her cloak more tightly around her shoulders and pattered up the broad steps to the gate. Since she had crossed the Void in his company, to come unwillingly to this other universe, she couldn't remember a time when she had been warm.

"Yes, my dear?" he asked, in a voice like raw whiskey and velvet. The face revealed by the restless light had never been more than nondescript, but sixty-odd years of existence had given it an extremely lived-in look, seamed and wrinkled and mostly hidden behind a close-clipped, rather scrubby white beard. When she stood beside him, her eyes were level with his.

"What is it?" she asked him quietly.

He only said, "I think you know."

She glanced nervously over her shoulder at the dark steel of the gates. Here the horror was stronger, a sense of brooding malevolence in the night. Here she felt the strange, chill terror, the irrational sensation of being watched from across unknowable gulfs of time by a malign and incomprehensible intelligence. "They've come," she whispered, "haven't they?"

Ingold rested a hand gently on her shoulder. "I think you had better go arm."

Her eyes dark in the wan bluish witchlight, Minalde watched Rudy dress. "What's wrong?" she whispered.

"I don't know." His voice was low, so as not to wake the royal infant who slept in his gilded cradle in the shadows on the opposite wall. "But I think I'd better be getting back." After a month in this world, the alien clothing was more or less familiar to him, and he no longer felt self-conscious in the homespun breeches and full-sleeved shirt, tunic, knee-length boots, and gaily embroidered surcoat he'd scrounged off a dead nobleman after the great massacre by the Dark Ones at Karst. But he still mourned the simplicity of jeans and a T-shirt. He buckled on his sword and leaned across the tumble of variegated silks to kiss the girl who watched him so silently. "Will you be at the gate in the morning to see us off?"

His hands framed her face. She caught his wrists, as if to hold him to her for a few minutes longer. "No," she said quietly. "I can't, Rudy. It's a long way to Quo and a dangerous road. Who knows if you'll even find the Hidden City or the Archmage, once you reach the end?" Her blue eyes shimmered suddenly in the pale phosphorescence of the witchlight. "I never could stand good-bys."

"Hey!" Rudy leaned over her again, his hands gripping her neck and shoulders, the dark hair spilling heavily down over his fingers as he drew her mouth to his. "Hey, Ingold's gonna be with me. We'll be okay. I can't imagine anyone or anything crazy enough to take on that old geezer. It won't be good-by."

She smiled crookedly up at him. "Then there's no point in making much of it, is there?" Their lips met again, gently this time, the loose strands of her hair tickling his face. "Go with God, Rudy, though the Bishop would die in her tracks if she heard me say that to a wizard."

Through their next kiss Rudy mumbled something about the Bishop. "Which probably wouldn't do her any harm," he added as their mouths parted. He reached up tenderly and brushed the tear from her cheek. In all his twenty-five years, he couldn't remember anyone, man or woman, who had ever been concerned about what he was going to do. *Why did it have to be a girl in another universe?* he wondered. *Why did it have to be a Queen?* Another tear stole down her cheek, so he whispered, "Hey, you look after Pugsley while I'm gone." His way of referring to Prince Tir, the last heir of the House of Dare, made her laugh in spite of herself.

"All right." She smiled shakily.

"We'll find the Archmage and his Council," Rudy whispered encouragingly. "See if we don't." He kissed her once more quickly and turned and fled, the bluish feather of light dying behind him.

In darkness he hurried through the mazes of the Royal Sector, misery in his heart.

She was afraid for him, and more than that, he was all she had—he and her baby son. In the past month she had lost the husband she had worshipped, the Realm she had

9

ruled, and the world she had grown up in. Yet she had never said, "Don't go."

And what's more, you selfish bastard, he cursed himself, *it never crossed your mind not to go.*

She had never questioned that his need to be a wizard took precedence over his love for her. Wretched as the truth made him, he understood it for what it was; he was first and foremost a wizard. Given a choice of what to do with the limited time remaining to him in this universe, he would rather seek the sources of his own power and the teachings that Ingold and the other wizards could give him than remain with the woman he sincerely loved.

Why did I have to find them both at the same time? he wondered miserably. *Why did I have to choose?*

Even her understanding of his choice was like gall in the raw wound of his guilt.

Yet there had been no possibility of another choice.

He stopped at the head of the main east stairway, leading down to the first level.

The sensation of wrongness, of unnamed horror lurking in the black mazes of the Keep, was stronger now, teasing at him like a half-heard sound. He shivered like a dog before the thunder, the hair at the nape of his neck prickling. All around him silence seemed to move through the branching corridors. Glancing nervously behind him, he started down the stairs.

Somewhere below him, a door must have been opened. Faint as a drift of incense, he caught the sound of chanting, the sweet murmurous richness of monks' voices singing the offices of the deep-night. Rudy paused on the stairs, remembering that the Church headquarters lay directly below the Royal Sector and that, to the fanatic Bishop of Gae, wizards were anathema.

As far as he knew, his love for Alde was unknown to any, except perhaps his fellow exile Gil. He doubted anything serious could happen to Alde because of it—she was, after all, Queen of what was left of Darwath, and the King had perished in the holocaust of the burning Palace at Gae. But he knew too little of the mores and taboos of this place to want to risk discovery. *And hell,* he thought, *maybe there's some kind of noninterference*

10

directive in force, since I'm from another universe and really shouldn't be here at all.

But if there was, he did not want to know.

At the moment it wasn't critical—there were plenty of other stairways down. Some of them had been part of the original design of the Keep, built like the walls of black, massive, obsidian-hard stone. Others had evidently been rigged millennia ago by ancient inhabitants who had simply knocked holes in the floors of the corridors where it suited them and let down jerry-built steps of wood. The same process had clearly been in force with the walls and cells of the Keep, for in places the black walls marched into darkness in rigid rectilinear order, while in others makeshift chaos prevailed. Passages had been blocked to build cells across the right of way, access routes had subdivided other cells, and partitions of brick, stone, and wood had chopped the original plan into literally thousands of self-contained units whose forms had shifted with their functions, with a result, over three thousand years, that would have challenged the most worldly rat in all of B. F. Skinner's laboratories.

Optimistically, Rudy set off into the maze.

"I feel nothing," Janus of Weg said quietly. The big Commander of the Guards of Gae sat on the edge of a bunk near the guardroom hearth, his face grave in the loose frame of coppery-red hair that surrounded it. He glanced across the hearth at Ingold. "But I trust you. If you say the Dark are outside, I would believe you, even if the sun were high in the sky."

There was a stirring among the other captains and a murmur of assent. The Icefalcon, like a foreigner among the Guards with his long white viking braids, said softly, "The very smell of the night is evil." Melantrys, a diminutive girl with the eyes of a ninja, glanced nervously over her shoulder.

"Smell, hell," rumbled Tomec Tirkenson, landchief of Gettlesand, a big craggy plainsman whose domains lay on the other side of the mountains. "It's like the nights when the cattle stampede for no reason."

The Icefalcon glanced coolly across at Ingold. "Can they break in?" he asked, as if it were a matter of no more

11

moment than the outcome of a race on which he had bet only a small sum.

"I don't know." Ingold shifted his weight on his perch by the hearth and folded sword-scarred hands on his knee. "But we can be certain that they will try. Janus, Tomec— I suggest that the corridors be patrolled, on all levels, to every corner of the Keep. That way . . ."

"But we haven't the men for it!" Melantrys protested.

"We've enough for a patrol of sorts," Janus admitted. "But if the Dark effect an entrance, it's sure we've not enough to fight at any one place, spread so thin."

The Icefalcon cocked a pale eyebrow at the wizard. "Are we going to fight?"

"If we can," Ingold said. "Your patrols can be eked out with volunteers, Janus. Get the Keep orphans as your scouts. They're always into everything anyway; they might as well be put to use. We need to patrol the corridors, simply to know if and where the Dark break in. It isn't likely that they can," he went on gravely, "for the walls of the Keep have the most powerful spells of the ancient world woven into their fabric. But whether the spells have weakened, or whether the Dark have grown stronger in the intervening years, I do not know." Despite the calm in that deep, scratchy voice, Gil thought he looked grim and driven in the uncertain flicker of the hearth-light. "But I do know that if the Dark Ones enter the Keep, we shall have to abandon it entirely, and then we will surely be lost."

"Abandon the Keep!" Janus cried.

"It stands to reason," the Icefalcon agreed, leaning back against the wall behind him. He had a light and rather breathless voice that sounded disinterested even when discussing the loss of the last sanctuary left to humankind. "All those little stairways, miles of empty corridors . . . We could never drive them out." The captains looked at one another, knowing the truth of his words.

"It's not only that," Gil put in quietly. Their eyes turned to her, a quick glitter in the room's shifting shadows. "What about the ventilating system?" she went on. "The air in here has to travel somehow. The whole Keep must be honeycombed with shafts too small for a man to fit through. But the Dark can change their size as well as

12

their shape. They could fit through a hole no bigger than a rat's, and, God knows, we have rats in the Keep. All it would need would be for one of them to get into the ventilation—the thing could attack at will, and we would never be able to find it."

"Curse it," Janus whispered, "that the Dark should rise at the start of the worst winter in human memory. If we quit the Keep, those as aren't taken at first nightfall would freeze before they came to shelter. These mountains are buried in snow."

"Rats . . ." Tirkenson said softly. "Ingold, how do we know the Dark aren't lurking somewhere in the upper levels already? The Keep stood empty for nigh two thousand years."

"We would have known," the wizard said. "Believe me, we would have known by this time."

"But their eggs?" Tirkenson went on. "How do the Dark Ones breed, Ingold? As Gil-Shalos said, it would need only one to go through the air tunnels, laying eggs like a salmon along the way. We could be sitting on top of a spawning ground of the Dark." Though the Guards were not as a rule nervous people, a ripple of horror seemed to pass through the assembled captains. The instructor Gnift shuddered and exchanged a quick, worried look with Melantrys.

"You needn't concern yourselves with that, at least," Ingold said quietly. He picked a bit of straw from the frayed sleeve of his mantle and avoided all their eyes. "I have seen the breeding places of the Dark beneath the ground, and I assure you that they do not multiply in any fashion so—tidy—as that." He looked up again, his face carefully calm. "But in any case, we cannot allow the Dark entrance under any circumstances. The corridors must be patrolled."

"We can get Church troops," Janus said, "and Alwir's private guards."

"I have my own men," Tirkenson added, rising. "The lot of us can take the south side of the Aisle."

"Good." Ingold stood and lifted his head to search the faces of those crowded into the narrow barracks, seeking someone in the uncertain yellow light. "I doubt that the

13

Dark will be able to breach the walls themselves, but if they do, we must know it."

"Can we know?" Melantrys straightened her sword belt, glancing up at him with chill black eyes. "The Dark can swallow a man's soul or blood or flesh between one heartbeat and the next, a yard from his fellows, before he can cry out."

"A Guard?" Ingold inquired mildly.

She bridled. "Of course not."

"There you are." He picked up his staff, his shadow looming behind him like the echo of the darkness waiting beyond the gates of the Keep. Once more he scanned the room, the figures there fading into milling confusion of preparation and departure. It might have been a trick of the firelight, but the lines seemed deeper in that calm and nondescript face. Whether this was from weariness, apprehension, or sheer annoyance, Gil could not tell.

All around them men and women were slinging on swords and finding cloaks; voices called to one another through the dark, narrow doors of the barracks. The air seemed somehow heavier, the fear in it as palpable as electricity; if she had touched Ingold's cloak, Gil thought, sparks would have jumped from the fabric. Janus remained for a moment at Ingold's side, towering over him, his broken-nosed, pug face grave.

"That is for the corridors," he said quietly. "What of the gates?"

"Yes," Ingold said. "The gates. I feel that is where they will concentrate their attack. But with the height of the ceiling in the Aisle, once inside they can strike from above, and ground defense will be almost useless."

"I know," Janus said softly. "They'll have to be fought in the gate tunnel itself, won't they?"

"Maybe," the wizard replied. "Gil—I shall need your help at the gates." Then he frowned and cast a swift, raking glance over the remaining Guards. Bright azure eyes hooded like a falcon's glittered in the shadows. "And where," he asked grimly, "is Rudy?"

At the moment, it was the question uppermost in Rudy's mind as well.

He knew he was still somewhere on the second level,

14

but that was about all he could be sure of. Having missed the turning for the stairway he sought, he had tried to double back along an allegedly parallel corridor, with disastrous results. A makeshift hall through what had once been a large cell beckoned, only to dead-end him in a black warren of crumbling brick and dry rot that spiraled him eventually into the center of the maze, a long-deserted outlet for the Keep's indoor plumbing system. Cursing those who had designed the Keep and those who had felt called upon to improve it alike, he crossed through the dark, water-murmuring privy and out into the corridors beyond.

He walked in the darkness without light. This was another ability which had surprised him, like being able to call fire from cold wood, or light to the end of his staff. Ingold had told him that this wizard's sight had been born in him, like his other talents, the seeds of a magedom that could bear no possible fruit in the warm, lazy world of Southern California.

And still he felt it—the building of tension, like water mounting behind a weakening dam, the brooding horror that seemed to fill the dark mazes through which he walked. His step quickened with his heartbeat. The conviction grew in him that the Dark were outside, focusing inhuman lusts and will upon the smooth, impenetrable walls of the Keep. Beyond human magic or even human comprehension, their numbers and power were so great that their presence could be felt through the ten-foot walls wrought of time and stone and magic. He had to find Ingold, had to find his way somehow out of this maze . . .

He found himself in a short neck of corridor that bore every sign of having been part of the original Keep. A flow of warmer air indicated a stairway somewhere nearby, leading down to the first level. Rudy paused, trying to get his bearings. Directly in front of him loomed the end of the passage, black and seamless, as if poured from a single sheet of dark glass. That would be the back wall, he realized in surprise, of the Keep itself.

Fantastic, he thought. *I've come in a bloody circle and, after all that wandering around, I still get to come down in the middle of Church territory anyway.* He shrugged. *But it beats hell out of wandering around up here all night.*

He did not go forward, however. A short stairway of a few steps branched up to his right, with a door at the top. The mirror-smooth blackness of the stone proclaimed steps and wall as part of the Keep's original design, but the setting of the door caught his attention. It was so placed as to be absolutely shadowed, thrown into virtual invisibility, from any light carried in the corridor itself. Only a wizard, walking like Rudy without light, could have seen it at all.

Fascinated, Rudy moved forward. His sense of the mounting peril and terror of the Dark grew no less. They would strike, and strike soon—he felt that much in his bones. But he knew that, provided they survived the night, he and Ingold would be setting out on their journey in the morning, traveling hundreds of miles through the barren plains and desert to seek the City of Quo where it lay hidden on the Western Ocean. Concealed as this room was, he was not altogether sure that he'd be able to find it when he returned.

But above all, pure curiosity drew him as a string might draw a cat, the unslakable curiosity that was the leading trait of any wizard.

The door was shut, the ironwork of the lock so rusted as to be almost unworkable. But it was no worse than the oil pans of some cars Rudy had wrestled with in his time. The chamber within was circular, unlike the uniformly rectangular cells elsewhere in the Keep. A bare work-bench ran halfway around the walls; under the bench, wooden boxes proved to contain miscellaneous rusted junk.

But in the center of the room stood a table, rising from the floor itself and built of the same hard, black, glassy stone. It was about four feet across, and inset in its center was a plug of heavy crystal, like the glass covering of a display case. But when Rudy perched himself on the table's edge and called a ball of witchlight over his shoulder to look, the white gleam glared back into his eyes, for the crystal was cloudy, showing only a kind of angular glitter underneath. First with his nails and then with the tip of his dagger, he tried to pry the cover off, without results. But there was something under there, of that he was sure. Elusive glimpses of angles and surfaces

16

whispered in those frosted depths. An observer, watching him as he examined the impenetrable stone, would have been reminded of a large and gaudy cat frustrated by a mirror.

To hell with it, he thought in disgust and made as if to rise. *This is no time to be messing with toys.*

But he was drawn back again. His shadow lay hard and dark over the gray glass, sharp-edged in the cool, steady light of the ball of phosphorous that hung behind his shoulder. After a moment's thought, he dimmed and diffused the light, trying to peer past the flickering crystal, but the thing still denied his gaze. Gradually he let the witchlight die entirely and sat looking at the thing in the dark.

Around him the room had fallen utterly silent. He knew that he should go but did not. He sensed that the thing was magic, of a deep and mechanistic sorcery far beyond his natural talents. Was this the magic, he wondered, that he would learn at the school at Quo?

His fingers probed at the crystal again, finding no seam between glass and rock.

Another thought came to him. Hesitantly, he projected a thin sliver of light into the crystal itself.

White and blue and lavender reflections blossomed forth around him like the three-dimensional tail of a celestial peacock. He shied back, shielding his eyes from that bursting fountain of light, then dimmed it, working awkwardly with the few light-spells he had been taught, like an artist's child with his first crayons. He suffused the crystal with a dim light and leaned over again to look inside, to the glittering bed of colored rock salts that lay at the bottom of their crystal cylinder.

A toy? A trip-light? An enchanted kaleidoscope?
Or the magic tool to further magics?

Staring down into those bright depths, he relaxed his mind, slowly emptying his soul of all concerns for the Dark, for Ingold, for Alde, and for the answer to this riddle itself. He let the soft, bright glitter of the gems below have its way with him, to do whatever it did.

For a time the images confused him. He did not understand what they were—incoherent scenes of blowing sand, rock hills on which nothing grew, rolling seas of brown

17

grass invisible in the overcast night. He sensed rather than saw a dark place take shape, roofed with clouds and drifted deep in snow, walled in by high cliffs of black rock crowned with twisted pines. Beyond the black clouds he sensed gorge-riven peaks, knife-edged heights, and the endless miles of glaciers where the ice winds skated, screaming . . . *Sarda Pass?* he wondered. *Tomorrow's road?* The images grew clearer—ragged foothills and then an endless brown plain, with tawny grasses waving under the lash of the wind. A black sky was sheeted with cloud. A pale thread of road stretched out of sight into pitiless distance.

Frozen and bitter vastness swallowed his soul.

And, as if the images moved with his heart, he saw the soft glow of reflected candlelight and the starred embroidery on the changeable colors of a silken quilt. The colors shifted, aqua to teal to river-reed green, as they were shaken by the sobbing of the woman who lay there, her black hair thrown about her like scattered silk.

I can't leave her, he thought in despair. *I've known her such a short time.*

And miss Quo? the other half of his mind asked. *And not speak with the Archmage? Not have Ingold teach you the ways of power?*

He closed his eyes. Like a tingling through his skin, he became aware again of the Dark and the building fury of them, riddling the night like the coming of an electrical storm. *I have to go,* he thought, with a sudden chill of panic. But still he stayed, paralyzed between his choices—Minalde on the one hand, Ingold and the Archmage Lohiro on the other.

He opened his eyes, and the image in the crystal changed again.

Small and distant, the stars were visible—more stars than he had ever imagined, filling a luminous sky that hung low and glittering over the endless roll of the blue-black sea. Their piercing brightness touched the curl of foam on the silver curve of the beach. Outlined against that burning sky, he thought he could make out the shape of a tower, looming storey on turreted storey from the trees that crowded an angular point of land thrusting out into the ocean. But the tower seemed strangely elusive, slipping his eyes past it, turning them again to the stars. He tried to look inland, but found his gaze eluded there, too. Half-guesssed shapes of buildings clustered there, twining patterns of color on stone columns muted by darkness, briefly visible and then swallowed by mists. Try as he would to focus on the land, he found his eyes coming back to the sand, the sea, and the midnight sky, as if in a gentle refusal to answer his questioning.

Against the dark bulk of that square knoll and half-seen tower, he glimpsed the sudden flash of starlight on metal, winking momentarily and then gone. He looked again, releasing all thoughts of striving from his soul. The metal twinkled once more, and he caught the long swirl of a cape brushing sand, the scuff of a foot above the tide line. Like a sudden wash of spilling opals, the stroke of a wave eradicated footsteps from the sand. The man whose prints they were walked slowly on, and Rudy could see the starlight now on his bright gold hair—hair the color of sun-fire.

It surprised him, for he had expected the Archmage Lohiro to be old.

But this man wasn't. He was surely less than forty, with a young, clean-shaven face. Only the firm lines of the mouth and the creases in the corners of eyes that were a flecked and changeable kaleidoscope blue betrayed the harshness of experience. His hand around the hard, gleaming wood of his staff reminded Rudy of Ingold's hand, nicked with the scars of sword practice, very deft and strong. The staff itself was tipped with a metal crescent some five inches across, whose inner edge glinted razor-bright. The starlight caught in it, as it caught in those wide blue eyes and on the spun-glass glimmer of foam that washed the beach in a surge of lace and dragged at something half-buried in the sand.

Looking down, Rudy saw that it was a skeleton, old blood still staining the raw bones, crabs crawling grue- somely through the wet, gleaming eyes of the skull. The Archmage barely turned his steps aside from it. The hem of his dark cloak brushed over it as he passed and swept the sand as he went on down the beach.

Rudy sat back, cold with sweat and suddenly terrified. The light died out of the crystal below him, leaving the

19

room pitch-dark but for the bluish echo in its heart. Then he heard a sound, faint and distantly booming, a vibration that seemed to shake the Keep to the dark, ancient bones of its agelong foundations.

Thunder, Rudy thought.

Thunder? Through ten-foot walls?

His stomach seemed to close in on itself. He got up and headed quickly for the door. A second booming reverberated through the Keep, setting up a faint, sinister ringing in the metal junk heaped in the corners and shivering in the mighty walls.

Rudy began to run.

CHAPTER TWO

"Damn the boy," Ingold whispered, and Gil thought that he looked very white in the wild jumping of shadows. The first blow of that incredible power smashing at the outer gates had jarred the torches in their sockets, and they guttered nervously, as if the light itself trembled before the coming of the Dark. Behind her in the Aisle, utter chaos prevailed.

Men with torches ran to and fro, calling mutually contradictory rumors to one another and brandishing makeshift weapons in frightened hands. Little flocks of children and old people, the nuclei of small families, huddled like frightened birds along the watercourses, as close to the center of the great space as they could get, having fled their cells in terror when the pounding started. Others, mothers and fathers who had left their dependents back in the close darkness of their cells, crowded around Janus and the small knot of Guards who had remained in the Aisle, waving their arms, demanding what was being done, pleading for even lying assurances of safety. Janus towered above these lesser people in the torchlight, his voice deep and intense, allaying fears and recruiting patrols as best he could in that whirling chaos of noise and lamplight.

It was a scene out of Dante's Hell, Gil thought, with darkness like velvet and a random frenzy of flickering light. *Thank God, the Keep is solid stone. Maybe we can get out of this without immolating ourselves by morning. If the Dark don't get us first,* she added.

But Ingold was there, and Gil had never found it possible to be truly afraid when she was at the wizard's side.

So she felt only a kind of cold detachment, though her blood rushed violently through her veins and her body

21

tingled with a cold excitement. The separation was physical as well as emotional, for she and Ingold stood together on the steps before the gates, with the pounding, sounding roar of the beaten steel at their backs; none would come near them there.

The noise in the Aisle was tremendous, the repeated bellowing clang mingling with the wild keening of voices, to rise and ring in the huge ceiling vaults until the whole Aisle was one vast sounding chamber. Men and women rushed wildly about, purposeful or aimless, the bobbing of the torches and lamps in their hands like the storming of fireflies on a summer night. Behind Gil, the pounding of the Dark upon the gates was a bass vibration that sounded in her bones.

Ingold turned to her and asked quietly, "Is Bektis here?" He named the Court Wizard of the Chancellor Alwir, the only other mage in the Keep.

"Surely you jest," Gil murmured, for Bektis had a most solicitous concern for his own health. Ingold did not smile, but the quick flicker of amusement that lightened his eyes turned his whole face briefly, elusively young. It was gone as quickly as it came, the lines of strain settling back again.

"Then I fear that I shall have no choice," the wizard said softly. The blue-white glow from the end of his staff touched his face in shadow; the flicker of the torches beyond might have been responsible for the illusion Gil had of bitter self-reproach in the old man's expression, but she could not be sure. "Gil, I had not wanted to ask this of you, for you are not mageborn, and the danger is very great."

"That doesn't matter," Gil said quietly.

"No." Ingold regarded her for a moment, and a curious expression that she could not read overlay the serenity of his face. "No, to you it would not." Taking her hands, he placed his staff in them. The wan white glow remained at its tip, though she felt no sense of power or vibration in the staff itself. It was only wood, grip-smoothed over decades of use, and now warmed from his hand. "The light may fade if the spells of the Dark draw off too much of my power," he warned her. "But don't desert me."

"No," Gil said, surprised that he should even mention the possibility.

Ingold smiled at the self-evident tone in her voice. "I am not saying that either of us will survive this," he went on. "But if the outer gates go, the inner ones will crumple like thin tin. Icefalcon!" he called, and the thin young captain ran to them from where he had been among Janus' Guards.

It was thus that Rudy saw them as he dropped the last few feet down a makeshift ladder from a rickety second-level balcony. They looked like scouts in enemy territory, framed in the sooty jumping shadows of the gate torches, their faces revealed by the white light of the staff. The clamor of the gates redoubled, the separate blows merging into one continuous assault, roaring like an earsplitting cannonade that set the inner gates visibly vibrating and stopped Rudy's breath with horror.

Someone close to him screamed. The Icefalcon mounted the steps at a light-footed run, braids white in the shadows against his black surcoat, and began to turn the locking rings that closed the inner gates. The thought of the pounding fury in the night outside made Rudy's blood run cold, but he would not for any reason whatever have gone close enough to the gates to stop them. The gates moved open, inward on their soundless hinges; the bellowing roar of the assault on the outer gates rolled from the ten-foot passage between, a howling tidal wave of sound. The black square gaped, a clanging maw of darkness and roaring horror.

In the white circle of the magelight, Ingold and Gil stood like lovers, wizard and warrior, their nicked, bruised swordsman's hands joined on the wood of the staff. Then Rudy, his soul cringing, saw Ingold turn away and mount the steps. Gil followed with the glowing staff upraised like a lantern in her hand.

She can't be doing that! Rudy thought desperately, running to the foremost edge of the scattered and horror-struck groups that stood in the Aisle. *She hasn't got any magic of her own. If the Dark break through the gates and swamp Ingold's power, she has nothing!*

But he could not go toward them. He stood helplessly on the edge of the darkness.

23

The blackness of the passage framed the old man in his stained and rusty brown mantle and the girl in faded black with the white emblem on her shoulder and the wan light glowing above her head. The bawling roar of the power of the Dark surrounded them in the midnight of that enclosed space, but neither Gil nor Ingold looked around. Ingold's eyes were on the gates, Gil's, unquestioningly calm in the midst of that unearthly roaring, on Ingold's back.

She's crazy, Rudy thought in horror. *Never, never, never . . .*

Ingold had reached the end of the narrow tunnel. By the swift-waning glow of the witchlight, Rudy saw him put out his hands, touching the shaking steel of the outer gates. Only inches of metal separated him from the wild blood-hunger that haunted the night outside—separated everyone in the Keep from instant and hideous destruction. The witchlight flickered, fading . . .

And like fire, spreading from Ingold's fingertips, Rudy could see the runes that spelled the gates. They seemed at first to be only a faint reflection, swimming within the metal like schools of fish below the surface of clear water, visible only to his wizard's sight. But under Ingold's touch they brightened, flickering into life in a webwork of shining graffiti, spread over the gates from top to bottom and across the walls beside them. They were incomprehensible in their complexity, meshing tighter and tighter as more of those faint silver threads glimmered into view. The light from them outlined the old man in silver and bathed his scarred hands in a quivering foxfire glow. Silenced by the beauty of it, Rudy forgot the danger and the wrath of the Dark outside. He watched Ingold's hands move across the surface of that phosphorescent galaxy, his touch calling forth the woven names of ancient mages, tracing his own name among those lattices of light.

Impossibly, under the harsh, wild roar, Rudy could hear him speaking, his scratchy, velvet voice weaving his own spells of ward and guard there, placing his power on the doors. As he had felt it on the road down from Karst, Rudy felt again the force of the power filling and surrounding that nondescript little man.

"What the hell does that old fool think he's doing?"

24

The words were screamed out a foot from Rudy's ear. He could barely make them out above the din of the gates. His concentration broke. For an instant he saw Ingold as nonwizards would see him, an old man in a patched brown robe, standing alone in the darkness, tracing imaginary patterns on the door with his fingers. Then Rudy swung around to see the Chancellor Alwir at his side, the man's face dark and clotted with anger.

"He's spelling the doors!" Rudy shouted back.

The Chancellor brushed past him, striding forward up the steps. "He'll have us all killed!" Alwir strode through the darkness and the roar of sound like a man facing blinding rain, to seize the edge of the great door in order to shove it to. The counterweighted steel moved easily, swinging smoothly before another hand stayed it. Cool and arrogant, the Icefalcon looked across into the Chancellor's jewel-blue eyes.

Rudy couldn't hear what passed between them. Alwir's shout was lost in the roaring fury from the passage beyond, and the Icefalcon did not raise his voice to reply. The cacophony was hardly so much sound anymore as an elemental force that blotted sound. In the sickly pallor reflected from the staff in Gil's hands, the scene before the gates had an air of nightmare unreality blurred by the dirty redness of the torches. The two black-clothed men faced each other soundlessly, the one raven, the other pale as ice.

Though Gil, within the tunnel of the gates, must have known what was taking place, Rudy could not see that she so much as turned her head. The light of the staff she held was dying.

Looking beyond Alwir and the Icefalcon into the darkness, Rudy saw to his horror that the light of the runes had entirely died. Ingold stood alone in a dark hollow of sounding metal, the only marks visible on the shivering steel the silver tracing of his own spells. Still Rudy saw him moving in the darkness, tracing signs that flickered and were swallowed by the malice of the Dark. Over the furious hail of blows on the gates, Rudy heard Alwir yell, "Shut the gates! I order you to stand off and shut them!"

The Icefalcon only stood, regarding him with cold, colorless eyes. Behind him, the tunnel had grown utterly dark.

The Chancellor cried something in his great battle voice, and his hand went to the hilt of his sword. Metal flashed in the reddish shadows of the torches as it swept free of its scabbard . . .

. . . and the faint hiss-*ching* of the edge singing clear was as audible and distinct as a note of music.

The sudden, utter silence that fell upon the hall was like a roaring in the ears. It was like an outdoor silence in so huge a place, for the first second unbroken even by a drawn breath among the several hundreds of people who had come to take problematical refuge in the Aisle. So deep was the hush that lay over them all that Rudy could hear clearly the soft, light tread of Ingold's returning feet.

The wizard stepped through the dark gate, with Gil moving quietly at his heels. The old man took the door edge from Alwir's clench and pushed it gently to. The faint, hollow boom of its closing reverberated to the ends of that soundless hall.

"The gates will hold against the Dark now." Like the sound of the gates, Ingold's grainy voice was low, but it carried to the farthest corners. "It may be that they will try to break in elsewhere tonight, but . . . I think the main danger is past."

"You—foolish—old—bastard!" Alwir's resonant voice grated over the words like a file. "Opening the inner doors could have been the death of us all!"

"They would never have held if the Dark Ones had forced the spells on the outer," the wizard returned mildly. His face was very white, and his hair was matted dark with sweat, but only Gil stood close enough to him to see that his hands were not altogether steady. Quietly, she returned his staff to him and stood close by his elbow.

Alwir spoke as cuttingly as a flaying whip. "And is that something else that you, as a wizard, speak of with sole authority? As the only wizard in the Keep, do you feel justified in every crackpot scheme you care to pursue?"

Ingold raised heavy-lidded blue eyes to meet Alwir's. "Not the only wizard," he replied softly. "Ask your court mage Bektis."

Alwir swung around. "Bektis!"

The word was snapped in the way a dog-handler might

26

crack a whip on his boot to bring his dog belly-down to heel. The court mage disengaged himself with great dignity from the crowd that had formed itself before the western doors and came forward, the jumping torchlight salting fire over the bullion embroidery of his velvet sleeves.

"Whether the gates would have broken or not," he said, stroking his waist-length silvery beard with delicate fingers, "it would have been perhaps better, had you consulted with others before any course was decided upon." He looked haughtily down his nose at Ingold. Rudy could see his high, domed forehead all pearled with sweat.

"Indeed it would have," another voice purred suddenly, low and dry and as thin as wind through bone, "had you been here."

Bektis turned as if bitten. Govannin Narmenlion, Bishop of Gae, moved up the steps toward them at the head of a small company of the Red Monks, the bald-shaved warriors of the Church. Above the gory crimson of the episcopal robes, the Bishop's face was thin and bone-hard, a skeleton with living coals burning in the dark eye sockets. Only the fullness of her lips betrayed her sex. Her harsh voice rode easily over the court mage's indignant reply. "I commend your courage, Ingold Inglorion. But it is said that the Devil guards his own."

Ingold bowed to her. "As does the Straight God, my lady," he replied. "You know better than I in whose hands rest the people of the Keep." He looked ready to pass out on his feet, but he met the chill, fanatic eyes levelly, and it was Govannin who turned away.

"And he was not the only one conspicuous by his absence, my lady Bishop," Alwir added with sweet malice.

"Indeed," the Bishop replied calmly. "Many were absent from their appointed posts. Others remained—to guard their stores of food, lest those be looted while they were gone."

The Chancellor's brows shot up, then plunged, hooding eyes that were the same morning-glory blue as his sister Minalde's, but hard as the sapphires he wore around his neck. "Looted?"

"Or inventoried," the Bishop went on softly, "to be marked for future—" Alwir's mouth hardened dangerously. "—reference."

27

He lashed out, "And you think that in the midst of an attack by the Dark Ones—"

"The Faith must protect itself as it can," she shot back at him. "To preserve our independence, we must be beholden to no secular power for bread."

"As Lord of the Keep, I have the right to control—"

"Lord of the Keep!" Govannin spat scornfully. "The brother of the Regent for the true King, my lord, and that only. A man who consorts with wizards, who seeks to bring the Archmage, the very left hand of Satan, here among us. If you expect the blessings of the Straight God upon your endeavors . . ."

"The Straight God works in many ways," Alwir grated. "If our strike against the Dark in their Nests is to succeed, we shall need both the troops of the Empire of Alketch in the south and the wizards of the west."

Like flint, his words struck fire from those steely eyes. "The Straight God has no truck with the tools of Satan," she snapped, "nor with those who foul their hands with such tools."

"We are beyond the time when a ruler can pick and choose his tools."

"There is never a time when siding with the Crooked One is excusable."

Quietly, Gil took Ingold's arm, and they descended the steps to the main body of the shadowed Aisle. The old man moved slowly, stiffly, leaning on his staff. Those who had crowded around to see the confrontation between wizard and Chancellor fell back from him, murmuring and making the sign against evil. Rudy fell quietly into step with them. He nodded back to where the Chancellor and the Bishop were still squabbling and shook his head. "I don't believe this."

"Oh, come, Rudy," Ingold said mildly. "They haven't any proof that I did more than endanger the whole Keep by opening the inner gates." He glanced sideways, sunken eyes amused.

"But I saw the motherloving runes!" Rudy exploded. "They *disappeared*, goddammit!"

"Did they?" Gil looked across at him curiously. "You know, I didn't see anything at all. I could feel—things, forces, in the air. But it was just—darkness."

Frustrated, Rudy turned to Ingold for support. "Of course they did," the wizard said. "But you were the only person in the Keep capable of seeing—you and Bektis."

"And it would be worth Bektis' job to say so," Gil added wryly.

She looked tired, Rudy thought, and no wonder. Coming down from Karst and training with the Guards, Gil had begun to have the look of a half-starved alley cat. He had never understood her, either as an intolerant, intellectual scholar in California or now as a warrior of the Keep. But having seen her standing behind Ingold as he faced down all the armies of the night, Rudy felt an awe of her that amounted almost to fear.

"That's how we wizards get our reputation for eccentricity," Ingold went on in his mild, scratchy voice. "We do things that people don't understand, for we see things differently and act as we deem fit. Those who are not mageborn cannot comprehend us and perforce must mistrust us or, rarely, trust us implicitly. It's no wonder wizards have few friends and that those few are mostly other wizards." They crossed a footbridge, fragments of lamplight glinting on the silent spill of ebony below. "And then, too, horrible things have been known to happen to those who befriend mages."

The groups of people, the huddled families and restless, prowling watchers, were slowly trickling from the Aisle to return to the black mazes of the Keep. From the doorways on the lower levels, voices could be heard as patrols called to one another. Alwir and Govannin, each surrounded by a separate retinue, were making their way back up the Aisle, the venom in their voices audible, though distance and echoes blurred the words. By the gates a line of guards had been set, their drawn swords flickering eerily in the red torchlight. The opposed terrors of both noise and silence no longer filled the Keep. Rudy wondered how long it was until dawn.

"I can't imagine what it's going to be like if you guys do bring the Archmage and the Council of Wizards here," Gil went on as they approached the darkness of the barracks. "Alwir's going to try to use them against the Bishop, even as he'll use the troops of the Empire of Alketch, if he can get them."

"I have no doubt that he will get them," Ingold said quietly. "But since the Alketch is practically a theocracy, he will be lucky if his precious allies don't take his power and hand it over to the Church. He'll need Lohiro on his side to balance that threat if he hopes to invade the Nests of the Dark and still have any sort of kingdom to rule afterward."

"Ingold," Rudy said uneasily, "I think I've seen the Archmage."

The old man's attention narrowed and focused like the beam of a laser. "Where? How?"

"Here, in the Keep. In this crystal kind of thing. I—I got lost." The wizard raised a quizzical eyebrow at that, but said nothing. Rudy hesitantly described the room, the table, the crystal, and the visions he had seen.

Ingold listened intently until Rudy was done and then asked him, "Where was this room?"

"I don't know," Rudy said helplessly. "Someplace on the second level is all I know."

Ingold was silent long enough for Gil to wonder what arcane curses revolved through his mind. Finally he sighed. "That is Lohiro," he said. "I have seen him walk so, down the beach at Quo. But the thing that you speak of I have never seen before." They stopped before the doors of the barracks. Ingold glanced over his shoulder, back into the darkness of the Aisle. Flickering lights ran to and fro there on hurrying ghostly feet, like spooks on a deadly earnest Halloween. He turned back to them. "I have sought for some word, some contact with Lohiro for a month now, ever since the fall of Gae."

"Could you put off your departure?" Gil asked. "Worst-case, it wouldn't take more than two days to find that room."

The old man hesitated, obviously torn. At last he shook his head. "In two days, the storms will have moved down from the high glaciers to bury the Pass again." He sighed. "If we leave tomorrow, I shall be turning them back the last day down the foothills as it is. After that it will be weeks before we can get out."

"Wouldn't it be worth it?" She glanced around, as if at the bleak world beyond the windowless walls of the Keep. "If you could make contact with him, he could start on his way here tomorrow and you'd cut your time in half."

"Maybe," the wizard said quietly. "If we find the room again. And if the crystal there is actually a means of communication, rather than simply observation. And if the image that you saw, Rudy, was not merely the echo of events long gone, or part of the illusions that surround Quo. Divination by crystal is by no means sure. You remember the Nest of the Dark in the valley to the north of here, Gil. By fire and crystal, it is still shown as blocked up, when you and I have been there and have seen that it has been open for years. And after all that," he continued somberly, "we may still have to set out on this journey, when deep winter has locked down upon the plains. But I will ask you this, Gil . . ."

Their eyes met, and he grinned suddenly, as rueful as a schoolboy. "It seems to be my night for asking things of you."

She grinned back. "I'll ask you something someday."

The old impish expression flitted briefly across his tired eyes. "God help me." He smiled. "When we are gone, as your duties with the Guards give you time—look for this room for me. Lohiro will certainly want to see it when he comes."

"All right," Gil agreed quietly.

"Yeah, but she'll have a hell of a time finding the place," Rudy argued. "I mean, since she isn't mage-born . . ."

Ingold and Gil exchanged a glance, a quick glitter of eyes in the light of the staff that stood between them. Then Ingold smiled. "That's never stopped her."

There was a moment of silence, then the wizard turned abruptly and vanished through the barracks door.

Gil sighed and looked back out into the random flurries of dark and light in the Aisle. In repose, Rudy noticed, her face had acquired a network of fine-penned lines around the eyes that hadn't belonged to the shy, gawky scholar in the red Volkswagen. It had been a long night, and was wearing on toward dawn. Outside, if the Dark Ones waited, they waited in silence.

Nothing like starting out on a walk of more than fifteen hundred miles with only two hours' sleep, he thought

31

tiredly and prepared to turn into the barracks to see to his packing. But another thought crossed his mind, and he stopped. "Hey, Gil?"

Her attention came back from other things. The pale schoolmarm eyes turned to him.

"What would you think of somebody who—who'd leave someone he loves, to go after something he wants?"

Gil was silent for a moment, considering. "I don't know," she said finally. "Maybe that's because I don't understand love very well. I see people act out of what they say is love, but it's like watching someone act from a really deep religious conviction—it's incomprehensible to me. My parents—my mother—wanted certain things for me and couldn't understand that all I wanted was to be a scholar. Couldn't see that I'd rather live in a crummy little office in the history department of UCLA than in the classiest hundred-thousand-dollar home in Orange County. And she said she loved me. Over and over and over. So I'm the wrong expert to ask about love, Rudy. But as for leaving someone to go after something you want . . . Leaving them for how long? How badly do they need you to stay? It's all situational. Everything's situational."

Manlike, Rudy shied from the specific. "Well, like if you had only a short time together and had a choice of spending it with this person you loved or being separated from them because of—of something you wanted. Something you wanted more than anything in the world, except them."

Gil shook her raveled braid back over her shoulder. "What makes you think you have a choice?"

Rudy gulped. "Hunh?"

Her voice was as chilly and neutral as her eyes. "Only a wizard can find the City of Quo, Rudy. Ingold's got the Dark Ones on his trail, God only knows why. He needs another wizard to back him up. If you hadn't volunteered to go looking for the Archmage with him, Rudy, you'd probably have been drafted."

A long moment of silence followed, while Rudy digested that one. Love and the loneliness of exile fought in him against the burning memory of that first instant of the knowledge of his own power, the instant he had called forth fire from darkness. The double need in him for love

32

and power seemed to rise over him like the tide, with a confusion of memories: Ingold standing in a shining web of runes; the darkness of Minalde's watching eyes; and the sweep of pearlescent waves washing over a half-buried skill.

In the end it all meant very little. He would go because it was required of him that he go.

"You got a great way of putting things, spook," he muttered tiredly.

Gil shrugged. "Booklearning," she explained. "It rots the brain. Get some sleep, punk. You have a long walk in the morning."

It was a small and very tired group that gathered on the steps of the Keep three hours later in the gray chill of dawn. Standing, shivering, beside Ingold in the misty snowlight, Rudy reflected to himself that in some cases it was better to have no sleep than too little. As far as he knew, Ingold hadn't been to bed at all. Every time he'd waked up through the confused remainder of the night, he'd seen the old man sitting beside the fire with the demon-smoke of his foul-smelling tea in wreaths around his head, staring into the yellowed chip of crystal he carried, while Gil and the Icefalcon assembled provisions for the journey with their usual silent efficiency.

After three days of storms, the Vale of Renweth lay bleak and snowbound all around them, a white, rolling sea breaking against the black rocks of the surrounding cliffs. To the west, the shallow trace of the road climbed toward the dark notch of Sarda Pass, almost hidden in roiling gray cloud; to the east, it wound, descending through what a week ago had been sun-tinted meadows of long grass and a scattering of woods, on out of the Vale past the broken bridge of the Arrow Gorge and down to the Dark-haunted lowlands by the Arrow River. Northward the land rose, mile after forested mile, like a fjord between the high cliffs of the Rampart Range and the greater bulk of the Snowy Mountains, to meet the cold meadows of the timberline and the white walls where the glaciers began.

But around the Keep itself, the ground was clear. Hunks of snow mixed with chopped dirt had been ripped up by the violence of the Dark Ones' assault and lay scattered, like the spew of a frozen volcano, hundreds of feet from the walls. The walls themselves were unmarked, the black gates that had roared like gongs under that power and fury unscratched.

Winds sneered down the Vale, roaring in the trees. Rudy shivered wretchedly in his damp cloak and wondered if he'd ever be warm again. Beside him, the Icefalcon was saying to Ingold, "I hope you packed shovels, unless you plan on turning yourselves into eagles and flying over the Pass. Winter's hardly begun and they say Gettlesand across the mountains is buried deep in snow."

Even as a rank novice in the arts of wizardry, Rudy knew that few mages would risk changing their being into the being of a beast, and then only under conditions of extreme emergency. But to nonwizards, magic was magic; and from the outside, shape-craftiness looked much the same as simple illusion. On the other hand, Rudy did think longingly of conjuring up a snowmobile.

The Icefalcon continued in the same light, uninflected tone. "I imagine my own journey will be easier—provided I don't get my horse stolen."

"Your journey?" Gil asked, surprised.

Pale eyebrows elevated fractionally. "Hadn't you heard? I'm the one who has been chosen to ride south to the Alketch with my lord Alwir's letters to the Emperor, asking his help with troops."

Ingold laid a hand gently on Gil's shoulder to stop her next angry words. "It was a logical choice," he said smoothly. "Alwir picked the messenger with the best chance of survival."

Who coincidentally happened to be the man who kept him from shutting the doors on you last night, Rudy added. But, like Gil, he held his peace.

Unruffled, Ingold searched through his voluminous robes and eventually located a small hand-worn token of carved wood that he gave to the pale captain. "I leave you with this," he said. The Icefalcon took it and turned it over in curious fingers. It was dark and smoke-stained, obviously old. Rudy had the impression that it was shaped like some living thing, but it was neither human nor any animal that he recognized. "It is imbued with the Rune of the Veil," Ingold explained, "the rune that turns aside

34

the eyes and the mind. It will by no means make you invisible, but it may help you on your journey."

The Icefalcon inclined his head in thanks, while Ingold pulled on his worn blue mittens and wound ten feet of knitted gray muffler around his neck, so that the ends fluttered like banners in the chilly winds. Around the corner of the Keep, a gaggle of the herdkids appeared, Keep orphans in charge of looking after the stock. Most of them were running aimlessly, shrieking with laughter and hurling snowballs as if they hadn't been playing keep-away with death through the night. But a couple of them were leading a donkey, a scrawny miserable beast with the Earth Cross of the Faith branded on one bony hip. The donkey represented a major victory for Alwir and Ingold, since the Church owned most of the stock in the Keep. Rudy suspected Govannin had had the thing exorcised and blessed.

Other shadows appeared in the darkness of the gates. Alwir stepped forth into the wan light, dark and elegant and as unmarred as the walls, followed by Janus, Melantrys, Gnift of the Guards, and Tomec Tirkenson, who in a few days would himself be leaving with his troops, his stock, and his followers, to take the long road over the Pass to Gettlesand. Of Govannin the Bishop of Gae, there was no sign. True to her word, she would have no truck with the tools of Satan, nor lend her countenance to their endeavor.

Ingold left his friends and walked up the steps toward the Chancellor, Rudy heard the drift of words, Alwir's voice deep and melodious, Ingold's reply warm and grainy. He glanced sideways at Gil and saw her looking hard and strained, her eyes narrowed and cold. He felt the tension rising off her like smoke, misery and worry and fear. *Well, hell, why not?* he thought. *If the old man buys it out on the plains, she's in for a long stay.*

We both are. The thought was frightening.

"Hey, spook?"

She glanced forbiddingly at him.

"Take care of yourself while we're gone, okay?"

She evidently told herself to relax and did so, slightly. "I'm not the one who's gonna need taking care of," she said. "All I have to do is sit tight and keep the door shut."

It was on the tip of Rudy's tongue to ask Gil to look after Alde for him, but on second thought, he couldn't imagine someone as tough and hard-hearted as Gil getting along with the shy, retiring Minalde.

Gil sighed. "Have a good trip, punk," she added. "Don't screw up and turn yourself into a frog."

"At this point, I doubt he could manage even that," Ingold said judiciously, coming back down to them. The rulers of the Keep were disappearing back into the shadows of the gates. After a moment the Icefalcon followed them, his dark cloak sweeping the loose powder snow that sprinkled the steps. "For the present he's quite harmless."

"Thanks loads," Rudy grumbled.

"Enjoy it," Ingold urged. "There's a great deal to be said for being unable to destroy inadvertently those whom you love. And you surely will not be harmless by the time we return, if we return."

"The pair of you," Rudy sighed, "are the worst couple of pessimists I've ever met in my life. No wonder you get along so well."

Gil and Ingold unconsciously closed ranks against the common foe. "Clear analysis of any situation," Ingold declared, "is often mistaken for pessimism."

"The two shouldn't be confused," Gil added.

"I'll explain the difference to you one day."

"Thanks," Rudy said glumly. "I'll look forward to it."

He turned and started down the steps. For a moment Ingold and Gil stood alone before the doors of the Keep, but Rudy was collecting the lead-rope of the burro from the head herdkid and did not see what, if anything, passed between them there. A moment later the wizard came down to join him, huddling deeper into his dark mantle against the stinging wind. As they plowed their way along the buried path toward the road that would take them through and over Sarda Pass, Rudy glanced back once, to see Gil standing on the steps, her bruised hands tucked into her sword belt, watching them go. An icy skiff of breeze dashed blown snow into his eyes; he thought he saw another shape, black-cloaked and small, standing in the vast shadows of the gates; but when he looked again, there was no sign.

CHAPTER THREE

Forever after, Rudy's memories of the journey to Quo were memories of the wind. It never ceased, as integral a part of that flat, brown, featureless world as the endless ripple of the dried grasses or the bleak, unbroken line where the dark planes of ground and overcast sky met in an infinity of cold and emptiness. The wind blew from the north always, as bitterly cold as the frozen breath of outer space. It streamed down off the great ice fields where, Ingold said, the sun had not shone in a thousand years and where not even the wooliest mammoth could survive. It roared like a river in spate down eight hundred miles of unbroken flatlands, to bite the flesh to the bone. Ingold said that he could not remember a winter when it had blown so cold or so steadily, nor a time when the snows had fallen this far south. Neither in his memory, he said, nor in the memory of any that he had ever spoken to.

"If it's usually even half this bad, it's no surprise we haven't met anybody," Rudy commented, huddling as close to their wind-flattened fire as he could without the risk of self-immolation. They had made camp in a rolling depression of ground that Ingold identified as a beast wallow of some sort—bison or gelbu. "Even without the Dark Ones, this part of the country would be a hell of a place to try and make a living."

"There are those who do," the wizard replied without looking up. Wind twisted their fire into brief yellow ribbons that licked the dust. By the restless light, only the prominences of his curiously reticent face could be made out—the tip of his nose, the wide-set flattened triangles of the cheekbones, and the close, secretive mouth. "These lands are too hard for the plow and too dry for regular farming, but in the south and out in the deserts, there are colonies of silver miners; and here, close to the mountains, lie the cattle lands and the horse lands of the Realm. The plainsmen are a hardy breed," he said, strong fingers twisting at the leaves of the fresh-water mallows he was braiding into a strand, "as well they have to be."

Rudy watched him weaving the plants together and picked out by the leaping glow of the fire the shapes of the seeds, the petals, leaf and pod and stamen, identifying and fixing the plant in his mind and recalling what Ingold had told him about its curative properties. "Are we still in the Realm of Darwath?" he asked.

"Officially," Ingold said. "The great landchiefs of the plains owed allegiance to the High King at Gae—in fact, as a legal entity, the Realm stretches to the Western Ocean, for the Prince-Bishop of Dele takes—took—his laws from Gae. But Gettlesand and the lands along the Alketch border have carried on a long battle with the Empire to the south, and I doubt that the breach will be healed, whatever Alwir's policies may be." He glanced up, a bright glint of crystal blue between the shadows of his hood and the muffler that wrapped the lower part of his face, the firelight reddish gold on his long, straight eyelashes. "But as you can see," he went on, "the plains themselves are all but deserted."

Rudy selected a long stick and poked at the tiny fire. "How come? I mean, I see all these animals, antelope and bison and jillions of different kinds of birds. You could make a pretty good living in this part of the country."

"You could," Ingold agreed mildly. "But it's very easy to die in the plains. Have you ever seen an ice storm? You get them in the north. Once in the lands around the White Lakes I found the remains of a herd of mammoth, chunks of frozen flesh scattered in head-high snow. The beasts had been literally ripped to shreds by the inferno of the winds. I've heard stories that the cold in the center of those storms is such that grazing animals will be frozen solid so swiftly that they do not even fall, but stand, turned to ice and half-buried in snow, with the flowers they were eating frozen in their mouths. And the storms strike without warning, out of a clear sky."

"That would sure kill the property values," Rudy assented with a shiver. But something undefined stirred in his memory, something he had read, or had heard read to him . . . Wild David's Body Shop in Fontana came back to him, with himself slouched in the erupted mess of split vinyl and filthy padding of David's old swivel chair, leafing through decayed copies of the Reader's Digest while a crowd of the local bikers argued profanely about what they wanted him to paint on the tank of somebody's Harley . . .

"And if you haven't seen the effects of an ice storm," Ingold continued, "at least you have seen the work of the White Raiders."

An almost physical memory returned to Rudy in a rush—the sweetness of the opalescent mist of the river valleys below Karst, and the sour tang of nausea in his throat. The drift of smoke in the foggy air, the bloody ruin of what had been a human being, the raucous laughter of the carrion crows, and Ingold, like a gray ghost in the pewter light, his robe beaded with dew and a tag of bloody leather in his hands, saying to Janus, "This is the work of the White Raiders . . ."

Rudy shivered. "Who are the White Raiders?" he asked.

The old man shrugged. "What can I tell you of them?" he replied. "They are the People of the Plains, the kings of the wind. They say that once upon a time their home was only in the far north, in the high meadows along the rim of the ice. But they haunt all the northern plains now and, as we have seen, have begun to invade the river valleys at the heart of the Realm."

On the edge of the narrow circle of the firelight, the donkey Rudy had named Che Guevara snorted and stamped at some sound in the distant night, his long ears laid back along his head. Distantly, Rudy caught the howling of prairie wolves. "You know," he said with forced casualness, "I don't think the whole time we were on the road down from Karst I ever actually saw a White Raider. I knew they were following the train, but I never saw one."

"Well, they're most dangerous when you don't see them." Ingold smiled. "And you're wrong, in any case. You did see one. The Icefalcon is a White Raider."

Of course, Rudy thought, more surprised by the fact that

39

the Raiders didn't resemble the Huns or the Sioux than he was to learn that the Icefalcon was a foreigner among the dark-haired, blue-eyed people of the Wath. And now that he came to think if it, the Icefalcon wasn't of Bishop Govannin's Faith; at least he'd only sniffed in disdain at Gil's question on the subject. Rudy remembered the farmhouse in the mists again and shuddered.

"That's the chief reason Alwir sent him on the mission to Alketch," Ingold continued, setting aside his herbs and rising. "Of anyone, a Raider would have the best chances of surviving the journey." He picked up his staff, preparing to make his usual brief inspection of their campsite before settling down to guard duty.

"Yeah, but if he's the enemy, how did he get to be a Guard?" Rudy protested uneasily, and Ingold paused in the act of turning away, a shapeless dark blur against the paler sand of the bank beyond.

"What is an enemy?" His scratchy voice seemed to come disembodied from the surrounding darkness. "A great variety of strange people find their way into the Guards. I'm sure if the Icefalcon wanted you to know, he would tell you." And though Rudy could not see him move, the wizard seemed to fade from sight.

Rudy shook his head in a kind of amazement. Ingold could be the least visible man he had ever met, seen when he wanted to be seen and otherwise all but invisible. It wasn't that he was shy, Rudy knew. The wizard observed the world like a hunter from an unseen blind; concealment appeared to be his second nature. Rudy wondered if all wizards were like that.

He huddled, shivering, next to the tiny fire. The cold of the night was so intense that he could feel only a little of the fire's warmth, even at a distance of twelve inches. Already in the treeless plains, wood was scarce, and they were burning brushwood and buffalo chips. Unlike the more volatile wood fires, the chips gave off a steady, cherry-red glow, and the heart of the fire was like a rippling amber well of heat. In that well, images took shape under his idle attention—the jeweled darkness of Alde's rooms at the Keep, with the single sphere of gold floating around the flame of the candle as pure and beautiful as a fruit of light or a single note of music, and Minalde's face, bent over a book, the sudden gleam of a tear on her cheek.

Although he was fairly certain the tear was not for him, but for the fate of the heroine of her book, Rudy still ached to go to her, to be with her and comfort her. At first he had shied from seeking her image in the fire this way, not wanting to spy on her. But his longing to see her, to know that she was all right, had proved too much for him. He wondered if Ingold knew.

For that matter, had Ingold ever sought the image of a woman he loved in the fire?

Sudden wind lashed at the fire, tearing the image from its heart. Like ripped silk in a cyclone, the fire twisted first one way, then another . . . And Rudy realized that the wind was not from the north.

It came from no direction—thin, cold, twisting. He looked up, light-blinded, at the sky; but by the time his eyes adjusted, he could see only the chaos of darkness. He started to rise, and a voice said quietly behind him, "Stay where you are."

Somewhere in the night, he saw the flutter of trailing muffler ends and the glint of eyes. Wind stirred at the fire once more, and the renewed light flashed in the burro's glassy green stare and picked out the shape of Ingold's cloak. Turning his eyes skyward again, Rudy saw them, black against the black of the churning sky, a sinuous ripple of movement and the glint of claws and wet, shining backs. The Dark Ones rode like a cloud, north against the wind.

Rudy realized his hand had gone to his sword hilt and slowly released it as they passed on by. His heart was hammering irregularly, his flesh cold. "We were lucky," he whispered.

"Really, Rudy." Ingold stepped from the darkness to join him. "Luck had nothing to do with it."

"You mean you made us invisible?"

"Oh, not invisible." The wizard settled down by the fire and set his staff within easy reach of his hand. "Merely persistently unnoticed."

"Hunh?"

Ingold shrugged. "Surely you've had the experience of not noticing someone? Perhaps you turned your head, or

41

were momentarily distracted by something else, or dropped your keys, or sneezed. It is very easy to arrange for that to happen."

"To all of them at once?" There was something a little awesome in such a collective lapse of vigilance.

Ingold smiled. "Of course."

Rudy shivered. "You know, those are the first Dark Ones we've seen on the plains?"

"Understandably." The wizard fished in his many pockets and located the yellowed crystal in which he was wont to seek the images of things far away. "I have reason to believe those Dark Ones have followed us since we left the mountains, or at least have been patrolling the road across the plains."

"You mean, looking for us?"

"I don't know." The wizard glanced at him across the dim glow of the fire. "Because if that were so, it would mean that they know that we have lost contact with the wizards at Quo."

"But how could they?"

Ingold shrugged. "How do they know anything?" he asked. "How do they perceive? What is the nature of their knowledge? They are utterly alien intelligences, Rudy, strangers to the very pattern of human thought."

Rudy was silent for a moment. Then he said, "But I'm thinking that the easiest way for them to know we've lost contact with Quo is if they know what happened to the wizards there." He looked hesitantly across the fire. "You understand?"

"I understand," the old man agreed, "and I would say so, too, but for one thing. I do not know what has befallen Quo, nor how the Dark Ones have contrived to hold the wizards under siege there. But if Lohiro were dead, I would know it. I would feel it."

"Then what do you think has happened?" Rudy insisted.

But to that Ingold had no answer.

Neither had those they asked, the few straggling bands of refugees that they met upon the road, fleeing east through the searing iron wind. For days at a time the pilgrims would travel absolutely alone through a universe of brown, rippling grass and shallow sheets of water—

42

water pocked like hammered silver by rains, or more often frozen in bleak and shining expanses of gray ice. But twice in those first few weeks, Ingold and Rudy encountered the decimated remains of clans or villages, fleeing cold and fear and darkness. The stories those men and women told were always the same: of small things that crawled down cold chimneys, or slipped between the window bars; of huge things that ripped doors from their hinges, or blasted down stone walls with the wrath of all the devils of the night; and of chill, directionless wind and the scatter of stripped bones upon the ground.

"And wizards?" Ingold asked of those circling the low glow of the dim campfire light.

"Wizards." A fat, heavy-muscled woman with a face like a leathery potato spat scornfully into the fire. "Lot of good their wizardry did them or any of us. I talked to a student out of Quo. They're all gone, hidden, locked up in a ring of spells, and they've left us to fend for ourselves. We won't see them till the Dark have gone."

"Indeed?" Ingold said, wrapping together and stowing away his packets of medicines. He had returned the band's hospitality within the makeshift circle of guards by healing the wounds either incurred in battle against the Dark or the White Raiders, or the effects of exhaustion and exposure. "When was this?"

She shrugged. "Months gone," she said. "He spent a night with us. We buried his bones and my husband's in the morning. Never knew his name."

"Fled, I say," the big patriarch of the clan rumbled. In the firelight, his greenish eyes, so common in Gettlesand, regarded them askance, but he did not ask how they came to be traveling alone and westward in these bitter times. "Fled south, to the jungles and the Emperor of Alketch."

Ingold paused in surprise. "Where did you hear this?"

The big man shook his head. "Stands to reason," he said. Far out over the plains rose the thin silvery chorus of wolves crying the moon. The camp guards shifted, calculating their distance; nearby an ox lowed in fear and jingled its tether chain. "There are no Dark in the Alketch, they say. But I'd sooner die free than live there."

43

"What do you mean, there are no Dark in the Alketch?" Rudy asked, startled.

"So they say," the patriarch told him. "But to my mind, that's just the kind of thing the Emperor would put around to get slaves cheap."

The second band they met, many days later, was smaller, two men and a couple of skinny towheaded kids, all that was left of a village of silver miners from the south. The children watched them from wary eyes through tangles of fair hair and stole a hatchet and packet of cornmeal when Rudy's back was turned, but to Ingold's question of wizards, the older of them only said, "Dead, I reckon."

"Why do you say that?" Ingold asked gently.

The boy looked at him with bleak scorn. "Ain't everyone?"

"In a way it isn't surprising," Ingold said later as he and Rudy trudged on westward through that dry, silken sea of hissing grass. In the buffalo wallows and the ditches beside the road, last night's snow drifted in cold, gritty mounds or blew like sand over the pavement. "Lohiro called all of the ranked wizards to him, to gather at Quo. I don't wonder that nothing has been heard of them."

Rudy was silent for a time, remembering the long road down from Karst and Ingold in darkness before the sounding doors of the belabored Keep. "You mean," he said quietly, "that no one else has any kind of magic help at all?"

"Well—not necessarily." The old man scanned the skyline for a moment; then his eyes returned to Rudy's. "There are those who never went to Quo at all, village goodywives, or self-taught spellweavers, or the closet-mages who never developed their powers, as well as the small-time fortunetellers whose art and ambition were insufficient to take them through the mazes to Quo. And below them there is a third echelon of wizardry, people born with a single talent—firebringers, finders, goodwords; children who can light dry tinder just by looking at it, or who can find things that are lost; women who say, 'Bless you,' and it seems to stick; healers who pretend their power comes from their learning, rather than from the palms of their hands; people who generally suppress such powers in childhood and deny them in the confessional; and people whose powers are so slight as to deny them the dubious prestige of wizardry, who seek to avoid the social stigma of being mageborn. These are the only wielders of magic left to defend against the Dark."

"And you," Rudy said.

"And me," the old man agreed.

As day followed day and the silver westward road dwindled out of existence under a black-clouded sky, Ingold spoke more of wizardry. He told Rudy of its long conflict with the Church, of its ancient strongholds, and of the great mages of past eras, Forn and Kedmesh and Pnak, who ran with the wild horse herds of the northern plains. Sometimes Ingold would point out animal signs, or identify the few creatures hardy enough to be abroad in the savage cold—huge, shaggy-coated bison, gelbu like short-necked, humpless camels, tabby-striped wild horses, or the many birds of the endless grasslands. He spoke of their ways and habits, not as a hunter would see them, but as the beasts saw themselves, with their narrow intelligence and their cautious world wisdom. In time Rudy found himself understanding even some of Che the burro's thought processes and motivations, such as they were, though it didn't make the balky and chicken-hearted animal any easier to live with. Now and then the old man would ask about something he had mentioned earlier. After the first few times Rudy was forced to admit he hadn't been paying attention, he listened more closely. And as he listened, it made more sense, as with any branch of knowledge as more is learned of it.

Often in the course of that journey, Rudy wished he hadn't been so successful in avoiding the efforts of a well-meaning school system to educate him. Most of what he learned seemed to him to be not magic at all, only a prerequisite course in knowledge he should have had but didn't: how plants grow, and why; the shape of the land and the sky; the motions of the air, and why wind blows as it does; how to meditate, to still the restlessness of the mind and focus it on a star, or a flame, or a single wisp of grass twisting in the wind; how to listen; and how to see the subtle differences in the silence and emptiness of the plains, the variations in the shapes of pebbles, the subtle shifts of wind and color and the pitch of the ground. Besides being a wizard, Rudy figured, Ingold must be at least an Eagle Scout, for he understood survival, how to set up a camp unseen, how to find water in the dry places, and how to scrounge food from this most barren and unyielding of countrysides.

As they walked, Ingold would occasionally stop to pick a plant from the roadside or point one out where it grew in the arroyos that laced the land as they moved south. After he had pointed out such a plant and described its growth and uses if any, Rudy found he had damn well better be able to repeat back everything about that plant. As a sometime artist, he had learned to observe; and after studying eight or ten different plants, he found he knew what to look for when he came across new ones. After a time it got to be a game, and he would seek them out for himself, asking Ingold about the unfamiliar ones and coming to the sudden enlightenment that any biology major could have introduced to him years ago—namely that there are similarities of structure and function in different groups of living things. The orderliness of it amazed and delighted him, as if he had walked for twenty-five years in a world of black and white and, turning a corner, had discovered color.

"Wizardry is knowledge," Ingold said one afternoon as they sat on the white boulders that lined the bottom of an arroyo where they had taken shelter from the wind. The land was growing higher and less grassy, the waving fields of long brown grasses giving way to short bunchgrass and huge, scraggy-barked sagebrush. Dry washes cut the land, scattering it with stone and gravel. At the bottom of this one, a thin trickle of water ran, edged with ice even at high noon. It burned Rudy's fingers through his gloves as he filled the drinking bottles. Ingold sat on the rocks behind him, idly drawing the dry, yellowish blossoms of a dead stalk of kneestem through his fingers as he scanned, without seeming to, the banks of the gully against the pallid sky. "Even the most talented adept is useless without knowledge, without the awareness of every separate facet of the world within which he must work."

"Yeah," Rudy said, sitting back and stoppering the flask with stiff, clumsy fingers. "But a lot of what you've been

46

teaching me sometimes seems kind of useless. Like that kneestem you've got—I mean, it doesn't have anything to do with magic. It's just a weed. You said yourself it's worthless."

"It is worthless to us and to animals, having no value either as medicine or as food," Ingold agreed, turning the dry wisp in his mittened fingers. "But we ourselves are useless to other forms of life—except, I might point out, as sustenance to the Dark Ones. Kneestem, like you and me, exists for its own sake, and we must take that into account in all our dealings with the world that we hold in common with it."

"I see your point," Rudy said, after a moment's consideration of how much of what he loved and valued was, objectively, pretty useless. "But I didn't know jack about anything when I started magic. I called fire because I had to."

"No," the wizard contradicted. "You called fire because you knew it could be done."

"But I didn't know that."

"Then why did you try? I think you knew in your heart that you could do it. I think you might even have done it as a child."

Rudy was silent for some time, sitting on the bleached bones of the rock. The wind moaned faintly along the banks above them, and Che flicked his long ears at the sound. There was no wind in the gullies. It was so still he could hear the water clucking softly at the ice. "I don't know," he said finally, his voice small and a little frightened. "I dreamed about it, I think. I used to dream about a lot of stuff like that when I was a real little kid, like three or four years old, I remember dreaming—I think it was a dream—I picked up a dry branch in our back yard and, holding it in my hand, I knew I could make it flower. And I did. These white flowers budded out all over it, just from my holding it, just from my knowing they would. Then I ran and told my mother about it, and she hit me upside the head and told me not to imagine stuff." The memory came back to him now, as clear as vision, but distant, as if it had happened to someone else. There was no sorrow in his voice, no anger, only wonderment at the memory itself.

47

Ingold shook his head. "What a thing to tell a child."

Rudy shrugged it away. "But I was always interested in how stuff was put together. Like cars—or anyway, I think that's why I was good with cars. How they work, and the sound and feel of whether they're right or wrong. The human body's the same way, I guess. And I think that's why I drew. Just to know what it was and how it all fits."

The wizard sighed and laid the dead plant stem among the rocks. "Perhaps it's just as well," he said finally. "You could never have gotten the proper teaching, you know. And there are few more dangerous things in the world than an untaught mage." New winds threaded down the gully. Ingold stood up, shivering, and pulled his hood over his face once more, wrapping his long muffler over it so that all that showed of his face was the end of his nose and the deep-set glitter of bright azure eyes. Rudy got up also, hung the water bottles over the various projections of the pack-saddle, and led Che up the narrow trail that had taken them down into the draw. Ingold moved nimbly ahead of him.

"Ingold?"

They scrambled up the last few feet to level ground and made their way back toward the road. A covey of prairie hens went skittering away almost under their feet. Che flung up his head in panic. The skies had darkened perceptibly, and in the distance Rudy could see the rain sheeting down.

"Why is an untaught mage so dangerous?"

The wizard glanced back at him. "A mage will have magic," he said quietly. "It's like love, Rudy. You need it and you will find it. You will be driven to find it. And if you can't find good love, you will have bad, or what passes in some circles for love. And it can hurt you and destroy everyone you touch. That is why there is a school at Quo," he went on, "and a Council.

"The wizardry at Quo is the mainstream, the centerpoint of teaching. Since Forn the Old retired there and began to gather all the lore of wizardry in his black tower by the sea, the Archmage and the Council of Quo have been the teachers of all those who were capable of understanding what was taught. Its principles are the principles handed down from the old wizardry, the legacy of the empires that existed before the first coming of the Dark, three thousand years ago. They are older than any kingdom of the earth, older than the Church."

"Is that why the Church has it in for us?"

Wind had begun to blow down rain upon them, mixed with hard, tiny spits of hail. Rudy pulled up his hood resignedly. He had long since gotten used to the idea that if it rained, he got wet. There was no shelter in the open plains.

"The Church finds us unbiddable," Ingold said mildly. "They talk of the power as a manifestation of the illusions of the Devil, but it all comes down to the fact that we have the power to change the universe materially and we owe neither them nor their God allegiance. As you've already guessed, we are excommunicates, ranking with heretics, parricides, and doctors who poison wells to drum up business for themselves. If the Church wanted to press the point, they could give Alwir considerable trouble for employing Bektis or even associating with me. The Church will make no marriage when one of the parties is mageborn; and when we die, we are buried like criminals in unhallowed ground, if we aren't simply burned like murrained beasts. Whatever happens, Rudy, remember that no law protects wizards."

The darkness of the vaults beneath the palace at Karst came back to Rudy's mind—the narrow doorless cell and the Rune of the Chain, spelled to hold Ingold there until he starved. *No wonder,* he thought, *those with only a single power choose to lie about it. The surprising thing is that anyone becomes a wizard at all.*

Rain drummed down around them, black and freezing, from a dark sky. It pooled in the ditches beside the road, sheeted the low ground, and ran in rivulets down Rudy's cloak, slowly soaking him through. He tried to remember the last time he'd seen a clear sky and wondered wretchedly if he ever would see one again.

Ingold was still speaking, more to himself than to his companion. "This is why the bonds between us are so strong. We are the only ones who truly understand each other, as Lohiro and I know one another's mind. It's why he and I traveled together, bound as allies against all the

49

world, why he was like a son to me, and why he picked me to be his father. We are all we have, Rudy—wizards, and those very few people who, not mageborn themselves, understand. Quo is more than the center of wizardry on earth; it is our heart-home. It is all we have."

The cloudburst was slackening. Light and mists rolled in the lowering air, but no sign of sun or sky. It seemed as if all the world were blanketed in cloud and the sun would never break through again.

Rudy asked, "Do wizards—uh—marry among themselves? Or could a wizard, like, marry an ordinary person?"

Ingold shook his head. "Not legally. There is no legal marriage with excommunicates such as we, at least not anymore, though matters used to be different in times past." He glanced sharply sideways at him, and Rudy had the uncomfortable feeling, as he often did with Ingold, that his mind was being read. "There used to be a saying, 'A wizard's wife is a widow.' We are wanderers, Rudy. We make that choice in accepting the power, in admitting to ourselves what we are. There are those who are not mageborn who understand us, but mostly they also understand that we cannot be like them. It's a rare person, woman or man, who can accept a long-term relationship on that basis. In a sense we are born damned, though not in the way the Church means it."

"Do wizards love?"

A look of pain crossed behind the blue eyes, like a quick shiver in the wake of a draft. "God help us, yes."

All of this strange miscellany of knowledge and information only served as a background to quiet Rudy's mind and help him to focus and understand. The step between understanding the world and understanding magic was a very small one.

One night Ingold scratched the runes in the dust by their tiny campfire, and Rudy, who had guessed by this time that the wizard did not repeat himself, spent the evening studying their shape and sequence in the dim, ruddy light. After that he periodically drew them out for himself while he sat his guard watches, laboriously memorizing shapes, names, and attributes—the constellations of forces which centered on each separate symbol. Ingold

50

sometimes talked about them as the two men ate supper or settled down for the night, explaining how they might be used for meditation or divination, telling where they came from, who had first drawn them, and why. Slowly their pattern came to make sense to Rudy, until he saw how a single rune, properly made with the appropriate words and thoughts, could draw its attributes to itself and surround itself with them. This was how Yad would protect and turn aside the gaze of a seeker from that on which it was drawn, how Traw would make invisible things visible, and how Pern would focus the thoughts of those who looked upon it for rationality, justice, and law.

Ingold never drew them all out for him again.

He taught Rudy other things as the plains country gave way entirely to the fringes of the cold sagebrush deserts. He showed simple tricks of illusion that could be woven around a wizard to make other people see things they did not really see. A mage could spot the illusion, but most people, who operated on surface impressions, could easily be led to think that they saw a person of different appearance, or a tree, or an animal, or a flaming whirlwind—or simply nothing there at all. It was less like magic, Rudy thought, than it was like acting, or storytelling, or drawing, but done differently. Rudy could already call fire and mold the white witchlight into a ball to illuminate without heat, like St. Elmo's fire on the end of his staff. He had learned to use his ability better to see in darkness and, by experiment, to draw visible things in the air with his fingers. As they came into the true desert and water grew scarcer, Ingold showed him how to make a water compass by witching the twigs of a certain plant and how to tell by magic if a plant were poisonous.

One night they spoke of power, of the central key of each person or being or living thing—and Ingold's definition of living things was very different from Rudy's. He spoke of the focus of all being, the innermost truth that Plato had called the essence; the understanding of that was the key to the Great Magic, and the ability to see it was the mark of a mage. Watching those bright crystal eyes across the fire, Rudy saw reflected in them the vision of his own soul, lying, like the silver runes on the Keep doors, beneath the surface of the familiar body. He saw with calm and pitiless detachment his own feelings about himself, the interlocking of vanity and love and yearning and laziness, a kind of bright, glittering perpetual-motion machine of affection, cowardice, and sloth that drove his restless soul. He saw it with Ingold's pure, unforbearing gaze, seeing faults and virtues alike, and was neither surprised nor ashamed. It only existed, being what it was. And in that timeless and bodiless trance, he became aware of that other essence beside him, like a lightning-riddled rock, lambent with power, fired within by a magic that permeated from its visible core. *Ingold,* he thought, startled and shocked, for the momentary vision of those scarred depths of love and grief and loneliness dwarfed his own bright, shallow emotions to insignificance. He felt an overwhelming awe of the wizard again, as he had before the ringing doors of the assaulted Keep and as he had one night in the valleys of the river, when Ingold had asked him why he wanted to be a mage. It was an awe that Rudy usually kept hidden, half-forgotten in the face of that shabby little old man with his scarred hands and mild, sarcastic humor. But the awe never fully left him; it increased as he came to understand this scruffy old pilgrim. He would now no longer question how Ingold knew whether Lohiro of Quo were alive or dead.

"Magic isn't like I thought it would be," Rudy said much later that same night as he gathered his blankets about him, while Ingold settled down by the fire to take first shift at guard. "I mean, I used to think it was like— oh, people turning themselves into wolves, or slaying dragons, or blasting walls down, or flying through the air, or walking on water—stuff like that. But it's not."

"But it is, really," Ingold said easily, prodding at the ashes of their tiny fire. "You yourself know that one does not turn oneself into a wolf—for to transpose your personality into the heart and brain of a wolf, aside from being very dangerous in terms of the structure of the universe, might prove too great a temptation to you."

Distantly, the wolves answered his words, their faint howling riding down the night wind. In the darkness of their arroyo camp, Rudy caught the bright, hard glitter of Ingold's eyes and heard the dreamy edge to his voice.

"Wolves love what they are, Rudy. To be strong—to

kill—to live with the wind and the pack—it would call to the wolf in your own soul. There would always be the danger, you see, that you would not want to come back. And as for slaying dragons," he went on in a milder tone, "well, dragons are really rather timid creatures, tricky and dangerous, but only likely to attack humans if driven by hunger."

"You mean—there are dragons? Real live dragons?"

The wizard looked startled at the question. "Oh, yes, I have actually even slain a dragon. Rather, I acted as decoy and Lohiro did the sword work. As for the rest of it— blasting down walls and walking on water . . ." He smiled. "Need has simply not arisen."

"You mean," Rudy said uneasily, "that—you could? If you had to?"

"Walk on water? I could probably find a boat."

"But if there wasn't a boat?" Rudy pursued.

Ingold shrugged. "I'm quite a good swimmer."

Rudy was silent for a time, his head pillowed on his hands, staring up into the black and featureless sky, hearing the belling of the wolves on their hunting trail, sweet with distance and incredibly lonely, and remembering the men he had known who had chosen to live as human wolves on a hunting trail of steel and gasoline. *To live with the wind and the pack* . . . That he understood. That mind he knew.

Another thought came to him. "Ingold? When you said that the Dark Ones are—'alien intelligences'—you meant that humans can't understand their essence, didn't you? And because of that, we can't comprehend the source of their magic?"

"Exactly."

"But if—if you took on the being of the Dark, if you took the form of a Dark One, then wouldn't you under-stand them? Wouldn't you know then what they are and how they think?"

Ingold was silent for such a long time that Rudy began to fear he had offended the old man. But the wizard only stared into the fire, drawing the stem of a dried stalk of grass through his restless fingers, the flame repeated a thousandfold in his eyes. When he spoke, his soft, scratchy voice was barely audible over the keening of the winds.

"I could do that," he said. "In fact, I have thought of it many times." He glanced over at Rudy. Gleaming from the wizard's eyes, Rudy could see the overwhelming temptation to knowledge, the curiosity that amounted in the mageborn to an almost unslakable lust. "But I won't. Ever. The risk would be too great." He dropped the grass stem he held into the fire and watched it idly as it curled and blackened in the veils of burning gold like a corpse upon a pyre. "For you see, Rudy—I might like being a Dark One."

CHAPTER FOUR

"I never thought it would come to this so soon." Gil lobbed a hunk of snow down at the trampled muck of the valley road below.

Seya set down her bow and quiver, shook the powdered snow from her black cloak, and gave a perfunctory glance at the dark pine woods that rose behind the little watchpost. "Come to what?" she asked.

Gil got to her feet, cramped from her long watch in the icy afternoon. "Come to guarding the road against our own people."

Seya said nothing.

"I've been watching the smoke of their campfires," Gil went on casually, gathering up her own weapons, bow and sword and spear. "I figure they camped at the ruined watchtowers where the road comes into the Vale, the ones Janus called the Tall Gates. There were several thousand when they came up the road yesterday. By the fires, I don't think there's near that many today. The Dark must have come in the night." She turned, prickled by the older Guard's silence. "You know, we didn't have to drive them on like beggars."

Seya looked uncomfortable. She hadn't cared for it, either. The newcomers had been nearly frozen, in rags and starving, when they'd trudged up the valley road. It hadn't taken much of a show of force to send them on their way. But she only said, "When you put on the emblem of the Guards, Gil-Shalos, you gave up the right to have an opinion. We serve the King of Gae—in this case, Prince Altir. Or the Queen."

Gil folded her arms, trying vainly to warm her hands under her dark, shabby cloak. In the distance she could still see the thin plumes of bluish woodsmoke rising in the clear, freezing air. *It wasn't the Queen who gave the orders*, she thought. *It was Alwir. But it might as well have been her Majesty, for all the difference it made.*

She thought of the Queen, a shy, dark-haired girl standing in her brother's elegant shadow. She saw the two now as they had been yesterday, standing in the dark gateway of the Keep with their guards ranged around them, the bullion on their embroidered robes flashing palely in the wan sunlight. *We have neither food nor space to take you in*, Alwir had said to the tall, ragged monk who had led the refugees up the Pass and who had stood at their head with his stained red robes as brown as old blood against the snow. *What food we have will barely take us 'til spring.*

There had been a stirring among Alwir's guards and a leathery rattle, like a dragon's scales, of fingered scabbards. The refugees had turned away, retracing their plowed tracks through the crusted snow.

"Look." Seya's voice broke Gil from her reverie, and she turned her head quickly, following the older Guard's pointing finger. A single rider had appeared on the road, his tall, bony bay horse picking carefully through the slippery mess of ice-scummed potholes that was all that remained of the way. Even without the ivory braids that lay on the man's dark shoulders, Gil would have recognized the tall, thin body and the easy way he sat a horse. The colorless eyes sought the women; a gloved hand was lifted in hail and farewell.

Gil raised her hand in answer, not certain whether to laugh or feel sadness. It was typical of the Icefalcon that he would set forth on a journey from which he might never return with no more than a wave at his closest friends. It would be a long journey and a slow one—he had only the single horse. Stock was precious in the Keep of Dare.

As the dark woods of the Pass swallowed him again, she glanced worriedly at the blur of campfire smoke veiling the black trees and said, "You think he'll have trouble passing their camp?"

Seya raised one eyebrow. "Him?"

Given the Icefalcon's coldblooded ferocity, Gil had to admit it wasn't too likely.

Seya went on. "It's more probable that Janus and the foragers will have trouble. When I left, Alwir and Govannin were still going at it hammer and tongs about how big a guard should go with the wagons and how many of them should be mounted. Alwir kept saying we can't afford to strip the Keep of any more manpower than we can help—and he has a point, considering the attack the Dark Ones made on us last week—and Govannin's on the verge of apoplexy because most of the wagons they're sending with the foragers are hers."

"I agree with Govannin," Gil said. She set aside the weapons of guarding—the bow and spear—for Seya's use and shook the snow from the blanket. "The refugees didn't look as if they were in any shape to take on even a small band of armed men; but once Janus hits the river valleys, he may have to contend with the White Raiders. There's supposed to be a band of them there."

Seya scrambled down the rocks and settled herself into the one niche under the overhanging boulders that provided both a view of the road and shelter from the biting winds. Four hours of guard duty had given Gil ample time to scout it out. "It's anybody's guess what's in the river valleys now," she said quietly. "They'll have enough problems with brigands and wolves and the Dark Ones."

Gil resettled her sword belt around her waist. "Where are they heading, do you know?"

Seya shook her head. "Anywhere there was stored food. Deserted towns, well-known farms—anywhere they can find stored corn or straying stock." She laughed suddenly, wrinkles stitching her lined face like the folds in wet silk. "That's the other thing they've been warring about all morning. Tomec Tirkenson and his people finally got on their way over Sarda Pass for Gettlesand."

"I knew they were planning on leaving as soon as the snows let up." Gil shrugged into her damp cloak, drawing its dark, heavy, smoke-smelling folds about her. "Alwir should be pleased; it makes for fewer mouths to feed."

"And fewer defenders." Seya pulled the spare blanket over her feet. "But what really stuck in Govannin's craw was that Tirkenson took all his own cattle with him. She forbade him to take them, since the people of the Keep had greater need; she threatened to excommunicate him if he did. He said she'd excommunicated him ten years ago, he was walking around damned anyway, the cattle were his, he'd bought them in Gae, and he'd break the neck of anyone who tried to stop him from taking them back to Gettlesand with him. He had all his cowpunchers lined up behind him, so there wasn't much her Grace could say, and Alwir wasn't about to start a fight with the only landchief still loyal to the Realm. When I left, the Bishop was burning candles in the pious hope that he fries in Hell."

Gil laughed. She liked the landchief of Gettlesand. But if he had left, taking not only his cattle but his horses, it was no wonder Govannin was anxious about those that remained. Starved as the refugees encamped in the Pass were, they might try to kill the horses simply for meat.

The wind veered around the shoulder of the mountain, blowing a light skiff of snow down upon them from the rocks above. The cloud-cover lay high that day, just skimming the tips of the white-blanketed peaks; when it shifted, Gil thought she could see the cold flash of the glaciers. *Growing or retreating?* she wondered idly. *Growing, I bet, if they've had many winters as cold and overcast as this one. Just what we need to add to our problems. A goddam ice age!*

She looked back down the Pass at the churned, muddy slop of the frozen road, the spatchcocked landscape of sterile black and sterile white, and the gloom of the woods that even deer had deserted. In the distance, the camp smoke made a little white streak, like a finger smudge in the murky air. "Where were they from, do you know?" she asked Seya.

The Guard shrugged. "Penambra, maybe. The monk who talked to Alwir had a deep-south accent. Probably some of them had been wandering around in the valleys for weeks."

Maybe Alwir was right, Gil thought as she climbed the muddy path and started back through the woods toward the Keep. The vast quantities of corn, wheat, and salt meat stored in the top two levels of the Keep, or secreted in the mazes of cells in Church territory, looked to be a lot, until one realized that they would have to last some eight thousand souls through the winter. It was only early

October. Whatever forage Janus could find in the valleys below was an unknowable quantity. Perhaps it was necessary that she and the other Guards had been a party to denying food and shelter to emaciated children and to leaving them for the Dark. It was the other side of the warrior's coin. The clean joys of warfare were part of a larger picture, and what to her was a way of life was to others above her simply an instrument of policy.

But, she reflected, she was hardly alone in that. In her light, tuneless voice she began singing "A Policeman's Lot Is Not a Happy One," and the Gilbert and Sullivan melody floated on the drift of an alien breeze through the dark, stony woods of another universe.

The road circled a stand of pines, and the smells of the Keep reached her from afar, the stinging woodsmoke, as women rendered used fat and ash into soap, and the warm reek of cattle. Children's laughter mingled with the confused bleating of sheep and goats, with the ringing of an ax in the woods, and with the sound of a deep bass voice lifted, like Gil's, in song. Half-frozen mud squished under her boots as she picked her way around that last turning of the path. And there it lay before her, its sleek walls sheened by the pallor of the dull sky.

It wasn't as big, maybe, as the monster high-rises Gil was familiar with as a child of the twentieth century. But the Keep was well over half a mile in length, hundreds of feet in breadth, and close to a hundred feet in height. Enormous doors were dwarfed by the monolith in which they were set. Its teeming inhabitants swarmed the broad steps and trampled snow at its base. Black and enigmatic, the Keep of Dare guarded its secrets.

What secrets? Gil wondered. *Who built it, and how?* She was aware that it lay far beyond the technology of the present age, with its constant soft currents of air and dark, ever-flowing streams of water. *Was it raised by magic or only by superb engineering?*

And her infinitely distractible scholar's mind scouted the thought: *Who would know?*

Eldor, maybe. In a long-ago dream she had overheard the dead King speak of the memories he had inherited from the House of Dare, whose founder, Dare of Renweth, had raised those midnight walls. But Eldor had

59

perished in the destruction of Gae. *His son, Altir?* The memories had been passed to him, to make him the target for the malice of the Dark. But he was an infant, too young to speak. *Lohiro?* Maybe. But the archmage was hidden at Quo, and it would be weeks before he came to the Keep, if he ever did.

Gil considered. Ingold had said that records did not go back to the time of the building of the Keep. The chaos of the first incursion of the Dark into the realms of humankind had been followed by centuries of ignorance, social dislocation, famine, and violence. But how far back *did* they go? And did they carry in them some memory of an oral tradition, like Merlin and his dancing giants who reared Stonehenge? What was in the wagonloads of Church records that Bishop Govannin had risked civil war with Alwir for on the road down from Gae?

A flicker of movement caught her eye and drove that thought from her mind. Someone was slipping through the trees to her right—someone who was furtive without being particularly skillful about it. Gil got a brief glimpse of a peasant's fluttering rainbow-colored skirts, all but hidden in the dark swirl of a cloak. She wondered if it was any of her business.

The shadow flitted from tree to tree, working through the woods above the road. *Probably headed for the refugee camp,* Gil guessed. *That's the only thing in that direction. At least somebody's showing a little compassion, for all the good it's likely to do.*

In that case, it *was* her business. There was barely time to make it there and back before darkness fell. Gil paused in the road and, for the benefit of the fugitive, snapped her fingers and cursed as if she had forgotten something, then turned and hastened back. Once out of sight of the watcher's probable course, she doubled back through the rocks at the road's edge and scrambled her way to higher ground. She slipped between two shaggy-barked fir trees to wait, her dark cloak blending with the gloom of the shadowy afternoon, the white quatrefoil emblem of the Guards on her shoulder like a patch of snow on wet-darkened wood. In time she saw that cautious figure emerge from the trees, hurrying along the path above the road, keeping a wary eye on the backtrail, and huddling for warmth in the folds of a black fur cloak. The hood had fallen back. A great jeweled clasp glittered like stars in the raven knots of hair.

It was the cloak Gil recognized. Only one woman in the Keep had a cloak like that.

"My lady!" she called out, and Minalde stopped, eyes startled and wide. Gil stepped from between the trees.

"Please go on back," Alde said hastily, brushing the stray ends of her hair away from her face. "I'm not going far, and . . ."

"You'll never make it there and back by dark," Gil said bluntly.

"I—I'm not going to the refugee camp." The younger girl drew herself up, standing on her dignity. Her expression reminded Gil of her own younger sister when she lied.

"And you shouldn't be going there alone," Gil went on, as if she hadn't heard.

Alde would never make the big leagues as a liar. "But I have to," she protested. "Please don't stop me. There's plenty of time . . ."

"They're camped outside the Vale, down at the Tall Gates," Gil stated unequivocally. "It will be dark in a little over two hours. And besides . . ." She took a step toward Alde, and the girl fell back, like a deer on the edge of flight. Gil stopped herself and spoke more softly. "And besides," she continued gently, "if they learned who you were, you might never make it back at all."

"They won't know," Alde insisted, still keeping her distance. "I'll be all right."

Gil sighed. "You can't know that." She took another step, and Alde retreated warily.

Rudy had said once that Minalde's crazy courage was equaled only by her stubbornness. Gil saw now what he meant. "At least don't go alone," she said.

Alde flushed a little and began contritely, "You don't have to . . ."

"Christ knows, somebody should!" Gil turned on her heel and started back toward the entrance to the Vale, cutting through the snowy woods. "This way's quicker, and we can circle to avoid being seen from the watchpost on the road." Alde followed in her wake without a word.

It took the girls a little over an hour to reach the camp. As Gil had surmised, the newcomers had taken over the Tall Gates, ancient watchtowers that in former times had guarded the principality around the Keep from the smaller, less organized realms of the valleys below. As the Realm had spread, the towers had ceased to be a frontier and had been allowed to fall into ruin. As ruins they remained, vine-grown cliffs of mortared stone dominating the narrow neck of the muddy road, strongholds only of bird and beast.

The girls were met on the road by a thin, gray man—who had once been very fat indeed, to judge by the sack-like wrinkles of his deflated chins—carrying a spear and wearing over a scarecrow assortment of rags a soiled cloak of gold-frogged velvet. Alde gave their names as Alde and Gil-Shalos, from the Keep of Dare, and asked to speak with his lord.

Ankle-deep muck pulled at their feet as they crossed the square before the northern watchtower. The place smelled like a privy, wreathed in a perpetual haze of woodsmoke. The pitiful flotsam of flight littered the ground. Meager bundles of possessions, stray cook pots, and little heaps of firewood were scattered over the dirty snow. Men and women sat huddled miserably around their fires or moved among them slowly. The place seemed very quiet, except for the weak, persistent crying of a child. Gil felt ashamed of her cloak, her strength, and the marginal ration of food she'd wolfed down at noon. Beside her, Alde looked very white.

Their escort halted before a brush shelter. In the shadows at the back of it, Gil thought she could discern a small, stiff figure, lying completely covered by a ragged quilt; a man sat on a bed of cut pine boughs near the open end of the shelter, quietly holding the hands of two boys who with tear-blotched faces slept huddled at his side. He looked up inquiringly as the shadows of Gil and Minalde fell across the light.

"M'lord?"

The man got slowly to his feet, careful not to wake the boys, and limped from the shelter. Gil recognized him at once as the monk who had spoken for the refugees when Alwir had turned them away at the gates of the

Keep. "Yes, Trago?" Dark eyes sunk into leathery hollows moved past him to Gil and Alde, then rested for a moment on Alde's face. "Yes," he said quietly. "You may go, Trago. Get someone to stay with the boys, if you would."

Trago saluted and moved away through the camp.

The man turned back to them, and Gil noticed how waxy his skin looked under the black tangle of unkempt beard. "I am Maia of Thran," he introduced himself in that same quiet voice. "Bishop of Penambra." Alde started to speak, startled, and he smiled suddenly, his teeth very white in his beard. "I believe my predecessor assisted at your wedding, my lady," he said. Color flooded into Alde's cheeks that no cold could account for. He continued gently. "I was captain of his Guards." He inclined his head to her, a sign of reverence to her rank. There was no irony in his voice as he said, "Welcome to what is left of the city of Penambra."

"I'm sorry," Alde said quietly. "Please don't think I came—idly, or—or—"

"I do not," he replied reassuringly. "But I assume that, as you did come incognito and without retinue, your visit is less than official."

Only a fool could have watched the interplay between Alwir and his compliant sister at the Keep gates yesterday and remained ignorant of how the land lay, Gil thought; and this tall, gaunt scarecrow in his ecclesiastical rags did not look like a fool. It was within a few percentage points of certainty that he knew that Alde had come here without the Chancellor's approval or knowledge.

Alde raised her eyes to meet his. "I'm sorry," she said again. "But I couldn't *not* come."

"I understand," Maia said, "and I thank you for your compassion." He glanced around them at the camp. Men in the muddy rags of uniforms were making arrows by the warmth of smoky fires; women were tending children as best they could. There was the ripe smell of carrion cooking, the bubbling of thin soups, and the grating, persistent wailing of a child. "Still and all, I don't advise you to come again. As legal ruler, I can still hold most of us from turning bandit. But by your next visit I may be dead or ousted. Tomorrow you may find yourself dealing with anyone. The Dark have taken a very heavy toll."

Alde's voice was timid. "Is Penambra truly destroyed, then?"

"Truly," the Bishop said quietly. "Close to nine thousand of us left the city with wagonloads of goods, food, and all that we could carry away. You know Penambra—a city of bridges, built on a hundred islets in the bay. Rains flooded the town and trapped us in the cellars; and the Dark haunt those cellars, even in daylight. Half our provisions were lost to floods and half our people to the Dark before we even got clear of the town. Through the delta it was the same. The lands are flooded by the unseasonable rains and by the Dark, who have broken the levees on the rivers. What used to be the richest part of the Realm is deserted or peopled by ghouls who live by plundering the houses of the dead. It lies under terror of the Dark. They carry off as many as they kill outright. Did you know that?"

"Yes," Alde said. "I knew."

He looked at her closely, then nodded. "If you know that, my lady, and are still among us, you are more fortunate than I had thought."

He folded long, bony arms. A singularly gentle man, Gil thought, to have been commander of the Church troops. A group of ragged warriors passed them, changing the camp guards, lank, dirty men and women with bows and axes. They saluted him as they walked by.

Maia sighed. "So. People spoke of the Keep of Dare, the old hold up at Renweth. In some places, enclaves of farmers have made little Keeps, fortified buildings along the river. Your brother is not the first to turn us away. But even those don't seem to be proof against the Dark. We've found their fortresses smashed like eggshells, the defenders dead or wandering mindlessly. We've been beset by wolf packs, or dog packs hundreds strong. There was even a rumor of White Raiders in the valley . . . At times on the march here I felt it was the end of the world." White teeth gleamed briefly through the tangled beard. "In some ways I think the end of the world would be a simpler matter to deal with. If what the Scriptures tell is true, at least that would be quick."

"Oh, but it has been quick." Alde looked around her at the desolate camp, her jewels glittering in her hair as she moved her head. "This summer all of us were sitting on our terraces, watching the sun in the leaves and dreaming of sledding and parties at the Winter Feast. Now, before the night of the Winter Feast, we may all be dead. That's quick."

Something in the black humor of this amused him, for he chuckled. "Possibly. Possibly." The gray sky darkened overhead; he drew the rags of his cloak a little tighter about him. "But to have come here and to be told that there is neither food nor space by one with that monolith of the Keep at his back and his fat merchants in their ermine cloaks all around him . . . I do not know what I expected, my lady. But not that."

Alde said nothing, but Gil saw the fire of shame burn her face.

A girl came running through the mucky confusion of the camp to the shelter by which they stood, calling, "M'lord! M'lord Bishop!" He stepped toward her, and she said, "Troops, m'lord. From up the road."

Maia cast one quick look at Alde, meeting her blank surprise. Then they all hastened to see.

Before they reached the road, Gil could hear the sounds of the troop clearly over the unnatural silence of the camp. Behind the clinking of brass scabbard buckles, the soft slurp of boots in half-frozen slush, and the light jingling of mail shirts, she heard the whuffling breath of overworked horses and the creak of harness-work and wheels. The land on which the watchtower stood overhung the road, and the brink of it was jammed with silent, ragged watchers, but they made way for the Bishop and the two girls. Down below, Gil could see the troops hastening through the twilight—Janus on his stocky bay gelding, his red hair hidden by mail coif and helm, his eyes darting to take in every possible danger of the camp and the crowding woods beyond, Alwir's troops in their scarlet livery, leading the horses that drew the empty wagons, looking uncomfortable and ashamed as they passed before the hungry eyes of those to whom they had denied food and shelter, and the double file of Red Monks walking guard, faceless in their masking helmets. The men and women around Gil watched this show of force pass by in silence; only one child in the back of the crowd cried out, asking if those men were going to give them food.

Beside her, Maia said softly, "They are fools to set forth anywhere this late in the day."

Alde shook her head. "They had planned to be gone at noon. I don't know what delayed them."

Gil did, but held her peace. The latest quarrel between Alwir and Govannin had left its marks; though the force around the empty forage-wagons looked formidable, she would have doubled it, had it been up to her. She, too remembered the farms burned down by the Raiders.

The Bishop of Penambra did not move until the last wagon and the last of the rear-guard had vanished into the obscurity of the snowy woods. Then he said, "So they do not only harvest—they glean also, so that those who follow after must make a meal off the chaff."

Alde glanced up at his tall figure, her face flushed with shame. She stammered, "We—we have need of all we can find. Alwir is raising an army, sending to the Emperor of Alketch for troops. They will burn out the Nests of the Dark at Gae, and so establish a place of safety from which we can reconquer the earth from the Dark."

The straggly eyebrows raised, sending a whole laddering of wrinkles up the high forehead. "On several occasions the Empire of Alketch has been likened to the Devil, my lady, and it is true in this regard: they say that the Devil cannot enter any man's house unless he is first bidden, but afterward, no man may bid him to leave. I think your brother would profit to take in the seven hundred or so warriors left to me, who are loyal to the heir of the House of Dare, before he gives his bread to enemies."

"My brother says . . ." Alde began. She stopped, too ashamed to go on.

"Your brother is a man who keeps his own counsel," Maia finished gently. He reached out his big, bony hand with its two crippled fingers, to rest on the black, soft fur that fell over her shoulders. "I understand, my lady. But speak to him for us. Tell him he will need our swords. Tell him anything. We cannot hold out here long, and there is no place on the face of the earth left to which we can go."

66

"I will tell him." Alde looked up into the gaunt, waxy face towering above her own.

"Speak for us," Maia said, "and if ever you should need them, my lady, you may count on our swords and our hearts."

"We can't just leave them to starve!" Alde said fiercely. The twilight of the lonely road had closed down around them. Evening lay like a veil over the dark trees.

"Alwir can," Gil pointed out.

"He wouldn't!"

"He's already done it. To bring in the Penambrans without starving our own people, Alwir would have to institute some kind of rationing system. Govannin will never stand for that."

"But she's the Bishop!" Minalde insisted passionately. "She's the head of the Church!"

"Sure," Gil agreed coldbloodedly. "You think she's going to welcome another Bishop into her bailiwick? And a commoner at that?" Gil had learned enough of the name structures in the Wathe to recognize what that "of Thran" meant on the end of Maia's name: farmboy; plow-tailer; sharecropper, maybe; someone to be looked down upon by those scions of the ancient Houses who could boast that semiroyal "-ion" tacked onto their titles.

Alde sighed dispiritedly. "I wish you wouldn't say things like that."

"I can't help it." Gil shrugged. "I'm a born devil's advocate. I'm not saying it can't be done." Something rustled among the dark trees, and Gil swung her attention to the sound. An owl flitted silently from a branch. She turned back, trying to pretend her heart wasn't doing double time. "Alwir has a point—you have to draw lines somewhere," she went on. "But there's room in the Keep, if the newcomers don't mind living up in the back reaches of the fourth level or under the tiles on the fifth. And I'm not sure what the foragers Alwir's sending out will find. If there's plenty of forage stored in the valleys, it could make a lot if difference, and it's something he isn't taking into account. Okay, maybe he's thinking worst-case." She shrugged again. "But I know damn well all the food in the Keep hasn't been reported and isn't in the main depots.

Walking patrol, I've come across dozens of deserted cells that are all locked up and barred, and I'd be willing to bet that, come spring when everybody's starving, people like Alwir's friends Bendle Stooft and Mongo Rabar are going to make a sudden bundle. But I'm not an expert."

Alde frowned. "If the Penambrans do come, where can we store the food? They'll need all that space to live in."

"Easy," Gil said. "Put it outside. That's been talked of before—build a giant compound out past the cattle byres and wall it against deer and wolves. The Dark don't eat dead meat or grain."

"Do you think Alwir will?"

"Alwir would love it. He would be tickled to death to know where all the food in the Keep is. Govannin will block it, and they'll start fighting over whether the Keep needs all those nonwarriors."

Alde looked at her reproachfully. "Has anyone ever told you that your logic is appalling?"

Gil grinned in the dusk. "Why do you think I never got married?" She stopped, catching Alde's arm to make her halt also. But the sound she'd heard had only been the sigh of wind, rubbing bare branches in the icy cold. She was aware that it was suddenly very dark. They went on, quickening their pace.

"There," she said as they rounded a curve in the slushy road. Far off against the black flank of the mountains, a square of reddish light was visible. "They'll have built fires around the doors and left them open."

"They can't do that!" Alde protested. "It's against Keep Law! If the Dark came in force . . ."

"It means they know you're gone," Gil said quietly and glanced up at the leaden sky. On either side of the road, the trees had faded into misty darkness, forming a murky cathedral through whose endless mazes of dark pillars an occasional black-flecked beech shone like silver in the gloom. The last fading of the daylight would leave them walking almost blindly.

"But Tir's in there," Alde insisted. *It was like her*, Gil thought wryly, *to think of her child before her own safety*. "Alwir should have . . ."

"Oh, come on," Gil said roughly. "Do you really think he would?" She stopped again, this time certain. She could feel it in her veins, a rush of electricity that had very little fear in it. Gooseflesh rose on her arms. Like the breath of agelong night, she felt the restless stirring of air on her cheek.

She sensed a movement in the air above; but looking up, she saw only the blackness of clouds. Yet she felt something in the shadows, haunting the snowy darkness with malignant watchfulness. In the utter silence, the faint ringing of her drawn sword seemed very loud.

"There!" Alde whispered. Gil swung around and saw the drift of darkness like a ghost above the snow. Sinuous, inhuman, it flickered into brief visibility and was gone. Without being certain why she did so, Gil turned and glimpsed something—the suggestion of anomalous motion, the flick of snow swirling against the drift of the breeze—to their right. But it faded, like a word whispered into darkness.

Then something dropped from the dark air above, something that splattered acid from a monstrous mouth to melt the snow in stinging rain, something that stank of blood and darkness. Gil's sword whined faintly, a blur of razor-bright steel cleaving the sooty protoplasm and dousing them both in a stream of foul and gritty black water that gushed from the wound. She saw the creature now as it swung through the air, a formless darkness that grew as it moved, the catch of crustaceous pincers and the long, sudden slash of a spined tail, coiling like a whip and thicker than a man's forearm. She hacked downward, severing six feet of that thrashing cable, which began at once to disintegrate. Like a howling storm of silence, the creature turned on her, the dripping tentacles of its mouth reaching out for her, an eldritch, all-swallowing cloud of night. She slashed into the darkness, stepping into the slimy welter of beating membranes and knowing, the instant before her sword cleaved the thing, that she had it and had it clean. Then the sticky remnants of the severed creature were streaming and folding messily around her like wet, dissolving sheets in the wind. The snow around them stank.

Alde started to get up from the ground, where she had very sensibly thrown herself to give Gil a clear field. Her face was dead white under the bloody slime, but calm.

"No," Gil said softly, "stay down." Without a word, Minalde obeyed. Nothing moved in the darkness, but Gil felt the chill presence of the Dark still. Above the foetor of the mucky snow around them, she smelled the sharper odor of the living creatures. In a single motion, she turned and slashed, her body reacting to cues before her mind registered them. The creature that loomed so suddenly from the darkness behind her split on the bright metal of a long, one-handed side-cut that Gnift had told her only that morning looked like an old granny beating a carpet . . .

To hell with Gnift and his granny, Gil thought, turning in the storm of slime to cut downward at the third Dark One, delighting, as she always did, in that clean and terrible precision. Her face and hands smeared now with charred muck, she swung around, scenting the night for further signs of attack.

The night was still. She reached down quickly and hauled Alde to her feet, running for that square of burning orange light that was the only thing visible in the blackness of the overcast night. "Are there more?" Alde whispered, glancing back over her shoulder at the massed, windy darkness of the trees and mountains beyond. "Can you . . ."

"I don't know," Gil panted. She stumbled, her feet slipping in the trampled goo of the road, her drawn sword in one hand and her other gripping Alde's elbow. "There's a Nest of them in the valley twenty miles to the north—they haven't got far to come. I guess those three were strays from the main attack." The light was nearer now, warm and amber on the snow, hard as glass reflected from the black sides of the Keep. Against an orange whirlwind of fire, forms were recognizable—Alwir, like Lucifer in his winged cloak, the Guards' instructor Gnift with the firelight flashing off his bald head, Seya and the other Guards.

"Main attack?" Alde asked, horrified. "But where . . ."

"Can't you guess where the rest of the Dark are? Why we were attacked by only two or three?" They reached the last slope of ground, coming into the glare of the fires. The ruddy light gilded Alde's scratched, dirty face and shimmered like a live thing over the dark, rippling fur of her cloak. She shook her head, confused.

"They're all down at the Tall Gates," Gil said quietly.

Alde looked absolutely stricken. "Oh, no," she whispered. Dark figures massed within the slit of brightness that

70

was the gate. Alwir came striding down the steps toward them, looking relieved and concerned and, Gil thought, just a trifle annoyed. It didn't help that Alde immediately and automatically accepted the blame for herself and hung back like a schoolgirl caught out in a scrape. Her brother took her arm gently and led her up the steps.

In the gate passage, everyone was talking at once. The gates were closed—six inches of solid steel. The well-oiled locking mechanisms clicked softly as the rings were turned. There seemed to Gil to be hundreds of people in that ten-foot passageway—Guards and Alwir's red-uniformed troopers, volunteers and herdkids, and people who were idle, curious, or ineffectually helpful. The narrow space rang with their chatter and was filled with crowding faces and flaring torches. Gil heard herself gabbling out what had happened, explaining it to Seya and Gnift. Strong hands rested on her shoulders and back; her friends were all around her. Before her, barely visible through the massed backs, the jumping shadows played crazily over Queen and Chancellor, grimy little sister and tall brother sharing the big man's vast, dark cape.

As they crowded out from the inner gates into the Aisle, Gil passed them. She could see Alde talking earnestly, her wet hair shaken around her face with the intensity of her speech. Alwir stopped, listening gravely to her.

Gil was close enough to hear him say, "Alde, I'm sorry. There is nothing I can do . . ."

"You can try!" Minalde cried passionately. "You can at least talk to him! Not turn them away like tramps!"

"You are a mother," the Chancellor said quietly, "and easily touched by pity. I am a commander. Janus and his foraging party set out this afternoon for the river valleys, and it may be that we can reassess the situation when they return."

"It will be too late by then!" she insisted, and her brother caught her by the shoulders, looking down at her white, intense face, her burning eyes.

"Alde, please understand," he said softly. She turned her face away, her cheek resting against the soft beaded leather of his gauntleted wrist. He put a gentle hand to her cheek and brought her eyes back to his. "Alde, my sister —don't undermine me, I beg of you. If you go against me, the Keep will dissolve into chaos, and we will all perish. Please. Don't go behind my back again."

She nodded wretchedly, and Alwir placed a comforting arm around her waist. Alde leaned against her brother as if exhausted, her black hair spilling down over the velvet of his shoulder, and he led her back toward the Royal Sector that was their home.

Standing among the Guards, Gil watched them, two dark figures silhouetted in the leaping warmth of the torchlight. *Well, what the hell,* she thought. *Now that Rudy's gone, he's all she has. And I can even understand Alwir's not wanting to take in men who will hate him for turning them away before.*

But nevertheless, she felt as if she had just seen a death warrant signed for that gentle priest and his ragged congregation among the ruins of the Tall Gates.

CHAPTER FIVE

"Holy Christ!"

"Really, Rudy," Ingold returned, in the mildest of tones. "There's no need for concern. They're only dooic."

"Famous last words." Rudy stood irresolutely in the sunken roadbed, warily scanning the filthy host of semihumans that had appeared with such suddenness on the banks above. "That's what Custer said about the Indians." Ingold blinked at him in surprise. "Never mind." He drew his sword and set himself for a fight.

Back in Karst, Rudy had seen tame and enslaved dooic shambling along after their masters with frightened, doglike eyes; he had thought them pathetic. Feral and naked, baring their yellow tusks along both sides of the empty road, they were an entirely other matter. There must have been twenty or more big males in the band; the tallest of them, standing in the center of the road with a huge rock grasped in one distorted hand, was close to Rudy's own height. Ingold had told him once that the dooic would eat anything, including burros—possibly even including human beings, if they could kill them. He wondered how much effect his and Ingold's swords would have against so many.

Ingold clicked his tongue reprovingly and placed a comforting hand on Che's head. The burro was on the verge of hysterics—not that it ever took much to reduce him to that state—but he quieted under the old man's touch. Rudy, who stood a little in the lead, risked a glance back at them.

"Would those things attack people?"

"Oh, possibly." Ingold took Che's headstall in one hand and brushed past Rudy, making his way calmly toward the half-dozen or so hairy, two-legged animals blocking the route. "In this part of the country they're hunted and put to work on the treadmills in the silver mines. I don't be-

73

lieve the wild ones know where the captives are taken, but they associate humans with horses and nets and fire, and that is enough."

The big male in front of him raised its weapons with a threatening shriek. Ingold pointed unconcernedly toward the main mass of the band, the females and infants, grouped on the hillside above. "You see how the weaker members of the tribe travel in the ring of the stronger? It's for protection against the prairie wolves or the *hrigg,* the horrible birds."

Rudy took a deep breath, something seldom advisable in the vicinity of large numbers of wild dooic. *Okay, man, it's your game,* he thought grimly and hefted his sword, prepared to sell his life dearly.

Several paces in front of him, Ingold didn't even turn his head. "Gently, Rudy. Never fight if you can pass unseen." As he came close, the dooic seemed to forget why they were standing in the roadway. Some began looking aimlessly at the sky, the ground, and each other; others wandered off the road, scratching for vermin or picking among the skimpy brush for lizards to eat. Ingold, Rudy, and Che wound their way among them, but the only assault was olfactory.

"Always take the easiest way out," Ingold counseled pleasantly, scratching the burro's ears as they left the sub-humans behind them. "It saves wear and tear on the nerves."

Rudy glanced back at the scattering Neanderthals, who had returned to the usual primate occupations of hunting bugs and picking lice. "Yuck!" he said succinctly.

Ingold raised his brows, amused. "Oh, come, Rudy. Barring rather crude table manners, they aren't the worst company I can think of. I once traveled through the northern part of the desert with a band of dooic for nearly a month, and though they weren't particularly elegant company, they did take care that I came to no harm."

"You traveled with those things?"

"Oh, yes," Ingold assured him. "This was back when I was village spellweaver for a little town in Gettlesand. It was hundreds of miles from their usual runs, but they evidently knew I was a wizard, for when the single water source in the midst of their territory went bad, they came

74

south and carried me off one night to go there and make it good again."

"And did you?" Rudy asked, both fascinated and appalled.

"Of course. Water is life in the desert. I couldn't very well force them to come in closer to the settlements for it, else they would have been trapped or killed."

Rudy could only shake his head.

They had left the high plains and had passed the borders of the desert itself. They moved through a dry, cold world where marches were measured from water to water and the wind whipped dust-devils across a barren horizon. In the great sunken flats that were like the beds of abandoned lakes, the wind played skeleton-tunes in the rattling bones of thorn and jumping cactus. But the high lands between were bare rock, clay, and lava, scoured into fantastic shapes by the unbroken cruelty of the elements, or ground to rock and pebble and sand. In places, dunes covered the road entirely, the sand printed with the laddering tracks of enormous sidewinders, six to eight feet long. Once Rudy glimpsed what looked like huge, two-legged birds dashing weightlessly along the red skyline. It was an eerie land, where for days, unless one of them spoke, there would be no sounds but the persistent whine of the wind, the tap of the burro's hooves on the roadbed, and the hissing slur of moving sand. It was like the silence of the hills back in Rudy's California home, the silence he had sought there on his solitary expeditions with shotgun or bow. In that unending stillness, the whirring of an insect was like the roar of an airplane engine and the only noises heard were those of the listener's own making—the creak of belt-leather and the draw and release of breath.

In all this empty vastness the travelers met no one, and the solitude, far from bringing loneliness, created a kind of measureless peace in Rudy's soul. They seldom spoke these days, but neither seemed to feel the lack. Sentences uttered two and three days apart took on the flow of conversation. Ingold would point out the burrow of the tarantula-hawk or the tracks of the little yellow cat-deer; sometimes Rudy would ask about an unfamiliar cactus or type of rock. Twice they felt the presence of the Dark Ones, seeking them on nights when the wind died down. But for the most part, they were utterly alone.

"How long were you in the desert?" Rudy asked, after a long time of walking in silence.

"Forever," Ingold replied and smiled at the startled look Rudy gave him. Since the start of their journey, the pale cloud-cover had not broken; in the shadowless light, the wrinkles in his windburned face seemed very dark. "You see, the desert is my home. Quo is my heart-home, the place of my belonging. But I was raised in the desert. I have traveled it from one end to the other, from the borders of the Alketch jungles to the lava hills that rim the northern ice, and still I do not know it all."

"Was this when you were village spellweaver?"

"Oh, no. That came much later, after King Umar, Eldor's father, had me exiled from Gae. No. For fifteen years I was a hermit down in the split-rock country, the land of empty hills and sky. I would be months alone there, with nothing but the wind and stars for company. I think I once went for four years without seeing another human being's face."

Rudy stared at the wizard, horrified but uncomprehending. It was inconceivable to him. Like most of his generation, he had seldom spent more than twelve hours alone at any one time. He could literally not imagine being alone, absolutely alone, for four years. "What were you doing?"

His feelings must have crept into his voice, for Ingold smiled again. "Looking for food. You do a lot of that in the desert. And watching the animals and the sky. And thinking. Mostly thinking."

"About what?"

Ingold shrugged. "Life. Myself. Human stupidity. Death. Fear. Power. This was—oh, years ago. There was another hermit there then, a man of great power and kindness, who helped me at a time when I needed help desperately." He frowned, remembering. Rudy saw in his eyes the brief echo of the young man he had been, wandering the solitudes of the wastelands alone. Then Ingold shook his head, as if dismissing an impossible thought. "He is very likely dead by this time, for he was quite old when he first found me, and I was only a little older then than you are now."

"Can you contact him?" Rudy asked curiously. "If he's

a wizard, he might have some word about the wizards at Quo."

"Oh, Kta wasn't a wizard. He was—I don't know what he was, really. Just a little old man. But no, it would be impossible for me or anyone to contact him. He would be found, if he wanted to be found, and if not . . ." Ingold spread his hands, showing them empty. "I haven't seen him in a good fifteen years."

They walked on in silence for a time, Rudy's thoughts chasing one another randomly, his eyes picking out tiny tracks in the sand, patterns of wind, and the shapes and natures of plants that flickered dry and yellow against the empty sky. He was trying to picture Ingold as a young man, trying to picture any situation in which the wizard would be in desperate need of help, trying to envision someone capable of giving the old man what he could not find for himself.

The road mounted a small rise, coming out of its sunken bed to crest a barren ridge above yet another flat of salt-bush and stone. The veer of the wind whipped Rudy's long hair into his eyes. For a moment he wasn't sure if he saw or only imagined the distant glitter of something far out in the flatlands. Even when he paused to shade his eyes, he wasn't sure what it was—only that vultures circled over it, high in the wan air.

"What is it?" he asked softly as Ingold came back to stand beside him.

The old man didn't reply for a time. He stood, his eyes narrowed against the distance, showing no visible reaction. But Rudy could sense a tautness that grew in him, as if in readiness for a surprise attack.

"White Raiders," Ingold said at last.

Rudy turned his eyes from the gruesome remains of the Raiders' sacrifice. It was nearly a week old. What the vultures and jackals hadn't gotten, ants had. But it was still fresh enough to be revolting. He concentrated instead on the cross that had been erected beyond the head of the stretched victim; it was seven feet tall and wreathed in complicated streamers of feather, polished bone, and glass. The cross itself was wood, rare in this treeless land, with a skull nailed in the join of the beams. The tufts of feathers and knotted grass twirled skittishly in the wind, reminding him weirdly of the candy skulls with roses in their eyes of the *Fiesta de los Muertos.*

"It's a magic-post." Ingold walked around it, cat-footed, leaving barely a trace of tracks on the dry crumble of the turned-up earth. His fingers caressed lightly the smoothed wood, as if to read something there by his touch, then brushed the dangling glass. "That's odd." He said it half to himself, like a man who found in his garden flowers not of his own planting. Rudy shivered and scanned the horizon, as if expecting to see the Raiders materialize like Apache from the pale wastelands of sand and thorn.

"Did the Raiders make it?"

"Oh, yes." Ingold went over to the remains of the sacrifice, hunkering down to examine the loathsome bones. Rudy looked away. "The Raiders will make a sacrifice in propitiation of something that they fear—you saw that in the valleys below Renweth—and usually, but not always, put up a magic-post to hold the soul of the tormented dead." He straightened up, frowning. "Generally they will make the propitiation against the ice storms, which they consider to be evil ghosts; lately they have begun to do so against the Dark. But this . . ." He came back to the cross, like a ghost himself in the pallor of the shadowless afternoon. "This I have not seen." He moved a little way off, poking with his staff at the hard, cracked clay of the ground, the knobby yellow twigs of the catclaw snagging at his mantle and the blown dust blurring his tracks. "They fear something, Rudy, and fear it enough to sacrifice one of their own band to divert its rage. But it wouldn't be an ice storm this far to the south—and it isn't the Dark."

"How can you tell?" Rudy asked curiously.

"I can tell by the pattern of the streamers and the marks scratched in the wood. This isn't the regular hunting ground of any tribe of Raiders that I know—they do not range the desert at all, but stick to the plains, following the bison and mammoth. Only the extreme bitterness of the winter and perhaps the coming of the Dark have driven them here." He came back and collected Che's lead-rope again, for all the world like a ragged old prospector hunting for the motherlode among the cactus and ocotillo. "We shall have to be careful and cover our tracks," he went on, turning back toward the road. "The Raiders prize steel weaponry and would in all probability cut our throats to steal our swords."

"Great," Rudy said fatalistically. "One more thing for us to worry about."

"Two," Ingold corrected him. "The Raiders—and whatever it is that the Raiders fear."

But in the two empty days that followed, they saw no sign of White Raiders. Toward afternoon of the second, Rudy thought he could discern a dust-cloud and movement on the road ahead and he suggested concealment.

"Nonsense," Ingold said. "Any Raider who raised dust higher than his own knees would be expelled from the band and left for the jackals."

"Oh." Rudy shaded his eyes and gazed into the clear grayish distance. "That's a hell of a dust for just one family, though."

As they drew nearer, Rudy saw that this was indeed far more than a single family, or even several families. An entire town was on the move, as the refugees from Karst and Gae and the ragged survivors of Penambra had moved. A long line of swaying wagons was surrounded by a skirmishing ring of riders and a broad scattering of scouts afoot. The creak of leather and the barking of dogs sounded weirdly unfamiliar to Rudy's ears. He had not been aware of how used he had grown to the silence of the desert. At the head of the wagon train, a cloaked woman walked afoot, and it was she who hurried her steps to meet them as the mounted scouts drew in from both sides. Something in the arrangement of the band reminded Rudy of the way Ingold had said the dooic traveled, and he smiled to himself at the thought.

The woman threw back the hood of her cloak as she came toward them, revealing a long, plain face that had been just short of homely before it had acquired whip-cut scars from the tails of the Dark and the blotched burn of acid. Her warriors fell in behind her, grim, dusty men and women in sheepskin jackets with seven-foot longbows in their hands. The woman herself carried a halberd, which she seemed to use as a walking stick, its enormous blade glittering in the pale daylight.

"Welcome," she called out to them as she came near.

79

"And well met on the road, pilgrims." Close up, Rudy could see she was about five years older than he was, with a long, straight mare's-tail of black hair and the hazel eyes so often found in Gettlesand. "Where have you come from, that you're moving west? Are you from the Realm?" Hope, eagerness, and anxiety struggled in her face and in the faces of those behind her.

Ingold held out his hand to her and inclined his head in mingled greeting and respect. "We have come out of the Realm," he replied. "But I fear we bear ill news, my lady. Gae has fallen. King Eldor is dead."

The woman was silent, the hope stricken from her eyes. Around her, the warriors, men and women, exchanged quiet glances. Back in the train, a baby cried, and a woman shushed it.

"Fallen," she said after a moment. "How fallen?"

"The city is a ruin," Ingold said quietly. "It is the haunt of the Dark by night, of ghouls and beasts and slave dooic gone feral by daylight. The Palace burned, and King Eldor perished in its ashes. I am sorry," he said gently, "to be the bearer of such news."

She looked down, and Rudy saw her big, rawboned hands tighten on the shaft of the halberd, as if to steady herself, or to cling to it for support. She looked up, and her eyes were sick with weariness. "Have you come from Gae, then?" she asked. "Because if you're bound for Dele in the west, if you'd hoped to find refuge there . . ." She gestured behind her at the train, which was slowly coalescing around the strangers in the road. "About two-thirds of these people are from Dele. The rest are from Ippit, or the country around the Flat River. I'm Kara of Ippit. I was—am—spellweaver of the village."

Ingold looked up at her sharply. "You're a spellweaver?"

She nodded. "The priest always understood. And I've been able to help, with what powers I have . . ."

"Are you ranked?"

"No. I had to leave Quo after my first year there because my mother was ill." Then she looked down at him with sudden eagerness, realizing what his question had meant. "Are you a spellweaver?"

"Yes. Is your mother?"

She nodded, and Rudy saw the quickening of new life

80

from the dead exhaustion of her face. "Have you had any word, heard anything at all, from Quo?" she demanded. "I've been trying so hard, trying for weeks, but I can't even get sight of the town. You're the first wizard I've seen since any of this began." She reached out to clasp his hand. "You don't know how good it is . . ."

"I know very well," he contradicted with a smile. "I haven't had word or sign from Quo or news of any other wizard but yourself since Gae fell. We're bound for Quo now, to find Lohiro and ask his help."

A faint stain of color flushed up under the burnt brown of her skin. "Well," she said, "I'm afraid your calling me a wizard is like calling that little burro of yours a battle-charger. In the same family, maybe, but different in kind." She looked at his face again, the black line of her brow kinking suddenly, as if she sought some lost memory.

He smiled again. "The colt of a battle-charger, perhaps," he said. "Where were you and your people bound for, Kara?"

She sighed and shook her head. "Gae," she said simply. "Or the river valleys, anyway. We left Ippit for Dele, which was the nearest city. We couldn't hold out in Ippit —too many buildings had been destroyed, and the raiding of the Dark was too heavy. Three days out of Dele, we met a great train of people fleeing that town, most of them half-frozen and starving. We shared what food we had . . . We've been on the road for three weeks. We thought if we could reach the river valleys . . ." Her voice trailed off hopelessly.

"The valleys are alive with the Dark. They're far thicker there than on the plains. King Eldor's son Altir has been taken to the old Keep of Dare in Renweth at Sarda Pass, where Chancellor Alwir has set up the government of what is left of the Realm. But they are hard-pressed, too," Ingold went on, passing over the scene that Rudy and he had both glimpsed in the fire, the sight of Alwir and his troops turning aside the refugees of Penambra.

Kara nodded despairingly. "I feared that," she whispered. "Have you heard of anywhere, anywhere at all . . . ?"

"Possibly. Tomec Tirkenson, the landchief of Gettlesand, has rebuilt the old Keep at Black Rock. I don't know

81

how crowded they are there or how well supplied, but it may be, if you went there and threw yourselves on his mercy, he could give some of you a home."

Kara glanced over her shoulder at the scruffy band of rangers at her back, and it seemed to Rudy that, without a word spoken, a motion was moved, passed, seconded, and voted—a swift council of desperation that had nowhere else to go. Her eyes returned to Ingold. "Thank you," she said quietly. "We will go there, and if he turns us away, at least it's better than remaining in Ippit to die." She straightened her broad shoulders and shook back her straight, heavy hair.

"Tirkenson has a bad reputation with the Church," Ingold told her. "But he is a man of what mercy he can afford as Lord of Gettlesand and he knows the value of having a wizard in his Keep. Is your mother with you also?"

Kara nodded.

"And did she go to the school at Quo in her time?"

A rare glimmer of humor flashed behind those greenish eyes. "And mix with all that highfalutin booklarnin'? Not her."

Ingold smiled, and the swift, sudden warmth of his expression captivated her completely. She continued to study him as if trying to place him. Her eyes changed from puzzlement to surprise and then to awe. She whispered, "You're Ingold Inglorion."

He sighed. "That is my unfortunate fate."

She was instantly covered in gawky confusion, like Gil when told that she'd done something right. "I'm sorry, sir," she stammered. "I didn't realize . . ."

"Please," Ingold begged her. "You're making me feel horribly old." He reached out and took her hands. "One thing more, Kara. There's a band of White Raiders somewhere in the area—I think a hunting band some thirty strong. We came upon a magic-post two days ago. I'd suggest you double your guard and widen your point-men. The Raiders are afraid. They may want one of your people for another sacrifice and they're certainly going to want your sheep."

One of the men in the group behind Kara asked worriedly, "Afraid? What do they fear? The Dark?" At the name of the Raiders, a whisper had passed through the train, like the smell of a wolf through a herd of cattle.

Well, Rudy thought, *they're desert dwellers. Maybe some of them have seen the leftovers from the Raiders' propitiations of the local spooks.*

"Possibly," Ingold said. "But the magic-post we found wasn't raised against the Dark. I have no idea what it is that they fear, but I do know that they fear it."

Kara frowned thoughtfully. "It's the wrong time of the year for fires," she said. "And it wouldn't be ice storms this far south. Unless they're a deep-north band with no idea how far south they've come . . ."

"I should hesitate to believe that a band of Raiders, under any circumstances, has no idea where it is," Ingold said. "But I've seen the propitiations for all of those. It isn't any of them. Have you heard any rumor, any story, any hint of tracks or signs of anything else abroad in the lands?"

A bearded farmer with a longbow grinned. "That would scare the Raiders? Maybe a million stampeding mammoth followed up by a flock of horrible birds, or a sun-cat with a thorn in its paw . . ."

Ingold shook his head and returned the grin. "No— they don't make magic-posts against anything they can kill."

"Disease?" the woman suggested doubtfully.

He hesitated. "Maybe. But the Raiders have a rather simple way of dealing with disease."

"Well," she admitted. "But in a big epidemic you can't leave *everybody* behind."

"I seen 'em dump as many as twenty out of a band, ma'am, and that's a fact," the farmer said, scratching his head. "And there has been a lot of sickness and famine this winter, what with this consarn weather."

"Maybe," Ingold said again. "But on the whole, the Raiders regard disease as an internal weakness of the will, rather than as an incursion from the outside. The Raiders don't see things the way we do. Sometimes they fear some very odd things. But in any case, there is something out there; and against it—and against all other ills of the road —may you be safe, Kara of Ippit, and those who walk in

83

your shadow." Reaching out, he made a swift sign above her head. "A good outcome to your journeyings."

She smiled shyly and repeated his sign. "And to yours—sir."

With this they parted, Rudy and Ingold continuing on their road, Kara and her village on theirs. The dust of the train swamped the two pilgrims, and they found themselves for a time surrounded in a white fog, moving among the crowding shapes of wagons, weaving among women, children, chickens, and goats. Craftsmen passed them with barrows full of tools, farmers bearing plows upon their backs, and makeshift warriors with swords and halberds. Dogs drove sheep along the fringes of the train, amid a faint, flat clatter of bells. More than one villager raised hands in greeting as the two wizards passed. An old granny knitting in the back of a wagon croaked cheerily, "You're headed the wrong way, boys!" Kara's voice was faintly heard to exclaim in shocked disapproval, "Mother!"

Rudy grinned. "So that's an untaught mage, than which there's nothing in the world more dangerous?"

"She knows her own limitations." Ingold smiled at the memory of that shy, homely woman. "As a rule, half-taught mages are worse even than the untaught, but she has the goodness of heart that wizards often lack. Among wizards she is an exception, in her way."

"Is she?"

Ingold shrugged. "Wizards are not nice people, Rudy. Kindliness of heart is seldom the leading characteristic of a mage. Most of us are proud as Satan, especially those with only a few months' training. That's the reason for the Council. Something must exist to counterblance the effects of the knowledge that you can, in fact, alter the paths of the universe. Haven't you felt it—that euphoria that comes with knowing that you can braid fire in your hands and twist the winds of Heaven to your bidding?"

Rudy shot him an uneasy glance and met eyes that were far too knowing and a smile of wicked amusement at having read his mind. He grumbled unwillingly, "Yeah—well—I mean, so what?"

The last of the herds was passing them, the whitish dust skating on the wind. Under a featureless sky, the stony emptiness stretched away to nothing. "So what indeed?" Ingold smiled. "Except that the ecstasy of power has a terrible way of getting out of hand. The Council and the Archmage have their work cut out for them to hold in check, not the power itself, but the souls of those who wield it."

Rudy thought for a moment about that, remembering the feeling that had sprung to his heart when he called fire, the quick, gleeful sparkle of triumph when his illusions worked. And he saw suddenly the trailhead of a path that could lead to evil past contemplating. But it was evil he understood. It was seeking knowledge for the sake of knowledge and power for power's sake, leaving Minalde to search for his own destiny, and staying in that hidden chamber to fathom a crystal's mysteries, while Ingold faced death and the Keep's destruction outside. He saw in himself the potential for unchecked power.

Even as his mind shied from that thought, he wondered, *Does Ingold feel it, too? Does Lohiro?* Like a young and golden dragon, with those empty, glittering eyes, the picture of the Archmage returned to him. *Has he wrestled with the ecstasy of unlimited horizons?*

He must have, Rudy thought, *if they made him Archmage. The most powerful wizard in the world, master of all the others. You really have to have your act together to stay straight under the weight of that one. Power—pure power. The rush from that must outdo any drug ever formulated.*

"How long does it take?" he asked. "How long do you have to study at Quo?"

"Most people stay there three to five years," the old man said, turning away from the vanishing dust-cloud on the backward road and setting his face to the featureless west once again. "But, as you see, not all mages take their training there. In times past, there were other centers of wizardry, the largest of which were centered around Penambra. And then, other mages learn by apprenticeship to itinerant conjurers, as Kara's mother probably did. The third echelon, the firebringers and finders and goodwords, operates purely instinctively, if it operates at all. But the center is at Quo. Its towers are our home."

The afternoon was wearing toward its pallid close, the darkness louring down upon the east. At the Keep of Dare

85

they would be shutting the great doors soon, under Govannin's prayers and Bektis' mediocre spells.

"So where does Bektis fit into all this?" Rudy asked idly. "Did he go to Quo, too?"

"Oh, yes; in fact, Bektis was about ten years senior to me. He feels I've come down in the world."

"So you learned to be a wizard at Quo, too."

"Well—not exactly." Ingold glanced across at Rudy, the evening shadows blurring his features within the shadows of his hood. "I studied at Quo for seven years," he went on, "and I learned a great deal about magic, power, and the shaping of the fabric of the universe. But unfortunately, no one there managed to train me out of my vanity and stupidity and my fondness for playing God. As a result of this, my first act upon returning to my home was carelessly to set in motion a train of events which wiped out every member of my family, the girl whom I loved, and several hundred other perfectly innocent people, most of whom I had known all my life. At that point," he continued mildly, into the silence of Rudy's shock and horror, "I retired to the desert and became a hermit. And it was in the desert, Rudy, that I learned to be a wizard. As I believe I said once before," he concluded quietly, "true wizardry has very little to do with magic."

And to that Rudy had no reply.

CHAPTER SIX

By command of her brother, Minalde did not return to the refugee camp by the Tall Gates. But a week after her first visit there, Gil took the downward road again, as cautious as a hunter of leopards, conscious of Maia's warnings about the kind of man who might succeed him in command of the Penambrans.

The watch on the road was still kept, but far less strictly. The numbers of the Penambrans had dwindled alarmingly; a Guard named Caldern, a big, deceptively slow-looking north-countryman, had visited the camp and said they were but a handful, huddled around their pitiful fires, cooking a fox they'd snared. He had seen nothing of Maia, and at this news Minalde had wept.

Why, then, Gil wondered, standing in the overcast gloom beneath the silent trees, did she feel this prickle of danger, this sense of being watched? About her the winter woods were hushed, a somber world of wet sepia bark and drab, snow-laden black pine needles, the bare, twisted limbs of shrubs sticking through the drifts like the frozen hands of corpses. It had not snowed in three days, and the ground was churned in muddy tracks where the Penambrans had been foraging and setting their snares. In the still air, she could smell the woodsmoke of the camp.

Why did the desolation have that sensation of hidden, watching life? What subliminal cues, she wondered, keyed her stretched nerves so badly? Or was it simply rumors of White Raiders and the old, half-buried wolf tracks she'd seen farther up the road?

The Icefalcon would know, she thought. The Icefalcon would not only sense the danger—if there was danger—but be able to identify its source.

But the Icefalcon was slogging his way down the drowned river valleys and dealing with dangers of his own.

Through the silence of the brooding woods, sounds came to her from the direction of the road—the *smuch* of hooves through frosty slush, the creaking of wheels, men's and women's voices, and the faint ringing of sword belts and mail—sounds comforting in their familiarity, if for no other reason. Gil hurried toward the road, thankfulness in her heart. The forage-train had returned in safety from the valleys below.

From the high bank of the road at this point, she saw them, the straining horses slipping in the frozen mud. She recognized Janus afoot, leading the way; his horse had been pressed into service to draw a wagonload of moldy, filthy grain bags and the smoked carcasses of half a dozen swine. The road was bad here, and the Red Monks and Alwir's troops had fallen to, helping to lift and force the sinking wheels through the knee-deep slop. Every wagon was laden.

She saw Janus stop and raise a hand to signal a general halt. He was almost directly below her, and she noticed that, in the week of foraging in the valleys, he'd visibly lost flesh; his square face under a grimy, reddish stubble was drawn and marked with sleepless nights and bitter, exhausting labor by day. He stepped forward, probing the road with a stick he carried; it sank in the ice-skimmed slush. His whole body, like those of his troops, was plastered in half-dried, half-frozen mud, his dark surcoat scarcely distinguishable from the scarlet ones of the men he led, except for the places where the mud had been brushed off. With a gesture of disgust, he summoned the troop to him; Gil heard his voice, assigning men to collect pine boughs and branches to lay over the road, to make some kind of footing so they wouldn't be stuck there until this time next week.

The men and women scattered, scrambling up the frozen banks, vanishing into the darkness of the woods. They were fewer than when they had gone down to the river valleys, worn, exhausted, and muddied to the eyes. Janus walked back to stand among the handful who were left, glancing uneasily at the crowding, close-ranked trees. There was something in all this that he, too, misliked.

Then he saw Gil, and some of the tension lightened from his eyes. "Gil-Shalos!" he called up to her. "How goes it at the Keep?"

"The same," she called back down. "Little word of the Dark; a few broken heads. Did you pass the camp at the Tall Gates?"

He nodded, and his taut, over-keyed face seemed to harden with regret. "Aye," he said, more quietly. "Curse Alwir, he could take in those who are left. There's few enough of 'em now; they wouldn't cause him trouble."

Another voice, soft and gentle and a little regretful, replied, "Perhaps more than you think."

Gil looked up. Maia of Thran stood on the high bank of the road opposite her, looking like the rag-wrapped corpse of a starving beggar whose hair and beard had grown after death. There was a stirring in the woods. Clothed in the skins of beasts, with their matted hair like beasts themselves, half a hundred of his men appeared from the monochrome darkness of the trees. Among them they pushed the bound, gagged, and unarmed dozen or so of the Red Monks who had gone to look for pine boughs.

Janus' call for help died on his lips.

"It is an easy matter," the Bishop continued in his soft voice, "even for starving warriors to ambush a warrior or two alone. Easier indeed than it has been to keep that road shoveled and churned into mud impassable by laden wagons and to watch here for you. If you had been gone three more days, I doubt we would have been able to keep it up. But now, as you see, we have food . . ." He gestured toward the stocked wagons. ". . . and the wherewithall, once we have recovered our strength, to go see for more."

Gil heard a noise behind her. Penambrans were coming out of the woods on her side of the road as well—grimy, wolflike, so thin that the women could be distinguished from the men only by their absence of beards. Those who did not have steel weapons had clubs or makeshift armament. One woman carried an iron frying pan whose blood-stained undersurface proclaimed successful use. They were already scrambling down the banks to the road to carry away the contents of the wagons.

"Once upon a time we trained together as warriors, Janus of Weg," Maia continued, his clawed, crippled hands

89

shifting their grip upon the staff that Gil suspected was all that kept him on his feet. "Perhaps you will do me a service now and carry a message for me to the Lord of the Keep of Dare."

Gil sighed and rubbed at her tired eyes. "I would sell my sister to the Arabs," she announced to the empty darkness of the Aisle around her, "for a cup of coffee." But no one heard this handsome offer, and only the echoes of midnight stillness murmured to her in response.

It was night in the Keep.

It was always night there. The dark walls held darkness inside as effectively as they held the Dark without. But in daylight hours the mazes of its corridors were alive with the flickering confusion of lights, grease lamps, pine knots, and the smolder of tiny fires in grubby and crowded cells. Voices echoed and re-echoed with laughter, song, scolding, Keep gossip, and Keep politics. The Aisle was always a circus of people working on what handicrafts they could barter for food or goods or simple good will, people washing clothes in the pools by the water channels, and people gathered to talk or to gamble for points, pennies, and love. In the deep night, one could feel the weight, the age, the mass of the Keep. Then the empty silnce reminded Gil of Ingold's descriptions of the Nests where the Dark bred underground.

The silence oppressed her, redoubling the loneliness in her soul. From the rickety second-level balcony where she stood, Gil could see very little of the cavernous spaces before her, for they were lighted only by the gate torches, weak and tiny with distance, and by occasional wall sconces down near the doors of the Church. A draft touched her face, clammy as the finger of a passing ghost. A tribute, like the murmur of the water below, to someone's long-past skill as an engineer.

Whose?

Gil flexed her stiff muscles and tried not to yawn. The last two days had been exhausting ones.

She had not been a party to the Council meetings called in the wake of the message that Janus had delivered to Alwir from Maia of Thran. But she had been there when the Chancellor and Govannin had met Janus on the steps

90

of the Keep; and she had seen the livid rage that had suffused Alwir's dark face at the news that several tons of food, plus every wagon and every spare horse in the Keep, had been appropriated by the Bishop of Penambra and his people. It had not helped the situation when, after a second of shocked silence, Govannin had said, "I told you to send more guards." Had Alwir been a wizard, Gil thought, the Bishop of Gae would surely have hopped, rather than walked, away from her glare.

A very plump merchant in green velvet who had come out as part of Alwir's entourage cleared his throat uncomfortably and ventured, "Is there any possibility, my lord, that the Dark Ones might destroy this—this shameful upstart?"

Govannin replied dryly, "The Bishop of Penambra would seem to be an able enough commander to forestall even that for quite a while yet."

The merchant toyed for a moment with the ermine tags that decorated his doublet. "Um—between the Guards of Gae and your own troops, my lord Alwir, we ourselves can field quite a force . . ."

"No." The harshness of the new voice startled them all. In the shadowless gray of the overcast afternoon, Alde's face was like marble, her mouth set and her nostrils flared with anger. None of them had seen her slip up, as quiet as Alwir's shadow, to join the group upon the broad Keep steps. "They are our people, Bendle Stooft, and they will be sharing this fortress with us. I shall thank you to remember it."

Against her rage, even Alwir had nothing to say.

There had been councils, of course, and negotiations. The earlier system of food distribution, personal barter, subsidy, and random charity had to be revamped, and Govannin fought tooth and nail against the suggestion of a general inventory of food in the Keep. But that same day outside storage compounds were laid out; every man, women, and child in the Keep, warrior and civilian, was turned out to help work on building them and to transport food to them to clear the upper levels. It was an exhausting task to those who also mounted watch through the dark hours of the night, but necessary. Gil knew that whatever

Alwir wanted to say in negotiations, Maia and his Penambrans would be admitted into the Keep.

And so they should be, she thought, stretching her shoulders to ease the kinks from them and fighting the ache in her muscles that came from too little sleep and too little food. Quite apart from the need for the extra warriors of Penambra to counterbalance the troops of the Empire, when they arrived, it had been monstrous to deny the refugees shelter in the first place.

She had watched through too many nights herself, on the road from Karst to Renweth, ever to be free of the horror of being in open ground in the dark. She thought of the Icefalcon, making his way alone through the flooded and peril-fraught valleys, with only the token of the Rune of the Veil to guard him, and of Rudy and Ingold, out in the emptiness of the plains. She found she missed Ingold more than she had imagined possible and wished that, like the wizards, she were able to see faces in the firelight. It wouldn't be the same—nothing was the same as Ingold's presence, his wry, tolerant amusement at the world around him—but at least she'd know if he were still alive.

She could think of no single person in her own world whose loss affected her so. The world itself, yes—the sunlit tranquility of the UCLA lawns, gilded by autumn evenings, and the warm peace of the library at midnight, surrounded by musty volumes as she traced a single reference through reams of medieval Latin and Old French. By this time, her women friends and her advisor, Dr. Smayles, would have reported her missing, and her parents would have instituted a search. The thought of what they all must be going through troubled her deeply. Of course they would have found no sign of any intention to leave anywhere in her cluttered apartment. Maybe they'd even come across her old red Volkswagen, rusting in the hills near where a deadbeat pinstriper named Rudy Solis had last been seen.

And how would she explain when she got back?

A cross-draft pulled at the flame of her torch, making her shadow leap nervously across the wall at her side. On the cross-draft, Gil smelled the scent of snow.

The doors of the Keep were open!

She held her torch aloft, her eyes narrowed with darkness and distance. Her heart pounded suddenly loud in her breast. It was the dead of night outside; the Dark could be anywhere. At this distance she couldn't tell whether there was any widening in the shadows of the gates or not, but the torches beside them, she saw now, were leaping and flickering in the draft, throwing irregular sooty patches on the dark wall behind. There was no sign of the gate Guard anywhere.

Fear chilled her. If the Dark had gotten in and seized the Guard . . . It would be Caldern, she thought rapidly, ducking through the mazes of stone-flagged passages at a run, the smoke of her torch trailing her like comet-hair. If the Dark had gotten in and seized Caldern . . . But how would they have gotten in? She counted turnings, left and right, dodging through a makeshift access corridor and down a splintery ladder, her sword already in her hand. The torchlight jerked crazily around her spinning shadow as she emerged into the Aisle and ran for the doors.

The inner gates stood a foot or so ajar, the slot of darkness between them like an eye slit in the visor of a black Hell. Gil sidled toward it, feeling the rushing of her own blood like fire in her veins. The steps where she had stood with Ingold, when he had asked her to hold the light at his back, were empty, and Gil frowned suddenly at the anomaly. If the Dark had gotten in and seized Caldern, there would have been something—bones, blood, his sword—to show it. Even if they had seized him, carried him off bodily . . .

She swung violently around. The empty Aisle stretched a thousand feet at her back.

Don't start that, she told herself grimly. *First things first.*

She pushed the inner gates a fraction wider and stood in the inky slit.

The misty starlight visible in the narrow rectangle of the open outer gates wasn't much, but it was enough to show her the ten-foot passage of the gates. There was no movement in the inky shadows clustering in the corners and the vault of the roof and, more importantly to Gil, no feeling of the presence of the Dark. She held up her torch; though it jittered in the draft, it revealed nothing untoward. Still her whole body was tensed like a cat's as she

93

slid noiselessly down the tunnel and stood in the open doors of night.

For the first time since Gil had come to Renweth, the cloud-cover had broken. Icy moonlight frosted the world outside, turning the snow to diamonds and the shadows to velvet. Frost lay like lace on the black stone of the steps. Three sets of heavily booted tracks led down the steps and through the frozen mud of the path outside, circling around toward the food compounds that had been built only that week and filled within the last two days.

Gil sighed tiredly. The story was now clear.

Maia and the Penambrans would be coming to the Keep within days. The food stored by Alwir's government and hundreds of large and small Keep entrepreneurs had been moved out to the compounds to make room for them. Probably not all, Gil guessed; there were still probably hoards cached in deserted cells and back corners by those who did not trust fate and would not admit to anyone all they had. Guards, Alwir's men, and Church troops were supposed to protect the compound by day—and fear of the Dark by night.

The wetness in the tracks was not yet frozen. Caldern could easily have been lured away; since the night of the Dark's great assault on the Keep, the Dark Ones had made no further attempt to break the gate, and the post of gate Guard was generally given to the captain of the watch, simply so the other members of the watch would know where to find their leader. Who would guess, Gil thought, that somebody would actually leave the gates open to venture outside at night to steal food?

There were three of them, she thought, considering the tracks, and a fourth to distract the captain. That argued a ring—not a single man or woman, fearful for some family's hunger after the arrival of the Penambrans in the Keep, but an organized group who would steal as much as they could and lock it away, holding it until the starving spring.

It was all as clear as the moonlight that edged the steps in crystal.

Gil stood for what seemed like a long time in the diamond night, the smell of snow and pine like ice water in her nostrils. Long ago, she remembered, she had been a

94

scholar, and it had never been her wish to harm anyone. All that she had ever desired had been the clean solitude of knowledge, the peace of mind and heart to read, to think, to unravel riddles and reconstruct past times, and to seek the truth behind the polemics of those whose business it was to lie about the dead. Alone in the hoarfrost cold of midnight, she remembered it clearly, for knowledge had been all she had ever wanted. She had chosen it over the husbands she might have had, if she had ever bothered to seek them, and the peace of family good will that she had let slip by the wayside in the wake of her parents' horror at her chosen course.

But since that time, she had come to other knowledge.

She stepped silently back into the blackness of the gateway. Putting her shoulder to the massive iron bindings of the door, she pushed it to.

The guttering light of her torch threw a fitful and tarnished gilding over the rings and levers that operated the locks. She heard the muted click of the mechanism, deep within the tons of poised iron, and, as if hastening to escape from what she had done, she took her torch from its wall holder and hurried back up the passage. She walked soundlessly, all her senses keyed. It was not impossible that the Dark had slipped through the open gates and were lurking somewhere in the darkness of the Keep. Above her own fear, she felt fury at the irresponsibility of the men who had done it—who had risked not only their own lives but the lives of everyone in the Keep and the integrity of the last sanctuary on earth for money.

In the weeks since the Guards had asked her to become one of them, Gil had killed dozens of the Dark Ones. The Icefalcon had said she was a born killer, a creepy sort of compliment that she wasn't sure she wished to accept. Maybe it only meant that she was naturally cold-hearted and single-minded and that she would, if put to it, rather kill than be killed. But she felt now as if she had cut a lifeline and let three men drown. She was glad she had not seen their faces and did not know who they were.

She never clearly identified the sound as she stepped out of the inner gates. It might have been cloth swishing, or the whine of something hard and heavy whistling through the air. But weeks with the Guards had given her hair-trigger reflexes, and the leaded stick meant to crush her skull cracked instead on her shoulder with splintering pain, throwing her forward to the floor. The torch skidded from her hand, and darkness seemed to swim down over her eyes, even as she rolled. Feet approached at a run, and she drew her sword with a long sideways hack at floor level, bracing her body as best she could against the impact. One of the looming figures in the darkness above her jumped. The other one screamed and fell on her, kicking and writhing in agony and screaming with a voice that rang in the hollow enormity of the vaulted Aisle. The weight of him crushed on Gil's injured shoulder, the screaming rang in her ears, and hot, slimy wetness gushed over them both.

Irrationally furious at him for wallowing over her like that, Gil twisted out from under, pain ripping through her shoulder as she moved. Her eyes cleared. A bearded man she vaguely recognized hopped around on the outskirts of the encounter, a short sword in his hand. There was another man in the shadows behind him, also armed with a sword, his fat face pallid with nausea. Without stopping to wonder, Gil tried to get to her feet, but the bearded man, taking his chance, stepped in on her with a brutal downward swing of his blade. Through a welter of pain and darkness, Gil recognized the blow as "coffin bait," a fool's move, and her reaction was as automatic as a blink. She took him under the sternum with a two-handed thrust of her longer blade and saw blood burst simultaneously from chest and mouth. His eyes glazed with shock and with the amateur's almost comical astonishment at death.

The fat little man dropped his sword and fled. On her knees, her head reeling, Gil watched him run all the way down the Aisle; she felt nothing but a cold, queer detachment, mixed with a little contempt for his cowardice. The man behind her was still thrashing on the floor, still screaming wildly on that same high note, still clawing vainly at his leg. Gil turned her head slowly and saw she'd cut his left foot off at the ankle. It was lying, still in its gold-stitched slipper of green kid, about four feet away. Then she fainted.

*   *   *

"She be all right?"

The voices around her were fuzzy and confused. Gil whispered, "Ingold?" through cottony lips, blinking up at the hovering shadows.

"You'll be fine, Babydove," Gnift's soft, hoarse voice said, and an encouraging hand patted her hair. "Just fine."

Gil sighed and shut her eyes against the smoky hurt of the dim lights. *I guess the Icefalcon was right after all.* So much for queasy considerations about closing the gates on those three poor thieves who'd gotten left outside and all that eyewash about the value of human life. Put to the test, she'd killed a man without so much as a token *what am I doing?*

Gil knew that at the time she had known perfectly well what she was doing. She was saving her own life.

Absently she thought, *Four for sure and one maybe, if the poor bastard bled to death.*

And she began to cry, as she had done when she had lost her virginity. She had crossed a line that could never be recrossed. It was no longer possible for her to be what she had been.

"Hey, Angel Eyes," Gnift's voice said again, and the sword-calloused hand wiped the tears from her cheek. "It's all over. Just a little broken collarbone. Nothing to that." But she could not seem to stop herself and wept, not for the pain, but out of a sense of loss and an understanding of herself.

The world returned slowly to focus. She lay on her own bunk in the barracks, the narrow room jammed with her fellow Guards in the blurred yellow glare of the grease lamps. Her shoulder was strapped and braced, and Gnift was wrapping up his crude surgical equipment on the next bunk, his elf-bright eyes kind. Melantrys was standing next to him, a bloody towel dangling from her hand. Caldern, who had replaced the Icefalcon as captain of the deep-night watch, towered over them both.

Melantrys glanced over at her. "You did nicely," she said. "Clean. I told you she had a strong side-cut, Gnift. Took the foot off through both bones and halfway through the other ankle." Her cold, careless eyes returned to Gil. "Was that a one-handed cut?"

Gil drew a shuddering breath and nodded. She wondered if her father had cried the first time he'd killed some Japanese he didn't know. In a voice that sounded hideously matter-of-fact, she said, "Yeah. What happened to you, Caldern?"

The big captain scratched his head. "Were had for chump," he drawled in his north-country accent. "Chappy come yellin' murder down the way, and 'twere no others to call. I followed, and a pretty chase he led me; and lost of him after a'. Sorry it is I am, lass."

Gil shook her head, closing her eyes again against the light. "You couldn't have known."

"Not something anyone would have guessed," Janus' voice said, and the Commander loomed suddenly from the darkness. "We never thought to be posting guards on the gate to keep folk from throwing them open at night." He elbowed his way through the press to stand behind her, as large and solid as a Mack truck. "Are you well, Gil-Shalos?"

"Fine," she said quietly. The one person who could have comforted the pain in her soul was camped somewhere in the middle of the plains; she wanted only to sleep.

She heard Janus say to the others, "Show's over for the night, children; time to clear out the College of Surgeons. The alarm's out—there's probably not a Dark One in a hundred miles, but it's an all-troops patrol of the Keep, just to be sure."

There was scuffling, moans, chaff and vivid curses in the pungent tongue of the Wathe. Through her closed eyes Gil heard them leaving, Gnift flirting outrageously with Melantrys, and Janus and Caldern conversing in their unintelligible north-country dialect. The noises faded, amid a jangle of sword belts and mail. Lonely darkness returned.

"Can I get you anything?"

Gil opened her eyes again, surprised. In her thin peasant skirts and black cloak, Minalde sat on the next bunk.

"You can get me some water, if you will." The girl turned away to dip some out of the communal tank. "What are you doing here?"

"They told me you'd been hurt," Alde said simply. "They woke me to sign the papers to arrest Parscino Pral."

98

She came back with the dripping cup in her hands. "Can you sit up to drink?"

"I think so. Who's Parscino Pral?"

"The man whose foot you cut off." Alde spoke very matter-of-factly as she helped Gil sit up a little further against the collected pillows of the entire barracks. The slightest movement ground the broken ends of the collarbone together in the bruised mess of the torn flesh. "He was one of the wealthiest merchants in Gae. The man you killed was Vard Webbling, his partner. Pral says the third man was Bendle Stooft."

"He was." Gil remembered now, the faces falling into place. Pral had been a member of Alwir's coterie of merchants, the day Janus had been released by the Penambrans. Bendle Stooft had been there, too, dressed in green velvet and ermine. She didn't remember Vard Webbling at all. But already it was only a matter of academic interest. Alde certainly didn't look upset. *But then,* Gil thought, *Alde has seen far more men die than I could ever imagine. Since the fall of Gae, her life has been nothing but a wilderness of flight and horror.* She was certainly less than likely to waste good guilt over a man or two killed and a shut door that condemned three others.

"Could you identify him before a tribunal?" Alde asked.

"Sure," Gil said, "no problem."

Alde blew out two of the room's three lamps. "Would you like me to stay for a while?" she asked.

Her eyes closed again, Gil said quietly, "No. Thank you, though." She heard the girl hesitate; then quick, light footfalls pattered through the empty barracks and out into the Aisle beyond.

Bendle Stooft was brought to trial late the following morning, in the big cell Alwir had taken over for his audience hall in the Royal Sector. Gil recognized him immediately. The soft, slack face and receding button chin had swum through the confusion of last night's dreams. He sat now in a carved chair, nervously fiddling with the jewels in his rings, so that his hands glittered with a fireworks display of topaz and green in the warm gold of the candlelight. It was a formal occasion; candles banked the long and strangely carved ebony table at which the tribunal sat, giving them the curious appearance of holy statues enshrined in votive light. The fire of bullion embroidery rippled and flickered over Alwir's breast and sleeves and wound like tattoo-work around the knuckles of his black kid gloves. The flame caught in a hard glint of hot red-purple in the amethyst of Bishop Govannin's episcopal ring and glowed in the crimson of her habit. Between them, Minalde looked very pale and composed.

Gil stood behind the prisoner, flanked by Janus and Caldern. She was exhausted from the walk here, and her head buzzed with fever. The room around her had a two-dimensional quality, unreal to her tired eyes. Colors seemed to drip as vividly as blood against velvet darkness, and sounds changed their quality, either louder than they should be or humming and distant.

Her own voice echoed strangely in her ears as she said, "That is the man."

"Are you sure? Alwir asked. Beside him, the Bishop unstacked her long, fragile fingers and stacked them together differently, as if observing the patterns made by the shadows of those bony knuckles.

"Yes," Gil said. "Of course."

"You understand the severity of the charge?" Alwir asked in that soft, melodious voice. "You must be sure there is no mistake."

Gil frowned. "He and his friends tried to murder me," she said. "It isn't likely I would forget him."

"And," Janus said quietly at her side, "if the charge is severe, the consequences of leaving the Keep doors open after dark are more so."

"Even so," Alwir agreed gravely. "And indeed, some kind of punishment is certainly in order."

"Some kind?" Govannin purred, her eyes slipping sideways at him, as dark as smoky agate. "By Keep Law, there is but one punishment."

Candlelight glittered a thousandfold in the dark-blue eyes. The Chancellor made a deprecating noise of general agreement in his throat, and Stooft turned fish-belly white. "Nevertheless," Alwir went on, "since there was no clear evidence that the Keep was in danger—"

"My lord," Janus broke in, "we found the bones of Stooft's three helpers outside the food compounds this

100

morning. It's sure that the Dark were in the Vale last night."

"But at what time, my lord Commander?" Alwir asked. "It may not have been until hours later. We want to see justice done here."

Justice? Gil felt the rush of anger heat her as the broken ends of her collarbone ground together. *That man tried to kill me.* And she looked over at Stooft in time to see him settle back into his chair; a just perceptible movement of relaxation told its story. He had spoken to Alwir beforehand. He knew he was not going to die. Rage went through her like a river of blood, rage greater than what she had experienced in the fight at the gate. She knew exactly what policemen felt when they heard a junkie or pimp or mugger they'd hauled in get off with a suspended sentence. Janus' fingers tightened over her good arm to remind her she was still in the presence of the Council of Regents.

"Indeed," Alwir continued smoothly, "I think the whole question of food theft and hoarding can be resolved by consolidating the stores under a single proprietorship. With Maia and his people coming within our walls, the danger of black marketeering is doubled. Proper guarding can nip the problem in the bud, and we will have no more troubles of this kind."

"Consolidation?" The Bishop's fine eyebrows rose, but her eyes remained like wet pebbles in a stream bed, as emotionless as a shark's. "Under the wardship of the Council, with yourself at its head, my lord Chancellor?"

Alwir's shoulders stiffened. He kept his voice suave. "Surely you can see that it would be better than the present chaos . . ."

"I cannot say that I do." The wind-dry whisper of her voice was mild, considering. "But if a consolidated storage of food appeals to you, my lord, what better centralizing agency can we find than the Church, which has a far larger and better-trained clerical staff than your own, as well as its own body of troops?"

"Out of the question!" Alwir snapped furiously.

"Then it isn't really consolidation you seek, is it?"

"We have been through this before," the Chancellor said, his voice suddenly tight. "With proper regulation . . ."

"By whom?" the Bishop rapped harshly. "People like Bendle Stooft, your good old friend from Gae?"

"In times past we have been friends," Alwir said stiffly. "But in no way will I allow his friendship to affect my judgment of this case."

"Then follow Keep Law," she said, "and leave him in chains at sunset."

"My lord!" Stooft croaked leaping from his chair with, Gil thought detachedly, remarkable agility for so pudgy a man.

"Be still!" Alwir snapped at him.

The merchant flung himself to his knees in front of the ebony table. "My lord—please—I'll never do it again. I swear it. The others made me. I swear, it was all Webbling's idea, it really was, Webbling's and—and Pral's— they forced me to go along . . ." His sparkling hands groped over the polished surface, the gold of his rings rattling on the gleaming wood. His voice babbled on, rising in pitch like an old woman's. "Please, my lord, I'll never do it again. You said you wouldn't let anything happen to me. I promise I'll do whatever you ask . . ."

"SILENCE!" Alwir roared.

The two Guards, coldblooded automatons, stepped forward in unison to take the man by the arms and set him bodily on his feet. Gil could see that he was trembling in the soft lamplight, sweat running off his face as if he were melting in the heat. He stood hanging onto the Guards, weeping.

Alwir went on, more calmly. "Now, there has been no talk of an execution, though of course some form of severe punishment is in order."

Govannin looked at her hands. "There is only one punishment."

"Really, my lady Bishop," Alwir said, "we do not wish to set a precedent . . ."

She glanced up. "I think it an admirable precedent to set." In the jumping light, her ageless face resembled that of some archaic vulture-god. "It will certainly cause like-minded thieves to reconsider their actions very carefully." The long, cold fingers smoothed a wrinkle from her scarlet sleeve.

"If the food supplies were consolidated . . ."

102

"Confiscated, you mean?" Her black eyes glittered maliciously. "There are hundreds of little entrepreneurs throughout the Keep who managed to haul grain and stock and dried goods down from Gae. There are others planning to execute forage missions of their own. How many would show that kind of initiative if it were all going to people like Stooft here? If, after their trouble, they found they would be robbed of what they already have, they might even fight."

"Fighting would be madness!"

She shrugged her angular shoulders. "So, in my opinion, would be confiscation."

"It is not confiscation!"

"A play upon words, my lord," she said disinterestedly.

With visible effort, Alwir got a grip on himself. The Bishop looked down at her hands with that little ophidian smile and said no more.

"I suppose it is a coincidence that the largest of those—entrepreneurs, as you call them—is the Church itself? That for all your pious talk about the care of souls, your real concern is with the wealth of the Church?"

"Souls inhabit bodies, my lord Chancellor. We have always cared for both. Like you, we seek only the greatest good for those whose charge God has given us."

"And is that why you, the representative of the God of mercy, demand this man's life?"

She raised her head, flat black eyes under heavy lids meeting his with self-evident calm. "Of course." Stooft made a desperate little crying noise in his throat. "And that is my final vote, as member of the Council."

"And my final vote," Alwir grated, "is that the merchant Bendle Stooft be publicly flogged with thirty lashes and imprisoned upon bread and water for thirty days. Minalde?" He glanced sideways at his sister, who had sat all this while in perfect silence, watching everything that had passed between the merchant, the prelate, and her brother.

She raised her head, dark, jeweled braids swinging against cheeks that had gone as white as paper in the reddish shadows. "I vote death."

"WHAT?" Alwir half-rose, speechless between shock and rage.

Stooft made an inarticulate whimpering cry and would

have thrown himself to his knees again, had not Janus and Caldern prevented him. He began to sob. "My lord! My lady!" Tears streamed down his trembling cheeks. Alde raised her eyes and regarded him with desperately held calm, her full lips taut and gray, as if with nausea.

Gil wondered how she could ever have given herself airs about killing one man and maiming another in self-defense. There had been no question about the rightness of her action then, no storm of protest over it. The man had not hung there wailing between his two guards, pleading for his life, for pity, for time. She had been upheld by the double supports of desperation and rage. Minalde had to do her justice cold.

Alwir started to speak to his sister in a hushed, angry voice, but she spoke over him, sounding strained and thin. "In doing what you did, Bendle Stooft, you endangered my life and the life of my son, as well as the life of my brother, who has shown, I think, great mercy in even asking for your reprieve. You have endangered the lives of your own wife, your daughters, your young son, and everyone in the Keep, from highest to lowest." Her voice gained strength and volume, but Bendle Stooft wasn't listening. He just sobbed, "Please, no! Please, no!" over and over again. Alde went on. "As Queen of Darwath and Regent for Prince Altir Endorion, I decree that at sunset tonight you will be chained between two pillars on the hill that faces the doors of this Keep and left there for the Dark Ones to take you. May God have mercy on your soul."

The merchant screamed, "You're a mother, my lady! Don't leave my children fatherless!"

Her chin went up; her face was as calm and chill as a frozen pond, but Gil saw the small upright line that appeared between her brows. Janus and Caldern were obliged to lift the prisoner bodily from his chair and half-drag, half-carry him, shrieking like a damned thing, from the room.

Dizzy and ill, Gil followed on their heels. As she passed through the doorway of the hall into the darkness beyond, she looked back and caught a last glimpse of Minalde, sitting in the soft glow of the ranks of candles, her face buried in her hands, weeping.

104

CHAPTER SEVEN

Gil drifted slowly to consciousness, with the puzzled awareness that she had been asleep. The smell of incense clogged her nostrils, choking after the things she had smelled in a dream—if it had been a dream. Soft chanting, strophe and antistrophe, mingled in her ears. She was aware that she sat in a kind of octagonal anteroom, shadowed, dark, and empty. Fishing in her clouded recollections, she thought she must have come here to rest after the other members of the procession had returned from the sunset execution.

Or maybe the execution had been only a dream.

She didn't think so. The mud and snow on her boots were fresh and dripping as they melted on the smooth black stone of the floor. She remembered stumbling in the wake of every man, woman, and child in the Keep across the road to the knoll that faced the gates, hearing the wailing of wolves and wind in the forest and the solitary weeping of the three of four women who would mourn Bendle Stooft and Parscino Pral.

Like a counterpoint to that melody, she'd heard the muttering in the crowds all around. "Good time, too. When we refugeed from Gae to Karst, the old skinflint charged me a penny for a loaf of bread—a whole penny! And me with six kids starving and no place to lay our heads!" "Penny for bread?" A man laughed bitterly. "Him and Pral charged me six coppers for a bit of space on the floor of a wash-house, to spend the night in shelter. I lost my wife that night. For all of me, that Guard could have taken his hands and head, as well as his sodding foot."

Support your local Guards, Gil thought, exhausted, and raised her head to look around her. Memory came clearer now. She'd been with Janus and Melantrys. Alwir had asked to speak with them up in the Royal Sector. She'd followed them, her vision graying, as far as the Church and then had fallen behind. *Let Janus deal with him,* she'd thought. *I'm not going to climb the goddam steps on his say-so.*

She saw now that the anteroom had been built like a turret against the back wall of the Aisle long after the Keep's original construction as an entrance-hall to the sanctuary itself. To Gil's historian's eye, this type of excresence denoted some period of overcrowding in the Keep's history, the same overcrowding that had caused the original passageways and cells to proliferate and tangle so alarmingly. The anteroom contained little but a few carved stone benches and an ikonlike painting of an unfamiliar saint being nibbled to death by snakes. On the far wall, a doorway led into the sanctuary itself.

Somewhere a door opened. Chanting drifted from the sanctuary, winding echoes of the monks' voices praising God in an archaic tongue. To Gil it was weirdly familiar, a confusing mirror of her medieval studies, a bizarre reminder of the Void that she had crossed to come here, as perhaps others had also done. The Scriptures Govannin had read in the place of execution had been familiar, oppressing her with the sense of dealing on two planes of reality.

The image of Govannin returned to her, silhouetted against the yellow sunset sky. Like a dark, hard heelstone between the massive pylons of the pillars, she had stood in her billowing cloak; the pillars lay like a gun sight between the gates of the Keep and the dark notch of Sarda Pass, and Govannin's cruciform arms had formed bony cross hairs, sighting on the small, baleful eye of the sinking sun. Parscino Pral had hung limply in his chains on one pillar, half-dead already with shock and loss of blood. Bendle Stooft had cried and whimpered and pleaded throughout the Bishop's prayers. All around them, the men and women of the Keep had stood like a dark lake of watching eyes. On the other side of the knoll, that silent company had been joined by a second, smaller group of refugees, some two thousand ragged men, women, and hungry children come in silence to observe the justice of the Keep.

Snow winds had whipped across the Vale. The chains

had clanked on the pillars, and the keys had rattled in Janus' hands. Alwir read out the charges in his trained, powerful voice, and Govannin spoke her prayers, formally requesting the Lord to forgive these men their sin, but implying by her tone of voice that it was all the same to her if He did not. Then, as the sun vanished into the bruised darkness of the banks of clouds, they had all turned their backs on the doomed men and returned to the Keep as the swift winter twilight enfolded the land.

Gil had a hazy memory of Maia of Thran, leaning on his staff as he limped up the Keep steps between Alwir, Govannin, and Minalde. She did not think she had seen anyone take the muddy downward road back to the Tall Gates.

But that, too, might have been a dream.

Restless with fever, Gil got to her feet and walked to the sanctuary door. From its shadows, she looked into the enormous cell, double the normal height, with a floor space, if cleared, of possibly ten thousand square feet, although Gil's judgment of such things had never been very good. That whole shadowy vastness was lighted by only three candles, burning on the bare stone slab of the central altar; by their spare, small light, the monstrous chamber dissolved itself into a chaos of climbing latticework. Pillars, galleries, and balconies hung suspended one above the other like stone lace, with miniature chapels balanced in fantastic hanging turrets and irregularly shaped platforms winding upward in stair-step spirals; over all of it brooded inanimate armies of demons, saints, angels, animals, and monsters peering from jungles of carved tracery. In the intense shadows, not a soul was visible, but Gil could hear them chanting, chapel answering chapel, throughout that eerie gloom.

She had heard it before, on the road down from Karst— blessings and requiems, vespers and matins. Where did the roots feed across the Void, she wondered, and in which direction? What was the evolution of ideas? Straight transfer or the doubled branches of an archtypical Platonic root? Or something else, something wholly inconceivable? She wondered about that saint in the anteroom, whose curiously elipsoid eyes held an expression of startlement

107

rather than pain. Was there a Christian saint who had ended his days to give pagan vipers their elevenses?

It was all scholars' games, she knew, and would not alter one whit the threat of the Dark, or the inevitable clash between Alwir, Govannin, and the Archmage. But Gil was a scholar, and no amount of training with the Guards, no matter how many men she killed or what she felt about it, would change that. It was what no one, with the exception of Ingold, had ever understood about her— her delight in knowledge for its own sake, in the Holmesian reconstruction of long-vanished events, and her nosing quest for the uttermost roots of the world.

"Gil-Shalos."

She swung around, startled. Through the haze of her delirium, backed by the lights of the antechamber, Bishop Govannin appeared like an angel in a fever dream, sexless and pitiless in the blood-scarlet of her episcopal robes, a creature of inhuman beauty, intelligence, and loyalty to her God. But her voice was a dry, woman's voice. "You are not well?" she asked slowly. "At the tribunal you seemed ill, and now it looks not to be going better."

"The wound's a little feverish, is all," Gil excused herself. "I'll get over it in a day or so."

The long, bony fingers indicated, without touching, the slings and strapping that bound Gil's shoulder. "More than that, I fear," she said. "Shoulders can be a bad business."

Beyond them in the holy place, a fresh wave of chanting rose—for the soul, Gil presumed, of Bendle Stooft. Beside her, the Bishop raised her head, listening with a critical ear. In the golden fog of the lamplight, Gil considered that face, the high, intelligent brow shadowing a deep fanatic's eyes, the stubbornness that scarred cheeks and lips like dueling cuts. Fine, small ears, dainty as shells, ornamented the smoothness of the bald pate where it ran into the old, wrinkled power of the ropy neck muscles. It occurred to Gil that in her youth Govannin Narmenlion must have been a strikingly lovely woman, the toast of a regiment— except that women with that kind of cold and driving intelligence were very seldom the toast of anything.

"Your Grace?" she asked softly, and the dark eyes returned to her as if from a reverie. "How was the Keep built?"

The Bishop considered the matter carefully, not as Gil's friends among the Guards had. Finally she said, "I do not know. Which in itself is strange," she added, her long fingers moving to caress the black stone of the doorway at her side. "For it is our shelter and our home."

"Does anyone?"

Govannin shook her head. "Not to my knowledge. I was considered grossly overeducated for an heiress, yet I can recall no word of that."

Gil had to smile. "Yeah, I was—grossly overeducated, too."

A ghost of an answering smile touched those full ungiving lips. "Were you?"

"Oh, yes. I was a scholar in my own lands. I suppose in a way that's what I will always be. Would the Church records have any mention of the building of the Keep? How it was done, or by whom?"

The Bishop folded her arms, thinking. Past her, Gil saw movement in the sanctuary, gray-robed monks ascending narrow steps, dimly lighted by the amber glow of a censer. They vanished in shadows, but their voices remained, like the sound of winds in the rocks. "Perhaps," Govannin said finally. "Most of the Scripture comes from the Times Before, but it contains teaching and wisdom, rather than engineering. The records that, no thanks to my lord Alwir, we brought here to the Keep go back to the time when the see was here at Renweth, but I do not think they extend into the Time of the Dark itself. But some might." She must have seen the brightening of Gil's face. "Is this important to you?"

"It could be," Gil said. "Those records could contain in them some clue, some information, not only about the Keep but about the Dark. What they are—why they came—why they left."

"Perhaps," the Bishop said again, after a long moment's thought. "But for the most part, I think you will find them simply tales of how much the harvest was, who was born and who was buried, and if the rains were light or heavy. As for the coming of the Dark to the Times Before . . ." She frowned, her dark, fine brows drawing together and the lines in that strong, crepy face hardening. "I have heard that the civilizations of Before were wicked

109

and debased. Amid their pride and their splendor, they practiced abominations. It is my belief, now as then, that the Time of the Dark was just punishment, which lasted for the span allotted by God. The Book of Iab tells us that God will let the Evil One have domination for a time, for the Lord's own purposes." She shrugged. "I have lived a long time and have learned never to question the motivations of God."

"Maybe," Gil said. "But it seems like a lot of suffering and pain to go through, when perhaps it could be averted. If God didn't want us to learn from history, we wouldn't have hands to write with, nor eyes to read."

"A wizard's sophistry," the Bishop replied calmly. "One by which they are all tempted and all fall. No, I do not criticize the argument, though I do know you are loyal to your wizard friends. But I doubt the utility of struggling against the intent of God. His ways are slow but as sure and inescapable as the coming of the ice in the north."

"But who," Gil insisted, "can know the intent of God?"

"Not I, certainly. And I do not think it evil to learn from history. I am not yet one of those monks who preach the burning of all books and the telling of Scripture from memory alone. Knowledge is power, whether over the Dark Ones, over Kings who would usurp unto themselves what is rightfully God's, or over sorcerers and mages who do not believe in God at all and whom the Devil uses for his own ends. We can combat knowledge with knowledge and their power with ours."

"Like the Rune of the Chain?" Gil countered a little bitterly. She got a dark, enigmatic look in return.

"The use of such devices is unlawful," the Bishop said. "The Rune of the Chain can be spelled to bind and cripple a wizard's power, and I have heard of its being so used. But using evil's work in any way defeats the good of the cause. Only evil can come of this quest for the Archmage of Quo."

"You don't think a wizard's power might be given to him by God?"

Her tone was perhaps more heated than she had intended. Govannin regarded her for a moment expressionlessly, seeming through the fog of fever and lamplight to be nothing more than a bodiless shadow and a fiery gleam

110

of eyes. "You rush to his defense," she said at last, and her voice had only the calm interest of a python that watched the world and chose what prey it would. "Beware of him, my child. He has great ability and much personal charm for a man who has traded his soul to Satan—which is what he has done, though he will not own it. Satan uses such men also, who from ignorance or pride will not see what they have done by giving in to the temptation to power. But I am old, Gil-Shalos. I have seen the other kind of wizard, evil wizards, renegades, headstrong, ambitious, and self-seeking. If you had ever met such a one, who worked for and openly welcomed the powers of Crookedness, you would never again think that the talents of a mage come from or have anything to do with God."

"But he isn't like that!" Gil protested hotly. Images rushed to her mind and unwise words to her lips. She remembered Ingold standing in the brilliance of the magelight, holding blizzard and darkness at bay until the Guards could get Tir and Alde to the Keep, the old man walking into a tunnel of sounding blackness, surrounded by runes of power that no one else could see, and the look in his eyes when he had handed her his glowing staff and asked her to guard his back. "He would never bend to evil, never use his powers for ill. There can be good and bad wizards, the same way there are good and bad men . . ."

Govannin raised dark, elegant brows. Gil stumbled and broke off her words, her cheeks suddenly hotter than even fever could account for, glad of the veiling shadows. "I'm sorry," she stammered, confused. "I spoke disrespectfully, and all you have done has been kindnes to me." It had doubtless been decades, Gil reflected, since any member of hoi-polloi had so lashed out at Govannin Narmenlion.

But the Bishop was only silent for a time, a curious, considering light in her eyes. When she spoke, her dry, cracked voice was kind. "I like you, my child," she said. "You are a warrior as you are a scholar, single-minded, and never without purpose. Your heart is very pure—pure in its scholarship, pure in its violence, and pure in its love. Such hearts can be hurt and can do measureless good and measureless evil, but they cannot be bought or cowed." She put out her hand, her fingers ice-cold against Gil's

111

cheek. "I shall send you the Church records, if you desire it, and also someone to interpret the writing for you. The knowledge is my gift to you, with the consequences of what that knowledge shall bring."

She held out her bony hand, and Gil dropped to one knee to kiss the dark bezel of the episcopal ring.

Later, waking in the barracks from feverish sleep, Gil wondered if this, too, had been a dream. But after supper, Minalde appeared in the barracks, bearing a heavy book which, she said, the lady Govannin had asked if she would take to Gil-Shalos.

"I was coming over anyway," she explained, seating herself at the foot of Gil's bunk.

Through the doorway beyond her, Gil could hear the noises of the night watch going out, the creaking of leather, the faint clink of buckles, and Melantrys' light, bantering chaff.

Minalde ran her fingers along the metal-clasped edge of the cover. "What is it?"

Gil explained briefly her desire to probe the origins of the Keep to learn something of its secrets. "I mean, hell," she said, "there's so much more to the Keep than meets the eye. Like—how come there's a flow of water in the latrines and fountains? Even if the Keep was built over an underground river, the stuff doesn't run uphill. Why is the air fresh in most places, not foul and stuffy? How was the Keep built in the first place? I know it was built three thousand years ago by Dare of Renweth, at the time of the first rising of the Dark," she went on, "but how long did it take? Where did everybody stay during construction, if they didn't start on it until after the Dark began appearing? Or were the Dark only down in the river valleys and the mountains safe?"

"No," Alde answered simply. "Because there's a Nest of the Dark not twenty miles from here, as you know."

Gil remembered the tilted slab of black stone in the midst of those clinging woods and shuddered.

"And for the rest of it," Alde went on, "you've already told me more than I knew before. I have heard that the magic in Times Before was different from the magic now, but I don't know what that means. I do know that centuries ago there used to be magic places, sort of temples of wizardry, in many cities, not just at Quo—so maybe back then it was the same way. Rudy says that magic is fused into the walls of the Keep."

At the mention of her lover's name, Alde's cheeks colored faintly, and Gil hid a grin. In many ways this dark-haired girl reminded her of the freshmen she'd taught; she was sweet, shy, pretty, and very unsure of herself. At such times it was difficult to remember that this soft-voiced girl had passed through fire and darkness, had seen her husband die in the flaming ruin of the battle-broken Palace, and had gone against the forces of the night, armed only with a torch and her own wild courage. She was the Queen of Darwath, the true ruler of the Keep, sitting at the foot of the disordered bunk with her legs crossed under her multicolored peasant skirts.

"So anyway, the Bishop offered to lend me the books to look for the answers," Gil said, edging herself up against her makeshift pillows. "Gnift's already told me that training or walking patrol is out for at least three weeks . . . I suppose he's right," she added regretfully, looking down at her strapped shoulder. "I'll have to get someone to read them to me and teach me the language, though."

"Oh, I can do that," Alde said. "Really, it would be no trouble. I know the Old Wath and the High Tongue of the Church, which is very different from the Wathe. It would be the first time, you know, that I've ever really used anything that I learned in school."

Gil regarded her for a moment through the barracks gloom, fascinated. "What did you learn in school?"

Alde shrugged. "Needlework," she said. "Songs, and how to write the different modes of poetry. I did an entire tapestry once of Shamilfar and Syriandis—they're famous lovers—but it nearly drove me crazy and I never did another. Dancing, and playing the harp and dulcimer. Something about the major parts of the Realm and a little history. I hated history," she admitted, shamefaced.

"Most people do," Gil said comfortingly.

"You don't." Alde's slim, well-kept hands traced the curve of the leather cover's embossing.

"I always was a freak that way." Rudy's teasing nickname of "spook" was hardly a new one.

113

"Well, the way you talk about it, it's as if—as if it has a point," Alde said. "As if you're looking for something. All they ever taught us about history was these little stories that were supposed to be morally uplifting, like the one about the man who died in a valiant rear-guard action for the sake of his comrades, or the story about all those old patriarchs who let the enemy slaughter them rather than be enslaved. That kind of thing. Things that I suspect never really happened."

The image of a stiff little boy in a powdered wig confessing to his father about who axed the cherry tree floated through Gil's mind, and she laughed. "Maybe."

"But if you need someone to read to you, I'll be glad to do it."

Gil studied Alde's face for a moment in silence. She herself had closed out the UCLA library, the way some people close out bars, far too many nights not to understand. And as for having a Queen as a research assistant— *Alwir,* Gil reflected, *will hardly miss her.* "Sure," she said quietly. "Any time you can get away."

They took over the little cubbyhole in the back of the barracks of the Guards, which Ingold had once used as his quarters. It was private, yet close to the center of things, and, Gil noted to herself, at the opposite end of the Keep from the Royal Sector and its politics. Alde took to coming there every day, usually bringing Tir with her, to work laboriously through the ancient chronicles, while Gil scribbled notes on tablets of wood coated with beeswax that she'd found in an abandoned storeroom. In another storeroom she found a desk, spindle-legged and archaic, small enough to fit into the narrow confines of her study. She used a couple of firkins of dried apples for a seat.

Thus she entered into a period of quiet scholarship, her hours of transcribing and sorting notes alternating with long, solitary rambles through the back reaches of the Keep in search of some sign of the mysterious circular chamber Rudy had described before his departure. It was from one of these that she returned one day to find Alde sitting at her desk, studying one of the tablets in the dim light.

"Is this what you do?" the younger girl asked, touching the creamy surface with a doubtful finger. "Is this all?"

Gil looked down over her shoulder. She habitually wrote with a silver hairpin as a stylus, in a combination of English and the runes of the Wathe. The tablet had written on it:

Swarl (?) s. of Tirwis, ss. Aldor, Bet, Urgwas—
famine, snows Pass 2, Tl Gts grsnd 4 (—)—no mtn
Dk—pop Kp 12000 + 3 stmts (Big Ring, ??)—buried
gaenguo (?)—Bp. Kardthe, Tracho

"Sure," she replied cheerfully. "That's from the chronicles you were reading to me yesterday. It's just a condensation—Swarl, whenever the hell he ruled Renweth, had three sons named Aldor, Bet, and Urgwas . . ."

"Bet's a woman's name," Alde pointed out.

"Oh." Gil made a notation. In the Wathe, pronouns had no gender. "Anyhow, in the second year of his reign there was a famine, and snows heavy enough to close Sarda Pass. The population of the Keep at that time was estimated at twelve thousand, with three settlements in the valley, one of which was named the Big Ring—don't ask me why. There was no mention of the Dark in the chronicle, which isn't surprising, since we have yet to find any word of the Dark in *any* of these chronicles, and right around the fourth year of his reign there is a statement that the Tall Gates were garrisoned, though they might have been so for years. The Bishops during his reign were Kardthe and later a man or woman named Tracho—"

"That's the old spelling for Trago. It's a man's name."

"Thanks." Gil made another notation. "And in his reign they buried the gaenguo, which I meant to ask you about. Isn't gaenguo the old word for a—a lucky place, or a good place?"

"Well—not so much good as just—I guess awesome would be the best word." Alde reached out with her foot and gently rolled Tir's ball back toward him where he was playing happily on the floor. "There were supposed to be places where certain powers were concentrated, where people could see things far off or have visions."

Gil considered, while Tir came crawling busily back across the crackly mat of straw and old rushes that strewed the floor. Alde bent down and let the infant catch her fingers, then lifted him to a standing position beside her knees. Tir threw back his head and crowed with delight.

"You know," Gil said thoughtfully, "I bet what they buried was the old Nest of the Dark." She picked up the tablet and turned it idly over in her fingers, the touch of the wax as cold and smooth as marble. "God knows, the place is creepy enough. But it's really sort of an opposite to a gaenguo. The atmosphere disrupts magic rather than channels it. Interesting," she murmured.

"Interesting how?" Alde glanced curiously up at Gil, holding her son's hands in her own.

"Because it looks as if by that time they had completely disassociated the idea of the Dark from the Nests. Which is less surprising than it seems," she went on, "when you consider that the bonfire was the first line of defense against the Dark. Which, of course, is why we have no records at all from the Time of the Dark itself."

Alde let Tir down, and the child crawled determinedly away in pursuit of his ball. "How vexing," she said, inadequately.

"Well, more than that." Gil sat on the narrow bed of grain sacks and covered her cold feet with her cloak. "It left everybody completely unprepared for it when it happened again. I mean, before last summer nobody had even heard of the Dark."

"Oh, but we had," Alde protested. "That's what— In a way it worked against Ingold, you see. When I was a little girl, my nurse Medda used to tell me not to get out of bed and run about the house at night because the Dark Ones would eat me up. I think all nurses used to tell their children that." Her voice faltered—in the end it had been Medda who had been eaten up by the Dark. "It was something you grew out of. Most little children believed in the Dark Ones. It was only their parents who didn't."

Gil momentarily pictured the probable fate of any shabby and unlikely pilgrim who tried to convince the authorities that the bogeyman was really going to devour America. "I'm surprised Eldor believed him," she murmured.

"Eldor—" Minalde paused. "Eldor was very exceptional. And he trusted Ingold. Ingold was his tutor when he was a child."

Gil glanced up quickly, hearing the sudden tension that choked off Alde's voice. The younger girl was looking determinedly away into the distance, fighting the film of tears that had appeared so abruptly in her eyes. *Whatever her love for Rudy,* Gil thought, *there is a love there which can never be denied.* In the strained silence which followed, Melantrys' voice could be heard, arguing with Seya about whether or not she should get rid of her cloak in a sword fight.

Then Alde forced a small rueful smile and brushed at her eyes with the back of her wrist. "I'm sorry."

"It's okay."

"No," Alde said. "It's just that sometimes I don't understand what there was between me and—and Eldor. As if I never understood it. I thought I could make him love me if I loved him hard enough. Maybe I was just being stupid." She wiped her eyes again. "But it hurts, you know, when you give everything you have and the one you give it to just—just looks at it and turns aside." She glanced away again, unable to meet Gil's eyes. Gil, clumsy-tongued and unhandy with her own or anyone else's emotions, could find nothing to say.

But Alde seemed to take no offense at the silence. In fact, she seemed to find a kind of comfort in it. Tir, having reached the end of the room, came crawling back toward the girls with his usual single-minded determination, and Alde smiled as she bent to help him stand once more. He was very much like Alde, Gil thought, watching mother and child together—small-boned and compact, with her wide morning-glory-blue eyes. *Just as well,* she added to herself, *that there's so little of Eldor in his only child. When you're carrying on an affair with a man the Church says is a servant of Satan, it's no help to have the echo of his predecessor before your eyes every time you turn around.*

Alde looked up suddenly, as if deliberately putting aside the pain and confusion of that first, hopeless love. "So where were you?" she asked Gil. "The Guards said you'd left right after breakfast."

"Oh." Gil shrugged. "Exploring, looking for something,

117

really . . . You've never run across any mention anywhere of a—a kind of observation room in the Keep, have you? A room with a black stone table in it, with a crystal kind of thing in the middle?"

"No." Then Alde frowned, her black brows drawing down into two swooping wings. "But that's funny—it sounds so familiar. A table—has it a crystal disc, set into the top of the table?"

"Yeah," Gil said. "It's part of the table. How did you know?"

"I don't know. I have the feeling I've seen something like that before, but—almost as if I dreamed about it, because I know I've never seen anything of the kind. That's funny," Alde went on quietly, sitting back against the desk, her face troubled. Tir, whom she had lifted onto her knee, promptly reached for the jeweled clasp that held her hair, and she undid it and gave it to him, her dark hair falling in a river down over her shoulders and her child.

Gil propped the arm in the sling against her knees. "Why is it funny?" she asked.

"Because—I've had that feeling a lot of times in the Keep," Alde said in a worried voice. "As if—as if I remembered things, remembered being here before. Sometimes I'll be walking down a staircase or along a hall, and I'll have this feeling of having been there before."

"Like *déjà vu?*" There was a technical term in the language of the Wathe for that—a circumstance which Gil found interesting.

"Not entirely."

"Like the inherited memories that are passed on from parent to child in certain families?" Gil asked quietly. "You did tell me your House was a collateral branch of the House of Dare."

Alde looked over at her worriedly in the gloomy yellowish lamplight. "But the memories only pass from father to son," she said softly. "And Eldor told me once that his memories of other lives were like memories of his own. Very clear, like visions. Mine are just—feelings."

"Maybe women hold inherited memory differently," Gil said. "Maybe it's less concrete in women and therefore hasn't been called upon for centuries, because there was

118

always a male heir of the House of Dare. Maybe you haven't remembered because you didn't need to." Gil leaned forward, the grain in the sacks she sat on scrunching softly and giving off a faint musty odor into the tiny room. "I remember a long time ago, Ingold said that Eldor's father Umar didn't have Dare's memories at all, because there was really no need—that the inherited memory will skip generations, one or three or sometimes more. But he said that they woke in Eldor because it was necessary."

Minalde was silent, looking down at the child who played so obliviously in her lap. Her unbound hair hid her expression, but when she did speak, her voice was soft and filled with doubt. "I don't know," she said.

Gil stood up briskly. "I think it's neat," she announced.

"Do you?" Alde asked timidly.

"Hell, yes. Come on exploring with me. See what you can remember."

As the winter deepened and the snows sealed the Vale into a self-contained world of whiteness, Gil and Minalde conducted their own rather unsystematic exploration of the Keep of Dare. They wandered the upper reaches of the fourth and fifth levels, where Maia of Thran had established his headquarters. He greeted them amiably in his own church down near the western end, with his own armed troops about him. They explored the crowded slums that huddled around the stairheads on the fifth level, hearing nothing but the liquid southern drawl of the Penambrans in their ears, and probed the dark, empty halls that stretched beyond. Armed like Theseus with a ball of twine, they traversed miles of dark, abandoned halls that stank of mold and dry rot, with the dust of ages drifting like ground fog about their feet.

They found storerooms, chapels, and armories filled with rusted weapons in the back halls of all levels. They found the remains of bridges that had once spanned the Aisle at the fourth and fifth levels, thin spiderwebs of cable heretofore hidden by the clustering shadows of the ceiling. They found cells stacked halfway to the ceiling with spiky mazes of piled furniture, carved in unfamiliar styles and painted with thin running lines of hearts and

119

diamonds picked out in gold leaf. They passed locked cells scurrying with rats, food stores cached by unknown speculators. They discovered things they did not understand—moldering parchments overwritten in debased and unreadable bookhand, or what looked like puzzling little white polyhedrons made of milky glass, three-quarters the size of Gil's fist, their function unknown and unguessable.

"You should let Alwir know about the bundle of parchments we found," Gil remarked at one point as they retraced their steps back from a remote corner of the fifth level. The puddle of yellow lamplight wavered around their feet. The air up here was warmer, the crowding walls of the empty warrens of cells pressing down on the girls in silence. Grotesque shadows lumbered along the wall, bending around the flame like pteranodon moths about a diminutive candle. Gil felt wryly envious of Rudy and Ingold's blithe, unthinking ability to summon light. *Damn wizards probably never gave it a second thought.*

"I will," Minalde agreed, holding the lamp up for better visibility. "He and Bishop Govannin are already quarreling about writing materials. Alwir wants to make a census of the Keep."

"He should. And he should be keeping his own chronicles."

"I know." Alde had imbibed enough of Gil's historical sense to realize that the Church accounts of certain events differed radically from secular records. "But because there's almost nothing to write on, nobody's keeping any kind of chronicles at all."

"Great," Gil said. "So when in three thousand years all this happens again, everybody's going to be in as rotten a shape as we are now."

"Oh, no!" Alde protested. "It couldn't—I mean—"

Gil raised her eyebrows and paused in a shadowy doorway. "Like hell it couldn't. This could all be part of a regular cycle. We don't know why the Dark came before or how many times it has happened. We know they have herds of some kind below the ground; we know they're taking prisoners. Are the herds descended from prisoners they took three thousand years ago? Did people drive them back underground, or did they just go away of their own accord?"

"But why would they?" Alde cried, much distressed.

"Beats the hell out of me." Gil paused, catching a faceted glimpse of something in a deserted doorway. She picked up another one of those little white glass polyhedrons and turned its uncommunicative shape thoughtfully in her good hand. "But that's what we've got to find out, Alde. We've got to get a handle on this somehow—and right now the Keep and the records are the only starting places I can think of." She shrugged. "Maybe we're wasting our time, and the Archmage will have all the answers when he comes back here with Rudy and Ingold. And then again, maybe he won't."

They continued on down the corridor, Gil caching the polyhedron in her sling for further investigation later. Echoes whispered at their passing, mocking footfall and shadow and breath. But the Keep hid its secrets well, furled tightly within the spiral and counterspiral of the winding halls, or revealed them in enigmatic or incomprehensible ways.

Early in their endeavors, they decided to ask Bektis about the observation room with its crystal table, on the off chance that his lore might have preserved some clue to its whereabouts.

The Court Wizard of the House of Dare, however, had little time to spend on the games of girls. He looked up with a frown as they came quietly into his room, a large cell tucked away in the warren of the Royal Sector. The light of the bluish witchfire that burned above his head shone on his high, bald pate and the bridge of his proud, hooked nose. Dutifully, he made a stiff little bow. "All my pardons, my lady," he said in his rather light, mellifluous voice. "In such a gown as that, one might easily take you for a commoner." Rigid disapproval seemed to have been rammed like a poker up his backbone.

Still he listened to Gil's description of what they sought, nodding his head wisely with his usual expression of grave thoughtfulness, which Gil suspected uncharitably that he practiced daily before a mirror. As she spoke, Gil looked around the room, noting the few black-bound books lining the shelves in the little sitting room area at the far end of the cell, and the richness of the single chest and carved bedstead. Unlike the table in her own minuscule study, the bedstead was newish, and the latest style current in Gae at the time of the coming of the Dark. It had clearly been brought down from Karst in pieces and reassembled, rather than scrounged from the old storerooms at the Keep. What sympathy she had once cherished for Lord Alwir's transport problems faded. He couldn't have been doing too badly if he could afford to cart along his Court Conjurer's bedroom set. In the cool brightness of the witchlight, Bektis' sleeves twinkled with scarlet embroidery, stitched into a pattern Gil recognized as the signs of the Zodiac. She picked out her own symbol, the tailed M of Virgo, before it occurred to her that this was yet another unexplained transfer, in one direction or the other, across the Void.

Bektis coughed solemnly. "The men of the ancient realms, my lady," he intoned, "had powers far exceeding our ken. Very little is known of them, or of their works."

Alde broke in hesitantly. "My lady Bishop says that the people of the Times Before were evil and practiced abominations."

A gleam of spite flickered in the old man's dark eyes. "So she says of all things of which she does not approve. In those times wizardry was a part of the life of the Realm, rather than a thing to be tampered with at risk. There were more wizards then, and their powers were much greater. Even in our own memory, my lady, wizardry has not been anathema, for did there not used to be citadels of wizardry, not only at Quo but in Penambra and in Gae itself, on the very spot where the Palace now stands?"

"Did there?" Gil asked curiously.

The dark eyes slid sideways at her. "Indeed there did, Gil-Shalos. We had respect then, in the great days of wizardry; it was wizardry that helped to build the Realm. But the Church drove us out, playing upon the sentiments of the ignorant; and one by one, those citadels closed, and such wizards as were left them took to the road. It was centuries ago," he continued, his words soft and light but suddenly fraught with impotent malice, "but we do not forget."

Gil shifted her arm uncomfortably in its grubby sling. "And your learning preserves nothing of their deeds?"

"Nor does anyone's, my lady." The old man looked

down, his voice turned smooth again. "The Archmage Lohiro made a study of some of the works of the Times Before, but even his knowledge is fragmentary."

Probably because he didn't have a mechanized worldview to start with, Gil thought, rising from her chair. She caught Alde's eyes and signaled her away, and they left the Court Wizard carefully pestling pearls to mix with hogwort and fennel as a charm against indigestion, the blue witchlight falling over the spiderlike movement of his hands.

They searched, not only through the dark halls of the Keep itself but, in Gil's patient, scholarly fashion, through all the ancient records they could lay their hands on. But matters that were of interest to contemporary chroniclers were not always the things that historians sought. Gil found herself wandering through a second maze of trivial information regarding the love lives of vanished monarchs, petty power duels with long-dead prelates, accounts of famines and crop failures, and how high the snow stood in Sarda Pass. Often her efforts took on a strangely surreal quality, as if she wandered back and forth through time as well as space, crossing and recrossing the myriad layerings of the universe on some curious quest whose meaning she only vaguely understood.

It was in this that she longed more than anything else for Ingold. She felt herself at sea, wrestling with facts and languages and concepts she barely comprehended. Alde's help was invaluable, but her breeding had been upperclass and her education orthodox; there was much about the history of the Church, the Realm, and wizardry that she simply did not know. As Gil patiently decoded the masses of filthy and overwritten palimpsests in her tiny study far into the watches of the night, she missed the old man's presence, if not for actual help, at least for moral support or for his company. At times when the voices of the deep-night watch could be heard in the distant corridors and weariness made the unfamiliar words swim before her eyes in the smutty yellow gleam of the lamp, she'd prop her injured arm on the slanted surface of the desk and wonder how she'd gotten where she was. How in a matter of six weeks or so had she gone from the lands of sunlight and blue jeans to a freezing and peril-circled citadel in the midst of alien mountains, digging through unreadable parchments for mention of something he had asked her to find? And she wondered if he watched her in that little magic crystal of his, or if he cared.

Between the two mazes of present and past lay a third maze, far less comprehensible but, she sensed, far more important than the other two. It was a maze of memory, as elusive as a whiff of smoke or the faint sounds one might think one heard in the night—a maze only barely to be glimpsed by that inward remembering look in Minalde's eyes.

"That's interesting," Gil said as she and Minalde emerged from the back entrance of a boarded-up cell crammed to the ceiling with old furniture and dozens of those useless, enigmatic white polyhedrons. Clouds of dust clung to their clothes; Alde sneezed in it, fanning it away from her face. Both of them were gray with it, like urchins playing in the construction yards. "From the furniture we found in there, it looks as if this area was growing increasingly crowded at the same time the fifth level was being abandoned."

"That doesn't make sense," Alde said, puzzled, trying to wipe the dust from her arms and only succeeding in putting huge, blackish smudges on her white sleeves. "If they were having such a space problem, why not move onto the fifth level?"

Gil shrugged and marked another arrow on the wall. "It takes forever to get up and back there," she said. "The second level was just more popular. In cities of my homeland, people will live in worse crowding than this, just to be in a fashionable part of town." She looked around. "So where the hell are we?"

Alde held the lamp up high. A short neck of corridor dead-ended twenty feet away in a blank wall—by its composition, part of the Keep's original design. Shadows shifted around them with the movement of the lamp, and Gil shivered a little in the draft.

A warmer breath of air from somewhere nearby brought the voices of monks chanting. "Close to the Royal Sector, I think," she answered her own question. "There should be a stair . . ."

"No, Gil, wait a minute." Alde stood very still, pale and small in the impenetrable shadows. "I know this place, I'm positive. I've been here before."

Gil was silent, watching the struggle on her face.

Alde groped helplessly for a moment at the memory, then shook her head in despair. "I can't bring it back," she whispered. "But it's so close. I feel I've passed this way before, so many times. It was part of my life, going to do something . . . something I did so often I could go there with my eyes closed."

"Then close your eyes," Gil suggested softly, "and go there."

Alde handed her the lamp and stood, eyes closed, with the darkness hemming her in. She took a hesitant step and another. Then abruptly she changed her direction, her stride lengthening smoothly as her thin blue and purple skirts brushed the ancient dust of the floor. For a moment Gil thought she was going to walk slap into the wall. But the angle thrown by shadow and lamplight was deceiving; just as Gil cried, "Whoa! Watch it!" the shadow seemed to swallow Alde. She tripped and cursed in a mild and lady-like fashion. Coming to her side, Gil saw that, instead of the wall, she had met with a short flight of black steps that mounted to a dark door with a rusted and broken lock.

"Is this it?"

Gil looked up from angling the lamp, trying to see down into the cloudy crystal inset into the table. "Of course," she said. "This is the observation room Rudy found the night before he left; this is what Ingold asked me to look for. And you found it." She hesitated, seeing the puzzled doubt still on Alde's face. "Isn't it what you were looking for?"

Alde walked slowly along the workbench against the wall, running idle fingers over its smooth edge. She picked up a white polyhedron that perched there, the reflected lucency of the lamp making it glow faintly pink where her fingers touched. "No," she said quietly.

"Don't you recognize this?" Gil swiveled around, sitting on the edge of the dark table.

Alde looked up from the small faceted thing she was

125

examining, her dusty hair hanging in tendrils around her face. "Oh, yes," she said matter-of-factly. "But I have the impression of having walked through here on my way to—somewhere else."

Gil glanced around the room. There was only the single door. Their eyes met again, and Alde shook her head helplessly. The silence lengthened between them, and Gil shivered with the sudden sense of coming close to the unknown. In that silence she became slowly conscious of something else, a faint, barely perceptible humming or throbbing that seemed to come from the dark stone of the walls themselves. Gil frowned as it gradually worked its way into her perceptions. It was familiar, as familiar to her as the beating of her own heart—something she ought to recognize, but had not heard since . . .

. . . When? Puzzled, she rose and went to the wall opposite the door, where the soft thrumming seemed the loudest. She reached across the narrow workbench to place her fingers against the stone.

"Oh, my God," she whispered as the realization struck her. Vistas of possibility for which she had been unprepared seemed to gape like chasms before her startled feet.

Alde saw the look in her eyes, snatched up the lamp, and came hastily to her side. "What is it?"

Gil turned her head to look at Alde, the chill gray of her eyes kindled almost to blue in the wavery glow. "Feel the wall," she whispered.

Alde obeyed, hesitating, and at once a frown of puzzlement that was half-fear and half-recognition touched her brow. "I—I don't understand."

Gil's voice was barely a breath, as if she feared to drown out that almost unheard sound. "It's machinery."

The trapdoor was not hidden, as Gil had feared it would be. It was merely set out of the way. The workbench, built centuries later, had been laid right across it. The hollow tube, like a wormhole through the darkness of the Keep's black wall, seemed to go up forever.

As she emerged at last into the vast space of warmth, dust, and the soft, steady throbbing of metal and air, it was borne upon Gil that she had, indeed, crossed a threshold and entered realms unknown to anyone else in this world—including, she was positive, Ingold himself. It came to her that the Keep of Dare, far from being a simple stronghold, was in itself a riddle, as black and impenetrable as the Dark.

She reached down the shaft and took the lamp that Alde carried. As she held up that single point of brightness, dark shapes limned themselves from the blackness around her—monstrous pipes, oily and black and shining, coils of twisting cable strung like vines from the low ceiling, and the gaping maws of enormous ducts that breathed warm air like the nostrils of some inconceivable beast. The noise, though not loud, drummed into her bones like the beat of a massive heart.

Alde emerged from the ladder shaft and stared around at the labyrinthine vista, barely to be seen in its cloak of shadows, with huge and frightened eyes. Gil suddenly realized that she was dealing with someone who had been brought up at approximately a fourteenth-century level of technology—and of the nobility, at that. A few minutes ago, she had felt no difference between them, as if they were contemporaries. Now the gulf of time and culture yawned like a canyon. She herself, theoretically acquainted with Boulder Dam and the wonders of Detroit, was silent before that endless progression of lifts and screws and pipes whose shapes the lamplight only hinted at. To Alde it must be like another world.

"What *is* it?" Alde whispered. "Where *are* we?"

"At a guess," Gil replied in tones equally soft, as if she feared to break the silence that lay on those stygian metal jungles, "I'd say we're at the top of the Keep, up above the fifth level. That ladder in the shaft seemed to go on forever. And as for what it is . . ." She held up the lamp and sniffed at the faint oily smell of the place. There was no dust here, she noticed, and no rats. Only darkness and the soft, steady beating of the Keep's secret heart. "It's got to be the pumps."

"The what?"

Gil stood up and walked along the perimeter of the little clearing by the trapdoor. The light in her hand played over sleek, shining surfaces, and the warm drafts stirred her coarse, straggling hair. "Pumps to circulate air

127

and water," she said thoughtfully. "I knew they had to exist somewhere."

"Why?" Alde asked, puzzled.

"As I said, the air and water don't move themselves." She stopped and bent down to pick up another white glass polyhedron from where it lay half-hidden in the shadows of a braided mass of coils as big around as her waist.

"But why wasn't any of this mentioned in the records?" Alde asked, from her perch on the edge of the trapdoor.

"That, as a very great man of my own world would say, is the sixty-four-dollar question." Gil slipped around a massive pipe of smooth, black, uncorrupted metal and passed her hand across the mouth of a huge duct. Deep within its shadows she could see a grid of fine-mesh wire. Evidently she wasn't the only person who'd worried about the Dark Ones getting into the air conditioning. "And here's another one. What's the power source?"

"The what?"

"The power source, the—what makes it all move."

"Maybe it just moves by itself because it is its nature to move." Which, Gil reminded herself, was a perfectly rational explanation, given a medieval view of the universe.

"Nothing lower than the moon does that," she explained, falling back on Aristotle and sublunary physics. "Everything else has to have something to cause it to move."

"Oh," Alde said, accepting this. The unseen walls picked up the murmur of their voices and repeated them over and over again, behind the sonorous whooshing of the pipes.

"Alde, do you realize . . ." Gil turned back, grubby and dusty in her black uniform, the lamplight glowing across her face. "There could be other places in the Keep like this, other rooms, laboratories, defenses, anything! Hidden away and forgotten. If we could find them . . . God, I wish Ingold were here. He'd be able to help us."

Alde looked up abruptly. "Yes," she said. "Yes, he would. Because—Gil, listen, tell me if this makes sense. Could the—the power source—be magic?"

Gil paused, thinking about it, then nodded. "It must be." *After three thousand years*, she thought, *it was an easier solution than a hidden nuclear reactor*.

"Because that would explain why none of this was mentioned in the records." Alde leaned forward, her dark braids falling over her shoulders, her eyes wide and, Gil thought, a little frightened. "You say the Keep was built by —by wizards who were also engineers. But the Scriptures of the Church date from long before the Time of the Dark. The Church was very powerful even then." Her voice was low and intense. "It's so easy to fear wizards, Gil. If they held the secret of the Keep's building—once the secret was lost, there would be no finding it again. And that could happen so easily. A handful of people . . . If something—something happened to them—before they could train their successors—"

Gil was silent, remembering Ingold before the spell-woven doors of the Keep and the fanatic hatred in Govannin's serpent eyes.

Alde looked up, the lamplight shining in her eyes. "I was raised all my life to distrust them and to fear them," she went on. "So I know how people feel about them. I know Rudy has power, Gil, but still I'm afraid for him. And he's out there somewhere, I don't know where. I love him, Gil," she said quietly. "It may be unlawful and it may be foolish and hopeless and all the rest of it, but I can't help it. There used to be a saying: *A wizard's wife is a widow.* I always thought it was because they were excommunicates." She put her feet on the descending rungs of the long ladder back to the second level. Her eyes met Gil's. "Now I see what it does mean. Any woman who falls in love with a wizard is only asking for heartache."

Gil turned her face away, blinded by a sudden flood of self-realization and tears. "You're telling me, sweetheart," she muttered.

Alde, who had already started her descent, looked up. "What?"

"Nothing," Gil lied.

CHAPTER EIGHT

The smothering sense of impending horror woke Rudy from a sound sleep. Wind screamed overhead, but the arroyo in which they'd made camp was protected and relatively still. He sat up, the rock against which he'd leaned to take his turn at guard duty digging sharply into his back, his breath coming fast, his hands damp and cold. His heart chilled with the knowledge that Ingold was gone.

A hasty look around confirmed it. He could see nothing of the wizard in the shifting darkness of the fire.

Rudy scrambled hastily to his feet, the terror of being left to his own devices in the midst of the wind-seared desert night fighting the horror born of guilt for falling asleep on duty. A thin shiver of wind lashed down on him from above, but it wasn't that which made him shudder. He knew himself incapable of surviving without the wizard. And—who or what could have snatched Ingold so silently?

Panic seized him. He caught up his bow and quiver and scrambled up the steep, rocky bank. At the top, the seething turmoil of the winds struck him, his wizard's vision showing him nothing but the wild movement of tossing sagebrush and cloud. Despairing, he cried against the winds, "INGOLD!" The winds threw his voice back upon him again.

The cold up here was incredible, burning like a sword of ice run through his lungs. Raging winds ripped the sound of his cry from his lips, throwing it at random into the darkness. He yelled again, "INGOLD!" His voice was drowned in the maelstrom of the night.

What was he to do? Return to the camp to wait? For what? Beat his way back to the road a few dozen yards away to look for some sign of the old man? Wait for morning? But he might as well give up hope then, for tonight's storm would scour all sign of Ingold from the face of the earth. A kind of frenzy took him—the terror of being alone in the dark. He knew he was helpless without Ingold, unable to go on and probably unable to return to Renweth either, set down in the midst of a hostile and terrible place. He fought off the overwhelming urge to run, to flee somewhere, anywhere. The wind shrieked curses in his ears and tore at his face with claws of frozen iron. Ingold was gone—and Rudy knew he could never survive without him.

Then he heard the wizard's harsh, powerful voice, torn and twisted on the deceiving fury of the winds, calling his name. Rudy swung around, facing what he thought was the direction of the sound. He strained his eyes, but could see nothing in the utter darkness of the howling desert night. The winds were screaming so fiercely that he could barely have heard himself shout, but he heard the call again.

Leaning against the force of the wind, he struck off into the darkness.

It took him less than half an hour to realize he had been a total fool. Wherever Ingold was, whatever had become of him, searching for him in the wild blackness of the storm was tantamount to suicide. Staggering blindly under the flail of the elements, frozen to the bone and gasping with the mere effort of remaining upright, Rudy cursed the panic that had sent him away from the hidden camp in the arroyo. He had utterly lost sight of it, wandering helplessly, chasing every will-o'-the-wisp of movement he fancied he'd seen or a sound on the wind that he took for his name . . .

Turning around in despair, he struggled back toward where he thought the camp ought to be. But nothing in all that wind-ripped landscape was familiar. Wizard or no wizard, he could not see in the dark when the wind blinded his eyes. Against his numbed cheeks, he could already feel the stinging bite of powder snow.

If you lie down, you'll die, he told himself grimly. *Keep moving till daybreak, for Chrissake, or it's one more contribution to the Starving Jackals' Benevolent Fund.* But the lure of sleep enticed him, the thought of that warmth beyond the dark wall. He thought of Minalde, of the sweetness of her arms, of the warm, golden afternoons of California, and of talking endless rounds of nothing with his buddies, throwing beer bottles at the trash can . . . *Keep going, turkey,* he commanded, forcing his mind from those soft temptations. *Think about fingernails on the blackboard. Think about jumping in water. Think about anything but sleep.*

He made himself move on.

There was no question of going anywhere or finding anything now—only of putting one foot in front of the other, of keeping his blood circulating until morning. In the morning there would be time enough . . . *For what?* To find Ingold, when in all probability the old man was walking straight away from him and would continue to do so for however many hours it would be until dawn? To sleep, out in the middle of nowhere, exposed to the dangers of the desert without the old man's cloak of magic and expertise to cover him? He wondered if this was the ice storm Ingold had spoken of, the searing hurricane of cold that could freeze-dry a grazing mammoth complete with the buttercups in its mouth . . .

He fought back the urge to sleep. Gil's image returned to him, shouting through that other snowstorm that had covered their last flight to the Keep of Dare—three weeks ago? A month ago? He pictured Gil dragging him up out of the snow and forcing him to move on when he would have lain down and died. *I don't care if you are a goddam wizard,* she had said, *you're a coward and a quitter.* And he was. He had always been. Only now he couldn't afford to be. Neither he nor anyone else could allow him that luxury. If the Dark Ones had taken Ingold from the camp, it would be up to him, Rudy Solis, the mage of San Berdoo, to find the Hidden City and present the problem to Lohiro.

The despair he felt at that idea was enough to make him think about lying down right there and letting the snows have him.

Coward and quitter, Gil had said. He couldn't feel his feet or hands; his whole body was numb and sluggish, his mind darkening under the inexorable grip of cold and fatigue. He stumbled and went down, feeling the snow winds ride over him.

It was the tingling in his numbed fingertips that woke him. Without opening his eyes, he flexed his hand; he

132

heard the thin crackle of the ice that had formed on his glove and the swift-flying whisk of animal feet fleeing across the snow. Through his eyelids he could see light. He knew he'd made it.

Rudy sighed. He was still cold and damp clear through to his bones. But the bitter cold of last night's storm had lessened, and the wind had dropped to its familiar steady whine. He was starvingly hungry, sore in every limb, and exhausted. It would be nice to lie here in this relatively sheltered space—had he dragged himself to the lee side of a dry wash last night or something?—and wait for rescue.

Only there wasn't going to be any rescue. It came back to him with chilling and horrible finality that Ingold was gone.

If Ingold is gone, he thought with sudden horror, *how the hell am I going to get back to California?*

Lohiro, he thought. *Lohiro is Archmage and head of the Council. He's Ingold's superior. He'll know.*

But grief took hold of his heart as he lay in the shaded snow. The old man was gone, never to sit across the flickering light of the campfires with that wicked humor in his sleepy eyes—never to blister Rudy with sarcasm if he mixed up the seed pods of kneestem and crannywort— never to stand with cupped palms filled with white light, blazing in an aura of brilliance out of the darkness. Rudy bowed his head against the icy slush. He had loved the old man, not just for his magic, or because the wizard was his teacher. If Ingold had been some old, pensioned-off steelworker living next door to him in San Bernardino, he knew he would still have loved the man.

Rudy thought of Lohiro and the vision he had seen in the crystal table at the Keep—the serene, emotionless face in its frame of fire-gold hair, the emptiness of those kaleidoscope-blue eyes. What had Ingold said to Lohiro? That he was like a dragon, a creature of fire and power, gold and light. But the Archmage was nothing like the shabby, old, beer-drinking maverick whom Rudy had first seen stepping out of the blaze of silver glory into the dawn stillness of the California hills.

Rudy knew it was time to go on.

He opened his eyes and found himself stretched out in the shelter of the dry wash's overhanging bank. Snow lay drifted all around him, melted by the warmth of his body into a kind of hollow that had further protected him from the winds. He lay in the long blue ribbon of shade thrown by the bank. Just beyond its border, where the sun glittered brightly on the snows, perched half a dozen small animals with coats of white-streaked brown fur. They were about the size of cats but had the long-drawn-out snouts, wrinkled lips, and gleaming red eyes of rats. They sat up on their hind legs, whiskers twitching, and regarded him with malevolent disappointment. Rudy remembered the tingling of his fingers which had awakened him and looked at them quickly. The leather at the ends of his gloves had been chewed.

With a wholehearted shudder of disgust, he snatched up a rock and flung it at the rats, and they melted almost scornfully out of sight into the snowy brush. Irrationally, Rudy wiped the nibbled leather on the seat of his breeches. He had the ugly feeling that he had not seen the last of them.

Cautiously, he picked up his bow. He'd managed to keep that through the night, as well as his quiver of arrows. He had water in his flask, and there was enough snow on the ground so that this was not yet a problem. He also had a little dried meat and some fruit-leather in the wallet at his belt. In addition, he had a knife, a sword, and some extra bowstrings. Shivering in the wan, heatless light, he wrapped his damp cloak around him, to no great avail. The cold leaking through his wet clothes would be a further drain on his energy, but there was no way to get dry. He scrambled to the top of the bank to have a look at the lands around him.

Only desolation met his eyes. There was no sign of the road anywhere. The overcast sky had broken enough so that the sun was remotely visible as a whitish patch in the endless roof of clouds. The wind was still bitter. The land sloped away before him in a pale reddish expanse of stony sand, barren of brush, cactus, or grass. Here and there, snow patched the sands, blown into fitful little whirlwinds.

The wind from the north and the sun in the east were the only guides for direction in all that empty land. He tried to remember whether he'd crossed the road last night and if he were north or south of it; he tried to recall the map Ingold had sketched out for him one night in the dust beside the fire. All he remembered of that was that they'd have to leave the main road to Dele at some point and strike overland, due west, to reach the Seaward Mountains and the Hidden City of Quo.

That much he could do. Head straight west—and then what? Eventually reach the Seaward Mountains? How long? Two weeks afoot, lost and virtually helpless? *Dream on.* And supposing he did? The Seaward Mountains were now one great spider web of illusions. *What the hell am I gonna do, stand in the foothills and yell, "Let me in. Ingold sent me?"*

But that, he realized, was exactly why Ingold had brought him along. Punk airbrush-jockey and half-trained screw-up artist that he was, he was the only free and trustworthy mage in the West of the World. Ingold, over whose stripped bones the scavenger rats must be fighting by this time, was counting on him.

And besides, where else was he going to go?

He headed west. The emptiness of the desert engulfed him.

He had thought before, traveling with Ingold through the wastelands, that he had come to understand the solitude and silence of those empty places, but he saw now that this had been a delusion. He was totally alone, totally forgotten. He was the only human soul in all this great emptiness. The sun climbed, strengthening a little. His cloak dried, and his shadow drifted, pale and watery, before him. Once or twice in the rocky wastes, he glimpsed jackrabbits or huge lizards the length of his arm, and once in the distance he heard the unmistakable dry buzzing of a rattler. But he knew himself to be alone. If he shouted at the top of his lungs, his voice would roll unheard through those silvery distances and die without ever reaching a human being's ear. He moved through the emptiness like a tortoise, with slow, dogged steps in a single direction, not to be turned aside.

A distant thicket of mesquite and greasewood proclaimed ground-water; he found a catch basin of rocks there, half-filled with melted snow. In the empty silence of noon, he ate as little of the dried meat and fruit as he could manage, resting, letting his thoughts drift. He wondered what Minalde was doing, how Tir was. He wondered about the White Raiders and the ghost that they feared. Had it been that, he wondered, which had taken Ingold so silently from his own camp? Or had it been the Dark, who had dogged their footsteps from Renweth? Would Lohiro know that? Had Lohiro, who was like a son to Ingold, watched him in the fire, even as Rudy had watched Alde? The vision in the crystal flashed disturbingly before his thoughts, the cold, empty blue eyes and the brush of a cloak hem across the wet gleam of a crab-crawling skull.

A small movement in the mesquite caught his eye; a moment later a rabbit bobbled cautiously into view, nose and ears a-twitch with apprehension. *Poor little bastard*, Rudy thought, and his hand stole smoothly toward his bow. Many nights on watch he had observed the jackrabbits and felt rather a kinship with them. They didn't hurt anyone and, like himself, were mainly concerned with food and fornication and staying out of trouble. The rabbit's ears swung like radar receivers; the timid little creature stared around, hoping against hope that the scenery concealed no greedy, bright-toothed death, which would end those mild rabbitty dreams of sweet mesquite tops and nymphomaniac does. *It's a tough life*, Rudy thought, *but it's you or me, and I'd rather it was you.*

As he drew the bow to him, the end snagged on a root and the arrow rolled sideways. The rabbit, galvanized into instant frenzy, rocketed wildly into the distance, leaving Rudy once again alone.

Great White Hunter blows it again. He returned to his meditations.

Eventually he shot three rabbits, one where he sat and two later in the early twilight. He found another mesquite thicket, this one among rocks. After sweeping away his tracks, he made a kind of fort by piling thornbushes between the largest of the boulders to defend his camp. He built a small fire and wondered if it was safe to sleep. *Probably not*, he reflected, but he knew himself incapable of remaining awake all night. After a day of semi-starvation, it was hard not to eat all three bunnies the minute they were cooked, but he reminded himself that he didn't know where his next meal was coming from and crawled into his spiny shelter to dream of superburgers and sun.

136

Deep in the night, he was wakened by the muffled padding of animal feet and the soft scratching of blunt claws on the rocks. He lay sweating in the darkness, seeing nothing beyond the tangles of interwoven thorn. In the morning he saw wolf tracks as large as his own hands all around the shelter in the dust.

The next day was colder, sunless, and gray. By the scent of the wind, he decided the rain would hold off and he filled his water flask with snow gleaned from a hollow in the rocks. The land was lower, thinly grown now with mesquite, small sagebrush, greasewood, and ocotillo that rattled like dry bones in the wind. The wind grew bitter, clawing at his face and cloak. He saw nothing that could remotely be construed as edible and he began to feel desperately lonely and frightened.

By afternoon he realized that he was being stalked.

The knowledge came upon him gradually. At first it was only a vague sensation, a wariness about open ground, a subliminal wondering about the anomalous rustlings in the mesquite on both sides of him. He had lived long enough with the wind to recognize the pattern of its sounds. He knew when the pattern broke.

He stood still, quieting his breath to absorb the sound and smell of the land. He could hear nothing but the whining of the wind through the chaparral, which lay like a waist-high forest over the desolation through which he had moved all day. He looked slowly around him, searching for something, anything, to tell him what he was up against and in which direction he might flee. Like the jackrabbits, he had no other course of action; he only wished it were possible for him to go streaking madly away through the sagebrush at eighty miles an hour as they did.

A sound riveted his attention. He turned his eyes back toward a clump of brush he'd already scanned before. There had been no movement that he could see; but he now saw a big male dooic, squatting in its shelter, holding a huge wedge of rock in its hands, and staring at him with that same hungry malice he had seen in the eyes of the scavenger rats. Like them, it melted slowly backward and edged out of sight into the brush beyond.

Rudy swung around, hearing more surreptitious stirrings

137

in the brush. Another hunched body was making its stealthy retreat. He felt himself grow clammy with sweat.

He was now aware of them all around. What had Ingold said—that he'd traveled with a band of them? But these dooic didn't look as if they had that kind of friendly intentions; they were armed with crudely chipped hand-axes and had tusks like those of wild pigs. Rudy moved on cautiously. He'd come pretty close to getting killed several times since his arrival in this world; but freezing to death, having the Dark Ones put the munch on him, or even having Ingold run him through with his own sword suddenly seemed a whole lot more comfortable and dignified than being dirtily mauled to pieces by a gang of Neanderthals. He was scanning the skyline and finally found what he was looking for—a distant clump of trees marking a water hole. He wondered how well dooic climbed. But in the trees he could at least get his back to something and fend them off. As it was, with his being surrounded in open ground, it looked like a losing proposition.

As he moved, he was conscious of the whole ring of them on both sides of him as well as behind. He could hear them shifting up through the brush to get ahead of him. If he let that happen, he figured it would be kiss-off time. He quickened his pace toward the trees—cottonwoods, he saw now—some two miles off. Without breaking stride, he unbuckled his sword belt and shifted the weapon up over his back, getting ready to run for it. On second thought, he also pulled off his cloak, rolling it up and bundling it under the sword belt. All he needed, he thought wryly, was to trip over the damn thing. He tried to judge the distance to the trees but couldn't; the dry, clear air of the desert made things look closer than they really were. He knew that, once he broke into a run, he had damn well better stay ahead of the pack.

He glimpsed movement in the sagebrush ahead of him and to the sides—humped, skittering shapes making a dash across open ground. *Here goes nothing,* Rudy thought. He broke into a run.

On all sides of him, the ground seemed to erupt dooic. He hadn't thought there were so many of them—twenty-five at least, rushing toward him with shrill, grunting howls, some of them from much closer than he'd suspected. Those ahead of him tried to close in, but it was no race. Rudy's longer legs carried him past them, and he sprinted out ahead, running for the trees with the pack streaming at his heels.

Once, when he was a very young child, Rudy had been chased for blocks by the local dog pack; he still remembered the heart-bursting terror of that run. But that had only been for a few hundred yards. He saw almost at once that he'd have to pace himself. The dooic were well behind him, but their whistling grunts still carried to his ears, and he knew they would overtake him when he'd run himself breathless. He tried to judge their speed and slow his own to match it. Already the trees looked farther off than they had looked before, and he knew it was going to be a long run. He thought fleetingly, *Why couldn't I have been a jogger instead of a goddam biker?* His chest was aching now; his body, toughened though it had been by the endless miles of walking, burned with fatigue. *And to think there were people who ran twenty-six miles for the hell of it.*

He felt himself flagging before half the distance was run. The raucous yammering behind him grew louder; and risking a glance backward, he saw the leaders of the pack a dozen yards from him, running with a rolling, bandy-legged lope. The flash of bared yellow tusks sent a surge of adrenalin through him that carried him a few yards farther from them, but he was already stumbling, the strain telling in every muscle of his sweat-soaked body.

He hit the trees three strides in front of the pack, barely able to breathe or stand, and swept his sword from its scabbard in an over-the-shoulder slash that hacked the arm half off the nearest of his pursuers. The blade jammed between ribs and sternum, and the creature went down howling in a geyser of blood, while the rest of the ring broke and drew back. In sickened panic, Rudy put his foot on the still-writhing Neanderthal to pull the sword free, and the thing's teeth slashed the leather of his boot and the flesh beneath before it expired as the blade came clear. Rudy fell back against the tree as the circle closed on him, hacking desperately at hairy hands and faces, sobbing with exhaustion, and being splattered with blood and dust. A thrown rock caught him on the shoulder as the dooic drew back again out of sword range. He swung around, unwilling to leave the minimal shelter of the tree. The attackers were hurling rocks at him from all sides with deadly and practiced aim. A stone the size of his two fists took a divot out of the tree inches from his head; another one smashed his elbow, numbing his arm, and a third caught him painfully in the ribs. With more haste than efficiency, he shoved the sword through his belt—whose bright idea had it been to sling the scabbard on his back?—and jumped for the lowest tree branch, scrambling awkwardly upward and praying he wouldn't cut his leg off with the deadly, unprotected edge of razor-sharp steel. The dooic swarmed around the trunk, shaking it and screaming and flinging rocks at him. Rudy clung to the swaying branches and tried to remember how deep the roots of cottonwoods went. But none of the dooic attempted to climb up to get him. After a time, they subsided, their howls dropping to a fierce muttering snarl. They squatted down around the tree to wait.

Fantastic. Rudy settled himself cautiously a little more firmly into the main crotch of the tree and carefully altered the arrangement of his sword. *I am not only lost and abandoned, I am also treed. If there is no such thing as random events, I sure as hell can't see the cosmic significance of this. It seems like a pretty pointless way to die.*

He drew his left foot up and checked the gashes on his leg. The boot and legging were saturated with blood, but his foot was still mobile—no tendon damage. Still, his leg would get infected if he didn't put alcohol on it or cauterize the wound somehow. At the moment, that didn't look real easy to do. He flexed his left arm and found it hurt like hell but would also move; he felt tenderly at his ribs and winced when one of them moved, too. Below, the dooic watched him with greedy eyes. He wondered how long they would stick around and what would happen if he fell asleep.

The cold afternoon dragged on. The dooic sat hunkered on the ground around the tree, occasionally wandering away in quest of lizards or grubs, the wind ruffling at their coarse, dark hair. Rudy disengaged his cloak and wrapped it about him for what little warmth he could get out of it. His leg throbbed agonizingly, making him wonder how long it took for blood poisoning to set in; this fear finally made him wedge himself more firmly into the crotch of the tree, unlace his boot and, sweating and sick, call fire repeatedly to the blade of his knife until the metal grew hot enough to sear the flesh. The process was excruciating and, since Rudy hadn't sufficient resolution to make a one-shot job of it, lasted a long time. He ended up by dropping the knife and vomiting, hanging limply in the branches of the tree, wondering if he were going to faint and fall and be torn to pieces, anyway, and wishing he were dead.

He there remained until it was almost dark.

Twilight came early under the overcast sky. Half in a stupor, Rudy barely noticed the failing of the light until the sudden flurry of grunts from below brought him back to full consciousness.

The dooic were scrambling to their feet, whistling and coughing among themselves, their beady eyes alert and their stooped bodies taut with fear. From his point of vantage, Rudy could see a pair of tall, ostrichlike birds stalking silently through the twilight shadows of the sagebrush, almost unnoticeable, despite their size, because of their hairy, brownish-gray feathers and smooth, catlike tread. He had seen such creatures once in the distance and had found their tracks. Now he saw that they had enormous, hawklike bills and that their eyes were set forward in their skulls—the mark, Ingold had pointed out, of a predator.

The dooic had fallen silent. They began to fade into the brush until, even from his high perch, Rudy could barely see them. Keeping his own movements to a minimum, he sat up, tore a strip from the hem of his surcoat, and bandaged the swollen mess of his left leg, tying his boot together over it. He cursed himself as he worked; in letting himself be injured, he had halved his already minimal chances for survival. The thought of trying to walk on the leg made him sick, but so did remembering that the dooic would very likely be back in the morning.

He had no idea which way was west, but by standing up in the branches of the tree, he could pick out the distant shape of a tall rock promontory that would offer some protection, if he could scale it. He refrained from thinking about what was likely to happen, if he could not. The thing to do now was to get away from the tree and find some

141

place where the dooic wouldn't look for him the minute the saber-beaked ostriches were gone.

Below him, there was a flurry of movement in the twilight. A female dooic broke cover almost under the feet of one tall bird and fled at a sprint Rudy hadn't thought the things capable of. But the bird shot forward like a gazelle, its huge beak tearing at the quarry in mid-stride, sending it down in a kicking jumble of arms and legs and blood. The other bird had started after its own prey, a young male with a hundred yards' start, and Rudy watched, aghast, as the thing ran down the fleeing dooic with long, effortless strides and disemboweled it on the run, then stood on one foot, holding a limb in its claw and tearing at it in a businesslike fashion, for all the world like a parrot eating a strawberry. Rudy remained, immobile with fear, in his tree until the birds had finished their grisly repast and stalked away into the dusk. The rest of the dooic were utterly gone. The ripped remains of Rudy's two erstwhile hunters were surrounded by the scavenger rats that seemed to have risen from the earth to quarrel over the bones.

The rats barely glanced at him as he slipped gingerly from the tree at last. They did put on some show of interest when his feet touched the ground and his cramped knee buckled, but went back to feeding when he got up again. Rudy had a brief, queasy vision of what would have happened if he had not been able to rise. The painful weakness of his left leg frightened him. He limped around the trunk of the tree and found his knife, then cut a sucker from the roots the right length for a walking stick. He checked his bow, debated momentarily about shooting a couple of scavengers for meat—it would be like shooting fish in a barrel—but couldn't bring himself to think of actually eating the carrion beasts. Besides, he'd only have to fight their brothers for the corpses, and at the moment all he wanted to be was out of there.

Leaning on his staff, which, like most cottonwood, was so soft as to be almost useless for the purpose, he limped slowly on his way.

He awakened to the distant sound of trumpeting. For a moment he puzzled over it, wondering if it were part of the clinging fog of his dreams, like the very brief, very clear

142

vision he had had of Ingold, sitting as he had so often sat beside their campfire, scratching runes in the dust with a stick. Then the pain of wakening came, the pain of cramps, of bruises, the stabbing pinch of his cracked rib, and the sickening throb of his ripped ankle. He had slept in a semi-fetal position in a cranny high in the rocks, half-frozen after a walk that had seemed to last most of the night.

The trumpeting did not fade with his dreams. It came again, a living sound, shrill and brazen.

Elephants?

What in hell are elephants doing in the middle of the Gettlesand deserts? Or am I really delirious this time?

He dragged himself upright and scrambled to the top of the rocks.

Once on the road from Karst to Renweth—years ago, it felt like, though he knew it had been less than a month—the train had stopped on a high, green saddleback hill. The rain had cleared, silver veils of mist drawing back from the heartbreaking beauty of the lands below, revealing them holy and mysterious, pearled with rain and frost. He'd stood next to the small, hide-roofed cart that fluttered with the black pennons of the House of Dare, leaning on the wheel while Alde bent from the seat to talk to him, holding Tir in her arms. She'd pointed outward over those drenched green lands at moving brown shapes in the distance and had said, "Mammoth. There haven't been mammoth in the river valleys for—oh, hundreds and hundreds of years."

And now here they were.

In the cold, pale wastes of the desert, they moved like perambulating haystacks, far more vast than any elephant Rudy had ever seen. They looked absurdly like the artists' reconstructions in picture encyclopedias—enormous shaggy bulks sloping down from huge, blocklike heads and mountainous shoulders, little fanlike ears, and recurved tusks like the soundbow of an ancient harp, with small, black, beady eyes above the tusks. Their brown fur was speckled with the white spits of snow that blew down from a bleak, featureless sky. Rudy identified the herd bulls, as massive as freight cars, the smaller cows, and the little calves, the smallest of which was still considerably larger than a Winnebago, clinging like Dumbo the Elephant to mamma's tail. A fresh gust of wind stung his face and flurried snow into his sheltering rocks. The mammoth turned their gargantuan backs to the snow and strode off southward, driven before it as they had been driven, Rudy thought, from their home on the high, brown grasslands of the north.

He shivered and wondered how much farther he could get on this futile quest. To the west, the colorless horizon lay as straight as a ruled line. He doubted he would see the Seaward Mountains for weeks yet and he knew already that he would not be able to continue that long. *Ingold was right,* he thought bitterly. *I should have reconsidered, sat tight back at the Keep. But, dammit, I didn't know then I'd lose him.*

Ingold knew. He knew there was an odds-on chance of one of us buying it and he was afraid it was going to be he. And he knew there had to be someone else to finish the quest.

Despairing, Rudy leaned his forehead on his wrists against the stone and wished he were dead. *Why me?*

The question is the answer, Rudy. The question is always the answer. Because you're a mage. You wanted to come along to learn to be a mage. You came to be a mage, and he took you because only a mage can finish the quest. You still owe him.

I didn't want this! his mind cried.

You didn't want to realize that you can call fire from darkness?

Dammit, Rudy thought tiredly. *Dammit, dammit, dammit. Even when he was gone—lost—devoured by the Dark —you never could win an argument with Ingold.*

A change, a turning of the wind, brought to him the swift, steady drumming of hooves—horses, a troop of them. A distant beating murmur vibrated through the rock beneath his body. He inched his head over the lip of the crag once more and saw them, like ghosts streaming as gray as mist through the snow-flecked wind.

White Raiders!

Ingold had been right. They were undoubtedly the people of the Icefalcon. Pale braids like Vikings streamed out behind the lean, long-legged warriors bending over the curved necks of their mustangs. They turned in a single fluid line, manes rippling and nostrils smoking, less than

144

half a mile off, but barely visible except as a pounding sense of motion in the empty lands. There was nothing of them to catch the eye; the horses were mostly that wolfish gray-brown of the land; the riders wore the same color. Even the fairness of their braids was the echo of sun-bleaching on dry grass. The fluttering of tags, feathers, and chips of bright-winking glass on their harness seemed like the random twinkling of wind and leaves. In a wide curve, they headed along the tracks of the mammoth and vanished, driven south by the winds.

Rudy sighed. He'd have to hunt again that day, for his rabbit meat was nearly gone. He changed the bandage on his ankle, cannibalizing another strip from the hem of his frayed surcoat for the purpose, and examined the wound worriedly. He had no idea what blood poisoning looked like or how long it took for red streaks to show up. Ingold had taught him emergency spells to keep gangrene at bay, but Rudy had no idea whether he'd executed them properly or not. It was borne upon him how gross was his own ignorance and how much he would have to learn, provided he ever got out of this mess alive. He cringed at the thought of all the knowledge he had passed blithely by in the good old days when he could go to a doctor, a grocery store, or —God forbid!—the cops as a last resort. As he climbed down out of his shelter, he remembered Ingold's saying that he had wandered this desert alone for fifteen years. No wonder Ingold had been so utterly self-sufficient. Rudy picked up his worthless staff and headed west again.

He walked throughout the day. Keeping the wind on his right, he knew he was heading west, though no sun broke the eternal overcast of the clouds. At times he wondered what he would do when he came within sight of the Sea-ward Mountains. But what the hell was he worried about? he asked himself. *You'll be dead long before you get in sight of them.* There was no reason for him to go on, but he did, like an ant crossing a football field. He wondered what had become of Ingold, whether the Dark had gotten him or whether it had been something else, that unseen other power that the White Raiders feared. What would become of Gil, stuck here forever in an alien universe?

He crossed a high, treeless stretch of barren rock, and the lands around him were now mostly pebbles and sand, a desolation in which only an occasional scrap of saltbush would grow. Blown sand and snow stung his face, the cold cutting through the bandages to torture his leg. In their shabby gloves, his fingers were numb. Three days he had been alone, moving like a ghost through this empty land —longer than he had ever been alone in his life. Though solitude had always bothered him less than he knew it bothered most people, his soul had ached yesterday and the day before for companionship—someone, anyone, a total stranger; he'd even have settled for his sister Yolanda. But he found that he was becoming used to the company of his own spirit. Though he still shuddered at the thought of spending months and years alone, as Ingold had done, he could now imagine, as a faint echo of the reality, what it would be like.

Twilight was settling down again. He wondered where he would spend the night. The land around him was utterly flat and desolate, without rock, without tree, without more than a few isolated patches of thin brush. He felt weak and exhausted, but knew that he had to keep going until he found something. To lie down and sleep in the open would be death indeed.

A movement caught his eye. It bobbed, stalky and awkward, on the crest of a stony ridge, yet there was a curiously catlike quality to it . . . Rudy froze. It was a tricky time of day; the graying light fooled the eyes, and the threshing of the few bits of brush in the wind masked the steps of those that hunted in twilight. *Dooic?* he wondered. *Christ, not again.*

Then he saw it, a streak of gray in the distance. It ran weightlessly over the sand, a blurred ripple of wolf-colored feathers and the pale gleam of a beak like a scythe blade.

There was nowhere to run and no hope of outdistancing the bird, but Rudy ran. He felt the grinding pain in his leg and rib and ran anyway, sprinting desperately into the twilight, without any thought but hopeless escape, like trying to outrun a speeding car. Rocks bruised his feet, and his breath sobbed in his lungs. Behind him, he could hear the soft, light thud-thud-thud of clawed and padded feet. He couldn't look back; his mind blanked to everything but staying on his feet and running faster. He felt no pain, no

146

tiredness, only desperate terror. He ran blindly into the sinking twilight.

When he fell, his first thought was that his bad leg had given out. But the hands he threw out to catch himself met nothing, and he plunged over the shallow cliff and down through a yielding tangle of branches that had masked the pit beneath. In the half-light and confusion, he felt twigs tear his hair. He slammed into something wooden and rough-barked that took the skin off his face as he half-rolled, half-slid down the last two or three feet to land in the fresh-turned earth below. Too dazed to understand, he rolled over and looked up. Ten feet above him, skylined on the edge of the brush-fringed cliff, the horrible predator bird stood, cocking its head to look down at him, as if at a loss to understand how he had suddenly gotten down there. For a heart-stopping moment, Rudy wondered if it would jump down after him. He could never fight it in this pit, even if he hadn't broken his sword, or his arm, or both, in falling. But the bird only ruffled up its feathers in disgust, opened its swordlike bill, gave a hoarse honk of displeasure, and stalked away into the dusk.

Rudy leaned back against the post behind him and closed his eyes. He felt that he could sleep or faint or die—it didn't matter which. But after a time, he told himself he wasn't out of the soup yet and he'd better sit up and take notice if he didn't want to come to a bad end.

He opened his eyes and looked around.

Fantastic. I've fallen into a mammoth trap.

There was nothing else it could possibly be. Most of the overroofing brush had been pulled down in his fall, revealing the edge of the pit against the fading sky. The place smelled of new-dug earth, and white fingers of roots poked from the black walls near the top. In the center of the pit, three huge stakes had been driven into the floor, and it was against one of these that he'd fallen. He used it to pull himself upright and pressed his hand to his abraded cheek. *Cheer up,* he told himself. *You could have impaled yourself on the way down.*

Now who the hell, he wondered, *would build a mammoth trap out here? Is there a town of some kind . . . ?*

White Raiders!

Fantastic.

He slipped back down the pole to slump at its base, his head supported in his hands. *Maybe I should have impaled myself,* he thought. *At least that would be fast. How come just when things look blackest, I turn around and they get worse?*

All I really need now to make things perfect, he reflected bitterly, *is a mammoth.*

The ground shook.

Distantly, the high, squealing trumpet of a beast in pain reached him, along with the booming thud of massive weight in flight and the swift pounding of hooves.

If I stay right where I am, Rudy thought tiredly, *the goddam thing will land directly on top of me and then I'll be mashed flat and out of this whole mess.*

No, he decided. *With the way things have been going lately, I'd just be maimed and then I'd still have to deal with the Raiders. But Christ, they have horses. Even whole and healthy, I couldn't run from them.*

What the hell. He lurched to his hands and knees and crawled to the corner of the pit closest to the direction from which the mammoth was coming, where he would have the most chance of its falling over and past him as it went down. The ground rumbled with the earthquake of its feet; it was squealing like a bugle, the sound shrill in Rudy's brain. The noise was like an approaching Panzer division, inescapable, blotting him into a dusk-enshrouded nightmare of noise and fear. The vibration of it shook his bones. Then he looked up and saw it silhouetted against the sky—a massive brown head, a mountain of flesh as large as a two-storey house, its trunk unflung and its eyes red with savage pain and fury. Dark blood splattered its pounding feet to the knees. Trapped below it, Rudy could only stare upward in horror. The sound of its feet, its voice, and the sea roar of the hooves went round and round in his brain. A horse and rider flashed past on the very lip of the pit, the man's braids gleaming whitely in the gloom. Hypnotized, Rudy watched the mammoth balk and swerve from the edge; its teetering feet showered him with dislodged rock and earth as it hung suspended above him. In what looked like a slow-motion cinema, he saw the man on horseback remove an arrow from his quiver and nock it as the mammoth shied and raised its trunk in a deafening scream of rage. The horse reared in panic, hooves inches from the edge; the rider drew his bow and aimed through the thrashing mêlée of shadow and weight and motion, of flying mane and fur and the titan bulk of the thing bearing straight down on top of him. In slow motion the arrow left the bow, floating, it seemed to Rudy, with calm deliberation across the dozen feet of intervening distance, to bury itself to the feathers in the mammoth's glaring red eye. The huge beast flung itself upward with a final scream of agony, rearing on its treelike hind legs, and seemed to hover, weightless, over the pit in which Rudy sat, trapped and immobile with terror. Then, like a mountain avalanche, it fell.

CHAPTER NINE

At first there was only utter stillness and the low, incessant moaning of the wind. Rudy was aware of diffuse dappled light, the smell of cut mesquite and blood, and the damp cold of earth beneath his bruised cheek. He sighed and choked his breath short at the pain in his cracked rib. He tried to move and couldn't. *To hell with it, then,* he decided, and lay still. His head ached, but without the hallucinatory confusion of last night's chaotic dreams. Horses, noise, and the slow, graceful flight of a detached arrow against a twilight sky merged together in his mind, but his last clear memory was of that monstrous mountain of writhing, screaming flesh plunging down into the pit on top of him, blotting out the last of the light. He took two very slow, very careful breaths and did a mental stocktaking of his body, isolating it limb by limb, as Ingold had shown him how.

First, he was alive, a circumstance that rather surprised him. His head ached, and he had a massive lump on one side. His left leg felt weak and painful, but no worse than it had yesterday, and he thought, though he couldn't be sure because he could not move his hands to check, that there were a few more ribs cracked. And that brought up the last point—he couldn't move his hands.

They were tied behind him.

For a few moments, he wondered if the White Raiders had merely tied him up and left him for the scavenger rats. But a drift of smoke reached his nostrils from the other side of the cut brush that walled him in, and he heard the muted nicker of horses. He lay face down in some kind of brush shelter; that much he could gather, but his face was turned toward the wall, and all he could see was the tangle of gray-leafed twigs and the chain of ants

150

that crawled inoffensively along them. He wondered if he was alone, but didn't particularly want to give himself away by looking.

He listened instead, letting his mind grow quiet and his breathing still. He found that this emptying of the thoughts was easier after the days he had spent in the loneliness of the desert. All things receded except his sense of hearing. Slowly the sounds came to his listening ears—the soft scritch of dry grasses in the wind, the clicking of dead leaves, the infinitesimal whisper of feet passing close to his shelter, and the silken, crinkling shear of a skinning knife separating hide from flesh, accompanied by the sudden strong renewal of the blood-smell. *Skinning the mammoth?* There was a faint stirring of a garment nearby, and the thin creaking of leather as the guard at the door of his shelter shifted his weight. *So there was a guard.*

Rudy extended his senses, sending them like runners along the ground, blindly seeking by touch the nature and bounds of the camp. Some sounds made no sense to him— soft little shaving noises and then the muffled tap of rock on wood. He become aware of more feet and the smoke and wood smells of a fire being stirred. A gust of wind chilled through the camp, bearing a distant scent of snow, and he heard a kind of glittery clinking sound that he thought was familiar, like a wind chime made of bones.

For some reason, the sound frightened him.

Soft feet swished in the sand, with a smell of feral grime and sweetgrass. He heard another, almost soundless creak of leather as a second guard stood up. He heard no voices—*maybe they talked in sign?*—but he knew the roof of the shelter was too low to stand under. They would both be outside. He turned his head cautiously to be sure and saw two pairs of soft-booted legs visible through the low arch of the shelter's opening; beyond was the ghostly flickering of a pale daytime fire. On the other side of the fire stood a glass-festooned magic-post, its streamers twisting faintly in the wind, like a scarecrow set to frighten away the legions of Hell. In front of it, a woman warrior with long barley-colored braids was driving stakes into the ground for a sacrifice.

Rudy had a bad feeling about whom they'd elected for that.

Stay calm, he instructed himself over a blinding rush of panic. *Ingold taught you an undoing-spell, and it worked fine back at the camp.* Nevertheless, it took him three tries that nearly cut off the circulation in his wrists before he finally felt the bindings slip and was able stealthily to work his hands free. His ankles were bound as well, but it was quicker to work the knots loose by hand. He kept his movements to a minimum, aware of the guards still standing outside. He felt almost smothered with apprehension. He knew already what he had to do.

They'd taken his knife and sword, along with his cloak and gloves. But if he could get to the horse lines undetected, to steal two for himself and cut the rest loose, he stood a chance of getting clear away—and mounted, maybe making it all the way to the Seaward Mountains after all. Even covered by a simple illusion-spell, he knew it would be impossible to sidle between the nearer guard and the one standing by the front door, but the shelter was merely a kind of yard-high pup tent made of cut mesquite, open at the front and only loosely covered at the back. He could hear nothing close by.

The illusion-spell was simple, as all illusions were. *Stinkbug*, Rudy decided. *Harmless, black, little, trundling along minding its own stinkbug business. Who the hell looks at a stinkbug?* He had practiced illusion under Ingold's critical eye and had been rather proud of the results. To wear an illusion was to feel against his skin a wind made of cold fire, a soft, glimmering cloak of misdirection that made him appear, as so many things in this world appeared, to be something he was not.

He pushed the brush aside and slipped through.

If he hadn't been standing in the middle of the camp, he would hardly have known a camp was there. It was situated in a sagebrush flat, and the brush shelters blended with the surrounding mesquite, identical in positioning and size. From where he stood, only one fire was visible, but he could smell others, made of smokeless wood and half-buried in sheltered holes, as Ingold habitually made fires. There were White Raiders in evidence, men and women both, though the women, Rudy saw at once, were like Gil—virgins of war, clothed and armed like the men and as cold-eyed as combat troops. They were dressed alike, in

152

close-fitting tunics and trousers of wolf or cougar hide, the grays and golds merged with the colors of the ground. Some of them wore close-fitting coats of wolf or buffalo hide. All of them were armed with knives, bows, and a form of bolo. In front of several shelters, he saw spears stabbed into the ground, the shafts ready to hand. As he'd seen before, the magic-post stood in the center of the camp. An old man was decorating it like a Christmas tree, with strings of bone and braided grass, broken glass, and flowers, and at its foot a woman was sharpening a long skinning knife. Beyond lay the horse lines, the mustangs grouped so as to resemble to the casual eye a wild herd grazing.

With utmost stealth, Rudy the stinkbug began his walk across the open ground of the camp.

He moved slowly, staying within the parameters of the illusion. He passed a guard talking to one of the women outside his former prison at a distance of a few feet, and neither gave him a glance. High and pale, the silver disc of the sun had appeared, for the first time in many days, and the shadow that it threw on the dirt was an insect shadow, perfect of its kind. The chill desert winds tangled in the braided ropes of the magic-post, fluttering the petals of the winter roses twined through the eyes of the skulls. The Raider finished twisting feathers around the cross-beam and stepped back. He was an old man, his hair so white as to be almost blue and his face like an age-black-ened oak burl. Rudy stopped to let him pass.

But he didn't pass.

Rudy's blood turned to ice water in his veins. The ancient warrior was looking down at the ground where the illusion of the stinkbug would be, and there was a hint of puzzlement in that leathery, impassive face. Then, without removing his eyes from Rudy, he took a step or two toward one of the shelters and signed to a man and woman nearby to come. They did, bringing spears.

Rudy broke into a cold sweat. *Hey, come on, you can't suspect an innocent little bug . . .* But of course, now that he remembered, the Icefalcon was suspicious of everyone and everything. Rudy walked as much faster as he dared, circling to get around the old man. But the three Raiders held a quick, silent conversation in finger signs and half-

153

whispers, then moved in front of him once more. *This isn't fair!* Rudy thought frantically. He looked about for something to use as a weapon. He made one last try to get around them, and the old warrior stepped across his path again.

Rudy's nervousness triumphed. The illusion crumbled as his concentration broke, and the white-haired Raider jerked back, startled, as Rudy seemingly materialized from the air. That one instant of surprise gave Rudy his chance. He grabbed a stick of wood from the ground, and it blazed into the cold illusion of white fire in his hand. As the Raiders closed in, he slashed with his fiery club at the man's face, broke through the line, and ran for it.

The camp boiled into life around him, lean, pale shapes seeming to appear from nowhere in pursuit. Rudy dodged through them at a staggering run, hearing the soft thunk of an arrow and feeling the sting of the barb skim his ankle, still swinging his flaming club at the men who tried to head him off. They fell back from the burning weapon. One of the horse guards grabbed him from the side. Rudy writhed around to knee him in the groin and struggled free to run again. He caught the nose rope of a shying mustang as hands closed on his left arm. Whirling, he laid about him with the stick, and the circle widened for an instant. That instant was all he needed. He scrambled awkwardly aboard the horse's back, thanking God the thing wasn't really tall and slashing at the Raiders on all sides. He saw his chance, turned the mustang's head out toward the open desert, and dug in his heels.

The mustang reared once, dropped its nose, and bucked him ten feet into the chaparral.

The impact with the ground was unbelievable. It slammed the breath from his body, and the broken ribs stabbed his side like knives. He tried to roll to his feet, but a stone-headed spear drove into the ground beside him, pinning the slack of his dark tunic to the earth. The shadows of the Raiders fell across him, and the next spear came down straight at his chest.

It missed. Thrown at a distance of less than ten feet, it swerved suddenly, impossibly, in midair, wobbled, and smacked him harmlessly broadside. The Raiders froze, pointing past him with whispers of alarm at something far out in the brown distances of the desert.

It's the ghost, Rudy thought in despair, twisting his head around to look. But he saw only a dark robed figure that seemed to melt out of the wind and the silence, a fierce-eyed and familiar old vagabond who came striding toward the camp as if he owned the place. One Raider, the man who had shot the charging mammoth in the eye, fired an arrow at him. It missed by yards. Rudy almost wept with relief.

Ingold stopped beside him and jerked loose the spear that pinned him. A scarred, blunt-fingered hand reached down to drag him to his feet, and a familiar voice rasped, "What did you turn yourself into?"

"A stinkbug, for Chrissake!" Rudy sobbed. "How the hell were they suspicious of a lousy stinkbug?"

In the shadows of his hood, Ingold's eyes had a dry glitter. "Have you seen any stinkbugs since you've come to this world?"

Rudy was silent.

Ingold went on. "There are none—as you would have known, had you been paying attention to what goes on around you." He glanced from Rudy to the White Raiders, who were fanning into a circle around them, spears pointing, as they would surround a cave bear. He held the spear he'd pulled slackly in his hand, point-down, and made no move toward sword or weapon of any kind. "And even so," he continued, as if they were alone and safe, "you could have used a simple cloaking-spell to leave the camp by the back way and head out into the brush, without a fireworks display like the one you just put on. You didn't need the horse, Rudy. And now, of course since we've made ourselves as conspicuous as we possibly can without actually murdering someone, that is out of the question."

The circle tightened around them, a bristling hedge of stone and steel points, like the teeth of a shark. Ingold watched the warriors without making a move.

"I'm sorry," Rudy mumbled.

The wizard's voice grated. "You and I may be a great deal sorrier before all is said and done."

A slight sound made Ingold focus his attention behind

155

him. Several of the Raiders fell hastily back. Rudy could feel the tension in the wizard, the leashed power, the blazing potential that customarily hid behind that mild, unassuming façade. The Raiders seemed to feel it, too. At least none of them appeared prepared to try to rush him.

Then the circle shifted, and a tall Raider stepped into the center of the ring, raising his hands to show himself unarmed.

He was a magnificent viking of a man in his forties, pale braided mustaches hanging down to the pit of his throat. His eyebrows were tufted like those of a lynx, curling upward and outward; beneath them, his eyes were as cold as frozen amber. The bleached gray-gold of his cougar hide garments was unrelieved by any mark of rank; but without question, he was the chief of the Raiders. He wore that majesty like a cloak.

Chill eyes that deduced the coming of herds or the threat of a storm in the bend of a single grass blade studied Ingold and Rudy for a moment in silence, pale in the white fans of wrinkles that scored the dark-dyed skin. When he spoke, his voice was a foghorn bass, and he spoke with a sonorous accent in the tongue of the Wath.

"You are wise men?"

"*I* am a wise man," Ingold replied dryly. "*He* merely knows spells."

The cool eyes shifted briefly to Rudy, evaluated the distinction, and dismissed him. Rudy felt his face grow hot and wished he could truly disappear or return to his stinkbug shape and trundle off into the desert, never to be seen again.

"I thought that so it might be," the Raider said. "Seldom does Yobshikithos the Arrow-Dancer miss his aim, but it is said that wise men are sometimes difficult to hit. Zyagarnalhotep am I, Hoofprint of the Wind, and you are come among the Twisted Hills People, out of the land among the White Lakes."

"You are far from your homes," Ingold said gravely. "Do the mammoth then leave the northern plains, to draw you this far to the south?"

The foghorn voice rumbled, "Where we ride, we ride. The lands of all the plains and of the desert are ours,

156

ours to use without leave of mud diggers from the river, wise though they may be. But you," he went on, with a gesture of one scar-creased hand, "you read our magic-post on the road these ten nights gone, not merely to see it and flee away, as do the people of the Straight Roads. Are you, then, that wise man whose name was known in the south many years ago, the Desert Walker, who was friend to the White Bird and his tribe?"

Ingold was silent for a moment, as if the name, like the stones of the desert or the shackle-gall on his wrist, brought back the taste of another life and another self. "I am that Desert Walker," he said at last. "But I must tell you, Hoofprint of the Wind, that the White Bird died of knowing me."

"I was a friend to that White Bird," the chieftain said quietly. "And men die, whether known by you or not, Desert Walker." Bleached lashes veiled the glint of his eyes. "But if you are that same one and the White Bird spoke truly unto me, good it is for us all that my people did not kill you, but only waited for me to come."

"Fortunate it is for your people," Ingold returned gently, "that they did not try."

The gold eyes met the blue in arrogant challenge, but after a moment the mouth beneath the braided mustache curled in appreciation. "Yes," he said softly. "Yes, truly you are that same Desert Walker who stole the White Bird's horses . . ."

"I never did!" Ingold protested in quick indignation.

". . . and made a certain bet regarding the horrible birds . . ."

"That wasn't me."

". . . and lost?"

"I won. And besides," Ingold went on smoothly, "it was all many years gone, and I was a most young and foolish Desert Walker in those days."

"You who are old and wise enough now to come striding into the camps of war, in the time when there are evil ghosts abroad upon the land?"

As if summoned by the speaking of the name, winds rattled in the glass and feathers of the magic-post, the white sunlight winked from the spinning metal, and the wild rose petals tore loose to lie in the grass like sacrificial blood. There was a stirring among the Raiders; a head or two turned, not toward the post, but toward the emptiness of the desert. Yet there was nothing there, nothing but the arctic cold.

Ingold leaned upon the spear. "Tell me of these evil ghosts," he said.

Zyagarnalhotep regarded these two ragged pilgrims from the lands of his enemies for a moment in silence, as if gauging what each of them was worth. Rudy had the uncomfortable feeling that they were far from out of it yet. But the chief only said, "Come. Eat with me, you and your Little Insect who knows spells, and we will speak of this thing."

Hoofprint of the Wind's shelter was larger than others in the camp, but, like most of them, indistinguishable from a thicket of mesquite at more than a few feet away. The faintest drift of smoke marked its fire, with a whiff of meat cooking. Ingold unerringly picked out the concealed entrance and led the way into the dugout room. "Is it safe?" Rudy asked softly, with a worried glance back at the warriors still grouped and talking quietly outside.

"Is anything you've done for the past four days?" Ingold replied tartly. "Sit down and let me see your leg."

The place was narrow and low-roofed, intensely gloomy, and smelling of crushed sage, dirt, and woodsmoke. Bison and mammoth furs strewed the floor, and Rudy eased himself down onto one of these while Ingold sorted through the various pouches and packets he habitually carried concealed about his person.

Another horrible suspicion assailed Rudy. "Hey—"

Ingold glanced up.

"It wasn't all a test, was it? I mean, to see how well I'd get along on my own?"

"It was not," the wizard stated dryly and began to unwrap the crusted bandages on Rudy's ankle and calf. "For one thing, you aren't fit to be tested on anything yet, and a test of this sort would be tantamount to murder. When I have call to murder my assistants, I do so deliberately and after fair warning. For another, I should have failed you the moment you went haring off out of camp into a

158

storm without stopping to ascertain whether I had really vanished or not."

"Yeah, but I—" The sense of what the old man said sank in. "Hunh?"

Ingold sighed and sat back on his heels. "It's the oldest trick in the book, Rudy," he explained patiently. "If you want to separate two partners, one of the quickest ways of doing so is to throw a cloaking-spell of some kind over one of them when the other one's back is turned. You were asleep, weren't you? I thought so. The other partner is bound to go pelting away in the opposite direction, yelling his friend's name, without stopping to make a careful search of the place or even take a second look. Merely a few minutes unguarded would have suited their purposes. The storm only made the situation worse."

"They—who?" Rudy winced as Ingold applied the thin paste of powdered herbs and water to the half-healed mess of his scabbing wound.

The old man looked up at him again and dried his hands on a corner of his patched and fraying mantle. "The Dark Ones," he said somberly. "The same ones, I think, that have followed us from Renweth. There weren't many of them, but there were enough to keep me pinned in a cave in the bank till morning. I'm going to need another piece out of your surcoat, Rudy. We haven't anything else to bind this with."

Rudy obliged him, reflecting philosophically that at this point a few more tatters made little difference. He knew he looked like some gorily exaggerated beggar out of an Ingmar Bergman movie, with his filthy rags, long hair, bruised face, and four days' worth of black stubble on his jaw. Ingold looked little better, worn out, filthy, and shabby, like a St. Francis after a bar fight. The last four days hadn't been easy ones on him, either.

"It wasn't neglect that kept me from tracking you and catching you up immediately," Ingold went on, bending down to rewrap the wound. "The Dark pursued me for two nights, and I couldn't afford to be far from shelter. I ended by killing most of them—which is the reason I believe that they came from Renweth and have pursued us all along."

159

Rudy said, "Hunh?" and then yelped with pain as Ingold's fingers probed gently at his damaged ribs.

"Sit still and this won't hurt."

"Like hell it won't. How do you figure that about Renweth?"

"It is always difficult to count the Dark, Rudy." The wizard paused in his ministrations, kneeling before him in the murky darkness of the shelter, his face grave in the gloom. "But there were surely fewer on the second night than the first, and fewer still on the third. If the Dark can communicate among themselves and there had been others within call, there would have been more, not less. Hence their anxiety to separate us, rather than risk further decrease in their numbers by an open fight." He turned back to his medicine bag. "Those ribs are only cracked, by the way. I'll mix a gum plaster to hold them still while they heal, which they should do in a few weeks, provided you don't try any more spectacular feats like this afternoon's. I was also hampered in my pursuit of you because I had to keep track of Che."

"Have you still got Che?"

"Yes," Ingold replied mildly. "At the moment he's concealed up my sleeve." Seeing Rudy's expression, he grinned suddenly for the first time since they had met. "He's hidden out in the desert, not far from here," he explained "I couldn't lose him—I certainly didn't plan on journeying to the Seaward Mountains, grubbing for forage all the way. We're in too much of a hurry for that. Besides," he added, "the Bishop would excommunicate me twice over if I lost her donkey."

Rudy pulled the frayed remains of his surcoat back into place and tangled with the lacings, cursing the man or woman in this universe who had never invented zippers. "Ingold, listen," he said after a moment. "You say the Dark didn't bring in reinforcements. I was four days out in the desert alone and I never saw the Dark Ones at all." Ingold nodded, and Rudy had the curious feeling for a moment that the old man could read those solitary hours printed like the tracks of a piper on sand in the lines of his face. "And you know what else? I never saw this ghost thing, either."

"No," Ingold said quietly. "Neither did I." Meticulously, he gathered together his herbs and medicines, his hands deft and his face in shadow as he spoke. "And the odd thing is that I never even felt its presence. I spent last night sitting awake in the darkness, without fire, watching, hearing, and feeling, as wizards can, the threads and fibers of the air for miles over the desert, seeking the smallest sign that the Dark Ones might still know where I was. But there was no trace of the Dark, and no trace of—anything. No breath, no sign, no spirit moving over the sands, except those night-walking creatures that are one with the being of the earth."

Rudy nodded, understanding what Ingold had done. As he himself had extended his senses to reconnoiter the camp beyond his prison shelter of brush, so Ingold had done on a vastly greater scale. He had sought and understood the shift of every spear of wind-moved weed, every harsh little scattering of kicked sand, and every scent that rode the airs of night, with the web of his awareness thrown like a net over hundreds of miles, seeking danger in the night—and finding none.

"But in that case," Rudy asked, "where or what is the ghost?"

"This do all my people ask," a bass voice rumbled. Looking up, Rudy saw that Hoofprint had entered the shelter, bending his tall head beneath the low pitch of the roof. He was surrounded by the greasy aura of woodsmoke and stewed game. The warriors who entered behind him, lesser chiefs of the war band, Rudy guessed, bore a tightly woven basket plastered inside and out with hardened clay and filled with chunks of steaming meat. Others carried smaller vessels filled with some kind of green, sharp-smelling mush. Rudy took a second look and saw that some of the smaller vessels were the skulls of dooic. Others, judging by the shape of the cranium and the absence of a suborbital ridge, were not.

The lesser chiefs settled down in a group a little apart, sitting on the furs and talking quietly among themselves in their own tongue. Rudy overheard a drift of it now and then, a spare, quiet murmur, modulated like the sigh of the wind, half-augmented by signs and marked by subtle changes of inflection. Only Hoofprint of the Wind came to sit with him and Ingold, bringing meat and mush and a bottle of some kind of drink that had a nasty sweet-ish backtaste and an insidious alcoholic content.

"Now," the chief said, when they had eaten and the semidarkness of the shelter was deepening with the coming of evening outside. "You wise men, who read all the papers of the mud diggers beyond the mountains, what is this ghost that is more terrible than the Eaters in the Night, wise man?"

"More terrible?" Ingold asked softly. Rudy heard in the mellow, grainy voice not only apprehension but over-whelming curiosity. Pointed to its lair, Rudy thought, he'd investigate it or die.

"So must it be."

"Why? Have you seen it?"

There was a movement of denial and the glint of silver on a thick, gleaming braid.

"Then how do you know that it is more terrible?"

The Raider shrugged, a slight gesture reminiscent of the Icefalcon's curt movements. "They flee before it," he said. "All the holes in the ground from which they rose up have they deserted and they come no more to this part of the plain. If this thing has eaten up the Eaters, now that they are gone, will it not destroy us also? When the chosen prey of a thing dies out, will it not turn to other? We know nothing of this thing and never have we seen it. Yet why have the Eaters gone? From what would such creatures flee? Have you heard the name of this thing, Desert Walker, in all your lore?"

"No," Ingold said. "I have heard nothing of this. When did they depart, the Eaters in the Night?"

Hoofprint of the Wind paused in thought, counting backward in time. Outside, the wind grew to a shrill-voiced violence with the dropping of the ground temperature; a few inches above their heads, the hide roof of the shelter rattled angrily on its moorings.

"It was the time of the first quarter moon of autumn," the tall barbarian said finally, and Rudy, gifted with the dark-sight of a mage, saw Ingold look up suddenly, a strange eagerness illuminating his lined face. "Yes," the chieftain went on. "They rose in the last full moon of the failing summer, far away in the north, and hunted across the lands of us, the Stcharnyii, the Chasers of the Mam-

162

moth, the People of the Plains. And we moved south, the Twisted Hills People, the White Lakes People, the Lava Hills People, and all the others of the Stcharnyii. We have hunted the deserts, picking little bugs from the ground as the dooic do. And now the Eaters in the Night have gone away and rise no more from their holes. But what has driven them forth, Desert Walker? What is this ghost that they fear? For now it has come here and driven the Eaters forth out of their holes, even in the desert. We have camped the night beside such a hole, and they came not in the night. Now what shall we do if this thing will choose to hunt us?"

Ingold sat quietly for a time, as if he had turned to stone. But Rudy could feel the tension in him, like a current of electricity, and could hear it when he spoke, under the deep, scratchy calm of his voice. "When the deer depart, the lion does not feed on the grasses on which they fed," he said softly. "Nor does the *hrigg*, the horrible bird, eat the bugs and lizards that are the prey of its prey. It may be that humankind has nothing to fear from this ghost. But tell me, Hoofprint of the Wind, where is this hole where you spent so calm and dreamless a night?"

"From here," the chieftain of the Raiders said, "we could be there tomorrow, riding swift horses." His amber eyes gleamed a little, like a beast's in the dark.

Beside him, Ingold asked casually, "And have you not swift horses?"

CHAPTER TEN

In spite of his dashing attempt at Errolflynnery, Rudy had never been on a horse before his arrival in this universe. On the road down from Karst he'd ridden exactly once, when he'd gone with a patrol of the Guards to investigate a farmhouse burned out by the White Raiders. The memory of what he'd found there still turned him sick. But, raised as he had been on *Maverick* and *Paladin*, he had been under the impression that there was nothing much to leaping aboard a horse and thundering away into the sunset. He had recently found out he was wrong.

The horses of the White Raiders were taller and longer-limbed than those bred in the Realm of Darwath and, from foraging on the scant saltbush and wiregrass of the desert, they were narrow-built and of prominent vertebrae. They were also skittish and half-wild, and Rudy's humiliation was complete when, in the iron darkness before the freezing desert dawn, he got chucked unceremoniously off the mildest old mare of the herd, the one Hoofprint of the Wind had chosen for him deliberately on account of her gentleness. He looked up from the dirt in bitter envy at Ingold, who was sitting a fire-snorting buckskin stallion like a patriarch of the Cossacks.

"Were you ever in the cavalry, by any chance?" he asked, as several of the Raiders went to catch the mare, their soundless laughter almost palpable in the leaden gloom.

"In a manner of speaking," the wizard replied cryptically. His breath smoked faintly in the starlight; he held the single rawhide rein in one mittened hand, the other hand resting relaxedly on his thigh.

Rudy remembered hearing somewhere—from Gil?—the rumor about Ingold's having been in his youth a slave in

164

the Alketch and he also remembered how the Alketch cavalry trained. Being chained to a practice post and having the local hotshots try saber charges at him wouldn't improve his riding much; but, if the story were true, it would sure as hell account for the old man's iron nerves. He muttered under his breath. "It figures."

The Raiders returned, solemn-faced with inward amusement, leading the mild and gentle mare.

They were riding north before dawn and continued throughout the day. The clouds that had broken the previous afternoon regathered, and the day grew colder instead of warmer as the small band of horsemen galloped north beneath a pale and heatless sky. At midday their breath was visible smoke, and the backs of the horses were steaming. Patchy snow covered the red sands and grew thicker as they proceeded north. Here and there Rudy saw tracks unfamiliar to his experience, and Ingold told him they were the sign of creatures native to the far north. But deeper and more frightening than the cold was the silence that covered the land. Nothing seemed to move or live in these wastes of sand and snow. At a casual look, even the winds that whirled like dust-devils across them appeared to be gone. When the riders stopped to rest or to change horses from the small cavvy of spares they had brought, Hoofprint of the Wind prowled restlessly on the edges of the group, talking softly with the dozen or so of his warriors who accompanied them or listening across the plains for some sound Rudy could not hear. The warriors who had come with them were silent, edgy as animals before summer lightning, keeping close together in the endless expanses of the snowy waste.

"There," the chieftain whispered, pointing to where the mottled red and white of the land seemed to slope upward to a far and hazy horizon. "There it lies."

Rudy shaded his eyes against the distance. He could make out a flat, dark gleam, like a sunken lake of oil. Though he wore a coat of buffalohide that the Raiders had given him, he felt suddenly cold.

"Do you have such places in your home in the north?" Ingold asked Hoofprint of the Wind as they turned the heads of their horses toward the dark gleam.

"Not in our own lands," the chieftain of the Twisted

Hills replied. "The Lava Hills People to the south of our runs, they had such a p.ace. The *tuar,* they call them, and others spoke of them, out in the Salt Plain to the east."

"*Tuar?*" the wizard said curiously. "Seeing?"

"At such places it is said that the shamans, the wise men of my own people, can stand and, having made proper respect to the ghosts of the Earth, can see far away. They say, too, among the Lava Hills People that once they hunted in this fashion, the wise man seeing and leading the people to the track of the antelope; but they hunt so no more."

"Why not?"

Zyagarnalhotep shook his head. "They do not say. Healing there was also, worked upon those spots."

Ingold fell silent, deep in thought, and thus they came to the entrance of the home of the Dark.

It was the first such place Rudy had seen, an entrance such as all must have been before humankind had used the deep-founded stones to bear the weight of early temples and forts. A vast plaza, hundreds of feet to the side, lay before them, like a football field floored in black and shining glass. In its center gaped a rectangle of shadow, like an open and screaming throat pointed at the sky. From it, worn stairs led down to the depths of the world. Rudy shivered, at once repelled and curiously attracted, a fear that was oddly like acrophobia coming over him. He felt an uneasy desire to cover that inky pit, to cover it and chain down the cover, and to mark it with the rune of Darb, the rune that would not let evil pass. But side by side with the repugnance was the fear that, if he got too near, he would descend those stairs and, against his conscious will, go freely to the Dark.

The riders drew rein where the snowy ground sloped downward to that glassy pavement. Ingold nudged his horse forward down the slope, and the hooves clicked loudly on the stone as he rode to the very brink of the pit. There he dismounted and took his staff from where it had been tied across the horse's withers; he had fetched it when they'd brought the burro Che into the camp last night. From the bank of snowy ground where he sat his horse among the Raiders, Rudy watched him, feeling a kind of eerie uneasiness as Ingold stood for a few moments on the lip of the stair, his head turned, listening as Zya-garnalhotep had listened to the wind. Then he descended a few steps and listened again, his hands in their incongruous blue mittens folded around the wood of the staff, the white sky vast above his head.

Hoofprint of the Wind called out, "What think you, Desert Walker?"

Ingold looked up and pushed his hood back from his face. "I hardly know what to think," he said. He came back toward them, like a ghost himself in the blowing wasteland of cold, and his horse followed him like a dog with its single rein trailing. "I feel that they are gone. In fact, I do not believe there is anything living down there, good or evil. Will you come down with me, Hoofprint of the Wind, to see this for yourself, or will you remain on guard up here while I go?"

The Raider looked uneasy, a feeling which Rudy heartily shared. He trusted Ingold implicitly and had never seen him err. If the wizard said there was nothing down there, he was probably right. On the other hand, Rudy knew that the Dark had magic of their own. There was just the outside chance that Ingold was wrong. And if Rudy was jumpy about it, somebody who knew the old man only by reputation could hardly be expected to follow him down to the very heart of the darkness, no matter how macho he was.

"If you are right, and there is nothing below," the chieftain said, "better would it be that we remain to guard the road at your back."

"Even so," Ingold agreed without irony, since this was, after all, his expedition to begin with. "Rudy?"

"Uh—" Rudy said. "Yeah. Sure." He slid down from his horse's back, astonished at how sore he was. Nine hours of fast, steady riding was no joke for a novice. He wondered if he'd be crippled for life. He disengaged the spear shaft he'd been using for a walking stick from behind his saddle blanket and limped down the bank to join the wizard on the pavement below.

Ingold turned back toward the stairway. Then he froze, like a wolf startled by some sound, raising his head as if at some far-off scent of smoke. The daylight reflected, flat and white, off his eyes as he scanned the sky.

167

"It can't be," he said softly to himself.

Rudy looked about nervously. "What can't be?"

"We're much too far south." Ingold swung around, scanning the horizon, his brows drawn down with worry and puzzlement. At the same time one of the horses on the bank threw up its head with a snort and began to prance fretfully.

"Too far south for what?"

Ingold turned back to the Raiders. "I'm not sure," he said to Hoofprint of the Wind, "and I may be mistaken—but I believe there's an ice storm coming."

It was the first time that Rudy had seen the implacable Raiders show any emotion at all. Fear sparked into the chieftain's amber eyes. "Can you be sure?" he asked and made a quick sign to the warriors behind him, a swift hand gesture that sent a ripple of whispers and motion through them like a stone dropped in still water. They, too, were afraid.

"No— Yes. Yes, I am sure." Ingold looked in one direction and then another, the lines of his face deepening with concern.

Not, Rudy suspected, *so much because we're all going to get turned into popsicles in the next sixty seconds, but because he doesn't understand why it should happen this far south, for Chrissake.*

"Don't!" the wizard called out as one of the Raiders wheeled her horse to flee. "You'll never outrun it."

"No," Hoofprint of the Wind agreed. "We are with you after all, Desert Walker." He urged his mount down the bank at a quick, slippery trot and across the stone pavement toward the stairway and the pit, the others streaming down behind him. Ingold strode after them, with Rudy limping in his wake.

"How soon?" Rudy whispered, glancing up at the pale, empty sky. He could feel nothing, sense nothing but the chill lour that had prickled his hair all day.

"Very soon." Ingold switched his staff from his right hand to his left as he came to the group of Raiders and horses, and Rudy grinned a little to himself. Like the old Western gunfighters, Ingold did a lot of things with his left hand.

Rudy had heard Gil speak of the stairways of the Dark,

but before now he had never understood the eeriness that surrounded them, the sense of alien and incomprehensible gulfs of time. Even deserted—if it was deserted—there was something about that black and terrible stair that tensed his backbone with a sense of watching and malicious cold. Light had never touched that blackness, any more than it had the darkness of the remoter fastnesses of the Keep of Dare. Those who could bear no light could come and go at will in that darkness, as silent and undetectable as the air on which they drifted. And the stairs looked so worn. The whole emptiness of the half-buried, dark pavement was foot-smooth and slick, unreflective of the hard, white sky. How many little bare feet had been drawn over that open space? he wondered. How many had followed that whispering call to their deaths in darkness? And over what terrible span of years?

And yet Rudy noticed that the Raiders would rather go down a supposedly empty Nest of the Dark than stay topside on the off chance that Ingold might be wrong about the storm.

Ingold's staff flickered into phantom brightness as he descended the stair ahead of them. Like phosphorous, it illuminated the narrow walls, the curve of the low roof, and the endless, twisting steps. Even as he crossed the threshold on the wizard's heels, Rudy could catch the smell from below, the sweetish reek of old decay that made the horses shy and the men look askance at one another. That smell clung around them like a vapor as they wound their way toward the center of the earth.

They turned a corner, and the wan daylight was lost behind them. The pallid gleam of the staff flashed glassily and green in the eyes of the horses, and the surrounding silence whispered with the fears of the men. Looking up at the black ceiling overhead, Rudy saw that it had been carved with long, chiseling strokes upward from below. The steps were straight but disturbingly irregular as to height and width, as they would be, to have been carved out by those who had no feet. Cool, damp air wafted upward to touch his face and bore on it a death reek, the stench of ancient corruption. He shuddered, taking what comfort he could in the living smells of men and horses around him and in the warmth of the crowding bodies

169

and the whispers and occasional soft nickerings that broke the deadly silence of underground. Once or twice he heard the scritching of rodent claws on the walls nearby and caught a glimpse of lean, wary scavenger rats slipping like furtive shadows into the fissures in the dark walls.

Whatever lay below, it was dead, dead and rotten, the stink of it laid by the cold. Yet it seemed that they descended for hours. The stairs curved and doubled back, and the only light was the faint foxfire glow that fell on the shoulders of the old man before him. Rudy's legs ached, then burned, while his mind and senses strained to catch some sound, some movement in the darkness below. But there was nothing—only the faint foetor of decay.

Just as Rudy felt that his legs couldn't stand anymore of this, Ingold said, "Stop!" He halted so abruptly that Rudy almost ran into him. With hardly a rustle of his fur clothing, Hoofprint of the Wind slipped forward from among his troops to join them. Rudy tried to take another step to see what lay in the darkness beyond, but Ingold put his arm across the passage to block him.

"What is it?"

Silently the wizard gestured with his staff out over the void.

There were no steps beyond the one on which they stood—only darkness, heightless, widthless, and bottomless. Without the glow of Ingold's staff to guide them, they would have simply walked off the edge unseeingly. In that stygian pit, Rudy could hear the slip and skitter of movement, the scavenger rats' thin pecking squeaks; he could smell the last sickening whiffs of old and distant putrefaction. Then Ingold held his staff out over the darkness, and the glare of it slowly increased until it burned with the diamond-hard, white light of a magnesium flare. It was the first light to penetrate that gloom since the forming of the world, and it did so slowly, touching the lines of floor and arch and pillar shyly, like a hesitant lover, unwillingly delimiting water and stone from night.

Rudy had meant to sound facetious, but awe conquered him, and his voice was barely a whisper. "Holy hellfires, Batman," he breathed, and Ingold raised a bristling eyebrow at him.

"These hellfires, as you say, are holy indeed," the wizard

170

replied quietly. "For you look upon what only I have seen and lived to speak of. This is the domain of the Dark Ones beneath the earth."

Twenty feet below them, the cavern floor began, sloping downward to roll away in miniature hills into darkness that the light of the staff could not fathom. The cave itself was hundreds of feet in height and perhaps twice that in breadth, and its opposite end was lost in impenetrable shadows. Dark, narrow entrances could be discerned among the pillars of limestone foresting the grotto, leading to yet other caverns. Vast stalactites hung like the pendant vaults of a flamboyant gothic ceiling, and these gleamed oddly in the steady white light, as if they had been polished smooth. The floor beneath was covered in a deep carpet of withered, brownish moss, broken in places by black sheets of water whose still surface threw back the light like polished onyx. So complete was the silence that lay upon the eon-haunted cavern that the vast, twisted vaults picked up the breathing of the tiny group of invaders, who huddled like beggars on the threshold of the abandoned realms of their foe.

"Look." Hoofprint of the Wind pointed. Something moved down there—scavenger rats slipping, beady-eyed, along the marges of a pool whose waters were like obsidian. Barely discernible among the brown, shriveled mosses of the cave floor, bones could be seen, gleaming palely in the white blaze of the witchlight. It was hard to tell because of the fluted pillars of the stalagmites, but there seemed to be a lot of them. "This is perhaps their graveyard, their place to leave the bones of those they take?"

"Nonsense," Ingold said, and raised his head to gaze off into the limitless distance of the cave. "There are far too few of them, for one thing. If this were the regular place to deposit the bones of their herds, in all the years the Dark have kept their wretched flocks in this cavern, the floor would be dozens of feet thick with them. And besides, you see there—" He pointed toward the ceiling, all eyes following the movement of the light. "See how pitted and shiny the stalactites are? The claws of the Dark rubbed them smooth. And see how deep that pathway is, up into that hole in the roof? It must have been one of their main thoroughfares. They would never live in the same place as corpses. No animal would."

"You mean they just lived up there?" Rudy whispered. "Like bats on the ceiling? I thought you said they were intelligent, that they had a civilization."

"And so they did," Ingold said. "Of a kind. But I believe it to be a civilization of the mind, a civilization with virtually no outward expression at all. It is one to which our minds cannot penetrate; and even if they could, we could not comprehend it, any more than a sheep or a pig could comprehend a love poem or money or the concept of honor."

Rudy nodded, his eyes traveling slowly over those dark and gleaming walls. "You got a point there. I could name you a couple of people who'd have a rough time with two out of three." Beside him, he heard Ingold chuckle.

While they were speaking, Rudy became aware of the cold. It flowed down the stairway behind him, deepening and intensifying until he found himself shivering in his heavy buffalo-fur coat. Even the weather-hardened Raiders huddled together for warmth; their breath steamed in the diamond brilliance of Ingold's light. From the twisting tunnel of the endless stair behind them, Rudy heard the moaning of far-off winds, a thin keening shriek whose wildness chilled his heart. He knew they'd been descending for a long time—God only knew how deep in the earth they were. Yet the intensity of the ice storm penetrated even there. He could see the ice condensing from the moisture of their breath to frost the polished walls.

His teeth chattered as he spoke. "So why are the bones there? Can we go see?" It crossed his mind that deeper in the caverns they might have a better chance against the unearthly cold.

Ingold pointed his staff downward at the drop. Rudy saw almost at once that it would be impossible to take the horses down the sheer fall. He wondered if the dooic, or whomever the Dark lured to their Nests, broke their ankles going over that edge.

The wizard glanced back over his shoulder at the chief of the Raiders. "Have you ropes?" he asked.

The panther eyes under the chieftain's long, curling brows darkened. "My friend, it is not a good thing," Hoofprint said quietly. "Down there are the dead. The whole cavern stinks of them. You can smell the wind that rises from the tunnels below. Better it is that you remain here with us to wait out the storm."

Ingold turned away restlessly, as if he would pace the narrow step. His feet touched the very edge of the chasm. "Why are they dead?" he asked. "How did they die?"

The chieftain sniffed, as at the question of a fool. "You stand in the caverns of the Eaters in the Night and ask how men came to die in this place? Stay among us, Walker in the Dark. To know that the Eaters slay men is no new thing."

Ingold only said, "Give me a rope."

They gave it to him.

"Rudy?"

Obediently, Rudy called light to the tip of the spear he used for a walking stick. With his fingers numb and aching in their worn gloves, he held it out over the void while Ingold dropped his own staff over the edge, then shinned down the rope with the businesslike deftness of a mountain climber. As he watched the wizard picking his way back along the cavern floor, Rudy noticed that the scavenger rats gave Ingold a wide berth. He wondered if this were a spell in itself, or if they were merely under the carefully engineered impression that the wizard was a saber-toothed tiger. From here, he was simply a little old man, the white glow of his staff like a dwindling star above his bowed head, the brown of his robes blending in with the dry, flaky moss that crumbled to dust beneath his light tread. Rudy watched that bobbing phosphorescence play in the shadows of the stalagmites for a time, while the wizard explored what lay beyond and among them. Then it vanished abruptly through a claw-smoothed doorway, seeking deeper darkness.

Behind him, Rudy heard Hoofprint of the Wind murmur, "Not for all the horses nor all the hunting eagles nor all the willing women of the earth would I seek thus the Eaters in the Night. Death there is in that tunnel. Cannot he smell it? This ghost that the Eaters themselves fear, this has swept these caverns end to end and slain the Eaters and their victims alike. Yet he will go to seek it, like a little priest on foot."

The cold grew deeper and more bitter, driving men and horses together to huddle like sheep in the protection of one another's warmth. Rudy wondered if Ingold would freeze down there by himself among the rats and darkness. Now and then, searing winds shrieked along the tunnel from above, moaning through the cavern and sighing in the carpet of frost-bitten moss. Rudy had little sense of time, but suspected it was something over an hour before the light glimmered once again in the caverns below and Ingold returned, shivering like a frozen beggar in a killing snow. He handed his staff up to Rudy, who took the glowing end gingerly and found the blazing wood perfectly cold and solid to his touch. Ingold climbed the rope hand over hand, the powdering of frost on his cloak glittering like diamond dust. The Raiders made room for him among them.

"Well, Thief of the White Bird's Horses?" Hoofprint murmured. "Found you, then, what you sought?"

"I never stole the White Bird's horses," Ingold responded automatically. Even through the freezing cold, Rudy could smell the taint of corruption on his ice-encrusted cloak. In the pallid witchlight, he looked white and drawn—like a man, Rudy thought, who had just got done vomiting up his socks.

"And no," the old man went on. "I found only the dead. They're mostly skeletons by this time, but you can see they're all of the same date of death, not a gradual accumulation. Rats, worms, bloated white toads as big as your head . . . But that's all. Down to the farthest depths of these caverns, I can sense the presence of no living creature—neither the Dark Ones nor anything that might have driven them forth."

Rudy hastily shoved away the images he had conjured from his too-vivid imagination. But something in the old man's scratchy, tired voice told him that Ingold would wander those caverns for many nights afterward in dreams. The sound of the furtive scampering in the deeps below turned him suddenly sick. "But why?" he whispered.

"Why?" Ingold glanced over at him. "If something did kill off the Dark—which I'm not altogether certain it did —it could have killed the herds as well. But if the Dark simply evacuated the Nest to go elsewhere, they could hardly take their herds with them, now, could they?"

"But could they not have defended this place against any ghost that came against them?" Hoofprint asked, and the frost crackled on his braided mustache.

"Perhaps," Ingold replied softly. "But we cannot even be sure that there was a ghost. I don't think so. I am not even certain that they left in fear."

The Raider's dark, animal face grew thoughtful. "If not in fear—then why?"

"Perhaps at a command?"

"And who would command the Dark?"

"A good question," the old man said. "And one whose answer I will seek in Quo. If the wizards there cannot help me, perhaps that question and what I have seen here can help them. All I ask of you, Hoofprint of the Wind, is the leave to walk through your lands."

The chieftain laughed softly. "As if the leave of any man could bid the Desert Walker to go or stay. As soon can a man bid the Dark. Nevertheless, you have my leave. And what will you do, wise man, you and your Little Insect, together with all the wise men of the world in one place upon the Western Ocean?"

"Find a way to drive forth the Dark indeed," the wizard replied quietly. "Or perish together in trying."

They emerged from beneath the earth to a world blasted and changed. As they struggled toward the livid remains of the daylight through the drifted snow that all but blocked the last twenty feet of the stairway, the cold seemed to grip Rudy's bones. Even after the bitter chill beneath the earth, it took his breath away with its brutal intensity. The small band of Raiders and horses came out to a surface landscape buried under hard, powdery snow so cold that it shrieked beneath the foot and to a sky black with clouds, where twisting columns of tornadoes wavered between dark air and frozen earth. Smaller winds chased each other aimlessly across the desolation, blowing snow now from one direction, now from another, in the confused remnants of the hurricane blast that had entombed the land.

"I thought you said the storm would be over," Rudy managed to say through uncontrollable shivering.

175

"It *is* over." Ingold swung himself lightly up onto his borrowed stallion. His breath crystallized to ice in his beard even as he spoke. "This is only its aftermath."

On the way south through the sick darkness of the late afternoon, they passed a small herd of bison, half-buried in the drifted snow. The animals stood head-down, crusted with frost, their flesh and blood frozen to rock as they grazed. *No wonder,* Rudy thought, *the Raiders will sacrifice one of their own people, if necessary, to propitiate whatever evil ghost it is that can do that.*

It was long after dark before they made camp. Even the freezing desert night was warmer than the daylight after the ice storm. The Raiders set up a tiny war camp with silent efficiency, and Ingold sat awake for a long time by the fire, talking with Hoofprint of the Wind. Rudy could see them through the narrow entrance of his shelter, the flickering touch of the gold light on the chieftain's long braided mustaches and on the scars on Ingold's hands.

After a time Ingold came into the shelter and crawled under the fur robes. The fire outside had almost died. Rudy whispered, "Ingold? What do you think?"

Ingold's voice murmured back out of the darkness. "About what?"

"About the ghost, for Chrissake."

One blue eye and part of a beard appeared from under the shaggy furs. The wizard raised himself up on one elbow. "I don't believe there is one. Or at least, not as the Raiders fear it. At the bottom of those caverns, I could sense no living thing."

"You think the Dark left on their own, then?"

"I think it's possible."

"Could they have been driven out by an ice storm like today's?"

Ingold was silent for a moment, considering. Finally he said, "I hardly think so. To the best of my knowledge, there has never been a previous storm this far south, and the Dark left their Nests in the plains, according to Hoofprint of the Wind, at the time of the first quarter moon of autumn, some seven weeks ago. The Dark are not weather-wise, Rudy. Even the most skilled wizard cannot predict when and where an ice storm will strike more than a few minutes before it happens."

176

In the outer darkness, a horse whinnied, a comforting sound. There was no other noise except for the endless groan of the wind. Even the wolves were still.

"Is that what they mean when they say something's as —as unstoppable as the ice in the north? Or as sure as the ice in the north?" Rudy asked.

"Not in reference to the storms, no," Ingold said. "In the north you'll find the great ice fields, where nothing can live and where there is nothing but an endless waste of ice. In places the ice is growing as much as an inch a year. In some places, more."

"Have you been there?"

"Oh, yes. That was long ago. Lohiro and I had—I suppose you could call it an errand in the ice, and both of us very nearly froze to death. At that time, the rim of the ice lay along the crest of a fair-sized range of hills that the old maps call the Barrier. The last time I was there, the hills were almost completely buried."

"Ingold," Rudy said softly, "what's the connection? Seven weeks ago was the first quarter moon of autumn. Gae fell. Lohiro and all the wizards in the world cut off contact with everyone and anyone. The Dark disappeared from the Nests in the plains after murdering their herds. What the hell is going on, Ingold? What's happening?"

The old man sighed. "I don't know, Rudy. I don't know. Is this one more catastrophe in a tale of random catastrophes, or is it all part of a single riddle, with a single key? We have shared this planet with the Dark for all the years of humankind's existence, yet we know nothing about them except that they are our enemies. If there is a key, is it at Quo? Or does the key lie with the Dark themselves, beyond human understanding at all? Or is it in the last place we would look for it, back at the Keep of Dare?"

CHAPTER ELEVEN

The messenger from the Emperor of Alketch came riding up the valley on a rare sunny afternoon, after a week of snows. Most of the Keep was out of doors, working on repairing the mazes of corrals or building new fences for the food compounds, chopping wood or hauling rocks for the projected forge. The cohorts of warriors at exercise under various of the company captains ran, jumped, and swung weighted weapons with sweaty good will. Children of all ages scattered through the Vale, sledding, skating, or sit-down tobogganing on the frozen stream, their shrieks of delight like the piping of summer birds.

Gil had picked that afternoon to experiment with one of the little white polyhedrons that she and Alde had found in such numbers throughout the old storerooms and shafts of the Keep. These had remained a puzzle to them, turning up with ubiquitous regularity, businesslike and yet to all intents and purposes useless. Like the Keep, they were smooth and shining enigmas.

At first she had theorized to Alde that they might be toys.

"They'd break if they were dropped, surely," Alde objected. The girls were walking along the new-dug path back to the clearing in the woods where the Guards had spent the morning in practice. Gil had recently returned to regular training and was black-and-blue.

"Votives?" she suggested.

"For what?" Alde asked reasonably. "Votives are gifts of light, candles, scent, incense, or of wealth given to the Church, in which case you present little bronze or lead models of what you've given."

"Maybe they *were* toys," Gil remarked. "They do stack together." And they did, fitting facet against facet, like a cellular structure or a three-dimensional honeycomb. "Do they really break?"

But, from an oblique sense of uneasiness at what she did not understand, or merely from an overdose of science fiction films in her own universe, Gil had elected to wait for clear weather to perform the experiment outdoors. She and Alde found Seya and Melantrys at the clearing, sparring with wooden training swords, and warned the two Guards of their intentions. There was a flat rock in the center of the clearing, and Gil set one of the white glass polyhedrons on this, threw a piece of sacking over it, and hit it with a hammer. The result was unspectacular. The polyhedron shattered into six or seven pieces, releasing neither poisonous gas nor embryonic alien beings. Gil felt embarrassed over her own apprehensions, but she noticed that Alde, Seya, and Melantrys had all stayed a respectful distance away.

The pieces appeared to be nothing more than glass of some kind, heavy and slick, like white obsidian. They were vaguely translucent when held to the wan sunlight, but otherwise unremarkable.

"You have me beat," Melantrys remarked, taking one of them between her small, scarred fingers. "It's nothing I've even heard of."

"I know," Gil said. "The records make no mention of them. But we're finding them all over the Keep."

"Maybe you're right about their being toys," Seya said. "Tir certainly likes to play with them."

And indeed Tir, who was bundled up in black quilting and furs, so that he looked less like a baby than like a stubby-limbed cabbage, was solemnly rolling another one of the milky prisms back and forth across the side of the rock. Alde sat next to him, sending the thing back at him every time he pushed it toward her. She glanced up at Seya's words. "But the Keep was built by people fleeing a holocaust," she argued suddenly. "Would they have brought toys?"

"We can't know that these things are as old as the Keep," Seya pointed out.

"No," Gil said. "But on the other hand, we've found nothing to show how they were made."

Alde turned back just in time to keep her son from

179

crawling over the edge of the rock and tumbling into the snow beneath. Tir was growing into a quiet, compact infant whose calm demeanor and lack of fussing disguised an appalling capacity for mischief. He could crawl unnoticed for long distances, making his silent and efficient way toward any danger, gravely consuming whatever mouth-sized morsels fate placed in his path and his mother wasn't quick enough to get away from him. Sometimes he seemed preoccupied with the white polyhedrons, stacking and unstacking the dozen or so Alde kept in her room, examining them for hours in fascination. Gil wondered if this was simply a baby's marveling at the world or if he remembered something about them from some long-forgotten ancestor in the Keep.

"If the people who built the Keep came here in as bad a shape as we did," Melantrys commented, pulling the rawhide thong loose from her hair and shaking down the thick barley-colored waves over her shoulders, "it would stand to reason that the things were pretty important. Maia says that when his people came up the Pass, they found thousands of crowns' worth of jewelry that people had chucked away in the snow."

Voices came faintly to them through the trees. Looking up, Gil saw Alwir pass, his fine hands gesturing to the melody of his speaking voice. At his side, Maia of Thran was nodding, a seven-foot longbow held unstrung in his hand. The Chancellor glanced up through the thin screen of bare birches and saw the three Guards in their black, shabby uniforms and the young Queen with her son. He passed them by without a word. Gil heard the swift, ragged draw of Alde's breath; turning, she saw the quick misery that had crossed the girl's face.

A voice called out, young and shrill, and Tad the herd-kid came running up the path toward the Chancellor with a string of the Keep orphans at his heels. Alwir looked down his nose at the boy until he heard what Tad had to say; then Gil saw him bend forward, suddenly attentive. She didn't hear what Tad had said, but she saw the look that flashed between the Bishop and the Lord of the Keep. Then Tad and his little band were running toward the clearing, Tad calling out, "My lady! My lady!"

Alde got quickly to her feet. "What is it, Tad?"

The children roiled to a stop, red-faced and snow-flecked, in the steaming cloud of their breath. "It's the messenger from Alketch, my lady," the boy gasped. "Lyddie here saw him coming up the road from the valley."

What seemed like the whole of the Keep had assembled on the steps to watch the coming of the messenger from Alketch. But whether they were ones who had come from Gae or from Penambra, they were silent, a sea of watching faces. From her position among the ranks of the Guards, Gil could see that the messenger rode alone. The Icefalcon had not returned with him.

For a time, grief clouded her vision, and she saw nothing. The Icefalcon had been her friend, the first of her friends among the Guards. Cool, aloof, and self-contained, he had only once paid her a dubious compliment—if she wanted to take being told she was a born killer as a compliment; in the course of training with her as a Guard, he had given her welts and bruises enough to qualify in most circles as a deadly enemy. But they had both been foreigners among the people of the Wath, and that had been a bond. And they had both stood behind Ingold, the night the Dark had come to the Keep.

For that, Alwir had sent him south. And he had not returned.

The messenger was dismounting. The murmuring among the vast, dark crowd around the doors of the Keep was like the lapping of the distant sea. He was a youngish man, black-skinned, with haughty, aquiline features and great masses of curly raven hair. Under a patched scarlet traveling cloak, he wore a knee-length tunic stamped with gold, its pattern picked up again on his close-fitting, high-heeled, crimson boots. A small horn recurved bow hung at his back; on the saddlebow rested a spiked helmet of gilded steel, and a slim, two-handed killing sword was scabbarded below. In his dark face, his eyes shone a bright, pale gray.

He made a profound salaam. "My lord Alwir."

Standing above him on the lowest step, Alwir gestured him to rise.

"I am called Stiarth na-Salligos, nephew and messenger of his Imperial Majesty, Lirkwis Fardah Ezrikos, Lord of

181

Alketch and Prince of the Seven Isles." He straightened up, diamond studs glittering in his earlobes.

"In the name of the Realm of Darwath, I greet you," Alwir said in his deep, melodious voice. "And through you, your master, the Emperor of the South. I bid you both welcome in the Keep of Dare."

Gil heard the murmuring behind her rise at that, and a man's angry voice grumbled, "Yeah? And all his bloody damn troops as well?"

"Ration our bread to feed the damn southerners," someone else growled, the sound of it almost lost among the general whispering, and a third voice replied, "Murdering fags."

With this in her ears, Gil watched Minalde come down the steps to greet Stiarth na-Salligos, her head high and her face very pale. The graceful young man bent over her hand and murmured formal courtesies. She asked him something; Gil heard only his reply.

"Your messenger?" Those elegant brows deepened in an expression of concerned regret. "Alas. Our road here was fraught with perils. He was struck down by bandits in the delta country below Penambra. The land is rife with them, hiding by night to haunt the roads by day, stealing and killing whatever they find. Barely did I escape with my life. Your messenger was a brave man, my lady. A worthy representative of the Realm."

He bowed again, deeper this time. And as he did so, he swept his scarlet cloak back like a mating bird, its scalloped edges like blood against the snow. Gil had a brief glimpse of the token that hung on his gilded belt—small, oak, shaped to a man's hand. Hot rage swept her, more blinding than her former grief. She stood motionless as Alwir offered Minalde his arm, the massed troops and the populace of the Keep parting before them, and led her upward to the dark gates, Stiarth of Alketch trailing elegantly at their heels.

What the messenger wore at his belt was the token of the Rune of the Veil that Ingold had given to the Icefalcon for his protection before the man rode away.

"He murdered him." The tapping of Gil's boot heels sounded very loud in the arched roof of the great west

182

stairway. "The Icefalcon would never have given up that token."

"Not even to someone who was empowered to negotiate for the troops we'll need?" Minalde asked quietly. She and Gil reached the landing, where an old man from Gae seemed to have homesteaded with two unofficial wives and large numbers of caged chickens. "Not even in the case of an emergency? If it was a choice between one or the other of them? He'd fulfilled his own mission in summoning the messenger."

"The Icefalcon?" Gil sidestepped two chicken crates and a cat and continued down the steps. From the corridor below, dim yellow light shone up, marking the back door of the Guards' barracks; with it came a whiff of cooking odors and steam. "Believe me, there was no one he valued as much as he did himself. Least of all some—some scented Imperial Nephew whom he could have broken in half on his knee." They turned right at the foot of the steps, went down a short stretch of corridor whose walls looked to be of the original design, and then passed through a makeshift side door and into a jumble of rough-partitioned cells to the right again. "He never went in for that kind of altruism, Alde. The only way Stiarth could have gotten that amulet of Ingold's was by force, in which case he'd have had to kill him, probably by trickery. Stealing it from the Icefalcon would have been tantamount to murder; that was his first line of defense against the Dark."

Gil spoke quietly, but her anger was still hot in her breast. Maybe it was the memory of the messenger's creamy smirk, or the fact that the negotiations were first and last with Alwir, with Alde being used merely as his rubber stamp. Maybe it was only the memory of waking up in the rain-dripping dimness of that stable back at Karst, when the Icefalcon had come to check in his cool, impersonal fashion whether she was well. But something of it must have carried into her voice, for Alde touched her sleeve, bidding her to halt.

"Gil," she said, "whether the Icefalcon would have given it to him of his own free will or not—let it be."

"What?" Gil's voice had an edge, sounding sharp in the gloomy half-darkness of these deserted corridors.

"I mean—Gil, you're the only one here who knew about

183

that token. But you're not the only one who thinks that—that Stiarth na-Salligos might have had something to do with the Icefalcon's not coming back. And, Gil, please . . ." Her low voice was suddenly urgent, almost frightened, her eyes plum-colored in the grubby and flickering light. ". . . Alwir says we can't afford to let negotiations fall through. Not for that."

Gil bit back a cruel reply. She stood for a moment, struggling with her sullen rage, knowing that Alde was, in a sense, right. *What's done is done. The murder by treachery of one of the few friends I had is done. Past.*

"Maybe," she said slowly. "But if that kind of treachery is common coin, do we really want negotiations to continue?"

Alde turned her face away. "We don't know that."

"Like hell we don't! Alde, you've been reading those old histories and records as much as I have. Compared with some of the crap they've pulled on settling the Gettlesand border question, murdering the Icefalcon would be Scout's Honor."

Alde looked back at Gil, her face imploring. "We don't know that he murdered the Icefalcon."

"Don't we?" Gil asked. "He sure as hell lied about it. If bandits had killed him, they would have looted the body, and Stiarth never would have gotten that amulet."

Minalde was silent.

"All right," Gil said softly. "I won't talk it up with the other Guards, though Melantrys is as convinced as I am about it. And I won't take any kind of revenge that would wreck negotiations. But I can't answer for anyone else."

Silence and shadow lay between them for a moment, broken only by the distant random talk in corridors closer to the Aisle than this one. The great gates would soon be shut for the night; the Church had tolled its bells throughout the Keep, and no few participants had made their way to the nightly services in the great cell beneath the Royal Sector where the Bishop Govannin centered her scarlet domain. Among them, Gil knew, would be Stiarth of Alketch, like all the dark southerners, a fanatic son of the Church. Someone—Bok the carpenter, she thought—had told her the Imperial Nephew had supped with the old prelate and had been closeted with her for some hours before the Council meeting with Alwir, Minalde, and the other notables of the Keep. Now Alde looked strained and worn in the dim light of her clay lamp, her loosely bound hair kinked and wrinkled from her formal coronet. She was a royal princess and the source of her brother's power, Gil thought, looking at that white, withdrawn face. And she was as much a pawn as any one of the Guards.

"Thank you," Alde said quietly.

Gil shrugged. "I hope it's worth it."

"To establish a bridgehead for humankind at Gae?" Alde blinked up at her, startled. "Once the Nest there is burned out . . ."

"But will it be? With Govannin and the troops of the Alketch trying to get rid of the wizards, and the Archmage, whenever he shows up, and Ingold, and with all the other leaders fighting Alwir for power? With the old-timers in the Keep resenting Maia's Penambrans and the common people accusing the merchants of stealing grain? Alde, you have a gunnysack full of cats here, not a team of mules that's going to pull together."

"I know," the Queen said softly. "And that's why I thank you for not—not making the situation worse."

Gil paused in her steps, looking curiously over at the sweet, sensitive face on the other side of the lampflame, seeing a girl who in Gil's world would be barely out of high school, yet with all the experience of ruin, horror, and death, of judgment and the soiled meshes of political expediency, behind those tired dark-blue eyes. Gil's grievance against the Imperial Nephew seemed suddenly very personal and rather petty. "Better thee than me, honey." She sighed. "But you know I'll back you all the way."

"Thank you," Alde said again. Their footsteps chimed together as they turned down the black hallways toward the barracks. In the dark weeks of winter, the friendship between them had grown, a friendship born of loneliness and mutual respect. Alde stood a little in awe of Gil's learning and her quick, cold intelligence; Gil envied Alde's patience and compassion, knowing them as qualities which she herself lacked. The two women recognized each other's courage, and Gil, from her own disastrous family life, understood Alde's misery and confusion at her increasing isolation from her brother in the welter of Keep politics. But if

185

Alde understood the trouble that Gil had found growing in her own heart these dark, snowbound days, she never spoke of it.

After a time Alde asked, "Were you going back to your research tonight?"

Gil shrugged. "I don't think so. I've decoded most of that last chronicle, and there isn't a whole lot in it. It's late —I think Drago the Third was the last King to rule from Renweth, and that was centuries after the Time of the Dark. When he disappeared, they moved the capital back up to Gae, where the big citadel of wizards was in those days."

"He disappeared?" Alde asked, startled.

"Well—he took off with somebody named Pnak for some place called Maijan Gian Ko, and there was this huge fuss about it, and he never came back. Where's Maijan Gian Ko, I wonder?"

"That was the old name for Quo," Minalde said. "The greatest fortunate place or Great Magic place—the center-point of magic on earth. If Drago took off for Quo, no wonder everyone was upset. Was Drago a wizard, then?"

Gil shrugged. "Beats me. But his son was the one who started the campaign against the mages of Gae, which eventually got them kicked out of the city. Why do you ask?"

"Well," Alde said, "I've often thought about how we found the observation room—just by closing my eyes and walking. Sometimes at night I'll lie in bed and do that, just remember walking down halls, seeing things around me. Most of the time it's nothing. But once or twice I've had the feeling that there ought to be more levels in the Keep. Do you think there might be levels beneath this one, dug out in the rock of the knoll itself?"

"It makes sense," Gil agreed. "Even if the power source for the pumps was magic, they had to put the machinery for it *somewhere*, and we haven't found it yet. But as to how we'd find the entrances—you've got me there."

They stepped through the wide, dark archway into the Aisle, where the gates were being shut for the night. The warriors of the day and evening watches were grouped around them, the soft run of their talk carrying over the general noise of that great central cavern. Melantrys was making her dispositions for the night, sharp, small, and arrogant next to Janus and the head of Alwir's troops. In the shadows of the gates, the white quatrefoils of the Guards shone like a ghostly meadow of asphodel on the faded black of their massed shoulders; black stars strewed the scarlet heavens of the uniforms of the House of Bes like an LSD vision of the Milky Way; the ranks of the Church wore deeper crimson, somber and unrelieved.

Alde frowned in thought. "The best way to explore this, I think, is for you to get the tablets on which you're making the Keep map and for us to go back to the observation room. We can start from there and go . . ."

"Wherever," Gil finished. They headed for the barracks door, almost tripping over a woman who loitered in its shadow. She hurried away from them as soon as they came near, a tall, red-haired woman whom Gil found vaguely familiar, clutching a threadbare brown cloak around her broad shoulders. A few moments later, when they emerged from the barracks with Gil's maps, they saw her again, hanging around the fringes of the group by the gate. She looked about anxiously, rubbing her reddened knuckles and twisting at her cloak; but when Seya went over to speak to her, she fled again.

Starting from the corridor outside the observation room, Gil and Alde worked their way steadily back through the Keep, comparing the composition and design of walls, floors, and doorways, stopping repeatedly for Gil to scratch additions to her maps on the wax tablets she carried and for Alde to think. Her memories were not always reliable, but weeks of research and mapping had fleshed them out. By this time, there was probably no one who knew more about the Keep than the two of them.

When they could, they stuck to the places where the original structure of the Keep remained. They descended by one of the original stairways to the first level and followed the line of the original corridors. "We seem to be heading back toward the barracks," Gil remarked as they turned down a narrow access corridor to find themselves in a long, deserted chamber that appeared to be the center of its own minor maze. "In fact, I think we're almost directly behind them, in the southwest corner of the Keep."

"The observation room was in the southeast corner,"

Alde said. "That's where the main pump shaft seemed to connect."

"'I wonder . . ." Gil stepped through an obliquely set doorway and looked around her. Alde raised the lamp as high as she could for what better light they could gain. "Well, we're close, anyway. This was part of the original design, and I *think* that wall there is the inside of the front wall of the Keep. You can see there's no trace of blocks of any kind. If we've come three rows in . . ." Gil turned and pointed with her silver hairpin. "Through there."

"Through there" proved to be not a cell or a closet, as she had supposed it would be, but a tiny passageway that ultimately ended in a square corner room, so jammed with junk as almost to hide in shadow the wooden trapdoor in the floor. With a cry of delight and without the smallest consideration for what Frankensteinian horrors might lurk in the shadows below, Gil pulled on its rusted metal ring and was greeted by a black well of shadows, a great smell of dust, and a soft, billowing cloud of warm air.

"It's like a different world." The great dark space took Minalde's soft voice and echoed it back to her like the sighing murmur of a million past voices. "What kind of a place was this?"

Darkness yielded unwillingly to the feeble glow of the lamp. Shapes materialized: tables, benches, the gleam of metal, scattered polyhedrons, white or frosty gray, and the twinkle of faceted crystal. Gill stepped forward and was greeted by the leap and sparkle of the lampflame repeating itself in countless tiny mirrors. Fragments of gilding slipped over the close-curled edges of a scroll and flickered in glass vessels half-filled with ashy powders or pale dust. The black floor rose in the center to form an altarlike platform, its hollowed top lined with charred steel.

Gil turned around, her wheeling shadow turning with her. "At a guess," she said, "this isn't so much a different world as one that's more the same. I think it's still as it was when it was built, the work of the last generation born in the Times Before." She ran her hand along the smooth, obsidian-hard edge of the workbench. "This is one of the old labs."

"Like Bektis' workshop?" Minalde asked, coming timidly into the center of the room.

"More or less." Gil brought the lamp closer to the workbench, touching, first with light and then with hesitant fingers, the frosted glass of the polyhedrons that lay there in such disarray.

"But what is all this?" Alde lifted a short apparatus that looked like a barbell made of glass bubbles and gold. "What's it for?"

"Beats me." Gil set a smooth, meaningless sculpture of wood up endwise; the lamplight slid like water from its sinuous curves. She rolled a sort of big glass egg haltingly into the light and saw it crusted inside with whitish crystals that looked like salt. "It's one hell of a thing to find the laboratories of the old wizards at a time when all the wizards on earth are on the other side of the continent."

Alde laughed shakily in agreement. Her eyes in the shadows were wide and wondering, as if she remembered what she saw from another personality, another life.

"And it's warm down here," Gil pursued thoughtfully. "I think this is the first time since I crossed the Void that I have been warm." She pushed gently at the steel doors at the far end of the room, and they slid back on their soundless hinges, poised like the gates of the Keep itself. In the room beyond, she heard the faint echo of machinery pumping; the light of the lamp she bore touched row after row of sunken tanks, the black stone of their sides marked with vanished water and a climbing forest of steel lattices. Gil frowned, walking the narrow paths between them. "Could it be—hydroponics?"

"What?" Alde knelt to trace the water stain with a curious finger.

"Water-gardening. Alde, what in hell did they use for light down here? Light enough to get plants to grow?" She pushed open another door, and vistas of empty tanks mocked her from the shadows. She turned back. "You could feed the whole damn Keep down here if you had a light source."

"Are we going to tell Alwir?" Gil asked much later as they ascended the straight, narrow little stairway back to the hidden storeroom. Alde carried the lamp now, walking ahead. Gil's hands were full of bits and pieces of meaning-less tools, half a dozen jewels of varying sizes she'd found in a lead box, and two or three of the new polyhedrons, frosted gray instead of milky, but just as uncommunicative. She shivered as they came up from below and the colder air of ground level nipped at her rawboned hands.

"N-no," Alde said. "Not yet."

They dumped their finds on the dusty trestle table that ran down the center of the large, deserted room and set the lamp down among them in its pool of dim and wavery light. Through the door and down the corridor they could see the blurred echo of other firelight and hear a baby cry, with a man's deep, smooth, bass voice rising in the snatch of a lullaby. The smell of food cooking came to them there, together with the odor of dirty clothes. All the sounds and smells of the Keep were there, telling of life safe from the Dark. Here in this small complex of cells was only shadow, and dust, and time.

"Gil," Alde said slowly, "I—I don't think I trust Alwir." The confession of disloyalty seemed to stick in her throat. "He—he uses things. This—" She rested her hand on a frosty crystal before her, joined spheres of glass and a meaningless tangle of interwinding tubes. "This is part of something that could be very important when the mages come back. But Alwir might destroy it or lock it up if he thought he could get some kind of concession from Stiarth by doing so. He's like that, Gil. Everything is like cards in his hands."

Her voice trembled suddenly with misery. Embarrassed, Gil spoke more gruffly than she'd meant to. "Hell, you're not the only person in the Keep who doesn't think he's God's gift to the Realm."

"No," Alde agreed, her lips quirking in an involuntary smile that was instantly gone. "But I should. He's been very good to me."

"He ought to be," Gil commented. "You're the source of his power. He has no legal power of his own."

Alde shook her head. "Only the real power," she as-sented. "Sometimes I think even his friendship with—with Eldor was part of his games. But Eldor was strong enough himself to keep him down, strong enough to make Alwir work for him, like a strong man riding a half-wild horse."

She sighed and rubbed at her eyes with one long, white hand. "Maybe Eldor knew it," she went on tiredly. "Maybe that's why he always kept so distant from me. I don't know, Gil. I look back and I see things that happened then and I start to doubt everything. Sometimes I think Rudy's the only person who ever loved me for who I am and not for what I could be used for."

Gil reached out and rested a comforting hand on the slender shoulder. "That's what happens when you mess with power," she said softly. "We are what we are, God help us."

Alde laughed suddenly, tears still filming her eyes. "So why must I have all the disadvantages of power and none of its rewards?" She picked up the lamp, her expression wryly philosophic. "But you see," she said as she led the way back toward the corridor, "why I don't think Alwir should know of all this just yet."

They stepped into the Aisle again, into a confusion of lights and voices. There was a little group ahead in the shadows of the gates. Even from here, they could hear a woman crying. A quick glance passed between them, and they hurried up the steps.

By this time of night, not many civilians were in the Aisle. It was, Gil guessed, a few hours before the deep-night watch came on. Her own watch began at eight the following morning, but training was at six; she was uncomfortably reminded that she ought to get to sleep.

It was the red-haired woman she had seen earlier who was crying, huddled against the wall with a small group of Guards around her, the torchlight like fire over the thick, tangled rope of her hair.

Janus was saying, "Dammit, are we going to have to post a watch to keep the people inside at night? You'd think the Dark would do that."

"It's the food," Gnift said simply, and those elf-bright eyes flickered toward the closed gates. "Things are thin now. With the troops coming up from Alketch—"

"Surely the Emperor can't expect us to feed his armies!" one of Alwir's lesser captains protested.

Melantrys gave him a snort of derision. "Hide and watch him."

"What is it?" Alde asked. "What's happening?"

The woman raised a face smeared with tears in the yellow torchlight. "Oh, my lady," she whispered. "Oh, God help me, I never thought he'd do it. He said he would, but I didn't believe."

"Her husband," Janus explained briefly. "Man named Snelgrin. He hid himself outside the Keep when the gates shut to steal food and cache it in the woods."

"I never thought he would," the woman moaned. "I never thought . . ."

"Obviously he never thought, either," Melantrys retorted softly. Gil remembered the couple now—Lolli was the woman's name. They were the first instance of an old-time Keep dweller marrying a Penambran newcomer. Maia had performed the ceremony less than three weeks ago.

Lolli was speaking again, her voice low and muffled, an animal moaning. Alde knelt beside her and took her gently by the shoulders for comfort, but she scarcely seemed to notice. "He didn't mean any harm," she groaned. "I tried to tell him, but he only said there was a full moon and a clear sky and no harm would come of it. I prayed and prayed he'd change his mind . . ."

Gil turned silently on her heel and left them there. There was nothing she or anyone else could do, and privately, she agreed with Melantrys. The man's stupidity was his own business and he had evidently not given much weight to the possible sufferings of his wife.

On the other hand, she thought as she lay awake in the narrow darkness of her bunk, people did all kinds of things when impelled by fear or love. She found it impossible to dismiss them, as she once would have done, simply as silly people engaged in incomprehensible stupidities. The love and suffering and fear there were too real and too close to what was in her own unwilling heart.

In time she heard Janus and Gnift come in and return silently to their bunks. Somewhere in the Keep, she thought she could hear the woman Lolli wailing still, though it might have been her imagination or some other sound entirely. She wondered what they'd find of Snelgrin when the gates were opened in the morning.

She thought of the Icefalcon, cool, aloof, and very young, riding away down the river valleys, then of Ingold and Rudy, setting off like the hapless King Drago III on a journey to the greatest magic place, never to return.

Maijan Gian Ko.

Sleepily, her scholarly mind picked at the etymology of the words.

Gian Ko.

Gaenguo.

Her eyes opened in the darkness. What had Bektis said? ". . . in Penambra and in Gae itself, on the very spot where the Palace now stands?"

She felt the blood turn to water in her veins.

But it doesn't make sense, she thought. The terrible silence of the Vale of the Dark returned to her, the heaviness of the vaporous air and the louring sense of being watched. She remembered the hideous geometry of the place, visible only in the angled light of sunset from the tangled rocks of the cliffs above, the sense of breathless confusion there, and the disruption, rather than the magnification, of Ingold's spells.

But was the effect always negative with regard to magic? At one time, could it have been positive? Is that why wizards built their citadels and people their cities near those . . . fortunate places?

And in that case, she thought, *is that why the places were fortunate—the effects positive—to begin with?*

Gil did not sleep that night.

Gil had never had much of an opinion of humankind, and it went down several more notches when the gates were opened at dawn. Word had evidently circulated through the Keep, for over a hundred civilians had shown up, idling in the Aisle since before seven in the morning for no better purpose than to be present to see what was left of the hapless Snelgrin. Gil was on day watch, logy from a sleepless night and bruised and exhausted from morning training; she felt she could have turned in her tracks and cursed them all.

As she had hoped, Alde was there, half-supporting the taller and heavier Lolli. It was clear that neither had slept. Lolli's face was blotched red and swollen from weeping; Alde's was very tight and calm. It was only her manner that kept the people there from pushing and staring. Rather to

Gil's surprise, Alwir had shown up, too, and Govannin, keeping to the background but making their presence felt.

Quite an audience, Gil thought sourly, surveying them as Janus and Caldern worked the heavy locking wheels of the inner gates, then walked down the dark tunnel to open the outer. *I hope they find something worth their while.*

But in the end they were doomed to disappointment, of a sort. The Dark had had other fish to fry last night. Snelgrin was found, alive but stunned, on the steps of the Keep, half-frozen from lying in the snow. The Dark had been known to devour the minds of their victims while leaving the bodies living, but Gil had seen those pitiful remains; they stood still, like cataleptics, or moved if jostled by the wind. Snelgrin managed to get to his feet, his movements odd and jerky, and stumbled up the steps without assistance. His wife was screaming and sobbing with joy. In a way it was touching, Gil thought, shivering in the icy cold of the sunrise. But it must be poor exchange for a pile of ice-crusted bones to some of the spectators.

After the smells of grease and smoke and human frowziness, the ice-water clarity of the morning was a welcome relief. Mauve clouds piled the lower slopes of the peaks above. Beyond them, the sky was a pale bluish green, the light cool and holy on the tracked brown slush and ice-crusted mud. Gil stood on the steps, her cloak wrapped tightly about her, thinking of the three men on whom she had closed the gates—of the Icefalcon, when the slender protection of the Rune of the Veil had been stolen from him, of Ingold, journeying slap into the biggest Nest of the Dark in the West of the World, hoping to find the Archmage there, and of Rudy—

"Gil?"

Alde was standing at her elbow. Gil breathed a sigh of relief. "You're just the lady I want to see." As they walked together out of Gil's watchpost among the sprawling food compounds, Gil hastily outlined last night's conclusions with regard to the meaning of the words "fortunate place."

"So the guys are walking straight into that," she finished, her breath drifting in a white veil against the darkness of the inky trees beyond. "Bektis will be awake by this time, won't he? Can you ask him if he can get in touch with them? Ingold talked about getting in contact with Lohiro at

Quo, so there's got to be a way to do it. I mean, to talk back and forth by crystal. Get him to contact them and tell them not to go any farther until I can talk to them." She glanced up at the pale brightness of the sky. It was late October, she calculated, but the days were already shortening to the time of the Winter Feast. "I'll be off duty around sunset."

"All right." Alde wrapped her sable cloak more tightly around her and hurried off down the slushy path for the Keep once more, the thick fur rippling in the light. But in less than an hour she was back, stumbling over the slippery mess of the icy trail, holding her thin peasant skirts clear of the mud.

Gil, huddled like an undernourished blackbird at one corner of the compound, left off trying to warm her hands and strode toward the girl. "What did he say?"

"I'm sorry, Gil," Alde panted. A flurry of the Keep children ran past them, throwing snowballs and shrieking, on their way to pick up kindling in the woods. A drift of smoke came to them from the wash-pots or the smokehouses, and with it the thunk of an arrow in a practice tree. "I'm sorry. Bektis says they're there already."

"What?"

"He says they've reached the walls of air. His spells can't find them within the mazes."

Gil cursed, comprehensively and imaginatively. "How long have they been there? Or does that tea leaf reader know?"

"No—Bektis isn't very careful about things like that. But they've been gone only a little over four weeks, so I'd imagine they've only just reached the Seaward Mountains."

"Son of a—I've been stupid," Gil said. "Blind and stupid. I should have figured out the etymology before this." She picked up a chunk of snow from the ground and hurled it with vicious strength against the mud-slab side of the nearest shelter.

"So if they've reached the walls of air," she went on more quietly, "then by the time they come out, they'll already know anything we have to tell them."

CHAPTER TWELVE

"Do you see it?"

"See what?"

Ingold did not reply. He only tucked his mittened hands into his sleeves and watched Rudy with a close, speculative expression, as he watched the younger man when he practiced spells of illusion or made the waters of a creek rise or fall. A breeze shook the leaves of the yellowed aspens over their heads, spattering them and the sodden path underfoot with leftover rain.

"You mean the road?" Rudy asked, looking back.

The turning he'd seen—or thought he'd seen—was gone. Only the main road was visible, its hexagonal blocks unevenly worn and faintly silver under their carpet of tawny decay, winding away in silence through the wet cathedral stillness of the woods.

Rudy looked inquiringly at Ingold but saw that he wasn't going to get any help there. He turned again to the vine-tangled banks above the road, wondering why he was so certain a road ought to be there. He sensed for the first time that feeling of rightness about something that did not exist, or wrongness about something that supposedly did. But there was nothing to see. Only a damp, blackish clay bank, grown over with wild grape and soggy, brown fern, crowned with a thin screen of ghostly, black-flecked birches. Somewhere in the distance, a swollen river groaned and stormed through the trees that had once fringed its banks. The air was filled with its muted clamor and the scent of leaf-mast and water.

Cautiously, Rudy scuffed through the squishing yellow carpet of leaves toward the bank. A drainage ditch separated the road from the steepness of the overgrown cutting, brimming with water from the bright, unseasonable rains.

Impelled by he knew not what force—or maybe simply by the maddening itch of a wizard's curiosity—Rudy started to wade into the ditch.

His foot touched stone.

He wondered how he could not have seen the little bridge that spanned it. It was directly underfoot, old and moss-covered, a few feet wide by a few feet long, jumping the ditch like a humpbacked dwarf. Trailing vines almost hid the milestone at its head; but peering closely at the worn granite, Rudy could discern the rune Yad had carved there. The Rune of the Veil.

And beyond the bridge was the path.

Rudy was sure he hadn't seen it before, but he felt as if he had known it would look like that. The sense of *déjà vu* carried to the smallest details—the way the wine-brown tangles of wild grape cloaked the sides of the cutting like curtains in an untidy house, the ankle-deep mold of yellow leaves on the path, and the black-edged mushrooms that grew on the bank above. With his foot on the stone of the bridge, Rudy looked back to where Ingold stood, smiling, beside the burro. "Can you see it?" he challenged.

Ingold's smile broadened. "Of course." He came forward, leading Che at his heels.

It had rained throughout the day, sheets of twisting silver rain that froze and soaked the travelers even through the comparative shelter of the trees. These eastern foot-slopes of the Seaward Mountains were wooded, and the roaring of the rain on the leaves had called to mind the voice of the sea booming in a storm. All yesterday and the day before it had rained, blinding them to the road ahead and swelling the creeks to rivers, turning the low-lands to wrinkled gray marshes all prickled with the dark spears of reeds. Above the trees, the day was still gray, cold, and threatening, but for all that, warmer than the frozen reaches of the plains or the bitterness of the wind-scoured desert. Rudy shivered in his buffalohide coat and wondered if he'd ever be warm or dry again.

Even in the dying of the year, the Seaward Mountains were beautiful, lush and opulent after the spare grandeur of the treeless lands. Scuffing through the oozing leaves of the roadbed, Rudy found that beauty seeping into his

197

soul. He rejoiced in the quiet of the woods, in the color
and richness of the life among the bronze and fawn of the
carpeting ferns, in the black of the wet pine bark and the
dark red of the oak, and in the alternation of darkness
and silver. Movement and life surrounded them, the flick
of the red squirrel's tail as it vanished around a tree and
the high, harsh laugh of a jay. The path topped the cut
bank and wound away through the woods, climbing a ridge
cloaked in yellow tamarisk and leading down through a
little pass that Rudy would have sworn was not there
before.

The wet leaves underfoot made the ground slippery, but
his leg barely twinged. He still used as a walking stick
the spear shaft he'd gotten from the Raiders and wore the
sleeved coat of buffalohide they'd given him. Another
breeze shook down more rain and brought with it the
cold, wet scent of the heights. Cloudy pillars of vapor hid
the peaks, but the bright smell was like the distant music
that called to the soul.

Against all his expectations, he and Ingold had reached
the Seaward Mountains. It now only remained for them
to find their way to Quo.

"RUDY!"

The desperation in Ingold's shout jerked him back to
reality, and a split second later something collided with his
head, a beating madness of black feathers and a beak that
gored into his cheekbone and narrowly missed his eye. He
struck at the tearing claws and heard the whine of Ingold's
staff slashing down inches from his face. With a hoarse,
mocking caw, the giant crow eluded the blow. With a
bloody beak it went flapping heavily back toward its
native trees. Rudy stood trembling in the road, gasping
with shock and idiotically remembering a Hitchcock film
he'd seen on the late-late show. Blood dripped down his
fingers as he touched the wound. Beside him, Ingold
scanned the trees with cold fury in his face. Whirlwinds
of black crows rose from their bare branches. Their ob-
scene laughter drifted back down like stray black feathers,
along with the dead leaves dislodged by their wings.

"Are you all right?" Ingold turned back to Rudy, dug
a kerchief from somewhere in his robes, and dabbed at the
cut.

"Yeah," Rudy whispered. "Fine, I guess. What the hell did that bird attack me for?"

The wizard shook his head. "That happens here, if you take your guard off. That, or something like it."

Rudy's hands were shaking as he took the cloth. The wound stung in the chilly air. In a way, even getting his leg slashed open by the dooic hadn't been this bad. He'd been ready for that.

There was no way to be entirely ready for the walls of air that encircled the City of Quo.

Often there was only a sense of being followed. Rudy caught himself constantly looking over his shoulder, uneasy in the silence of the dripping woods. Sometimes he had the conviction that he did not see things that were there. He would stop in such places, letting his mind drop into that state of unconcern that saw all things with crystal clarity, as once in the desert he had seen his own soul— the shapes of dead leaves, straw-colored against the sepia background of decay, and the roll of the land under its cloak of fern. Often, while he sensed the illusion of such spots, he could not fathom it, though once he did find another path, threading away from the main one, winding around a thicket of thorn-choked aspens that he had thought lay wider and higher than was later proved. Ingold followed him down this new path without a word. Still other times, the illusion-spell took the shape of a curious, irrational fear, a loathing to continue at all, or a vile detestation at passing a certain tree. Once past it, Rudy looked back to see the faint outlines of the Rune of the Chain all but obscured in the overgrowing bark.

"If you ask me, it would be damn easy to get lost in these woods," Rudy muttered, after Ingold had stopped him from going on and had shown him a side turning through a dark glen that he had, for some reason, been completely unable to notice. Once on the path itself, it was completely visible, and he was not even sure that it had ever been out of his sight.

Ingold mimed a man shielding his eyes from too-brilliant light. "Dazzling," he murmured. "The boy's intellect is simply dazzling."

"What are they afraid of?" Rudy went on, ignoring him.

"Afraid?" Ingold raised his brows.

199

"I mean, they have their magic to protect them in case of trouble. If it came down to a fight, I mean, which it wouldn't. I mean, who'd take on a bunch of wizards?"

"Never underestimate human motivations," Ingold advised. "Especially under the impulse of the Church. Remember that the Archmage has been called the Devil's Left Hand. It wasn't so long ago that the Prince-Bishop of Dele mounted a major war on the Council and sent an expeditionary force to torch the town and burn as many wizards as might be found in the ruins."

"Did the wizards fight them off?" Rudy asked, awed at the thought.

"Of course not. The expedition never came anywhere near Quo. There was rain and fog, and the army became lost in the foothills. It was eventually deposited back on the main road, miles from where it had entered the hills. Wizards can fight, if need be. But we are all very good at evading the conflict. Stop a moment."

Rudy halted, puzzled. Ingold took him by the arm and led him forward along the narrow path toward the edge of a cloud-filled gorge visible through the smooth, bare boles of the gray trees. Ingold kept a little in the lead and advanced with what Rudy considered ridiculous caution—until it became suddenly apparent that the edge of the gorge was very much nearer than Rudy had thought. He found himself looking down a sheer drop of black-walled cliff to a bristle of torn rock and jagged, broken trees, half-hidden in the mists at the bottom. Head swimming, he stepped back hastily. He thought he had seen something else on the rocks below, like the broken limbs of the dead trees, but whiter.

He glanced around quickly. The path itself had changed. Fog was blowing softly down on them from the higher peaks, and the trees were receding around them like mocking spirits into the mists, the ferns spider-webbed in silver dew.

"We've come quite high," Ingold said, his soft, scratchy voice calm and strangely disembodied in that cool, two-dimensional world. "From here the way becomes more difficult. The illusions of the road alone will have turned aside the malicious or curious or idle. The only ones to come this high are those who seek to become mages and

200

who can see the traps before they close—or those with the motivation to do the wizards real harm."

"So—what can we do?" Rudy whispered, afraid.

"Do?" The fog had closed on them now, so that Ingold was only a flat shape in the mist, hooded darkness hiding his face. "Dispel the fog, of course."

Hesitantly, Rudy stammered out the words Ingold had taught him to summon and dismiss the weather. Chill as wraiths, the fog caressed his face. Now he could feel the spell that bound the mist, drawing it like a net around them. He put out his strength against it, but felt it greater than his own power, older and infinitely more complex. He stood alone, wrapped in mist, almost choked by its thickness, as if smothering in a wet shroud. Sweat as well as fog dampened his face. He fought the impulse to run shouting from it—it did not matter in which direction—only to be away from the malicious strength of the hands that held the net.

"I can't do it," he whispered in despair.

Ingold clicked his tongue reprovingly. "Can't! If you can't, then we shall stay here, or else walk sightlessly. It will be night soon."

"Dammit!" Rudy wailed. "Can't you give me a stronger spell?"

"Why? Yours is perfectly adequate."

"It is not! You know you could sweep this stuff aside like a cobweb!"

"With the self-same spell, Rudy." Ingold was no more than a dark blur in the mists, but his voice was warming, like a fire in a cold place. "The strength of your spells is the strength of your soul. Haven't you realized that?" Ingold stepped closer to him, the coarse fiber of his robe sewn with pearls of dew. "As you grow, your spells will grow also."

"But can't you feel it?" Rudy demanded helplessly. "It's—it's like a boy fighting a man. I'll never . . ."

"If you keep saying never," Ingold replied mildly, "you'll come to believe it. If his back is to the wall, a boy has to fight a man, doesn't he? And sometimes he can win."

Rudy subsided into silence. Above the fog, the sky was

201

growing perceptibly darker, the first chill winds of evening drifting down from the unseen heights ...

Winds. The endless winds of the plains.

With meticulous bounding-spells and limits, Rudy summoned the winds.

They were icy cold, but they smelled of the stone and glaciers above. Thin, steady, and strong they blew, riding gray horses up from the gully, breaking the fog before them like startled ghosts. Cloudy shapes rolled away from the path and retreated ponderously from the sloping land. Trees shook wetness down on the pilgrims disapprovingly in the new strength of the winds that whipped Rudy's long, wet hair into his eyes. He started down the path, Ingold leading the burro silently behind.

They camped that night in open ground, under the shadow of the higher peaks. Ingold circled the camp with spells of protection, visible to a wizard's sight as a faint ring of foxfire around the perimeter, but nothing threatened them throughout that whispering night. In the morning, the clouds had cleared somewhat, and Ingold pointed out the pass which they sought, a narrow notch in the blackness of the mountain wall. Throughout the day it seemed to shift unaccountably to the northward, and at times the trails Ingold chose appeared to lead nowhere near it.

They were in high, treeless country now, where rocks towered as proud as goddesses above the trail. An occasional twisted live oak or clumps of scented heather clung to the barren slopes, and water rushed down in veils of glimmering lace, or boiled in rock channels whose depths showed rust and pewter and the velvet green-black of moss. The trail here was perilous, switching back and forth across the steep stone of the mountain's flank, overhung by massive boulders. In places the trail was buried under single boulders or great spills of talus and boulders mixed, deadly testimony to the spells that guarded Quo. Rudy wondered what would have happened to him at this point, had Ingold not walked at his side.

Ingold led the way now, picking out the tangled trails with preternatural skill. Rudy was surprised at his own exhaustion following yesterday's efforts. Try as he would, he could not see half the illusions that Ingold did. It certainly would never have occurred to him to cross the boiling rapids of a swollen river, as Ingold did, wading through a ford at the place that looked to be the deepest and most deadly. Nor would he have found the trail that led over a seemingly sheer cliff.

And then there was the bridge.

"What's wrong with the bridge?" Rudy wanted to know. The great span of moss-grown stone arched proudly over the canyon, its curved blue shadow faintly visible on the thorn and boulders that choked the thread of stream far below.

"It isn't there," Ingold replied simply.

Rudy looked again, then walked to the threshold and struck the stone with his staff. Wood clunked solidly on rock.

"Pieces of this road are unfamiliar to me," the wizard went on, "and the road has changed recently—become more dangerous, I believe. But I have crossed this gorge here dozens of times. There is no bridge."

"Maybe it has been put up since you were here last?"

"At the beginning of this summer? I hardly think so, with all the moss that's grown on it. Look at how worn the stones are, there along the railing. The bridge looks as if it were there from the beginning of time. And since I know it wasn't . . ." He shrugged. "It was never there at all."

"I seem to remember," Rudy said judiciously, "something you once said to me about disbelieving your own senses because of something you believe to be true . . ."

Ingold laughed, remembering their first conversation in the old shack in the California hills. "I am paid," he said humbly. "If, when we cross by hardier means, the bridge proves to be real and not illusion, you may revile me in any terms you please, and I shall bow meekly to the lash." But when they scrambled, scratched and bleeding from forcing the recalcitrant Che up the impossible trail out of the gorge, Rudy looked back and saw that the stone bridge was only a single strand of willow withe, as frail as a spider web, on which the wizards had threaded their illusion. From there he could see the bone dump, too, at the bottom of the cliff below.

Kara had come this way, Rudy thought. And Bektis,

too, and Ingold, in his youth. Had it been this bad then? It was one hell of a price to pay for safety.

"Hey, Ingold? If Quo stands on the Western Ocean, and the walls of air defend the landward side—has anybody ever tried to assault it by sea?"

"Oh, yes," the wizard said. "It's been tried."

Rudy thought about it and of his horror of the ocean and of deep water and of the many things that could happen out on those dark depths. The thought wasn't pleasant.

This, then, was the other side of power—the power that isolated wizards, that made them vagabonds, exiles in their own world, the power that drew them together. He remembered the look in Alde's eyes the first time he had called fire from cold wood.

You sought wizardry, he told himself. *And here it is. A bridge of illusion and the bones below.*

They traveled for hours through narrow canyons or followed rock ledges on the high peaks, slippery with ice. Twice they tried to force shortcuts over the bare, tawny flanks of the mountain, only to be driven back by the steepness of the ground. In the end, the trail petered out entirely, vanishing into the stony wastes. As they stood panting on the dark slope of a tumbled ruin of shale, Rudy looked up toward the pass, only to find that somehow he and Ingold had overshot it by miles, and it now lay to the south of them, the glaciers that crowned it gleaming palely in the heatless sky.

Ingold leaned on his staff, as motionless as a statue, with only the tautness of his mouth and the angry glitter of his eyes betraying him. Somewhere in the distance, Rudy heard the whine of the wind and the angry buzz of a rattlesnake. Other than that, the world was utterly still, as barren of life as it had been when the sun had first sung the world up from the sea. The wizard turned on his heel and started back along the false trail without a word.

Early evening found them in a deep, narrow valley thick with trees, at whose lower end lay a black tarn of still and oily water. "This place is not familiar to me at all," Ingold said quietly, eyeing the gloomy wall of tangled trees that all but covered the trail. "I think the wood is wider than we suppose. Can you see there, that blurring along the farther edge? It deludes the eye. I should be surprised if we can cross it before full dark."

Rudy glanced uneasily over his shoulder for perhaps the thousandth time that day. He hated the smell of the woods, but he found he loathed the water more. A wet, white mist had begun to curl from its dark surface. Wreaths of it floated among the first of the trees. "Yeah," he said slowly. "But I'd sooner try that than camp near that water."

"So would I, if you want the truth." Ingold gathered the lead-rope to hand and led the way into the woods, spells of clearing on his lips.

The black trees grew very densely, the space between them choked with glossy-leaved holly, dark ivy, and wild grape that spilled across the path, tangling the pilgrims' footsteps. The valley mists seemed to follow them, sliding among the thorny trunks like white cats. Darkness thickened in the woods, and Rudy, tentatively adding his own clearing-spells to Ingold's, felt the magic that bound this place together into a single murky entity, a knot of hostility and evil. Twice they lost the path entirely, and Rudy began to wonder if the trees themselves were moving.

"This is getting monotonous," Rudy panted, after the fourth time they had to halt and hack Che's packs clear of brambles with the little hatchet. The burro stood in shivering panic, the whites of his eyes showing all the way in a gleaming rim. "We gotta back out of this and try going around. We're never gonna get anywhere this way."

"Again with your never," Ingold reproached. But in the deepening darkness, Rudy could see that the old man's face was lined with concentration and weariness under the bleeding thorn scratches. Having pulled the donkey free, they advanced a few feet and looked back. The path behind them was gone.

Rudy cursed. Ingold sighed patiently and shut his eyes as if in meditation, bowing his head like some strange species of moss-grown tree himself. After a moment, Rudy saw his brow tighten in concentration and heard the deepening draw of his breath. Darkness seemed to tighten like a net. Rudy became aware of restless rustles and scurryings in the gloom around them. Things whistled in the trees, signaling, he thought.

Finally Ingold's tense shoulders relaxed, and his eyes

opened. "In my day there was an enchanted wood in these hills," he said, "but not like this. Unfortunately, as you may have seen, the wood fills this valley from end to end, and the mountains on both sides are steep. But at this rate, if we went on, we would stand a chance of being trapped farther in. If that happens, I would rather it happened in daylight."

They turned back, and Rudy saw that the path they had taken into the woods had now disappeared ahead of them. He muttered a few choice curses at Lohiro and company and followed them up with clearing-spells that Ingold had taught him. The woods proved no easier to get out of than they had been to enter, and it was fully dark by the time they reached the edge. They made camp among the thinner trees by a stream, and Ingold drew the protective circle double and triple wide on the musty leaves underfoot.

It had been a great many nights since Rudy had called up Alde's image in the flames. But Ingold still studied his crystal by the flickering glow of the fire. Exhausted in body and spirit, Rudy watched him, following the movement in the blue hawk eyes as they sought whatever they sought among the glinting facets. His own visions in the crystal table at the Keep came back to him—bright blue eyes, as wide and cold as the sky, seemed to stare into his, glittering like the diamond surge of foam over raw bones. The image followed him down into a restless sleep.

He dreamed of bones—bones lying in darkness, though in the dream he could see in the dark; the faint gleam of witchlight touched the ever-repeating curve of skull, rib, and pelvis in thin slips of ghostly silver. The dry, brown moss that the bones lay upon was slimy here, wetted with corruption and crawling with nameless and unspeakable white life. Around him, the red eyes of scavenger rats flickered in the dark. Something moved, hopping awkwardly. An eyeless white toad burped greasily at him from the top of a deformed skull. More toads hopped among the bones, slipping in the muck as they fled the touch of the witchlight. Rudy moaned, trying to fight his way clear of the horror of the dream, to turn his eyes from the hideous spectacle that he now saw covered the blackness of the uneven cavern floor for miles like a rotting swamp. Stalagmites rose through the filth like ghostly trees, and red eyes flickered and dodged around their bases. He heard the sticky scrambling of furtive feet in the dry, brown moss that was decaying and turning to dusty gray powder, where it was not horribly damp. He moaned again, sickened and faint. This time, however, it was not he who cried out, but the man he saw leaning against the dark entrance to some cavern beyond. His face was turned from Rudy, but Rudy knew him—would know him anywhere, whatever happened. The witchlight gleamed on white hair and on the galled ring of flesh visible between mitten and sleeve. Then there was silence, broken only by the rustling of millions of tiny feet among the moss and bones . . .

. . . among the leaves of the forest floor!

Che's squeal of terror brought Rudy up, sweating. The burro was tugging wildly at his tether, ears flattened back along his narrow skull, eyes staring. Beyond him, Rudy could see Ingold on his feet, at the edge of the pale glimmer of the protective circle. And still beyond, among the trees, was a limitless sea of red eyes.

"Holy Christ!" Rudy rolled to his feet and groped for his staff.

"No light," Ingold said softly without turning his head. There was no wind, but the whisper of those tiny clawed feet was like the forerunner of a storm in the forest. Even where the darkness hid them, Rudy could sense the squirming of their packed bodies. Their dry, fetid smell was everywhere.

"Can they come through the circle?" Rudy whispered. He thought the white flame of it flickered brighter, dancing among the fallen leaves.

"No," Ingold said softly. There was a creak and rustle overhead. Rudy looked up. The branches of the trees were furred with the rats, like foul fruit.

"Ingold, we gotta get out of here."

"We'll do nothing of the kind," the wizard stated in a voice like stone. "As long as nothing breaks the circle, we are safe."

Trust him, Rudy thought desperately, fighting the urge to run. *He knows more about it than you do.* Throughout the dark woods the rats shifted; the ferns were alive with their unholy scampering. He saw them clearly now, flowing in a gray-brown stream over the humped knees of the tree roots and through and around hollow logs. They swarmed in the stream bed and slithered in the deep, matted leaves, wrinkled noses pulled back from sharp, white teeth. Che squealed once again, jerking at his lead, his nostrils huge with terror.

Rudy saw the picket pin start from the ground and grabbed for the rope. The burro gave an almost human scream and flung himself backward, the pin tearing loose in a small fountain of leaf mold and dirt. The rope slid through Rudy's fingers. The burro put his head down and bolted over the edge of the circle and into the darkness.

It was as if the circling white flame had never been. The kicked leaves had not finished pattering down when the rats poured forward like a dirty river, hissing and squealing with rage. Rudy heard Che screaming and ran after him, striking with sickened horror with his staff at the vicious furry things that stuck like burrs to his boots, his coat, and his arms. One of the things launched itself from a tree in the darkness and struck his face; he thought he screamed, but later he wasn't sure, for at that moment he heard behind him the unmistakable roar of fire, and the light of it streamed over him. Flame splattered across the backs of the gray sea that seemed to be on the point of engulfing him. Turning, he saw Ingold swing his staff like a weapon, fire erupting from the length of it like a spewing banner of napalm.

Che was squealing frantically, his coat matted with running blood in the firelight, three huge rats hanging like terrier dogs to his lacerated muzzle. Rudy struck them off with his staff, feeling at the same time claws and sharp little teeth ripping at his calves. He beat them away and grabbed the lead-rein, paralyzed with disgust and panic, desperate to fight free of the filthy things.

The fire was spreading, rushing uncontrollably through the autumn-withered ferns. The leaves underfoot were catching, their moldering dampness throwing forth immense billows of sooty smoke. The flame in the ferns licked through that blinding curtain like the burning backdrop of Hell. Blazing rats fled this way and that, their fiery coats igniting the dead underbrush, their shrill screams forming an overwhelming metallic chattering above the smothered roar of the blaze. Smoke seared Rudy's eyes and seemed to clog his lungs, blinding him and trapping him in a wall of heat from which he could find no escape. Screaming in panic, Che twisted at the lead, and Rudy felt the stickiness of blood on his hands as he fought to drag the terrified animal out of a closing trap of heat, suffocation, and flame.

Out of the rolling fog of the smoke Ingold burst, gasping, his muffler wound over his nose and mouth. He caught Rudy's arm and dragged him along the path. They waded through a surging inferno, floored in fire and roofed in blinding smoke, and echoing with the chattering shriek of rats burning alive. Against the blazing underbrush, the damp tree trunks stood like black, smoking pillars in the murk. Unable to breathe, unable to tell one direction from another, Rudy was conscious only of a desperate fight for air against the blinding heat and of Ingold's hand like an iron shackle on his arm. As they left the woods behind them, they could see the reflection burning in the dark waters of the tarn, like a thick stream of blood and gold.

They did not stop until it was almost morning. The light from the forest fire was far behind them now, but the smell of smoke and rats stuck to their clothing, and the roar of the blazing underbrush carried for miles. Half-unconscious from asphyxiation, Rudy could only follow where Ingold led, up and down stony trails in blind darkness and through streams that bit their feet with cold. Dawn found them lying, scorched and exhausted, on level, stony ground. Rudy was too weary to flee farther, his hands and face burned, unable to sleep because of the terror of his dreams. The gray light that leaked slowly into the sky revealed the road before them, its hexagonal silvery blocks all but hidden under the accumulated drift of the dirt of ages. Above them loomed the massive darkness of the Seaward Mountains, plumed in billows and ostrich feathers of smoke and mist that caught the first coral tints of the morning. Behind them lay the rolling, lizard-colored sands of the high desert, the thick rust-red scrub nodding in the chill backwash of the northern winds.

They were where they had been three days ago, before entering the walls of air.

Rudy sighed, scarcely caring. *All right, man, have it your way. I didn't want to visit your lousy town in the first place. Next year I'll go to Disneyland instead.*

But Ingold got slowly to his feet, leaning on his staff with singed hands, looking westward to the dark backbone of the mountains. Rudy thought the old man looked half-dead and felt suddenly concerned for him as he swayed like a drunken man on his feet. The first gleams of rare sunlight glinted in the wizard's hair. Ingold raised his head, and his voice rolled out over the wooded expanse of the foothills. "LOHIRO!" he called, and the echoes boomed it in the rocks. "LOHIRO, DO YOU HEAR ME? DO YOU KNOW WHO I AM?" Scrub and stone and water whispered a reply to his words. Somewhere a jay screamed. High up, a feather of smoke caught the new sun, like a vagrant rosy cloud. His shout leaped from rock to rock. "LOHIRO, WHERE ARE YOU?"

But the echoes died, and the silence mocked their passing.

They climbed throughout the day.

At first the road was the same as on the previous day, swifter and easier because they knew the spells laid on it, though occasionally some branching trail that he had not seen before would catch Rudy's eye. The weather turned bad again, the sky heavy with the threat of rain. Rudy sent the cold front concerned several miles to the north, to dump its pent-up waters on the stony gullies of the foothills. He figured they had enough troubles without that. They reached the wooded vale with its burned trees and tarn of still water well before sunset and began the climb over the flanks of the mountain at its sides.

Clouds still masked the high peaks. The gray rocks were damp and icy. Rudy scrambled wherever Ingold led, exhausted and half-frozen, dragging the unwilling burro behind. Night found them in a mist-drowned wood far above the valley. Rudy was so weary he could barely stagger. He mumbled something about being waked at midnight to take the second watch; but when he finally rolled over, stiff and smarting and aching in every limb, he found him-

210

self wet with the dew and frost of morning, and the world was opalescent in the clinging fogs.

"Hey, you shoulda kicked me or something," he apologized, sitting up amid a soft crackling of ice on his blankets.

"I did," Ingold replied easily. "Repeatedly. I could have beaten you with a stick with much the same results." He'd built a small fire and was making griddle cakes on the iron tripod they used for cooking. The dark smudges under his eyes had turned to bruises. He looked as if he'd been in a fight. "It doesn't matter," the wizard added kindly. "I needed the time to think."

Rudy wondered how much the old man had slept since seeing the empty Nest in the plains. He sat up, stretching his shoulders gingerly, and thought with dread of breaking the ice in the nearby stream to shave. The world smelled of newness, of wet grasses and snow and sky. But from the valley below, the wind brought up another smell, and Rudy turned his head quickly, not knowing what it was or liking it. He glanced over at Ingold. The old man was digging in the packs for the dried meat with which Hoofprint of the Wind had stocked them. His movements were slow and tired. *You may have needed time to think,* Rudy decided grimly, *but it's gonna be a damn long day of rock climbing, and you look as if six cups of coffee, ten hours of sleep, and a handful of whites wouldn't do you any harm.*

"I've been up this trail a little farther already this morning," Ingold continued, returning to the fire. "The trail itself ends about two miles from here; from there the ground gets worse. You and I might make it, but we'd have to leave Che. And aside from the fact that he would surely die in this wilderness, we shall have troubles enough before us without trying to live off the land as well."

Rudy sighed. His whole body ached with the thought of a trailless scramble over terrain worse than yesterday's. For one thing, he hadn't thought terrain could *get* worse than yesterday's. Gritting his teeth, he asked, "So what do we do?"

"Go back."

Relief flooded Rudy's muscles like the hot bath that was rapidly replacing food, California, and Minalde as the object of his most wishful fantasies. "I'm game," he said. "Maybe the woods will be easier to get through in daylight."

They weren't.

From the stream back for some distance into the woods, the fire had seared off the underbrush, though the wet bark and damp leaves of the trees themselves had defied its heat. Beyond the burned woods, the trees yielded at first to Rudy's spells. But through his magic he felt their strength, and the implacable power of it frightened him. In time, the trees crowded in thicker, brambles tangling at the travelers' clothing and vines catching at their feet, until it was all Ingold could do to force a path. Even so, it seemed that the underbrush closed in after the old man, and Rudy found himself struggling through the clutching hedges simply not to lose sight of his guide. The cloudy light of the overcast day sickened to murky gloom here, choked by mats of thrusting branches and tangled creepers, until the woods were almost as dark as evening.

Rudy cursed as Che's packs got hung up for the umpteenth time in the thick mazes of blackberry brambles. He pulled the little ax free and began chopping at the thick vines. There was ivy twined with the brambles, and the ax head became entangled as well. Rudy's hands and face were bleeding with scratches by the time he'd unraveled the mess. Turning to go on, he found the trail ahead of him entirely gone.

"Ingold!" he called out. "Ingold, hang on a minute! Where are you?"

But only the silence of the black trees pressed upon him. Thorn and bramble surrounded him like a net, vicious and impenetrable. He could see no trail, either forward or back.

"Motherloving trees—INGOLD!" he yelled again. Somewhere in the woods there was a furtive, greedy rustling, but it was not in the direction Ingold had gone, nor anywhere near. Fighting panic, Rudy called on all his powers for a clearing-spell to break him out of what felt like a closing tangle of barbed wire, but the spells on the woods sapped his power like a leech on a vein, and the dark trees whispered in a sound very much like laughter.

For nearly an hour he called, his voice cracking with

strain and terror, sweat running down his face and soaking his clothes. He began to wonder if something had happened to Ingold and the old man was never coming back for him. He remembered the rats. "INGOLD!" he yelled, and this time he could hear the panic edging his voice.

Gritting his teeth, he repeated the spells of clearing, to open a path, some path, any path. So gripped was he by the suffocating sense of panic that he might have thrown himself at random against the thorns and tried to claw his way out. But a whisper of the leaves behind him sent him swinging around in terror—and a path was there. It was a fairly broad trail, and he thought he could glimpse faint glimmers of sunlight on the leaves far down its winding curves. He wrapped his hand tighter around Che's lead-rope . . .

. . . and stopped.

Sunlight? It's been raining for days.

Stay put, Ingold had said. *It's the oldest trick in the book.*

Rudy stayed put, like a lost child, calling Ingold's name. Finally he heard a muffled reply, a hoarse, cracked voice calling, "Rudy?"

"I'm over here!"

There was a trampling noise and a great shaking among the dark branches. Rudy had a momentary panic-stricken scenario of some incredible, slavering monster seeking him out by calling with Ingold's voice, but a few minutes later the wizard appeared from a thinning among the trees, his face and hands scratched all over and thorns and twigs lodged in his cloak and hair. He looked white and strained, exhausted by the game of wits with shadows. Without a word, he caught Rudy by the arm, took the ax from the pack, and began methodically hacking a path through the wall of briars. The woods yielded grudgingly, snaring the ax, tearing their clothes, reaching clawed, greedy hands to rip at their faces or snatch at their eyes. Both of them were stumbling with weariness when they finally broke through the last of the dark trees, to find themselves on the rim of jagged boulders that overhung a deep canyon— forty feet of sheer-sided cliffs falling below them to a jumble of water-torn rocks and splintery trees.

Ingold slumped quietly down against a boulder and

shut his eyes. He looked dead and dug up, Rudy thought, sitting wordlessly beside him. Even the cold of the overcast day was welcome after the hushed, hot darkness of the haunted woods. Rudy also closed his eyes, glad to rest, to have a few minutes wherein he was not afraid of what was going to happen next. Wind snuffled down the canyon below them and set all the trees of the woods at their backs to whispering their angry curses. Spits of cold rain kissed his face, but he hadn't the heart to send the rainclouds elsewhere. The veering of the wind brought another smell to him, bitter and metallic, one that he had scented before.

He opened his eyes and looked down the gorge before them. The rocks along the stream, he saw now, were stained black, and the brush and paloverde along the stream were charred and rotted in long spoors, as if filthy and corrosive streams had trickled down from farther up the canyon. That stinging smell breathed up at them again, poisonous and overpowering. He coughed and glanced over at his companion.

Ingold had also opened his eyes. The sweat was drying in his hair, the blood caking in little rivulets on his scratched hands. He was staring out into space, and his eyes held a look of infinite weariness and a kind of tired despair.

"Ingold?"

Only his eyes moved, but they seemed to lighten and smile.

"What is it?" Rudy asked.

The old man shook his head. "Only that we'll have to go up the gorge. We can't go back through the woods. There is worse evil in them than I thought, and I won't risk being trapped there until nightfall."

"Ingold, I don't like this," Rudy said. "Who's doing this? What's happening? Did Lohiro really set up all this?"

Ingold made a tired little motion with his hand, "No. Not Lohiro alone. I set up some of it myself when I was at Quo. In fact, many of the spells on the woods were mine, though they've been changed now and made—much worse. All the members of the Council have put their powers into the maze, and the maze changes, the traps and illusions shifting with each new mind that goes into it.

214

It has never been this—this difficult. It has never been this perilous. But Lohiro and the Council intended to wall themselves in. Only one of the makers of the maze can shift it now."

Rudy sighed. He wondered what would have become of him if the Dark Ones had really made off with Ingold in the desert. Could he have found his way to the heart of the maze?

No way, he decided. *I'd have poked around the feet of the mountains till I died.*

"You're the Great White Scout," he said after a moment. "But I'm here to tell you I do not like that gorge."

Ingold chuckled briefly. "Most astute." He got stiffly to his feet, collected his staff and Che's lead, and started down the narrow trail into the gully.

At the bottom of the ravine, the hot metallic smell was stronger, the fumes of it burning the nostrils. Pools of fouled black water gleamed greasily in the wan daylight, fringed with charred, stinking vegetation. Even close to the canyon walls, the weeds had shriveled in the noxious air, like flowers in Rudy's native California smog. Farther along, the head-high thickets of tule and bullrush that had masked the stream could be seen to be colorless, rotting in the pollution of that narrow place. From the canyon rim above them, the dark trees of the haunted woods frowned down; before them, on the distant shoulders of the mountain, Rudy thought he could glimpse the pass.

They followed the windings of the canyon for some distance, through a wasteland of fetid puddles and crippled, dying trees. A final turning brought them within sight of the end—desolate, stinking, a dark cave mouth amid broken slopes of shale and boulders. The sand around the cave was cut by filthy runnels of black and violent yellow slime. An oily suggestion of a putrid, greenish mist hung low over the ground. Beyond, on the higher slopes above the cave, the trees grew clean. But the woods were silent, unstirred by so much as a bird song, and Rudy heard the intaken hiss of Ingold's breath.

"What is it?" he asked softly, and the wizard touched his lips for silence.

In a voice indistinguishable from the flicker of wind in grass, he cautioned, "They have excellent hearing."

Apprehensively, Rudy dropped his voice to a subvocal whisper. "What do?"

The old man had already begun to retreat soundlessly behind the rocks. He replied in a murmur of breath. "Dragons."

"There's no chance he's out hunting?" Rudy whispered hopefully.

He and Ingold stood side by side in the black shadow of a massive boulder of splintered granite that shielded them from the cave beyond. They had scouted the walls of the canyon back for miles, but the only trail leading out of it was the one they had come down from the haunted woods.

"Of course not," the wizard replied in a soft, almost inaudible breath. "Can't you hear his scales sliding on the rocks of the cave?"

Rudy was silent, listening, casting his senses into the dark pit that loomed before them. In all the world there seemed no other noises but the *hrssh* of wind through Che's dusty pelt and the nervous jitter of his little hooves on the rocks. Then he heard the dry grating of incalculable weight and the thick drag of fetid breath.

"How big is that thing?" he whispered, aghast.

Ingold drew himself back from the edge of the boulders. "Forty feet at least. I'm told the old bulls can get to almost twice that."

"Eighty feet!" Rudy wailed soundlessly. He calculated the distance from their rock to the boulders that flanked the cave—it looked like miles, with or without Godzilla lurking in between.

"It may be sleeping," the wizard continued softly, "but I doubt it. Judging by the amount of discoloration on the trees, it's laired here for a little over two months. Probably it was trapped here when the mazes surrounding Quo were shifted and strengthened. But there's little game in these mountains, and certainly nothing large enough to interest a dragon. You can see for yourself that there are no bones near the mouth of the cave."

"Wonderful," Rudy said shakily. "Our friend should be

216

just tickled pink to see us." He edged his way around the boulders and surveyed the ground before the cave.

Here at the ends of the canyon, the stink of the beast was overwhelming. The deep bed of river sand was littered with fallen or rotting trees, eucalyptus, cottonwood, or oak, whose roots had been eaten away by the poisonous fluids that dribbled from the mouth of the cave. Violently discolored tangles of weeds and distorted brush flanked the cave itself and grew halfway up the boulders on either side. Rudy felt a light touch on his shoulder as Ingold came around beside him.

"You bear left up the rocks there; I'll take Che and climb the talus slope to the right of the cave. Go as swiftly as you can in silence. If it does come out and attack you, dive for shelter—any kind of shelter—and I'll try to draw it off. On the whole, it's more likely to attack me, since I'll have the burro. If that happens, you've got to go in and do the axwork. Cut it behind the forelegs or through the belly or up behind the neck, if you can get that close. And stay away from its tail. It can club you senseless before you realize what's hit you."

Ingold started to move forward, and Rudy caught his sleeve. "It doesn't—it can't fly, can it?" he whispered anxiously.

The wizard appeared startled by the question. "Good heavens, no."

"Or breathe fire?"

"No, although its slime and spittle can be corrosive in wounds, and its blood will burn you. No—the deadliness of the dragon lies in its speed, its strength—and its magic."

Rudy whispered in horror, "Magic?"

One white eyebrow lifted. "After your experience with the Dark, you surely cannot believe that the seed of magic is limited to humankind. Dragons do not have human intelligence; their magic is a beast's magic, the magic that lures the prey to the hunter—a magic of illusion and invisibility, for the most part. No cloaking-spell will work against a dragon; no illusion will turn it aside. Remember that." His hand closed around Che's headstall, and he stepped out into the pale daylight, beyond the shelter of the rocks. Rudy gathered up his staff, preparing to make a run for the canyon's left-hand wall. Ingold's whisper stopped him. "And one more thing. Whatever you do—don't look into the dragon's eyes."

At a quick, steady walk, Ingold started for the talus spill that formed a steep gray slope up the mountain to the right of the cave. Che braced his feet and shook his short mane, unwilling to walk toward the chemical stench of the dragon's lair, but Ingold, Rudy knew, was a lot stronger than he looked.

Rudy moved in the opposite direction, skirting the discolored pools and the rotting stands of dying trees along the foot of the cliff, uncomfortably aware of the possibility of rattlesnakes in the rocks he'd have to climb. His hands felt tied up with the staff he carried. Across the seventy feet or so of sand that separated the canyon walls, Ingold and Che glided in an almost invisible medley of brown.

Ahead of him, Rudy heard the slithering noise of tons of slipping iron. Something round and gold and glassy flashed in the darkness of the cave, and he stopped in his tracks, paralyzed by something closer to fascination than by horror. A preliminary hiss came from the darkness, with a rolling breath of oily stench and fumes that stung his eyes. Rudy blinked, blinded, wiped at the burning tears . . .

And there it was.

He had never imagined anything so hideous or so gaudy. He had been expecting something green and vaguely crocodilian, like the dragons in picture books, not the product of an unnatural mating between a dinosaur and a calliope. It was enameled Chinese red and flaming gold, flickering with bands of green and black and white that mottled the lean-ribbed sides like a beadwork on a pair of slippers. The head was massive, horned, mailed, and bristling with flared scales of purple, black, and gold, which gave it a curiously beribboned effect; from the tufted whorls of streamers, spikes, and fins on that snake-like nape, a long ridge ran backward, up over the towering fulcrum of the mighty hind legs and down the counterpoised bulk of the spined, deadly tail. Green slime dripped from the armored chin as it champed and swallowed. The huge head turned, not with the slow, saurian deliberation

218

of a movie monster's, but as quick as a bird's. Rudy found himself looking into round, golden eyes.

The amber quicksilver of those twin mirrors drank his soul. He did not understand the vision that he saw in them, distant and clear, striking resonances of certainty within his heart. He saw the far-off image of his own chained hands silhouetted against the freezing arch of winter stars. An echo of bitter cold and blinding despair pierced him from what he knew, as surely as he knew his name, was his own future. Mesmerized, he could neither have moved nor looked away, had he willed it. He had to see, to understand . . .

He had never thought that anything that huge could move so fast. The dragon lunged like a lizard. Waking from his trance, Rudy could scarcely have moved if he had been ready. But instead of ripping, eight-inch fangs, all that struck him was a whiplash of kicked sand, for the dragon turned in mid-spring with a metallic hiss of rage and pain. Rudy threw himself aside to avoid the lashing hind foot, then raised his head from the ground in time to see Ingold leap away from the steaming deluge of blood that burst from the monster's slashed flank. From the end of that long neck, the armored head struck like a snake. Ingold sprang clear of it, his sword striking sparks from the mailed nose.

The dragon reared itself back on the massive fulcrum of its long hind legs, its belly gleaming like stained ivory in the sick gray light. It strode forward and lunged down again, snapping, then half-turned to slash with twenty-five feet of spined tail whose force could easily have broken a man's back. Ingold moved out of range, but a moment later his sword whined in again, cleaving through air rotten with the choking fumes of the dragon's breath, to strike at the slashing teeth and iron mouth.

Don't go for the head, dammit, Rudy thought cloudily. *There's nothing but armor there.* Then, as the wizard ducked back from the lash of the tail again, he realized what Ingold was doing. He was opening the dragon up, distracting its attention, so that Rudy could go in for the kill.

The fanning mane of its protective bone shield guarded the dragon's neck from the front, making it impossible for its victim to get in any kind of killing blow. But every time the monster brought its head down to snap at Ingold, the whole of its neck brushed the ground. From where he lay belly-down in the sand, Rudy could see how delicate were the beaded scales covering the pumping arteries of the throat. A single blow would do it—provided, of course, a man was willing to run in under that heaving crimson wall of angry flesh.

His knees weak at the thought, Rudy scanned that mountain of scarlet iron for another target.

He could see none. His scanty knowledge of anatomy didn't cover dragons. He had no idea where they kept their hearts; and anyway, he doubted his sword would pierce the polychrome mail of its side.

The spiked club of the tail cut the air like a whip, its barbs skimming Ingold's shoulder as he dodged it, with a force that spun him, bleeding, into the sand. The claws raked at him like swords; Ingold cut at them desperately from where he lay. Rudy knew that if the dragon pinned the old man, it would be all over for them both. He gathered his feet under him and drew his sword, watching for his chance. The wizard rolled to his feet somehow, staggering, but kept drawing the attack backward and in his direction, never letting Rudy get within the creature's line of sight. Absurdly, Rudy heard the old man saying far back along the trail, "I have even actually slain a dragon— rather, I acted as decoy and Lohiro did the sword work . . ."

If Lohiro could do it, Rudy thought grimly, *so can I.* Anyway, it was a curious comfort to know that the Archmage had been relegated to the butcher position, rather than the infinitely trickier post as decoy.

The dragon struck out with its claws again, and Ingold went down, his bloodied sword gleaming as he slashed at the snatching mouth. The huge shadow spread over him in the drenched and smoking sand. Rudy was on his feet as the massive head reached down. Ingold saw him coming, cut, and rolled, the great head swinging to follow, green drool splattering from the chisel teeth. Rudy's sword cleaved the air as if he were chopping wood. It split the jugular vein, and he barely ducked aside in time to avoid the firehose of blood that exploded outward, steaming in the air as it roared thickly against the rock of the canyon wall, some forty feet away. The dragon screamed, flinging up its head, its huge tail lashing as it clawed at the streaming wound.

Rudy plunged in under the writhing shadow to drag Ingold to his feet, hauling him toward the talus slope as the ground all around them was drenched in a burning rain of splattering blood. His hands felt scorched by it; his lungs were seared by the fumes. The lashing tail struck the ground so near that it covered them in a wave of thrown sand. Stumbling on the base of the slope, Rudy looked back, staring upward in horror at that huge, gaudy body swaying against the pallid sky.

Then the dragon fell, hitting the earth like a derailed freight train, and the ground shook under the impact of its weight. It heaved itself halfway up, screaming harshly and metallicly, its beribboned mane lashing in the frenzy of its death throes. The trees cracked where it heaved against them, their leaves shriveling in the scorch of its blood.

Rudy pulled Ingold a little farther up the loose rock of the slope, so weak with terror and reaction that he felt he could hardly move himself. The old man was a dead weight in his arms, the back of his mantle sticky where the claws had raked through to the flesh.

In malice or unknowing agony, the dragon reared and made one final lunge at them, the vast jaws snapping shut in a spew of blood and drool. Then the great body twisted in one last convulsive heave and lay still. Black liquid trickled from between the chisel teeth.

Rudy whispered, "Jesus Christ . . ."

But Ingold said softly, "Hush."

The gold eyes opened. They stared upward, baleful, inhuman, at the two wizards crouched out of its reach on the slope. Then they blinked, filmy, translucent shutters sliding down over the dying inner fire, and for a moment there was a blank, curious question in the dragon's eyes. The hideous mask of scarlet bone was incapable of expression; but for a fleeting instant, Rudy had the impression of some other personality looking out through the sunken eyes. A thin, dark, bearded face, he thought, whose

221

dragon gaze rested briefly on Ingold before those dim, amber lamps were extinguished forever.

Around them, the hush was like the draw of expectant breath. Rudy felt the air stir and change, though there was no breeze; it was like the shifting in a curtain of perception.

"Look behind you," Ingold said softly.

Rudy turned his head to look. A path, old and overgrown, wound on up toward the pass that was, he saw now, less than five miles from the end of the canyon. For the first time since they'd come to the Seaward Mountains, he had no sense of illusion or misdirection. He looked down at the crimson carcass where it lay amid the decaying broken trees and smoking sand, its gaudy tags and scales already beginning to blacken in the virulence of its own body chemistry. Then he looked back at Ingold's face, to see it white with shock, hollow and stretched and old.

"What is it?" Rudy whispered.

Bleak blue eyes shifted to his own. "It's the road to the pass, Rudy," he said quietly. "The road into Quo."

"It wasn't there before."

"No." Ingold got stiffly to his feet, catching his breath as he tried to move. "He—removed the illusion. Just before he died."

"He?" Rudy echoed, confused. "He who? The dragon? But how did the dragon have any power over the maze?"

The wizard turned wearily and led the way to the top of the slope, where Che could be heard, squealing in panic and fighting his tether. Ingold took his staff from where he'd left it propped against the scabby bark of a twisted oak and, leaning heavily on it, limped to free the burro. Rudy realized his own staff had been left down below, scorched to charcoal in the dragon's blood.

Ingold went on. "I think the inference is obvious. You and I, Rudy, have just killed one of the makers of the maze—one of the members of the Council of Wizards. I have told you before how easy it is to forget your own nature, once you have taken on the nature of a beast." He looked back down the slope to where the dragon lay, steaming faintly, gay colors quenched in darkening blood. "Having taken on the being of a dragon,

222

he forgot what it was to be a man and a wizard. He became a prisoner in his own maze. Only in death did he recognize me and remember, to do what he could for me in memory of our friendship." Under the slime of blood and dirt, his face was a bruised mass of cuts, the blood from them leaking slowly into his beard.

"You mean—that was a friend of yours?"

"I think so," Ingold whispered.

"But—why would he do it? Why would he change himself into a dragon in the first place?"

Ingold sighed, and the sound was like a death rattle in his throat. He wiped his eyes, and his sleeve came away fouled with red, gritty slime. "I don't know, Rudy. The answer to that lies in Quo. And I'm beginning to fear what that answer is."

CHAPTER THIRTEEN

Night walked the halls of Dare's Keep, bringing darkness and the soft stirring of sleepers, through cell on cell and corridor on corridor of those ancient and storied mazes. There was stillness, except for the uneasy breath of the moving air, and silence, except where, here and there, sleepers would wake with cries from hideous and identical dreams.

The small gleam of the lamplight gilded the round globes of a sandglass and licked with tiny flames on the scrollwork at the fancy end of Gil's silver hairpin. The worn wax of her tablets glowed a creamy yellow where the light touched, and the intricate fretwork of the tablet's narrow frame gleamed mahogany red, like old claret. Around her, the study was silent.

This was the new study, to which she and Alde had carried the increasing quantities of tablets, parchments, and artifacts scrounged from the lab levels below. The lamplight picked out shapes on the table: polyhedrons, milky white or crystal gray, a scattering of faceted jewels, odd, tubular mechanisms of gold and glass, and strangely shaped entities of metal and wood, some hard and angular, others sinuous, shaped to the hand. There were stacks of wax tablets and piles of dirty, mildewed, overwritten parchments—the stuff of failed scholarship, the jigsaw puzzle whose message, Gil feared, would be delivered the hard way.

The message was now, to her, very clear. She'd tracked it like a long-forgotten spoor through her notes, tangling on old words, old spellings, changes of dialect, and the language itself. The correlation was not invariable, but it was there. Not all Nests had had the citadels of wizardry built near them in the early days when the healers and seers and loremasters had held power, in these northern realms, comparable with that of the mighty Church of the south. But all citadels of wizardry—and the cities that had grown up around them—had been built somewhere near the Nests.

Gil threw her silver stylus aside and began to pace the room. Her shoulder ached, the muscles violently complaining of the renewed rigors of practice; her hands hurt, blistered from the sword hilt, her fingers so stiffened that it was hard to write. Her hair fell in a sweaty straggle around her face, to hang in a sloppy braid behind. And her head ached, blinded by fatigue and worry and fear. She knew how Ingold must have felt, trying desperately to contact Lohiro and unable to do so, forced to baby-sit the convoy down from Karst when he could have been on his way to Quo already. *And,* she reflected wryly, *getting damn little thanks for his trouble.*

Why do I care? she wondered desperately. *Why am I concerned, why do I fear this way for him and grieve with him in his grief? This world is none of mine and I'll be returning to my own, to a place where the sun shines and there's always enough to eat. Why do I hurt this way?*

But as Ingold always said, the question was the answer. *Always provided,* she added wryly, *you want an answer that badly.*

"Gil?"

She looked up. Minalde blew out the touchlight she carried and stepped through the thin veil of its smoke. She looked white and tired, as if from exhausting labor. As she stepped into the tiny circle of the lamplight, Gil could see she had been crying.

There was no need to ask why. Gil knew there'd been a Council that evening, and Alde was still dressed for it, the high-necked black velvet of her gown sewn with the gold eagles of the House of Dare that glittered as if she had been sprinkled with fire. The braided coils of her hair flashed with jewels. This was Alde as Queen, and very different from the girl in her thin peasant skirts and worn bodice who hurried so eagerly through the corridors of the Keep.

She brought up a folding chair and sat down, mechanically stripping the rings from her fingers and her ears, her face as unmoving as wax. Gil sat opposite her, watching in

225

silence, toying self-consciously with her curlicued silver hairpin.

After a long time Alde said shakily, "I wish he wouldn't do this to me." Her trembling fingers dropped a ring, a signet carved out of a single blood ruby.

"How did the Council go?" Gil asked gently, to get her talking.

Alde shook her head, pressing her folded hands against her mouth to keep it from trembling. Finally she steadied her voice. "I don't know why it keeps on hurting me when he gets like this, but it does. Gil, I *know* I'm right. Maybe I am wanting—wanting to eat my cake and still have it to look at, at the expense of our allies. But they can afford to feed their own troops. We can't, not if we're going to have enough seed in the spring to mean anything. And yes, I know we had trade commitments to them for corn and cattle, but those were made years ago, and everything's changed. And yes, I know I'm trying to welch out of a bad debt when the going gets tough, but God damn it, Gil, what can we do?" Her voice rose, cracking, skimming almost unnoticed over the first swearword Gil had ever heard her utter. "But I'm not going to buy our way out of those debts by signing away part of the Realm! I've learned enough from you and Govannin about legal precedents for that. If I sign that treaty . . ."

"Wait a minute," Gil said, trying to cut the rising flood of fury and pain and guilt. "What treaty? What part of the Realm do they want you to sign away?"

The words broke the flow of Alde's emotions as a rock breaks the coming of a wave, reducing its force. She sat still for a moment, her white fingers stirring at the little heap of jewels before her, like miniature coals dyed with reflected flames of crimson, azure, and gold. "Penambra," she said finally.

"Penambra!" Gil cried, horrified. "That's like selling New Orleans to the Cubans! That seaport's the key to the whole Round Sea. If you sign it over to the Alketch, they'd hold that whole coastline!"

Alde looked up hopelessly. "I know," she said. "And I know it's flooded and there's nothing there but the Dark and ghouls and ruins. It's worthless to us; we can't hold it if we don't get a—a bridgehead at Gae. Alwir says that

226

would be paying the Emperor of Alketch in counterfeit coin, and we can always take it back. He wants a bargain with Stiarth at any cost."

"You didn't sign, did you?" Gil asked worriedly.

Alde shook her head. "Afterward, he said I'd ruined us all." She sniffed and wiped at her nose, the fine-carved nostrils red and raw. "He said I'd condemned us to rotting here in the Keep while the Realm was hacked apart piecemeal between the White Raiders and Alketch, all because I wanted to cling to—to the pride of being Queen . . ."

The slight quavering of her voice told its tale. Alwir's accusations generally had their drop of truth, enough truth to plant doubt in his opponents' minds as to their own motivations. As a girl, Minalde had probably preened herself about being Queen—pride was part of the office. And, being Alde, she had probably felt guilty about it and maybe even handed her brother the wedge by admitting it to him. *Bastard*, Gil thought dispassionately.

"Well, look," Gil reasoned. "If Stiarth gets his nose out of joint and pulls out completely—which he won't, since the Emperor would love to have somebody else fight his battles for him—what have we lost? The whole scheme of invading the Nests is a gamble to begin with."

Alde's cheeks got very pink, and she looked away quickly. "That's what he said," she murmured. "That I—I wanted to ruin the expedition."

"Why?" Gil asked, more startled than sympathetic. A lack of sympathy was one of her less endearing traits, she told herself bitterly a moment later.

Alde leaned her face on her hands. "He says that Ingold's poisoned my mind. And maybe he's right. A year ago . . ."

"A year ago you had somebody else to carry the ball for your people," Gil said roughly.

Alde shook her head miserably. "Gil, he knows more about this than I do."

"Like hell! He knows a lot, but he knows only what he wants to know, and that's the truth." When Alde neither moved nor spoke, Gil went on more gently. "Look—have you eaten anything this evening? . . . Then your blood-sugar level's bottomed out hours ago. I'll scrounge something for you in the barracks, and you should have a glass of wine and go to bed."

But Alde still didn't move. Almost in a whisper, she said, "He cared for me, Gil. He used to care for me."

He cared for you the way a man cares for a twenty-dollar screwdriver, Gil thought coldly, *because it's a good tool.* But since that was what lay at the heart of her friend's wretchedness, she did not add to it by saying so. Instead she asked, "How did Maia take it?"

Alde looked up, her eyes suddenly almost frightened. "He was furious," she said softly. "I've never seen him so angry, not even when Alwir turned them away from the gates. He never showed it, not while Stiarth was there, but afterward . . . He's usually so gentle. Govannin will use that against Alwir." She shook her head again tiredly. "So that's one more thing," she went on. "I can't cause schism in the Keep by siding with them against him. I don't know why I'm still upset about it . . ."

You're upset because he wants you to be, Gil thought sourly, then turned, her quick ears catching the soft tap of feet in the passage outside. "Who's there?" The walk was that of a woman, not one of the Guards.

"Gil-Shalos?" A grimy little blear of flame appeared in the dark doorway, shining on an unkempt twist of dark-red hair. "They say my lady Alde's here."

"Come in, Lolli," Alde sat up straighter in her chair as the big Penambran woman came quietly into the room. "How's Snelgrin?"

It never ceased to surprise Gil how even the most humble of the Keep's inhabitants seemed to accept Minalde as Queen and friend at once. She'd seen Alde making her rounds of the Keep by day, usually with Tir on her hip, sitting on the benches by the pools along the watercourses of the Aisle, talking to the women as they did their washing. Gil had come into the barracks of the Guards, or those of the troops of Alwir's household, and found Alde sitting deep in sympathetic conversation with some scarred old veteran of a dozen sacked towns.

"My lady, he's not good," Lolli said quietly. "I had to come and see you. You know about people, about sickness, maybe?"

Alde shook her head.

"But you're learned? You've read books?"

"Some. A little. But I couldn't . . ."

"I've spoken to Maia, but he had no answer for me. And that Bektis, that wizard . . . Begging your pardon, my lady, for he's of your House, but he couldn't so much as charm away warts, much less—this."

"What?" Alde asked gently. "What's the matter with Snelgrin? Is he ill?"

"No!" the woman cried in despair. "He's fit as a fiddle, he's strong—but he's different. He changed, after that night."

"If he spent the night outside," Gil remarked in a quiet voice, "it's no surprise."

"No," Lolli insisted. "Bektis may say that, but not like this." Her brown eyes sought Alde's, pleading for her to understand. "It—sometimes there are times I think it ain't Snel there at all. That it ain't him."

"What?" both girls cried in approximate unison, and Alde asked, "How can you tell?"

"I don't know! If I knew, it would be easier." Lolli buried her face in her big, red-knuckled hands, and her voice came muffled through her palms. "He forgets things, things he should know, like—like passages around the Keep, or why he was out that night. Sometimes he just wanders. I don't know what to do, my lady! And he won't hardly speak. Only now and then, and it's—different."

Gil's eyes met Alde's over the bowed red head. "Shock?" she asked softly, and Alde nodded.

"It's not just the shock of it." Lolli raised her face to them, her eyes pleading. "It's not just the night he went outside, waiting for the Dark to have him. When he touches me . . ." A look of loathing passed across her face, her lips squaring back from her teeth in shuddery horror. "I can't stand it. We haven't been married but a few weeks, and we only wanted to be happy. Now it seems—I can't stand for it to touch me. It isn't him, and, by God, I don't know what it is. Oh, Snel." she whispered hopelessly. "Snel."

Alde's hands rested on the woman's shoulders, rubbing the taut, quivering muscles. Lolli lowered her head again, sobbing quietly under Alde's touch like a frightened beast. For a long time there was silence, broken only by her moans, but something in the quality of the silence prickled

Gil's hair, as if she felt herself being watched. Gold slivers of light moved in the tangled copper hair and picked out the knuckles of Alde's hands and the deep iris blue of her eyes as her gaze crossed Gil's. Her look was troubled, seeking advice.

"Lolli," Gil asked after a moment, "where is he now? Where's Snel?"

The woman only shook her head wearily. "The Lord, He knows," she murmured. "Walks all the time, nights. Just walks. Dead eyes in a dead face. He's my husband and I loved him, but I won't be alone with him in bed."

"No, of course not," Alde agreed. "Listen, Lolli, are you still in the same cell you were, up on the fifth level? Then what I suggest you do for now is move. Take your things and find another cell, preferably with someone else. Do you think Winna would let you sleep on her floor for the night?" She named the girl who was the head of the Keep herdkids, in whose company she and Gil had often seen Lolli. "I'll ask Janus to have his Guards keep an eye out for Snel, and when someone finds him, Gil and I will talk to him. Maybe it's just that he's still strange from the shock. It was only a day or two ago . . ."

"Two days," the woman whispered. "And two ghastly nights."

"Come." Alde reached under Lolli's arms and coaxed her to her feet. "You need rest now."

Alde's just had a political knock-down-drag-out and been cursed by the one man whose opinion of her she took as her own, Gil thought wonderingly, *and she's still got sympathy and more to spare for other peoples' marital problems.* Following in the wake of the two other women, with lamp in hand to locate the rabbit warren of the orphans, Gil could only shake her head in amazement at the young Queen's capacity for helping others.

At this hour the corridors were deserted, the cells that lined them silent. Gil shivered, oppressed by that terrible darkness, at the same time wondering at herself. She had walked deep-night watch many times and never before felt the weight of this eerie dread. Twice she started, turning in her tracks like a frightened cat, but the lamplight showed nothing in the massed shadows behind. Still she found herself prey to a curious sensation of impending horror and shrank from every blind turn of the twisting passageways.

The orphans' compound was up on the fourth level. Lamps had been lighted there. Winna, a girl of seventeen, sat among the heaped blankets in a ragged nightdress, trying vainly to comfort a sobbing child of not much more than Tir's age. Other children huddled sleepily around them, upset and uneasy, as all children were in the face of a nightmare. Winna looked up quickly as her second in command, Tad the herdkid, admitted the newcomers.

"What is it?" Alde asked.

Winna shook her head. "It seems to be the night for nightmares, that's all. First Lydris, then Tad, and now Prognor."

"I didn't have a *nightmare*," Tad protested, anxious to set himself off from his inferiors.

"No," Winna corrected, "you're too old for it to be called a nightmare—but a bad dream, anyway. How can I help you, Alde?"

Here was another one, Gil thought, *who, with all her own griefs, had concern to spare.*

Winna listened gravely to Alde's whispered explanations and Lolli's less coherent fears, nodding her head and stroking the fair hair of the child in her lap. The pale faces and wide eyes that floated disembodied in the thick shadows of the room were those of the orphans whose parents had perished in the ruins of Gae and the massacre at Karst. *Peter Pan's Lost Boys,* Gil thought; *tough little survivors of the ruin of the world.* As she and Alde left, her last sight of the cell was of Winna chivying a place among the children for Lolli to sleep, and Tad and some other child volunteering to share their blankets.

"What do you think?" Gil asked as she and Alde headed back into the darkness of the mazes. The single bobbing flame of their lamp threw monstrous gargoyle repetitions of them in the walls behind, trailing them like inept spies.

Alde shook her head, her fingers working loose the main coil of her hair, the braided knots of it falling like skeined silk over the blackness and fire of her gown. "I don't know," she said quietly. "But Lolli's afraid. Is it possible that the mere fear of the Dark could have driven Snelgrin mad?"

"It's what I was afraid of," Gil said. "And believe me, the idea of a madman wandering around the Keep at night does not do wonders for my sense of well-being."

"And *you're* armed," Minalde added. "I think the next thing we should do is talk to Janus. But if Snelgrin is mad, what then? Do we lock him up? Feed him through the winter on rations that could cut into the spring seed? Have someone cut his throat, like—" She broke off, but Gil could finish the sentence. *Like the Icefalcon cut Medda's.* Medda, whose mind the Dark had devoured, had been Alde's nurse from childhood. On the road from Karst to Renweth, no one could have looked after a stumbling zombie, and there would have been no point to it. Alde knew this, and had known it at the time. But Gil realized that she had never forgiven the Icefalcon for being the one assigned to the job.

"Is he dangerous?"

"I don't know. Is there a way to find out?"

"Sure," Gil said cynically. "The authorities in my part of the world used it all the time. If a man flipped out, they'd wait till he actually killed somebody, then lock him up. Otherwise they couldn't know for sure."

Alde stared at her in disbelief. "You're not serious."

"Cross my heart."

"That's abominable!"

Gil, who'd had a grandmother murdered by known drug addicts in a parking lot for the contents of her purse, shrugged. "Yeah."

They passed a makeshift stairway that led to the upper levels, the hole where it pierced the ceiling hung with laundry to catch the rising drift of warmer air. There was no light from above, but the next stairway, also a rickety wood one, leading down, admitted a faint glimmer of candlelight from a curtained cell door, and a man's voice singing a lullaby. The girls climbed down, the darkness of the corridor below yawning like a well to receive them. As the winds of the ventilation stirred at their long hair, Gil felt it again, that sense of impending evil—shivering horror like a subsonic note, just below the level of perception. She remembered what Winna had said about three of the children having nightmares.

"Alde," she asked quietly, "can you feel anything?"

"Like what?" Alde stopped. The shadows of the hallway closed around them.

"Just stand still a minute."

Perhaps forty seconds trickled by. The silence was as audible as the drawing of breath in a room that should be empty. Gil felt an intruding consciousness of the vastness of the Keep and of the darkness filling its halls and cells. Alde shivered. "No," she said. "Let's go, Gil. What do you feel?"

"I think the Dark are in force outside," Gil said. "It felt like this the night of their attack. Rudy felt it, and so did Ingold. Tad told me later he'd had nightmares that night."

Alde looked around quickly. "What about the gates?" she whispered. "Will they hold?"

"I think so. Ingold's spells are still on them." But remembering the terrible darkness of that roaring tunnel, Gil shuddered nonetheless. More than anything else now, she wanted Ingold back at the Keep for his power against the Dark and for the simple strength of his presence, his power against her own fears.

"Where would Janus be?"

"The barracks." They were walking again, hurrying past doorway after dark doorway, around blind corners concealing yet more darkness, then down another flight of stairs, this time of the original stone of the Keep, broad and black and smooth. The green eyes of cats flashed in the lampflame, swift, gliding movement beyond the circle of light. Gil found herself fighting the panic urge to draw her sword. "We should wake Alwir and tell him, too."

"Yes." Alde moved along quietly before Gil, holding the lamp, its flame leaping in answering glitters of gold from the embroidery of her gown. "He should not have long gone to bed. And if the Dark are outside— Oh!" she gasped as they turned into the main corridor of the Royal Sector and saw something small and white that moved determinedly toward them at floor level. "You little beast, you!"

Even down the length of almost pitch-black corridor, Gil could recognize Tir, crawling with his usual terrapin-like fixity of purpose toward the nearest precipice. He could not quite walk yet, but he had mastered the technique of escaping his cradle. Only his white gown showed through the darkness as a bobbing blur, like a bunny on a dark night.

Then they saw movement in the darkness behind him.

At first Gil wasn't sure—a man, she thought. He had something in his hand, and he had emerged without a sound from the room that was Minalde's. She never knew how she saw his eyes in the dark, but she did.

By the time Alde screamed, Gil was halfway up the corridor, her sword in her hand. Blurredly, she recognized Snelgrin, and saw that what he had in his hand was a hatchet. He must have seen her coming and heard Alde's screaming, but those fixed, empty eyes were on the baby a few yards in front of him, and he moved quickly. Gil wasn't sure how she managed, but she caught the hem of Tir's gown and bowled him out of the way against the corridor wall as the hatchet cracked sparks from the stone floor where he had been. Too close for blade work, she turned the sword in her hand and pommeled the man across the face with the weighted grip. She saw his nose break and the flesh gape open, but the dead eyes never blinked. Cold and paralyzing fear went through her. She tried to step back, but he caught her by the hair, his strength making nothing of her weight, and she felt her head hit the wall with a crack. Tir was screaming now, too, wild, shrill screams of terror, as Snelgrin turned back toward him with his hatchet, his empty face all glittering with blood.

Someone wrenched the sword from Gil's stunned hands. Like a berserker, Alde fell on the man, hacking inexpertly but fiercely in burning rage. Snelgrin staggered back, raising his arms jerkily to protect his face. People were pouring into the corridor, voices shouting, lights jigging crazily over the walls. Tir's screams spiraled through the darkness like a drill. As if in a fever-dream, Gil saw the thickset Snelgrin swat Minalde out of his way as if she had been a moth, duck his head, and race blindly into the darkness that swallowed him.

Gil scrambled to her feet and ran to gather Tir from where he huddled, shrieking, by the wall. He appeared to be unhurt. Then a wild-haired madwoman with blood trickling from her cut lip tore him from Gil's arms and crumpled slowly to the floor, clutching him to her breast.

234

"Alde," Gil whispered, putting her arms about the girl, "he's okay, he's fine. Are you all right?"

The dark, tangled head nodded, and somebody grabbed Gil roughly by the arm. "What is it?" Alwir demanded, his face drained of blood. Behind him, his troopers came milling into the corridor, not all of them dressed, but all of them armed. Stiarth was there, the smell of woman still on him, hurriedly wrapping himself in a night robe, his dignity much impaired.

"Snelgrin," Gil said shortly. "He's mad."

"Who?" the Imperial Nephew demanded.

"The man who was outside that night has gone mad," Gil explained breathlessly, as Alwir went to his knees to gather his sobbing sister into his arms. He made no attempt to lift her, only held her as she clung to him in storms of hysterics.

"But why?"

"Because . . ." Gil began, and stopped, her mind leaping to other things. Scarcely aware that she spoke aloud, she said, "He's gone to open the gates."

"What?"

But she had turned and was fleeing down the black corridors like a madwoman.

How well does Snelgrin know the ways of the Keep? she wondered, dodging blindly through the tangled mazes that weeks of investigation had made as familiar to her as the freeways of home. *Will he risk cutting through the Aisle to save time? Will Melantrys be able to stop him at the gate? How mad is Snelgrin? Is he ahead of me,* she wondered, *or behind me now?*

There was no time to think. She ducked through an empty cell that she knew had a ladder down to the Aisle, heedless of her horror of heights or her knowledge that the wood of the thing was several hundred years old and crumbling with dry rot. *It's the closest,* she told herself grimly, *and the most you can do is break your leg on the floor.*

The wood crunched faintly in her grip, and the ladder swayed drunkenly under her weight. The Aisle was a void of air around and below her, through which she could faintly hear voices calling, feet running, and the thin, distant cries of a terrified child. Training had improved her

235

reflexes; when the rung cracked under her foot, she automatically jumped clear, landing lightly and turning, listening to the darkness.

No footfalls. No panic flight. Torches burned by the gates, but there was no sign of the captain of the watch. *Had she run to join the hunt?* Gil wondered. *God help us, she'd be right to do so.* The idea of a homicidal madman wandering the labyrinths of the Keep was almost as terrifying as the thought of the Dark breeding there. If he went up instead of down, he could live for years on the fifth level without anyone seeing him at all.

Except his victims, Gil thought.

Yet she was certain he had not gone up. From where she stood now by the Church doors, she could see the gates, tiny and infinitely distant in their flickering halo of torchlight. Not quite knowing why, she broke into a run again.

She was halfway up the Aisle when she saw him. He must have learned the mazes of the Keep well, for he slipped from a doorway to the right of the gates, his face still gouted and sticky with his wounds. She could see that he still had his hatchet and now carried a heavy ax as well. Crouching like an animal, he twisted the locking rings and pulled on the inner doors. They opened easily on their soundless hinges. He pushed them fully wide, shoved something under the right-hand door, and swung the axe. Metal clanged on metal.

My God, he's wedging it open!

Gil shouted, an incoherent animal sound of fury, and threw herself those last hundred feet.

Snelgrin looked up, his body still bent. Sparks flew from the iron as he drove the last few blows at the wedge. Gil had a confused vision of his face, the expression all the more terrifying because of its oddness, as if a being without facial muscles were trying to counterfeit expression. Drool slobbered from the slack mouth. The man uttered a wheezing grunt and turned to plunge back into the pitch-darkness of the gate tunnel moments before Gil reached him.

Can it see in the dark? she wondered as she sprinted up the steps and hurled herself into the darkness at his heels. But with the inner gate wedged open, there was time for neither speculation nor delay.

She knew where the locking rings were on the outer gates, and her hands grabbed flesh there. She'd felt his strength before, and now in the utter blackness it was terrifying, overwhelming. Hands ripped at her, pushing and tearing; she felt the ax scrape her leg as she scrambled to catch hold of his arms and body. She was yelling, shouting wildly in the darkness, praying the other Guards would show up before she was overpowered. The heavy body thrashed against hers, breath rasping hoarsely in her ears, the stink of his unwashed jerkin filling her nostrils. For a moment, they were locked in unequal combat; then she felt herself falling; the breath was driven from her, and an avalanche of flaming stars seemed to roar before her eyes. As if those blinding constellations actually gave light, she could see Snelgrin's face twitching, piglike, above her own, the eyes popping with surprise. There was an arrow driven through his Adam's apple. He choked, pawed at it, and made soundless gobbling motions, sweat gleaming on his face. He staggered a step or two to maul at the locking mechanisms of the shut outer gates, and another arrow appeared as if by magic through his temple as he turned his head.

Ten points for somebody, Gil thought and fainted.

Everyone in the Keep seemed to be around her when she came to. The roaring of voices was like the sea in a narrow place, pouring through the bare bones of her aching skull. The torchlight was blinding. She shut her eyes again and tried to turn her face away.

A wet towel was laid over her forehead. Annoyed, Gil tried to strike it aside, and a bony hand grasped her wrist. "Easy, child," the paper-dry voice of Bishop Govannin whispered. Gil tried to rise, rolled over, and promptly vomited. The hard hands caught her shoulders and steadied her without a word.

"What happened?" Gil asked when she finally could speak. Her head felt light, her body ached. Her face, she found, was covered with the scratches from Snelgrin's fingernails where he'd clawed her. She hadn't even felt that during the fight.

"Snelgrin is dead." The skeletal fingers pushed aside the clammy straggle of hair from Gil's forehead. "As we all would be by this time, had you not followed him."

Beyond the Bishop's grave, narrow face, Maia of Thran swam into being in the torchlight, his longbow still strung in his crippled hand. "Snel vanished through the gates just as I emerged from the Church," he said. "I was afraid I would not get in range in time."

"Yeah, so was I." Gil looked around. It wasn't everyone in the Keep, just most of them, who crowded around her. All the watches of the Guards were there, it seemed, with most of the Red Monks, Alwir's whole private army, and most of Maia's. Melantrys' face was cut, and a lump the size of a walnut was forming on her left temple. Stiarth of Alketch now wore a kind of flowered sarong, and Alwir had his velvet cloak over his nightshirt, looking rather crumpled and human in his bare feet with their well-kept toenails. And apparently three-quarters of the men, women, and children of the Keep had all turned out in nightshirts if they had them and scantly draped in bedding if they didn't. Gil saw Tad, Bendle Stooft's rotund widow, and Winna with her yellow hair hanging in plaits over her back. And all were talking.

Janus came back from the gate. Caldern and Bok the carpenter were still trying to hammer the wedge free with a counterwedge driven in from the other side. Snelgrin's body had been hauled out of the passage. His face lay where the torchlight could fall on it, but its expression was nothing human. Gil turned away, feeling she would be sick again.

She heard Bektis' voice, speaking low and swiftly. "I am sure of it, my lord. The Dark are gathered outside in force. The emanations of their wrath must have driven him mad . . ." She turned her head and saw him standing with Alwir. Bektis was immaculate in his gray velvet gown, with every hair of his waist-length silken beard in place. *Interesting*, she thought. *Alwir came pelting to the battle, even if he did have to do it in his nightie, while Bektis hung tight in the Royal Sector until the all-clear sounded. Probably with a bed across the door. Well, well.*

"No," a soft voice said behind her, and she looked up, to meet Maia's eyes. The Bishop of Penambra sat back on

238

his heels, watching Alwir, Bektis, and Govannin begin to squabble in the orange circle of the torchlight. "Snel never recovered from the night he spent outside the gates, did he, Gil-Shalos?"

Gil shook her head. "His wife spoke to us."

"She spoke to me as well," the Bishop said. He glanced over at Lolli, his dark eyes gleaming in the shadows. When he and his people had come to the Keep, he had resumed the Church fashion of shaving his face and head; Gil had only recently become used to seeing that long, narrow, hollow-cheeked face without its tangled black beard. "She is a Penambran and, like me, knows what it is to sleep outside and await the coming of the Dark. I thought it might have been because he was alone . . . but I knew Snel, a little. He was a man absolutely without imagination. It takes a degree of sensitivity to be driven mad. But I did not know." He folded his crippled hands on his knees and rested his chin upon them, his long body rolled into an ungainly ball of bones as he sat on his heels. Gil leaned back against the wall behind her, her head aching, her whole body shivering with reaction.

The Bishop of Penambra went on in a lower voice. "Bektis, of course, is useless as a healer of minds. But I have heard that Ingold Inglorion is good at such things. It is heresy for me to say so." He grinned with his white teeth. "But I regret his absence."

"You and me both, friend." Gil sighed.

He looked at her curiously for a moment, then turned his eyes again to the sprawled body with its puckered, elongated expression and vacant eyes. "It is well known that the Dark devour the mind," he said softly. "But this is the first time that I have heard that they can put something else in its place."

CHAPTER FOURTEEN

Rudy Solis and Ingold Inglorion entered the City of Wizards just after noon of the following day. From the hills above, they saw the sea mists roll back, revealing that small town—a village, really, grouped around its famous school—as it slowly emerged from veils of pewter, pearl, and white.

Even from the hills, Rudy did not think he had ever seen a place so completely destroyed by the Dark.

In Gae, the houses had been crumpled, smoke-blackened, or had had holes blown in roofs and walls. Here he could not find a single dwelling that had been left standing, not a roof that had not been ripped from its walls and thrown with blinding violence into the rubble-strewn streets. In the damp sea climate, weeds were already rank among the broken stone.

He and Ingold stood for a long time on the last rolling summit of the hill. Silvery grass rippled around their feet, but there was no sound here but the mewing of the sea birds and the boom of breakers. The air smelled of salt. A drift of mist obscured the town, then blew clear, as if unveiling the bare bones with a mocking flourish. Screeching whirlwinds of gulls rose from the ruins, to settle back a few moments later. Other gulls, wailing in their thin piping voices, hung motionless on stretched white wings against a featureless sky. Rudy wondered what the place had looked like the day after the attack had happened. Had the gulls blanketed the town like a visitation of death angels to pick the corpses, or had the rats been there first?

He hardly dared look at Ingold.

The old man stood beside him like something that had been carved from stone. The gray of the sky seemed to bleed the color out of everything, leaving only the blue of his eyes under their short reddish lashes. There was no expression on his face, but not for anything in the world would Rudy have spoken to him then. After a time, Ingold moved off, taking the downward path without a word.

Bodies were scattered throughout the city. From the way the bones lay, it was clear that scavengers had fought over them, worrying them to pieces. Mechanically, Rudy identified tracks—fox, rat, coyote, and crow. After this long in the open, there was little stink and few flies. He could see Ingold checking the signs as unemotionally as an insurance inspector, studying how the fire blackening striped the walls where it had been thrown or swept from a staff, instead of crawling up them in a regular pattern to concentrate on the roof beams, as it did in other places where the inhabitants had simply set everything they owned alight, and how the bones lay in groups of two or three at most, where they had not fallen singly. The wizards, it seemed, had not even had time to band together to make a stand.

It surprised Rudy a little how small Quo was. At no time could the City of Wizards have housed more than a couple thousand, of whom, according to Ingold, about a third were wizards or students. Small, fanciful stone houses had grouped around a main square or bordered the crooked lanes that trailed on out of the town. Only in the center of Quo were there large buildings, whose splintered frames loomed before the belated pilgrims as they made their way through the overgrown rubble of the streets. There the school proper rambled along the edge of the cove, buildings alternating with a long colonnade, through whose tinted pillars could be glimpsed the iron-edged sea. At the far left, the gatehouse slumped like a smashed sand castle, flanked by the kicked-in ruin of some mighty building of many storeys and turrets, all but buried now under the trailing vines of its feral roof gardens. To the right, at the end of the long curve of the bay, the black stump of a truncated tower stood alone on the farthest point of land.

It was for this tower that Ingold unhesitatingly made.

Since they had entered Quo, he had not spoken, and his face was still and very calm, as if this ruin had belonged to strangers and had not been the only home his

241

heart had known for most of his adulthood. The torn hem of his mantle, stained with the dragon's blood, brushed passingly over a picked skull and broken staff that lay half-buried in rubble and weeds. Behind him, Rudy shivered with a frightened sense of *déjà vu*.

Forn's Tower was also smaller than Rudy had thought. The buildings surrounding it were little more extensive than a couple of good-sized houses put together, built on the big square knoll that jutted out into the sea. The tower itself, or what was left of it, looked no larger than one fair-sized room stacked on top of another. The black, curved shell of its walls extended thirty feet into the air. From the square below, Rudy could trace the broken stairs winding up its side. As he climbed behind Ingold through the ruins, he looked out over the half-moon beach and saw the steps leading down from the school with their twining patterns of inlaid stone and, half-buried at the tide line, the remains of a crab-eaten skeleton.

The two men reached the top of the knoll. The tower and the buildings surrounding it had been blasted and gutted, and the black stone spew of it lay scattered everywhere. *Granted, the place was built later than the Keep, and by another technology entirely,* Rudy thought, stooping to pick up a splinter of rock and then hurrying his steps to catch up with Ingold again. *But it might have been thought that the spells of the Archmage could have kept the Dark out, as the spells Ingold set closed the doors to them.*

Ahead of him, Ingold walked through the ruins, following the line of corridors he had traversed in other years with the light, unthinking tread of a man in a hurry to do something else, passing doors he had knocked at casually, back in the days when those rooms had housed people he knew. He barely glanced at the open ruins and the cracked walls.

He's like a man with a mortal wound, Rudy thought, frightened. *He's still numb from the shock. The nerve ends are still cauterized. God help him when he starts to hurt.*

In front of them the floor fell away.

It had been blasted upward, the torn beam ends clearly indicating that the explosion had come from below. Standing on the crumbling lip of the pit, Rudy could look down into the labyrinths of the lower vaults and see squat pillars and worn red tile floors, the dust of ages that had accumulated since the tower's founding, muddied by the sea rains. Below them the torn flooring revealed a second vault, founded on the ancient heart of the knoll. But instead of the gray of buried rock, smooth black basalt reflected the distant sky. From deep below, a draft of warmer air blew upward onto Rudy's face, bringing with it the smell of a yet deeper darkness.

Beside him, Ingold said, "I should have guessed."

Rudy turned his head quickly. The wizard looked calm and rather detached, with the rising breath from below stirring at his ragged white hair. Rudy said hastily, "There's no way you could have known."

"Oh, I don't know," the wizard said absently. "I certainly got myself into enough trouble for warning everyone else of the possibility. I don't know why it shouldn't have occurred to me that all of the old schools of wizardry were built in cities that were later destroyed by the Dark."

"Yeah, but a lot of cities were destroyed by the Dark," Rudy argued quickly, hearing, under the deep calm of that scratchy voice, a note he didn't like, like the first fissure of an earthquake. "They knew the direction your research took. Any one of them . . ."

Ingold sighed and shut his eyes. Very quietly, he said, "Go away, Rudy."

"Look . . ." Rudy began, and the eyes opened. In them was a black depth of pain that amounted almost to madness.

Gently the rusty voice repeated, "Go away."

Rudy fled, terrified, as if an idly lifted pebble had turned into an H-bomb in his hand. When he reached the bottom of the knoll and looked back, he could not see that the old man had moved.

For a long time, it seemed, Rudy wandered the empty spaces of the ruined City of Wizards, listening to the booming of the sea. The crash of the breakers was somehow comforting, an echo of California winters. Whether it was because of the familiar damp cold of the seashore, the salt smell, or the magic that still lay over the town like an enormous silence, he felt at peace, as if he had come home. *Home,* he thought, his boots making barely a sound on the colored marble marquetry of the pavement. *To find home in ruins, and family—the family I should have known and never did—dead!* He looked back at the solitary figure on the knoll, very dark against the white of the empty sky.

Quo—gone. Everyone you knew and loved and respected—gone. The Archmage gone—Lohiro, whom you loved like a son. The only ones left are novices like me, charlatans like Bektis, goodywives like Kara and her mother. Alwir's army is scratched, or worse, going into battle against the Dark with no backup, leaving the Keep unguarded for the Raiders or the Empire of Alketch or the Dark. And only you left, the last wizard, a lost soul like I was in California.

And yes, you might have guessed, but no, it wasn't your fault. But he knew already that Ingold would never believe that.

Heartsick, Rudy turned away. He explored for a time the roofless remains of the ancient school, lecture halls where the carved benches had been swept and scarred by fire, laboratories and workrooms whose furnishings were torn and twisted by wild and incomprehensible violence, glittering in the chill, pale light with shattered glass and broken gemstones, and libraries, their couches and seats ripped, charred, and acid-eaten, with the leaves of books strewing the rain-damp pavements or plastered like wads of crumpled leaf mast in corners. In one such chamber he found a harp, half-hidden in a wall niche and protected by fallen timbers, the only whole and untouched thing in that world of ruin and desolation.

As he carried it down the steps, on which moss was already beginning to grow, to where they had tethered the burro, it came to him what this ruin meant. Without the school, later generations of wizards, no matter what their inborn talents, would be like him, untaught callers of fire, hopeless dreamers groping for a mode of expression that they could not find.

Or worse, he thought. *A mage will have magic . . . If you can't find good love, then you will have bad.*

Wind rippled in his long hair and chilled his fingers as

he packed the harp onto Che's back. They could take at least one thing, he thought, from the ancient city by the Western Ocean. One thing, out of all this destruction. He pulled the coarse, heavy fur of his buffalohide coat tighter around his neck and stood for a time in the shifting, patchy light of white sun and opal mist, staring out at the sea.

He thought of the Keep of Dare.

Not as he had often remembered it—the candlelit darkness of Alde's quiet rooms and the mazes stretching in shadows within those ancient walls—but from outside, as he had seen it only once, the morning he and Ingold had taken the road for Quo. An almost cinematic image of it formed in his thoughts—black and square and solid against the snow that lay thick around its walls, impenetrable, enigmatic, self-contained. He saw the black loom of the Snowy Mountains behind it and smelled the cold, biting freshness of the pine-sharp glacier winds. And with the image, he felt a need blossom in his heart, a yearning to be there, as urgent as lust or starvation. But he felt it from outside himself, as if the thoughts of another had been projected into his heart.

Looking up, he saw again the black and curiously regular shape of the knoll by the sea, the dark stump of Forn's Tower. Through the lacework of the bare trees he saw the small figure standing, arms raised, mantle billowing in the freshening winds from the sea. And he knew that what he felt was a call, and that the calling came from the man who stood alone at the heart of the last ruined citadel of wizardry. The last wizard, an exile gypsy vagabond with a sword at his hip and his back to the wall, was calling them all—the second-raters, the flunk-outs, the novices, the charlatans, and the goodywives. He was calling anyone, in fact, capable of hearing—calling them to meet him at the Keep of Dare.

Ingold came striding down from the knoll soon after, his face set and harsh, his eyes bitter and frighteningly cold, a stranger's eyes. Rudy scrambled off his perch on the rail of the colonnade to greet him, but there was nothing to greet in that blind, icy stare. "Come with me," Ingold ordered briefly. "There is one thing yet we must do."

The wizard scarcely spoke to Rudy again that afternoon.

Rudy fetched the burro in silence and in silence followed the old man down the blasted shore to the collapsed ruin beside the gatehouse. The terraced roofs had supported storey after storey of incomparable gardens, and these had fallen in on one another, tangling trees, masonry, flowers, earth, tumbled pillar, and broken beam into one colossal pyramid of wreckage. Ingold hunted around it until he found what had been a wide window that would still admit them to the ruined lower hall, then slipped like a cat among the precariously balanced blocks of half-fallen granite, working his way downward and inward. Rudy followed unquestioningly, although Ingold had bidden him neither to go nor to stay. In places, they could walk beneath ceilings that moved and groaned with the weight pressing on the damaged arches. In places, they had to climb piles of fallen rubble. Once they crouched to slide beneath a mighty lintel stone that was cracked right through the middle, supporting by equilibrium alone literally tons of colored stone, decked incongruously with dangling curtains of trailing yellow leaves. As he scrambled, panting, to keep up, Rudy half-feared that Ingold was seeking his own death in this place, for the wizard had turned suddenly strange and frightening, remote in his bitterness and rage. It was possible—logical, even—that he would arrange to perish with the others, in the city that had been his home.

But as they wriggled from the last rubble-clogged stairway into the broken vaults, Rudy understood why Ingold had come.

The bluish glow of witchlight slowly filled the long, narrow hall. It picked out the gold on the bindings of the books there, the smooth sheen of cured leather covers, and the spark of emerald or amethyst on decorated clasps. Like a ghost returned to the land of the living, Ingold moved down the rows of the reading tables, his blunt, scarred hands touching the books as a man might touch the face of a woman he had once loved.

It was obvious they couldn't take all. There were hundreds of volumes, the garnered wisdom of centuries. But, fatally incomplete as it had been, knowledge was the heart of Quo, as it was the heart of wizardry. To protect that knowledge was the reason for the city's existence, the justification for the rings of spells that circled the place so tightly that even after the death of every person there, the image of Quo could not be called in water or fire or gem.

Silently, Ingold touched the locks and chains that bound the books to their slanted desks, and the chains clattered faintly as they fell away. He brought two volumes back to where Rudy waited in the doorway and handed them to the younger man as if he were a nameless servant. "You'll have to come back for more," Ingold said curtly and turned away.

In all, they salvaged two dozen books. Rudy had no idea which they were, or why these were chosen and not others, but they were all large and heavy and loaded Che down unmercifully. Ingold scavenged material from a curtain to make rough satchels for himself and Rudy to carry what could not be put in the packs; after one look at the old man's face, Rudy dared not complain of the extra weight. When they crept from the rubble for the last time, Ingold turned back and wove spells of ward and guard over the whole of the ruin, that neither rain nor mold nor beasts should enter there, that all things should remain as they were, protected, until he should come again.

By then it was dark.

They camped on the open beach. If the Dark still lurked in that dead city, the ruins offered too many hiding places for them. And, Rudy thought, as line after line of the spelled circles of protection faded, glittering, into the air around the camp from the tips of Ingold's moving fingers, too many ghosts walked those silent streets for comfort. The night was cool, with the smell of distant rain; but over the ocean, the clouds broke to reveal a moon as rich and full as a silver fruit, its light frosting the billowed clouds into ski slopes of dazzling white. The crackling of the driftwood fire mingled with the slow surge of the waves in an echoing whisper of California.

Home, Rudy thought. *Home.*

He took the harp he'd found from its makeshift wrappings and ran hesitant fingers over its dark, shapely curves. The fire caught in the silver of its strings and touched the patterns of red enamel inlaid in the black wood of the sounding board. Like most Californians of a particular generation, Rudy had mastered sufficient guitar chords to get himself through epics like "Light My Fire"; but this instrument, he sensed, was designed for music of a kind and beauty beyond his comprehension.

He caught the glint of Ingold's watching eye. "Do you know how to play this?" Rudy asked hesitantly. "Or how it's tuned?"

"No," Ingold said harshly. "And I'll thank you not to play it, either, until you know what you're doing." He turned and looked out to sea.

Quietly, Rudy wrapped up the harp again. *Maybe Alde can teach me,* he thought. *Anyway, somebody at the Keep should know.* He felt as if he half-knew already what its sound should be and understood Ingold's not wanting to hear it bastardized.

"Its name is Tiannin," Ingold added after a moment, still not looking at him.

Tiannin, Rudy thought, the way-wind, the south wind on summer evenings that sowed restlessness and yearning in the heart like wind-borne seeds. He strapped the harp into the packs, with mental apologies to the hapless Che, and started back toward the fire. In the dark beyond their camp, he could see the broken line of the colonnade, his wizard's sight picking the merged patterns of flowers, hearts, and eyes that flowed down the colored stone. Against the sky, the dark bulk of Forn's Tower rose, like the burned stump of a dead tree under the azure glow of the sea horizon. Westward, moonlight gleamed on the surge of the waves, opal lace on the white breast of the beach.

Against the black wall of the cliffs, the elusive wink of starlight flashed on pointed metal.

Rudy's breath, his heart, and time itself seemed to stop. As if he had heard something, Ingold looked up, then out into the darkness that even to Rudy's sharpened perceptions revealed nothing more. The leaping brightness of the fire showed hope in his face that was almost terrible to behold. But for a long while, there was nothing in the night but the surge of the ocean and the wild hammering of Rudy's heart.

Then in the outer dark, that twinkle of pronged gold came again, with a stirring in the shadows along the beach. Rudy started to move, but a hand touched his wrist, stilling him, and he felt Ingold's fingers shaking.

A distant flicker of moonlight shone on the crescent end of a staff and was echoed still more brightly on loose, fire-colored hair. The wind picked up the motion of a dark cloak, billowing it briefly behind the man who walked along the ocean's edge, his tracks dark, enigmatic writing in the sand behind him.

Rudy knew their camp was wreathed in cloaking-spells fully as elusive as the walls of air that still circled the tomb of Quo, but the man looked straight toward them; in the moonlight, he could be seen to smile. The long stride quickened. Ingold's hand closed like a crushing vise on the bones of Rudy's wrist.

A dozen yards from the camp, Lohiro broke into a run. Ingold was on his feet instantly, striding out to meet him, catching his hands in greeting. Moonlight showed the old man and the young together, and gleamed on silver hair and gold and on the gnawed skeleton that lay half-buried in the sand at their feet.

"Ingold, you old vagabond," Lohiro said softly. "I knew you'd come."

"Why did you stay?" Ingold asked later, when they'd drawn the Archmage into the circle of their fire. Lohiro glanced up from the meal of pan bread and dried meat he had been devouring. To Rudy's eyes, he looked thin and hunted; the sharp face was worn down to its elegant bones. In the bright gold mane that fell almost to his shoulders, scattered streaks of silver caught the firelight. His eyes were as they had been in Rudy's vision in the crystal—wide and variegated blue, like a kaleidoscope, flecked all through with dark and light, and containing that odd, empty expressionlessness Rudy had noticed before. After seeing Ingold before the ruins of Forn's Tower, it made sense.

"Because I couldn't get away." Lohiro laughed, briefly and bitterly, at the sharpness of Ingold's glance. "Oh, the Dark are gone," he reassured them, in a taut, ironic voice. "They left the same night, clouds of them, their darkness blotting the stars. But I— It took the lot of us to weave the maze, my friend. One man couldn't pick that mesh apart."

"Yet they left?"

The skeletal white fingers gestured upward. "Through the air," he said. "Over the maze itself."

Ingold frowned. "How could they? The mazes extend for miles above the town."

Lohiro paused, then shook his head wearily. "I don't know," he said. "I don't know."

"Were you taken by surprise?" Ingold asked quietly.

The Archmage nodded. Behind him, his staff was stuck upright in the sand like a spear, the firelight glimmering off its points.

"By the Dark Ones from the Nest in the plains as well?"

"No." Lohiro raised his head, a little surprised at the question. "No, they had left their Nest to join the assault on Gae. Didn't you— Of course you wouldn't know." He sighed and rubbed his eyes. "We knew they'd left the plains to attack Gae—oh, the night it happened, I think. We'd all been going crazy for weeks. We had councils, committees, and research throughout the watches of the night. Teams of first-year students dug through the old records in the library. Thoth the Recorder turned out his most ancient documents, things so old they were held together by cobwebs and spells alone. It reminded me of that old joke about the miser whose favorite camel had swallowed a diamond." He shrugged. The points of his shoulder bones stood out sharply under the dark cloth of his robe. "But we turned up nothing much to the point. Only . . ." He hesitated, as if struggling with himself, and the dark, swooping brows were knotted in momentary pain.

"Only—what?"

Lohiro looked up again and shook his head. "It was very late. Thoth, Anamara, and I were still awake, but I think almost everyone else had gone to his bed. We'd all seen the fall of Gae, one way or another. There was a great heaviness over the town. Still, I don't think any of us were uneasy for our own safety. It happened—suddenly." He snapped his long fingers. "Like that. A great explosion—I've never seen the like. You saw what it did to the tower."

Ingold nodded, and his voice was very tired. "Like the experiments Hasrid used to do with blasting powder," he agreed. "You remember the stone house he wrecked?"

Lohiro grinned wryly. "That was nothing," he said, "compared to this. This was like—I don't know. It shook the foundations of the tower to its roots. I don't think I did anything, just sat there like a fool, and that probably saved me. Anamara ran to the door and threw it open . . . The darkness rolled over her like a big wave. I don't think she had time to make a sound."

Ingold looked away, and Rudy could see by the amber glow of the fire every small muscle, from temple to jaw, thrown suddenly into harsh prominence.

Lohiro went on. "I think Thoth called one burst of light—I don't know. Then . . ." He stopped, seeing Ingold's face. "I'm sorry," he said quietly, looking down at his hands. For a long moment the terrible silence was unbroken except for the surge of the waves on the shining wetness of the sand. "I didn't know."

Ingold turned back to him. His face was calm, but something had changed in his eyes. "It's nothing," he said. "It never was." And Lohiro, catching his eye, half-smiled, reassured.

Like a fine beading of diamonds, Rudy could see the sweat that suddenly glittered along the curve of the old man's temples.

"And that was it," the Archmage continued quietly. "I threw the strongest cloaking-spell I could find around myself and went under the desk and prayed." His long fingers wound together, unconsciously caressing the strong bones of those too-thin hands. "The next second there was a roar as if the whole side of the tower were going out—which it was, of course—and from where I was, I could see nothing but a kind of dark hurricane as they ripped the room to shreds. There was nothing else I could do, not even come out and fight them, for the room was a buzzing blackness of them, swarming like monster bees. Through the break in the wall of the tower, I could dimly see that the whole town lay under a cloud, as if I looked down into a storm." Wind blew in from the sea, a sudden gust of it stirring the thick, shining hair. Lohiro shook his head and raised those tired, empty eyes to meet Ingold's. "They

251

never had a chance," he said softly. "I could see lights, fire. I could smell the power, thrown out into that storm and burned. But there were so many of the Dark—so many. Someone turned himself into a dragon. From where I lay, I could see it, like a giant red eagle surrounded by hornets. But mostly—they were taken in their beds so suddenly that none of them knew."

The sea wind blew stronger, the voice of the waves imperceptibly louder on the offshore rocks. Rudy saw the clouds piling together to blot the blazing moon.

"And after," Ingold said quietly, "why didn't you get in touch with me?"

"I tried." The Archmage sighed. "The makers of the maze are dead, but the maze lives. I've been trying to contact you for weeks."

Ingold started to say something else, then stopped himself. By the firelight, he looked suddenly harsh and old, and the dark lines of bitter care cut like wire into his mouth and eyes.

Darkness was drawing like a curtain over the beach as the moon was lost in swift, smothering clouds. Its dying light glinted on the white crests of the driven waves. Even in the shelter of the rocks, their small fire began to thresh wildly in the wind.

"Yeah, but why couldn't you . . . ?" Rudy began.

Ingold cut in. "What have you been living on?"

Lohiro chuckled bitterly. "Moss."

"From the Nest?"

Lohiro nodded, his long, triangular mouth twisting unexpectedly into a wry grin. "Oh, there was a certain amount of salvage, if you wanted to fight the rats for it. I lived on that for a while. But I went down into the Nest of the Dark at last and lived on the moss, like their poor, wretched herds. Not that it's done me any more good . . ." He stopped again, wincing as if at sudden pain. The long hands shut on each other, bone crushing bone.

"Yes?" Ingold asked softly.

The changeable eyes flickered up at him, startled and empty. "What was I saying?"

"About the moss."

"Oh." Lohiro shrugged again. "Sometimes I wondered—

I lived like a beast. Alone. In the dark, like a mole. There were times I thought I'd go mad."

"Yeah," Rudy broke in. "But why didn't you . . . ?"

"Rudy, be still!" Ingold snapped, and Rudy, startled at the hardness of the tone, relapsed into silence. Ingold was profiled against the dark sea, and Rudy saw the old man's nostrils flare slightly, as if in anger, or as if his breath had quickened in fear. But he went on calmly. "What about the herds of the Dark?"

Lohiro's eyes shifted. "What about them?"

"Were they down there?" The smell of the storm front moving in off the sea was suddenly strong, a cold rushing of winds.

"No," Lohiro said after a moment. "No. They were gone. I don't know where or how. There was no trace of them."

Ingold thought about that briefly, then leaned forward and picked up a stick of driftwood to poke at the fire. The embers leaped and the wind twisted at the ribbons of flame. "You were right about the dragon," he remarked casually. "It was caught in the maze as well. We had to kill it."

"Do you know who it was?"

"Hasrid, I think," Ingold said. "He always did like dragons."

The Archmage nodded. "So he did."

Puzzled, Rudy looked from face to face in the firelight. Unsaid things and sentences unfinished hammered at his consciousness; for no reason he could think of, he was suddenly afraid—afraid of Ingold, harsh and distant and drawn in upon himself, and afraid of the tall, slender Archmage, restlessly twining his long fingers as he sat on the very edge of the circle of firelight. Rudy was afraid of the tension that lay in the silence between them, of the things they were obviously not saying to each other, and of something he could not name. "Look," he said, "I'm going to go check out the town . . ."

Ingold didn't even glance around. "Shut up and stay where you are!" He looked up from the fire to Lohiro again. "Although, mind you, Rudy did a good job helping me. He worked decoy as well as you did against the dragon we slew in the north."

Lohiro nodded. "Yes," he said. "I'd forgotten that."

Across the fire, their eyes met. The silence stretched like tensioned wire, straining toward its inevitable breaking point, bitter and undeniable. It flashed across Rudy's mind that he stood in hideous danger; but, as when he had stood paralyzed, gazing into the dragon's eyes, he could not have moved, had he wanted to. In the changeable brightness of Lohiro's eyes he could see nothing human. Nothing at all.

Ingold said softly, "You never worked decoy in your life."

The eyes were blank, empty. The Archmage's stillness was that of an automaton; the restless hands ceased moving, and the long, sensitive muscles of the face suddenly slacked. For an eternity, there were no sounds except the cold roar of the ocean and the ragged draw of Ingold's hoarse breath.

Then Lohiro struck, blindingly swift. The metal crescent of his staff seemed to burn in the light as it lashed across the fire, aimed at Ingold's throat. Ingold's sword was in his hands. The old man parried from his knees and rolled to his feet seconds later as Lohiro rushed him, sand and cinders flying from the Archmage's ragged mantle, emptiness in his staring eyes. Immobile with shock, Rudy could only watch in horror.

Ingold parried Lohiro's rush so closely that the crescent's metal point put an inch of red line on the outer edge of his right cheekbone. He caught the back of the crescent on the strong part of his own blade and continued the momentum of the rush, tearing the weapon from the Archmage's hands. It skidded away into the sand. Rudy cried out, in terror or warning, he did not know which, as Lohiro threw himself, empty-handed, toward Ingold . . .

. . . and changed!

The long, clever body seemed to melt into the billow of his wind-torn cloak, and his white, reaching hands appeared to multiply and become snatching claws. Without stopping his movement, he became a falling darkness of gaping, tentacled mouth that slobbered acid onto the sand and a spiny whip of tail snaking out to wrap itself around Ingold's body. Then the storm winds hit them like a freezing avalanche, caught that dark, tenuous body like an immense kite, and whirled it away into the howling night.

The winds roared down around Rudy and Ingold, a universe of noise and spray. Slashed sand buried the fire. Rudy was still sitting, his mouth open in shock and horror, when Ingold reached him at a staggering run through the wild chaos of the elements and pulled him bodily to his feet. The old man paused long enough to grab his staff and Che's lead-rope, then shoved Rudy along ahead through the blinding hurricane toward Quo.

Lohiro was waiting for them on the steps up from the beach. His face was as white as that of a glass-eyed corpse in the wild darkness of wind and magic, and his gold hair lifted from his brow in a fiery halo. Under the booming of the breakers, his voice was clearly audible, cool and amused. "Well, Ingold? Will you really slay me?" He started down the steps, his pronged spear at the ready. "Me?"

Ingold whispered, "You above all, my son."

With a swift, snapping movement, Lohiro reversed the staff, slamming its iron-shod foot like a club at Ingold's temple. The old man ducked, slashing upward and inward. Rudy saw white flesh and a thin streak of blood as the Archmage stepped away from the blade and chopped the staff down like an ax. Ingold caught the force on his pommel, drove the whining hardwood down past him, and struck along the shaft in the split second that the spear was entangled and his opponent's balance upset. Fire exploded between them, thrown from Lohiro's hand almost in Ingold's face. The old man staggered on the steps, his arm flung up to protect his eyes, and the younger one reversed the staff again, catching him under the knees and throwing him down onto the sand. In the same motion, Lohiro turned the staff and struck downward with it like a pitchfork at Ingold's throat. The movement was unbelievably quick and smooth, as deadly as a striking snake. But somehow the old man was not under the razor edge of the weapon. He rolled and parried, catching the shaft with his hands and bringing his foot up in his opponent's groin, hurling the Archmage bodily over his head and into the dark beach beyond. Ingold rolled to his knees, gasping, with fire streaming from his open hand . . .

But Lohiro was gone.

Ingold scrambled to his feet as rain began to slash from the black, boiling skies. Rudy ran to him, as if waked from a trance. Without a word, Ingold caught his arm and half-dragged him up the steps. Lightning roared into the sky above them, laying bare the bones of the deserted town and blinding the fugitives in its passing, the thunder shaking the world like the crack of doom. Rain plastered their hair to their cheeks as they fled along the water-sheeted colonnade, the pillars on both sides leaping into electric-blue visibility and plunging into darkness with the bursting of the lightning. The gusting wind tore at their robes as they ran, and the rain drenched them. Che was squealing and jerking against the lead-rein, in terror at the smell of electricity and power. Rudy wondered desperately what they'd do if the stupid critter succeeded in bolting with all their food supplies and the books Ingold had risked both their lives to salvage.

Then light burned his eyes, the smell of ozone searing at his nostrils and his hair prickling with the crackle of the lightning. The ruined wall before them smoked with the blast. Turning, Rudy saw Lohiro behind them, with his empty eyes and mocking grin.

Lightning illuminated Lohiro's raised white hand in the rain. Earsplitting thunder came simultaneously with a burning white explosion; a ruined doorpost near where they stood shattered, the splinters tearing the thick baffalohide of Rudy's coat. A rain squall veered, blinding him. Through it, the Archmage was a dim, watery form, his soaked gold hair lying slickly on his head, slowly advancing with his razor-pronged spear. Rudy shrank back, too afraid to run further, knowing that if lightning hit the pavement, they would all be electrocuted from the inch of water that flooded it.

Between Rudy and the Archmage, Ingold stood, the blade of his sword gleaming eerily in the soaking darkness. The winds increased, hurling great sheets of horizontal rain. On the drowning pavement the two wizards circled, feeling each other out. *Thirty inches of blade*, Rudy thought dizzily, *to six and a half feet of dark, iron-hard wood. Slick footing and blinding rain.* Ingold edged to the right, feinting, testing; Lohiro swayed like a snake. There was a swift gesture of Lohiro's long, white fingers and Ingold's quick counterspell, followed by the murmur of stillborn thunder and the acrid stink of ozone.

There were two Lohiros. Rudy saw the second one step, catlike, from the shattered doorway not three feet from him; with swift and deadly silence, the double plunged the pronged blade at Ingold's unprotected back.

Che reared, screaming in terror at the apparition. Rudy yelled wildly, "INGOLD, LOOK OUT!"

The wizard whirled. Half-blind in the wind, Rudy drew his own sword and slashed at that second Lohiro, only to have the figure flicker out of existence. He saw Ingold twist too late away from the razor crescent and stagger back, hand to his side. There was a whine of air as the Archmage reversed the staff in his hands again and the crack of the wood against the old man's skull. Rudy stood for one instant in paralyzed horror as Lohiro reached down and wrenched the sword from Ingold's nerveless hands. The Archmage bent over the crumpled body with a look of chill, pitiless satisfaction in his inhuman eyes. Then, with an inarticulate cry of fury, Rudy flung himself at the Archmage, heedless of the consequences. His sword seared through the blinding curtain of rain, but met only darkness and the fading echo of Lohiro's mocking laugh.

Rudy turned and scrambled back to where Ingold was struggling to rise from a pool of rain and blood. Che had already bolted through one of the dark doorways. Rudy pulled the old man erect, collected the sword where it lay a few feet away, and half-dragged, half-carried him to shelter inside.

It was one of the few buildings in Quo still blessed with a roof. Rain and wind crashed against the piled ruins of the storeys above, like the pounding of the mad sea. Rudy was shivering with fright and exertion as he laid Ingold down on a drift of moldering leaves and the soaked and matted remains of books. He called a faint glimmering of witchlight; by its gleam, he could see two skeletons crumpled in another corner of the room.

Ingold's face was corpselike in the ghastly light, white with shock and pain and the effort to remain conscious. Rudy could see where the points of the spear had torn into his side when he'd turned at the distraction of Rudy's yell.

Just as Lohiro knew would happen, God damn it, Rudy thought furiously, working to pull off Ingold's mantle so he could get at the wound.

"Don't," Ingold whispered desperately.

"You're hurt, man," Rudy muttered. "I've got to . . ."

"No. I'm a healer, Rudy. I'll be all right." The old man was gasping for breath, his hand groping to press his bleeding side.

"You're gonna goddam bleed to death . . ."

"Don't talk like a fool." Ingold's eyes opened, a stranger's eyes again, hard, glittering, and furious. His breath came hoarse and ragged, but already Rudy could see the flow of blood slowing between his burned fingers. "What possessed you to bring me inside?"

The arrogance in his voice touched off Rudy's own temper. "I had to get you to shelter! You were bleeding like a pig!"

"And whose fault is that?" Ingold snapped. "To be taken in by one of the cheapest tricks known to man, and a poor version of it at that."

"Well, I'm sorry!" Rudy yelled, enraged. "Next time I'll let you fight your own goddam battle!"

Equally furious, Ingold slashed back at him. "And if you don't have the wits to realize—"

They both looked up as the witchlight faded. Rudy sensed the spell, then, the same strong force that had drained his power in the haunted woods. In the growing darkness, he felt Ingold's power reach out, trying to kindle light. It met with that same inexorable strength. By wizard sight he saw the old man sit up, then heard the rasping intake of breath at the pain. Outside, storms of hail clattered on the pavements. A blinding crack of lightning illuminated the swirling of wind-driven rain and silhouetted the tall, angular form in the black arch of the doorway.

Witchlight flickered into the room again, bluish and shadowy, playing like St. Elmo's fire over the linen-fold paneling, the charred ruins of chairs, and the glinting bullion in the decaying curtains. It threaded Lohiro's dripping gold hair with quicksilver and lost itself in his staring, inhuman eyes. The long, triangular mouth quirked up into a grin at the sight of the two bloody and sodden fugitives huddled in their corner. He came slowly down the steps into the room.

Rudy fumbled to draw his sword, but Ingold shoved him back. "Don't be stupid." The old man dragged himself to his feet, his own blade burning with a sudden, cold light.

Look who's talking, Rudy thought, as the wizard staggered and caught his balance on the remains of a twisted chair. Wisely, he kept his mouth shut.

Whether the stagger was a deliberate fake, Rudy didn't know, but it drew Lohiro. The prongs flashed inches from Ingold's eyes. But the old man caught the crescent with his pommel, driving the spear down and past him to stick into the wood of the floor. In the same movement, it seemed, he slashed along the haft. Lohiro released his hold on the weapon and sprang clear, empty-handed.

Ingold rushed him, the blade of his sword burning as it slashed. Then, to his horror, Rudy realized why the old man had been angry to find himself in shelter—why he had called the storm in the first place. Out of the danger of the winds, Lohiro's body changed, his form melting into the form of the Dark. Dodging the whining arc of the blade, the Dark One flickered aside and fell, not upon Ingold, but upon Rudy.

There was no time to draw his sword. Rudy flung himself flat on the floor against the wall and covered his head, choking on the smell of stone, mold, blood, and acid in the darkness that seemed to engulf him. A shower of pebbles and dead leaves was kicked over him, and he felt the edge of a ragged mantle brush his face. Somewhere in the darkness, metal whined very close to him. When he looked up, it was to see Ingold standing above him, the crimson stain spreading over his side again. Five feet away, Lohiro was pulling his spear free of the floor. He was smiling, but there was still nothing in his eyes.

The Archmage moved in again, light on his feet, agile as a cat. The mind might have been taken over by the Dark, but the body and its training were his own. And he was fresh, Rudy thought—fresher, anyway, than Ingold, who had the long labor in the library and the slaying of the dragon behind him. Also, the Archmage wasn't conscious of trying to kill a man who had been his friend.

Rudy glanced up at Ingold. Red-rimmed eyes glittered in the black-bruised hollows of flesh. There was no pity in them, no remorse. Like Lohiro, Ingold was a machine that existed for the kill.

He ducked a feint to the eyes and the lightning head-blow that followed, then twisted out of the way as the prongs gouged upward at groin and belly. Lohiro evaded the old man's rush, falling back to his own distance and driving in again. The prongs of the crescent glittered, catching Ingold's blade and scissoring it viciously from his hands, the metal flashing as it struck the far wall. Ingold took a step back, his hands empty.

Lohiro struck like a gold puma. Rudy never saw Ingold's hand move, but he knew it must have done so, for Lohiro, though the floor at his feet was clear, tripped and staggered in his rush. In that gained second, Rudy pulled his own blade from its scabbard and tossed it to Ingold's ready hand. If the wizard had been less exhausted, he might have been faster, but the Archmage sidestepped the rush and regained his balance. A muffled explosion of sound cracked between them, throwing Ingold back against the far wall of the room, and the spear whined in again, the crescent driving into the panels to pin Ingold's sword hand to the wood. Then the Dark One, who had been Lohiro the Archmage an instant before, struck in along the spear haft. In the closing gap between the darkness around the Dark One and the old man pinned to the wall, Rudy had a confused glimpse of Ingold's left hand reaching across his body to pull his dagger from his belt; in the inky shadows, he saw the glint of its needle point. Then he heard a cry, somewhere between a shriek and a moan, and for an instant, Rudy wasn't sure who had cried out or why.

The darkness retreated. Rudy saw Ingold again, flattened against the wall, his sword hand still pinned and his eyes shut, his face glittering with sweat. Slumped against him, slender white hands clinging to his shoulders for support, Lohiro's long body was already buckling at the knees, the gold head bowed next to Ingold's face. Slowly he slipped downward and crumpled at the old man's feet.

Ingold dropped the bloody dagger and reached across his own body to dislodge the pronged spear. By the time

Rudy got over to them, he was on his knees, gathering the Archmage's bleeding form into his arms.

Lohiro's eyes opened, blinking dazedly up at the face above his. "Ingold?" he whispered, then coughed, bringing up a trickle of blood. In the witchlight, his face was ghastly, bathed in sweat and suddenly pinched-looking, as if the flesh were falling in on the bones. Even to Rudy's inexperience, the wound was obviously mortal.

Ingold said nothing, only sat with his head lowered, his face hidden in shadow.

The Archmage whispered, ". . . lied. Dark here—below." He tried to draw breath and coughed again, a hideous gurgling sound. Bony fingers picked restlessly at Ingold's sleeve. "Trapped . . . maze. Coming." He gasped, choking, and a spasm of pain passed across the thin, fox-like features. "Healer . . . you can heal me . . . They've let me go. Free."

Softly the old man said, "I'm sorry, Lohiro."

"Didn't mean . . . they took . . . made me." He choked again, fighting for air with a horrible wheezing. His fingers clamped hard over Ingold's soiled mantle, shaking at it, like a tugging child. "Heal . . . you can. They let me go."

Ingold's voice was a murmur for the dying man's ears alone. "I'm sorry. They might be able to take you back, you see."

"No," Lohiro gasped; for a moment, his face twisted again, with anger as much as with pain. Then that passed, and he coughed, bringing up more blood. "Don't know," he whispered. "Stupid . . . I never could . . . beat you. They take you . . . but they don't know." He coughed again, struggling to draw himself up. Over Ingold's shoulder, Rudy could see that the younger wizard's chest bore a dark, glistening river of blood. "They want you," he went on, his voice fading. "You . . ."

"Why?"

The blue eyes closed and gold lashes showed sharply against white skin that was already growing waxy. Lohiro rolled his head from side to side, his face convulsed with pain. "One of them," he whispered. "Became one of them. They are not many . . . they're one. They want you . . ."

"Why?" Ingold demanded.

Lohiro went on as if he had not heard. "I know . . . But

stupid. I'm sorry. I know . . ." he whispered. "The moss . . . the herds of the Dark . . ." He coughed yet again, as if gagging on blood. ". . . the ice in the north . . ."

The gold head lolled back. A moment later the long, white fingers slipped down from Ingold's sleeves and the nimble, bony body became a dead weight in his arms. For as long, Rudy guessed, as it would take to count to a hundred, Ingold sat in the darkness, cradling the friend he had slain. Then he laid the body down gently and got to his feet, his face harsh, terrible, and as empty as that of a stone image.

"Come," he said quietly. "If the Dark are below, they'll be after us now." He disappeared through a doorway, to return a few moments later leading Che. He found and sheathed his sword, while Rudy collected his own weapon and the gold-pronged spear Lohiro had carried.

Outside, the storm continued unabatedly, rain and wind slashing the town with redoubled fury. Ingold pulled up his hood, shadowing his face, and wrapped over it his sodden muffler with its trailing ends. Then he paused, turning back, gazing at Lohiro's body. It lay crumpled in the shadows where the Archmage had fallen, blood pooling on the leaf-strewn floor.

For a long time Ingold stood so, as if fixing some memory in his heart. Then, without warning, the twisted body of the dead Archmage burst into flame, the red-gold light showing clearly the sharp-boned face, the long, elegant hands, and the bright hair now transmuted to real fire. The pyre roared ceiling-high, a spreading column of heat that licked the rafters, its glare illuminating Ingold's calm, almost disinterested face and tortured eyes. Rudy watched until the body began to blacken, flesh curling from the bones in the midst of those topaz veils of heat, then turned away, unable to bear the sight. The room was filled with the odor of charred flesh.

After a time, he heard Ingold lead Che up the stairs, and he followed them out into the rain.

Thus they slipped from Quo like thieves, under cover of the hurricane winds. The Dark they left trapped within the walls of air. They left also in that town the ruins of the world's wizardry and the hopes of magical aid for humankind. Toward morning they made a cold camp in the hills above, and Rudy slept the profound sleep of total exhaustion. He woke in the afternoon to see Ingold sitting as he had last seen him, knees drawn up and arms linked around them, staring sightlessly down at the ruins by the gray ocean and weeping without a sound.

CHAPTER FIFTEEN

Firelight touched the rocks of the arroyo and shivered like rain down the strings of Rudy's harp. He respected Ingold's dictum that he should not play it, but night after night, in the windy darkness of the desert, he was drawn to it, unwrapping it from its bindings and testing its twenty-six strings. He learned them as he had learned the runes, each note in its sequence, each with its separate beauty and use.

On the other side of the fire, Ingold was silent, as he had been silent going on five days now.

On the whole, Rudy preferred the old man's silence to his bitter sarcasm, or to that blistering politeness with which he had treated any offer of comfort regarding what had happened at Quo. If Rudy had even doubted that Ingold's nature had its cruel side—which, he supposed, he must have, back in the days when he had been naive—he did not doubt now. There were days when, if he had not been too afraid of the old man, Rudy would have told him to go to hell and left him—except that there was nowhere else to go in the midst of the winter-ridden plains.

Winter had locked down over the empty lands. The sky and ground were alike made of iron, the going slow, the hunting poor. Rudy did most of the hunting, as he did most of everything else. It was he who lay for hours in the brush blinds to shoot meat that Ingold seldom touched, he who washed the stains of Lohiro's blood from the old man's robe and patched the tears in his mantle. When Ingold did eat, it was because Rudy forced him to; when he spoke, it was with an impersonal bitterness that bordered on contempt. He seemed to be drawing further and further into some remote part of himself, walling himself into his private hell of guilt and grief and pain.

And why not? Rudy thought, his mind turning back to the illusion-circled city on the shores of the Western Ocean, and the body of the golden-haired mage blackening like a straw in the flames. *Who's to say Lohiro didn't have the answer? Who's to say he couldn't have given it to us, once the Dark Ones let go of his mind?*

If, of course, they really did let go.

And if Ingold didn't simply let him die when he could have saved him, out of rage at his having betrayed them all.

Rudy glanced across the fire once again. Ingold was staring into the flames that were multiplied a hundredfold in his bleak eyes. He looked old, exhausted, and shabby, his long white hair fluttering around the sunken cheeks and brooding eyes. Out in the darkness, the wail of a coyote curled, thin and hopeless, on the wind, the cry of a lost soul wandering dry and empty wastes. The cloud-cover had broken, and the full moon stared down upon them from the rim of the broken-toothed western hills. Rudy wondered what Ingold saw in the blaze.

Was it Quo as it had been in the warm beauty of that last summer, unaware of the horror underlying its heart? Lohiro's empty eyes? Things that could have been, had Ingold thought to send them warning of the Dark? Or the Keep, black amid the snows under remote and freezing stars, now that the wizards of the world could literally be counted on the fingers of one hand?

Ingold, Bektis, Kara, me, and Kara's mother, Rudy enumerated glumly. *What the hell kind of chance have we got against all the forces of the Dark? What kind of chance has anyone got?*

No wonder Ingold walked in silence, a tumbleweed ghost on the desert road.

Only occasionally would the wizard rouse himself to give lessons in power that were, for days on end, their only means of communication. But his teaching was like everything else, brittle and bitter and cruel. He seemed to care very little whether Rudy learned anything or not; for him, Rudy felt, the lessons were simply a means of temporarily forgetting. He would throw unexplained illusions into Rudy's path, or deliberately wrap himself in a cloaking-spell and leave Rudy to search. For two days he had blindfolded Rudy, forcing him to rely on his other senses as they marched on in sightless silence. Without warning, Ingold had called forth blinding torrents of wind and rain and deadly flash floods in the washes, with which Rudy must cope or drown. By scorn and sarcasm and vicious invective, he pushed the younger man to learn stronger spells and taught him the tricky and terrible secrets of divination by water and bone.

Everything Ingold taught, he taught as a stranger. For the rest, he could not be bothered to speak at all.

Experimentally, Rudy's fingers formed chords, thirds and fifths. The tones of the harp sounded true. *A wizard's harp,* he thought, *brought from the wizards' city. Did the spells that preserved it from harm keep it tuned as well?* Cautiously, first with melody alone and then with groping chords, he found his way through the saddest and most beautiful of the Lennon-McCartney ballads, his mind and body bending to the harp, his eyes to the firelight and starlight on hands and strings. The music was clean, pure, and incredibly delicate, like a star caught in crystal, and he hated his own awkwardness and ignorance as unworthy of such beauty.

In the desert the coyotes yipped again, a full-throated chorus in the windy night. Rudy looked up and saw that Ingold had gone.

The moon had set. Rudy had no sense of the presence of the Dark, nor of any creature in the wastes of stone and cracked, parched clay, save those that made the place their home. Che dozed on the end of his tether.

Rudy set aside his harp and made a slow, careful examination of the camp. It was safe and secure within its rings of protective spells. Ingold's staff was gone. So was one of the bows.

Dogging a wizard by starlight was one of the less easy feats of this life. But Ingold's brutal training had paid off; Rudy picked up the turn of a branch and the scatter of sand that lay the wrong way to the wind, pointing a possible lead. He belted on his sword and picked up the staff that had once belonged to Lohiro the Archmage, taking his bearings from a notch in the hills and the shape and roll of the land. He stepped quietly away from the camp; then, turning back, he laid a word of warning on the whole outfit. Six feet farther off, he glanced back, and there was no trace of burro, fire, or packs to be seen.

He moved through the windy darkness like a ghost. Casting his senses wide, he occasionally found a trace of the old man—a place where a kit fox had unaccountably veered aside, or the slight scratch in the dirt on a rock face. He heard no sound, saw nothing moving in all the vastness of the frozen rocks, but twice his eyes returned to a humped black shadow where bare boulders broke the raw silver of clay flats. It was off the course of Ingold's trail. He could see nothing of the wizard in that jumbled outcrop of rock. But long meditation had given him a sense of dividing life from lifelessness. And once, on another windy desert night, he had glimpsed the shape of Ingold's soul, and that he would never forget.

Nevertheless, he had to get very close before he could be sure.

He stalked Ingold like a drift of wind in the night, as he had stalked his friends the jackrabbits. By this time he had a certain amount of experience as a hunter. But before he could reach the rocks, he saw Ingold move, a single turn of his head and the glint of a bitter eye in darkness. Then the wizard turned away again, scarcely even interested.

Rudy emerged from the concealing shadows. "You planning on coming back to camp tonight?"

"Is it any affair of yours?"

Rudy leaned on his crescent-tipped staff, annoyed at that steely arrogance. "Yeah, I'd kind of like to know if the Dark Ones are gonna put the munch on you."

"Don't be stupid. We'll find violets in this desert before we find the Dark. Or haven't you been watching?"

"I've been watching." Their voices were pitched low for each other's ears alone. Their bodies blended with rock and shadow; an observer at ten feet would have passed them by, unseeing. "But I don't figure I'm that much more clever than the Dark."

"What's the matter, Rudy?" Ingold jeered. "Do you think I can't handle the Dark?"

"No, I don't."

Ingold turned his face away and leaned his chin once more on folded hands and drawn-up knees.

"I think if it came to that, you'd love to get eaten by the Dark," Rudy went on coldly. "That way you wouldn't have to go back and tell Alwir the whole thing was a bust, and you'd still get credit for not being a quitter."

Ingold sighed. "If you think I'd undergo something as unpleasant as that over someone as essentially trivial as Alwir, your sense of proportion is almost as poor as your harp playing." He glanced up, then continued impatiently, as if throwing a sop to a begging dog. "Yes, I was returning tonight."

"Then why did you take a bow?"

Ingold was silent.

"Or did you figure I could carry the ball from here?"

"That's your choice," the old man snapped angrily. "You've got what you want—you're a mage, or as much a mage as I can make you. *You* go back and play politics with Alwir. You go back and spin out the illusion that your power gives you either the ability or the right to alter the outcome of things. You go back and watch the people you care for die, either by your own hand or through your damned wretched meddling, and see what it does to you in sixty-three years. But until you do, don't sit there in self-righteous judgment of me or my actions."

Rudy folded his arms and regarded the old man silently in the starlight. Hidden in the darkness of his drawn-up hood, Ingold's face seemed to be nothing more than a collection of angled bones, bruises, and scars amid a rough mane of dirty white hair. *Halfway already to being a desert hermit again,* Rudy thought. *And why not? We blew it. The mages are gone. Whatever Lohiro might have been able to tell us, if the Dark did in fact release him, Ingold ended.*

Quietly, Rudy asked, "So what do I tell them at the Keep?"

Ingold shrugged. "Whatever you please. Tell them I died in Quo. There would be some truth in that, anyway."

"And is that what I tell Gil?" Rudy went on in a voice that shook with controlled anger.

The old man looked up, fury and the first life that Rudy had seen in him in weeks blazing into his eyes. "What does Gil have to do with it?"

"You're the only one who can get her back to her own world." It wasn't until Rudy spoke that he realized the extent of his own anger. "You're the only one in the world who understands the gates through the Void. And you were responsible for getting her here in the first place. You have no right to be the cause of her being stuck in this universe forever."

He felt the rage that surged through the old man, rage and some other emotion breaking the bleak passivity of self-torment in which he had been trapped since Quo. But, like his grief, Ingold's anger was silent and all inside. In a queer, stiff voice he said, "Perhaps it would be Gil's choice to remain in the world."

"Like hell," Rudy snorted. "For myself, I don't give a damn one way or the other. But she's got a life back there, a career she wants and a place in that world. If she stays here, she'll never be anything but a foot soldier, when she wanted to be a scholar; and she'll stay that way until she gets killed by the Dark or the cold or the next stupid war Alwir gets the Keep into. I care for that lady, Ingold, and I'm not going to have you stick her here forever against her will. You haven't got that right."

The wizard sighed, and the life seemed to go out of him again, taking away even the bitter leaping of his anger. He sank his head slowly to his hands and said faintly, "No, you're right. I suppose I must go back, if only for that."

Rudy started to say something else, but let his breath out with the words unspoken. Ingold's anger puzzled him, and this sudden capitulation bothered him even more. But he sensed the breaking of some bond of bitterness in the old man, a bleak self-hatred that had given him a kind of strength. Now there was nothing.

Quietly, he said, "I'll be back at the camp. Can you find your way there?"

Ingold nodded without looking up. Rudy left him there, walking slowly back along his own invisible tracks, the double points of his pronged staff winking in the desert starlight. Once he looked around and saw that the old man had not moved. The dark form was barely distinguishable from the rock itself, no more than a darkness against the muted, uncertain shape of the land beyond. As he walked

269

back to the camp alone, Rudy could not remember having seen anyone so lonely or so wretched in his life.

"You think there's anybody home?"

Moonlight drenched the town before them, a collection of little adobe boxes climbing the hills in back of the road. The distant trickle of water and thick clusters of date palms, black against the icy, glowing sky, marked where the stream came down out of the hills. Several houses had been blown apart by the Dark; but, by the look of them, it hadn't been recently. *First quarter moon of autumn?* Rudy wondered. Most of the bricks had been pillaged to reinforce the buildings that remained, turning them into little individual fortresses covered on the outside from foundation to rooftree with elaborately painted designs, pictures, and religious symbols. On the nearest one, a beautiful woman stood with her feet on the back of a crooked devil, her left hand raised against a swarm of inaccurate, fishlike representations of the Dark Ones, her right arm and cloak sheltering a crowd of kneeling supplicants. By the light of the waning and cloud-crossed moon, the painting had a startling and primitive beauty, the colors lost in the moonlight but the outlines of the figures strikingly clear. For some reason, it reminded Rudy of the runes on the Keep doors.

"Possibly," Ingold replied, in answer to his question. "But I hardly think they will unbar their doors at night."

"It's you and me for the Church, then," Rudy sighed, and started off through the shadows of the narrow streets, with Ingold drifting like a ghost at his heels. The poison, Rudy thought, was working its way out of the old man's system; if he seldom spoke, at least he seemed to realize whom he was talking to when he did. But Rudy missed his humor, the wry fatalism of his outlook, and the brief, flickering grin that so changed his nondescript face.

When they reached the Church, however, Ingold surprised Rudy by leading the way around to the back, where a narrow cell was built onto the rear of the fortresslike structure. He knocked on the heavy door. There was movement inside and the sound of sliding bars. The door was opened quickly and quickly closed behind them.

A short and slightly chubby young priest had let them

270

in, a candle in his hand. "Be welcome . . ." he began, and then saw Ingold's face. In the soft amber light, the blood drained from his own face.

The priest's sudden silence called Ingold from his thoughts, and he looked at the young man, puzzled.

The priest whispered, "It was you."

Ingold frowned. "Have we met?"

The priest turned hastily away and fumblingly set the candle on the room's small table. "No—no, of course not. I—please be welcome in this house. It is late for travelers —like yourselves—" He barred the door behind them, and Rudy saw that his hands were shaking. "I am Brother Wend," he said, turning back and revealing an earnest, young face for a man in his early twenties. He was wearing the gray robe of a Servant of the Church. His head was shaved; but, by the color of his black eyebrows and sincere brown eyes, Rudy guessed his hair had been black or dark brown, like his own.

"I am the priest of this village," Brother Wend said, babbling to cover up nervousness or fear. "The only one now, I'm afraid. Will you sup?"

"We've eaten, thanks," Rudy said, which was true—and besides, he reflected, if things here were as bad as he'd seen them in the Keep, food was tight all over. "All we ask is a bed on your floor and stabling for our burro."

"Certainly—of course."

The priest went with him to put Che in the stables. While Rudy bedded the donkey down, he filled the priest in on all the news he could—of the fall of Gae, the retreat to Renweth, Alwir's army, and the destruction of Quo. He did not mention that Ingold was a wizard, nor indicate his own powers. Ingold, after the briefest exchange of amenities, had withdrawn to sit beside the small fire on the hearth and brood in silence. But throughout the evening, as Rudy and Brother Wend talked quietly in the shadows of the little room, the young priest's eyes kept straying back to Ingold, as if trying to match the man with some memory, and Rudy could see that the memory frightened him.

Rudy was just settling himself to sleep on the floor near the hearth when hurried knocking sounded at the door. Without hesitation, Brother Wend rose and slid back the bolts to let in two small children from the darkness outside. They were a pair of girls, eight and nine years of age, sandy-haired and hazel-eyed like the people of Gettlesand. In a babbling treble duet they outlined a confused tale of yellow sickness and fever and their mother and their little sister Danila, and last summer and tonight, clutching at the young man's sleeves and staring up at him with wide, frightened eyes. Wend nodded, murmuring soothingly to them, and turned back to his guests.

"I must go," he said softly.

"One or the other of us will let you back in," Rudy promised. "Go carefully."

When the priest had gone, Rudy got up to bar the door behind him. "Are you going to sleep?" he asked the silent figure by the hearth.

Ingold, staring into the fire, shook his head. He seemed hardly to have heard.

Rudy slid back into his abandoned blankets before they had a chance to grow cold and pillowed his head on the heavy volumes he'd carried from Quo—the only use, so far, that he'd seen for them. "You know that kid from someplace?" he asked.

Again Ingold shook his head.

Rudy had carried on a lot of these one-sided conversations in the last three weeks. Occasionally, he'd pursued them until he got an answer of some sort, usually monosyllabic, but tonight he gave it up. When he closed his eyes, Ingold was still brooding over whatever it was that he saw in the flames.

Rudy wondered what it was he sought there, but had never asked.

His mind went back over the glimpses that his own firewatching had yielded, glimpses of Minalde mostly, scattered but comforting: Alde combing her hair by the embers of her small hearth, wrapped in her white wool robe, and singing to Tir, who crawled busily around the shadowy room; Alde sitting with her feet up in the dim study behind the Guards' quarters, reading aloud while Gil took notes, surrounded by a clutter of books and tablets; seeing Gil look up and grin and make some joke, and Alde laugh; and once, frighteningly, Alde in a passionate argument with her brother, tears running down her white, furious face while he stood with his arms folded, shaking his head in cold denial. The images followed Rudy down into darkness, mingling with others: the empty Nest on the windblown desert to the north; the empty streets of Quo; the startled look in Brother Wend's big dark eyes when he had opened the door; and the way he'd whispered in terror, "It was you."

"Yes," Ingold's voice said, soft and infinitely tired. "It was me."

Blinking in surprise, Rudy tasted the heaviness of lost sleep in his mouth and saw that the priest had returned. Ingold was barring the door behind him; in the shadows thrown by the waning fire, his robes seemed to be dyed in blood.

The priest spoke shakily. "What do you want of me?" Defiance and terror mingled in the young man's voice. Ingold regarded him quietly for a moment, his arms folded, his scarred hands looking very bony and worn in the red flickering of the light. But he only asked, "She's better, isn't she?"

"Who?"

"Those children's mother."

The priest licked his lips nervously. "Yes, by the grace of God."

Ingold sighed and returned to his seat by the hearth, drawing his patched, stained mantle, which he'd been using for an extra blanket, back up around his shoulders. "It wasn't the grace of God, though," he said quietly. "At least not in the sense that it's usually meant. They didn't come to ask for the sacraments, even though you know as well as I do that the yellow sickness, once it takes hold, is almost invariably fatal. They asked you to heal her, as you healed their little sister some months ago." He reached across, picked up the poker, and stirred the fire, its sudden, leaping light doing curious things to the lines and scars of his hollowed face. He glanced back at Wend. "Didn't you?"

"It was in God's hands."

"Perhaps that's what you choose to say, but you don't believe it." The priest started as if he had been burned. "If you believed it, you wouldn't fear me," Ingold went on reasonably.

"What do you want?" Wend demanded again in anguish.

Ingold set down the poker. "I think you know."

"Who are you?"

"I am a wizard." Ingold settled back against the wall, the shadows cloaking him.

The priest spoke again, his voice tense and crackling with passion. "That's a lie," he whispered. "They're all dead. He said so."

Ingold shrugged. "He is a wizard also. His name is Rudy Solis. Mine is Ingold Inglorion."

Rudy heard the harsh gasp of the priest's breath and saw him turn away, his face buried in his hands. His body shook as if with a deadly chill. "He said they were dead," Wend repeated in a thin, cracked voice, muffled by his hands. "And, God forgive me, I rejoiced to hear it. It was a terrible thing, but I was glad to hear that the Lord had finally removed the temptation from me, after all these years. You have no right to bring it back."

"No," Ignold agreed quietly. "But you know as well as I do that God cannot remove temptation. It comes from inside you, and not from any outer cause. And you would be tempted as long as you lived—every time someone called upon you to use your powers for healing, and in times to come, when one of your people begs you to put the runes on his door to keep the Dark at bay. How could you refuse?"

The young man raised his face from his hands. "I never would," he gasped.

"No?"

"I have no power," the priest whispered hopelessly. "I gave it up—sacrificed it. I have no power." He faced Ingold desperately in the wavering shadows, his full lips pressed tight together and trembling. "That power comes from the Devil, the Lord of Mirrors. Yes, God help me, I am tempted and will forever be tempted. But I will not trade my soul for power, not even the power to help others. That power comes from the Crooked Side, and I will have no dealings with it. And then—I dreamed—I saw that city that I have known in my heart all my life, how it would look . . . And you were there . . ."

"Do you know why you had the dream?" Ingold's voice was soft, coming from a form that was little more than a

274

disembodied shadow among shadows, with a sunken glint of azure eyes.

"It was a summons," Wend whispered. "A need. A call. To go somewhere . . ."

"To go to Renweth Keep at Sarda Pass," Ingold said, and that deep, grainy voice, though quiet, seemed to fill the tiny room. "To help me and Rudy—and whomever else we can find—to drive out the Dark."

"And what else?" The young man's face shone with sweat, his eyebrows black against the whiteness of his high, shaven crown. "To go openly to the Devil? To announce to my Bishop—if he survived—and to anyone else who cares to know that I am apostate? To put myself under judgment as a heretic?"

Rudy, remembering another pair of steely, dark eyes burning out of a shaven skull, reflected that the kid had a point.

"And wrongly," Wend went on in a whisper. "Wrongly. This world, when all is said, is an illusion. It will go on without me. My soul is all I have, and if I lose it—it will be forever."

A long silence followed, with priest and wizard facing each other across the dying ripple of the hearthlight. They were curiously alike, Rudy thought, in their colorless robes. He remembered his own days as a drifter on the California highways, drawn by yearnings that could find no expression, an outcast because nothing made sense in terms of what he knew to be true. He tried to picture a life of fighting those yearnings, tried to imagine deliberately putting the powers of wizardry aside.

A mage will have magic . . .

He could not conceive of putting it aside.

Ingold rose. "I am sorry," he said quietly. "You have temptations enough; to add to them would be poor payment for your hospitality. We will go."

"No." Brother Wend caught his sleeve as he moved to wake Rudy, though a moment before the priest would have cut off his hand rather than touch the old man. "Wizard or devil, I cannot turn you out into the night. I—I'm sorry. It's only that I've fought it so long."

Ingold moved his hand as if to lay it upon Wend's shoulder, but the young priest turned away, retreating into the shadows at the far end of the room where his own narrow pallet was. Rudy heard the creak of ropes as he lay down, followed by the slurred whisper of blankets. After a moment Ingold returned to his seat by the hearth, drawing his knees up before him and evidently preparing to stare broodingly into the fire until dawn.

Silence settled over the narrow cell as the fire burned low, but Rudy could hear no alteration in the young priest's shaken breathing and knew that he did not sleep.

"And he was right," Rudy concluded, speaking of it many days later. "That's the damn thing. You remember how Govannin's always saying, 'The Devil guards his own.' Well, he doesn't, not anymore." Snow lay deep around them, covering the foothills through which they had trudged for two laborious days, blanketing the steep, rocky rise of the ground. Above them the black cliffs were criss-crossed with heavy, white ledges of snow, and the dark furring of trees was weighted with it. A smother of clouds hid the higher peaks and filled the rocky notch of Sarda Pass with nebulous gray.

Rudy's breath burned in his lungs. His long, wet hair hung damply around his face and over the collar of his buffalohide coat. The steel points of his pronged staff winked faintly in the wan afternoon light. Under the burden of books they'd brought all that long way from Quo, his shoulder ached, but his mind circled gull-like around a confusion of thoughts.

We're home.

Home to Minalde.

And to what else?

By now, he was long used to carrying on both sides of the conversation. "You said to me once to remember that we were outcasts. But that was back when we thought we'd have the Archmage to help us. And now we've got nothing, literally nothing. Anybody who declares himself a wizard is asking for it." He shrugged. "I don't blame Wend for sitting tight."

"Nor do I."

He glanced around, startled at the response. Ingold had been silent for days.

To his surprise, the old man continued. "In fact, I

should be amazed if anyone shows up at all. Kara and her mother might," he added reflectively, "if nothing else happened to them. But—the opposition to wizardry will have redoubled. And those alive to hear my summoning would be those who could not overcome their fear of opposition in the first place."

Ingold came up beside him, leaning on his staff, bowed under the weight of his burden of books, like a very old and very wretched beggarman, with his long white hair, grubby beard, and stained and tattered cloak. In the shadows between the rim of his hood and his ragged muffler, his eyes still looked sunken and tired. But at least he was talking.

Ingold went on. "Maybe now you understand my impulse to become a hermit."

"Well, let me tell you, the way you've been acting, I was damn tempted to let you do it."

The wizard ducked his head. "I am sorry," he apologized quietly. "It was good of you to put up with the grieving of an old man."

Rudy shrugged. "Well," he said judiciously, "since I've been perfect myself all my life, I guess I can find it in my heart to forgive you."

"Thank you," the wizard replied gravely. "You are very kind. But having heard you play the harp, I feel your assertion of perfection is rather rash."

Their eyes met, and Rudy grinned. "I had to get back at you somehow, didn't I?"

Ingold shuddered. "In that case I doubly apologize," he said. "If that was meant as retribution, my conduct must have been execrable indeed."

"Hey!" Rudy protested.

"It's the first time in my life that I've been thankful that I'm almost completely tone-deaf," the wizard mused— not quite truthfully, Rudy knew. "So I suppose there is good to be derived from every state."

"Well, then you and I better think real hard about what kind of good is to be derived from being in the doghouse," Rudy said grimly. "Because that's sure as hell where we're gonna be when Alwir finds out what happened at Quo." Then, in a different voice, he asked, "What did happen at Quo, Ingold?" Wind keened through the trees above the

277

Pass, but only a breath of it touched the travelers laboring through the drifted snow. The clouds moved down the mountains, as gray and chill as the fogs that had surrounded Quo. "Was Lohiro acting for the Dark—or was that the Dark themselves?"

There was a long pause while Ingold scanned the tracks of rabbit and bird in the snow of the drifts, as if judging matters pertaining to wind and weather. When he finally spoke, his scratchy voice was tired. "I think it was the Dark themselves." He sighed. "To this day, I don't know if they did release him, there at the end. If they did, I could have brought him back with us. At least we could then have had the benefit of his wisdom and the knowledge of whatever it was that the wizards unearthed before they were destroyed. But I couldn't risk it, Rudy," he said in a soft, urgent tone. "I couldn't risk it."

"Hell, no," Rudy agreed. "With all his knowledge and the Dark behind him—no wonder every building in the town was smashed, the wizards destroyed, and Forn's Tower blown to flinders. If your power could hold them at bay before the gates of the Keep, his power could only double theirs."

"As their powers could baffle, or channel, the powers of wizardry near their Nests. I should have guessed that when Hoofprint of the Wind spoke of the Nest as a place of seeing. That was how Quo was spoken of, back in the old days—and of Gae, incidentally. It needed all the forces of the Dark to break Gae," he added. "It wasn't ill-planned, Rudy, the final blow at Gae, Quo, Penambra—Dele, too, from what Kara said—all within a few days. The back of organized resistance was broken, and the hope of magical aid destroyed."

Ingold sighed, his breath a thin rag of cloud in the fog. "I had to kill him, Rudy. I couldn't let them have his powers. Perhaps he was still some sort of prisoner in his own body. Certainly—whatever it was—it had his speech, his mannerisms, his skills. But it didn't have his knowledge. Lohiro would have known that Anamara the Red and I were old classmates from years ago." He held up his hands, the first faint smile Rudy had seen glimmering wryly through his overgrown beard. "She knitted me these mittens the year we were lovers, back at Quo. For the

278

fourth most powerful mage in the West of the World, she was very domestic. Lohiro would never have spoken to me casually of her death."

"Was that what tipped you off?" Rudy asked quietly.

"Partly. And—I didn't like his eyes. But from what he had been through, I didn't know."

"So you trapped him."

Ingold nodded miserably and trudged on through the snow. Che hung balkily back at the full stretch of his lead—neither of them had ever managed to train the stupid creature to follow, a failure that in his darker moments Rudy was inclined to atribute to the malice of the Bishop of Gae. "I trapped him," Ingold said, "and I killed him. Maybe they did let him go. He spoke of the Dark as he was dying—that they are not many, but one. Maybe he had been one of them and, if I had healed him, we could have learned from him what they know, why they rose—and why they departed."

"Yeah," Rudy assented bluntly, "and maybe if you healed him, the wizards of Quo wouldn't have been the only ones to seal the Dark into the citadel with them."

Ingold sighed. "Maybe."

"What else could you have done?"

Ingold shook his head. "Been more clever to begin with. Realized the connection between the so-called fortunate places and the Dark. Pursued my own researches at Quo, instead of playing politics halfway across the continent. But the answer is gone, if there ever was an answer. The Dark made sure of that. And perhaps there never was an answer to begin with."

"Sure there was," Rudy said. He glanced over at the old man as they clambered up the last steep grade of the road, the crusted snow squeaking under their boots. "And there is. There's got to be."

"Does there?" Ingold scrambled through the drifts at his heels, dragging the unwilling burro with his load of books behind. "At one time I used to think there was a reason for things happening as they do and that somewhere all questions have answers. I'm not so sure of that anymore. What makes you think this one does?"

"Because even after Quo was destroyed, the Dark have been after you. They've chased you from here to hell and back again to keep you from finding that answer. The Dark think you have it, and they've been one jump ahead of us through this whole game."

Ingold sighed and stood still in the drifted road, his head bowed and his face hidden in the shadows of his hood. A flurry of snow blew down on them from above and brought with it the smell of the high peaks, of glacier ice and rock. The fog surrounded them, gray, drifting wraiths haunting the gathering darkness in the throat of the Pass. "So we're back where we began," he said at last. "With the question and the answer. I'm the one they want, but they've wiped out everyone but me. Is that question or answer?"

Rudy shrugged. "Which one are you going to make it?"

Ingold glanced up at him sharply and continued walking without a reply. Rudy followed behind, testing with his staff the solid ground under the blankets of drifts. Evening was drawing on. The sharp, chill dampness of the mists seemed to eat into his bones.

Ahead of him, the old man stopped; and following his gaze, Rudy looked up to the gray boil of clouds that shrouded the Pass.

Out of the evening mists, dark forms were materializing there, melting into being from shadow and wind. A draft caught a cloak and blew it out into a great dark wing; the gathering forms solidified, massing against the fog. Ingold stood still, his hood fallen back from his face, doubt and fear and a strange, wild hope moving behind those still eyes.

Rudy came softly up behind him. "Is it the Bishop's people?"

Ingold whispered, "I don't know . . ."

Then a man's voice rolled down the Pass, deep and harsh, like the sound a stone might make when it was dislodged in an avalanche from the side of its parent cliff. "INGOLD!" the voice cried, and Ingold's face was suddenly white in the gray light, looking upward at that assembled host.

Suddenly he shouted, "Thoth!" and struggled forward through the drifts at a speed which Rudy knew he could never match. Like a gangling bird of prey, the tallest of the watchers detached himself from their midst, striding down to Ingold in a black billow of robes. They met like long-lost brothers and embraced in the flurrying fog and snow, while the others came streaming down the path on Thoth's heels.

Coming closer, Rudy saw Kara among them, her scarred face smiling hesitantly. The others he did not know, but he knew who they *must* be. There were at least thirty of them, of all ages, both sexes, and all kinds; many of them were old, but one or two seemed very young. Thoth and Ingold still had their arms around each other's shoulders. Thoth, with his hood thrown back, was revealed to be a grim old man whose shaven head and beaked nose reminded Rudy of Bishop Govannin; his eyes were the color of pale honey.

Out of the crowd, another form pushed itself, an incredibly tiny, impossibly ancient little hermit, so shriveled with age that he looked as if he'd dried and bleached for a hundred years in the desert sun.

"Kta!" Ingold cried delightedly, throwing his free arm around the narrow shoulders. "You came after all!" And the tiny old man smiled his sweet, toothless smile and nodded.

"Rudy," Ingold said, and Rudy mused to himself that in the last six weeks he'd probably seen more emotion out of the usually unruffled wizard than anyone else had seen in decades. "Rudy, these are our people." Ingold had one arm around Thoth and the other around the ancient Kta, and among and between them and this knot of enchanted strangers on the snowy Pass, there seemed to lie an unbreakable bond, a chain made of light that bound them together. Ingold's face almost shone with joy. "These are the wizards who came in answer to my call. They've been waiting here to welcome us back to the Keep. My friends," he said, "this is Rudy. He is my student and one of us."

CHAPTER SIXTEEN

Unlike the messenger of Alketch, Rudy and Ingold did not merit formal reception. But from the crowd that stood in the streaming light of the gates, two figures detached themselves, hurrying down the dark steps to halt, suddenly shy and confused, at the bottom.

Rudy's eyes met Alde's, and his whole soul felt as if it were trying to leap from his body and carry him, weightless, up the snowy path. Somehow he was holding her hands, the torchlight edging her braided black hair in fire, his heart hammering so loudly in his breast he wondered if everyone in the Keep could hear it, and desperately telling himself, *It's a secret. Our love is a secret that no one must know.* He felt he would stifle if he spoke, so he only stood, gazing into the cornflower deeps of her eyes.

He was broken from this reverie by Gil's little squeak of delight as Ingold flung one arm around her neck and took from her a resounding kiss of welcome, to the cheers of the Guards assembled on the top step. Looking up, Rudy recognized them—Janus, Seya, Melantrys, Gnift—along with a sizable bunch of civilians who had quite probably defied a specific Church directive and turned out to welcome the pilgrim wizards home. It was a nice gesture, but he earnestly wished them all in Hell and the steps vacant but for himself and the woman before him.

"Alwir's inside," Alde said, stepping back from him. The touch of her fingertips had kindled a fire of hunger through his body, and the light of it was echoed in her eyes. But, mingled with her joy and desire, he could see something else in her face—that curious sense of security of a woman who had felt all along that her man would return.

"He's been shut up with Stiarth of Alketch all day,"

Gil said, still pink with confusion. "You guys don't rate." She disengaged herself from Ingold's arm and came over to give Rudy a chaste, sisterly peck on the cheek. "But I'm damn glad to see you home, punk."

Home, Rudy thought. *I've been home, by the Western Ocean, and found it a haunted ruin.* He glanced down at her unsurprised eyes and said, "I guess you know, hunh?"

She nodded and glanced back at where Ingold stood, Kta still in tow, talking a mile a minute with Thoth and Kara and that chattering group of others. To half of them, Rudy had discovered, Ingold Inglorion was a legend—he could still see it in their eyes. They were a ragtag and bobtail crew, gathered around those three. Rudy recognized Kara's mother—Nan, somebody said her name was—a withered little white-haired woman with a bent back and a cackling voice, one of the very few who didn't seem to be particularly impressed by Ingold. Kta was another—he was beaming toothlessly at all and sundry— and Thoth was the third. But the others, from the fat little man in a brocade turban and overembroidered surcoat and the fey, red-haired girl-child in castoff rags to the scholarly black gentleman in an outlandish white and silver toga and the gaudy minstrel boy, were looking at Ingold with an awe that bordered on worship.

"And, Ingold—Ingold, listen!" Minalde cried suddenly. Her dark-blue eyes were wide with enthusiasm, and she had evidently forgotten that she had ever been terrified of the old man. She slipped through the crowd of wizards and caught his sleeve eagerly, her face like a child's at Christmas. "We've found things here, wonderful things!"

"The old laboratories are here, intact," Gil added, carried away, and Rudy was drawn with them into the general group as the girls plunged into an excited duet, accompanied by much repetition and gesture. "Things we don't understand .. .." "And Gil's been digging up the records . . ." "Air ducts and water pumps, and the old observation rooms . . ."

Like schoolgirls, Rudy thought, amused. *Schoolgirls who've turned the place inside out and maybe found the keys to the defeat of the Dark that Ingold and I traipsed all the way to Quo and did not find at all.*

". . . and Alde has the inherited memories of the House

283

of Dare," Gil finished in triumph, "which is how we found any of it to begin with."

Ingold looked curiously at the younger girl, so like a flushed, eager schoolgirl with her braided hair and thin, gaudy skirts. "Do you?"

Alde nodded, suddenly shy. "I think so. I recall things that I see, but they aren't—they aren't visions, like—like Eldor had."

There was the slightest break in her voice, and Ingold passed over it without giving a sign that he had noticed. "A woman's memories, or a man's?"

She hesitated, not having thought of that aspect before. "I don't know. A man's, I suppose, if they come from Dare of Renweth. And they're less memories than a sense of recognition, of having been somewhere before. It was Gil's scholarship that helped us more, and her maps."

"Interesting," the wizard said softly. "Interesting." He looked for a moment longer at the girl, the child-wife of his dead friend, shoulder to shoulder with Rudy now, her hand seeking his, half-hidden by the folds of her skirts. Ingold's brow kinked swiftly, as if with passing pain, but it smoothed again; he turned back to Gil and put his arm across her angular shoulders. "And where have you put all this?"

By this time, Janus and the Guards had come down the steps to join them, and it was Janus who replied. "They've taken over the rooms at the back of the barracks. It started out as Gil-Shalos' study when she outgrew the storeroom; it's quite a complex now."

"The wizards started arriving only last week," Gil informed them as the whole group trooped in a body up the steps and through the dark, echoing passage of the gates. "Dakis the Minstrel was the first, then Gray and Nila the weatherwitches . . ."

"And Bektis was absolutely livid," the minstrel declared, pirouetting delightedly over the narrow span of a bridged watercourse. "I thought we should surely lose him to apoplexy."

Eyes followed them as they crossed the dim reaches of the Aisle, idle or curious, hostile or sympathetic, noting, perhaps, the number of Guards that walked with them, or who were the civilians in the crowd. They moved in a

284

shifting blur of witchlight, the glow of it stirring around them like a luminous fog.

Ingold stopped, startled at the chaos that prevailed in the wizards' complex. "We haven't had time to get things straightened out yet," Gil apologized.

"It comforts me to hear that," the old man said, surveying the long, narrow room. Fleeces, skins, and crates seemed to make up most of the furnishings; staffs leaned in corners like rifles in an armory; makeshift shelves had been set up, stacked with dilapidated books. The bluish witchlight slid like silk over the round body of a pearwood lute and winked on the angles of white and gray glass polyhedrons that were scattered across the table, the floor, and everywhere else. Parchments, wax tablets, dusty chronicles, and scrolls of yellowed paper littered every horizontal surface in sight, and over one of the room's few chairs lay a great pile of homespun brown cloth, and with it a tiny satin pincushion sparkling like a miniature hedgehog.

The wizards had evidently made themselves very much at home.

"And we have to show you—" Alde began.

But Thoth broke in. "Let them rest, child, and eat." His voice was as harsh as a vulture's, slow and heavy. He glanced once at the crescent-tipped staff that Rudy leaned in a corner and looked back down at Ingold. "You found Quo, then?"

Ingold shut his eyes and nodded tiredly. "Yes," he said.

"And Lohiro?"

"Dead."

Thoth's eyes flickered to the staff, to the bundles of books that Rudy and several volunteer helpers were placing on a small cleared corner of the table, and back to the ravaged face of his friend. "So," he said.

Ingold's eyes opened. He studied the other man's narrow face. "What happened, Thoth? Lohiro said you had been killed."

"No." The Recorder of Quo laid a long, bony hand on Ingold's shoulder. "The others . . . yes. Your girls have been telling me," he went on slowly, "of their—findings—regarding the fortunate places of ancient times. These were similar to your own discoveries, I am sure."

Ingold nodded wretchedly.

"But deeper, since they had access to things to which you did not."

Only those who stood nearest heard Ingold whisper, "I should have guessed."

"Perhaps," the tall wizard said evenly. "But you are wrong if you suppose that Lohiro did not have such knowledge."

Ingold looked up quickly; though all reason for fear was past now, the reflection of it suddenly aged his sunken eyes.

"From the outset, as you know, I sought the oldest of the records for reference to the Dark—largely without result," Thoth continued. "The records there did not go much farther back than Forn's time, but your mention of Nests at Gae, Penambra, and Dele—all the great centers of the wizardry of old—seemed to fit into a disquieting pattern. Shortly after Lohiro and the Council closed Quo to all, I went to him with my suppositions, and he, Anamara, and I searched the town and the Seaward Mountains for miles. We suspected that a Nest lay under the tower itself, under the subfloors of the old vaults, though we could find no sign of it. Still we three spelled and respelled the foundations of the tower. Believe me, Ingold, not even the winds of the Dark could have risen through the cracks in the floor, had we not been betrayed."

Those strange eyes rested for a moment on the old man's haggard face. "It was when we were spelling the mountains, I think, that Lohiro first spoke of the Dark as being of a single essence. We found little concerning them in the books, though my students turned the libraries inside out, breaking spells of opening on volumes whose very languages had been long forgotten and combing for something, anything—to little avail. But Lohiro watched in Anamara's mirror and saw the Dark Ones fight ·at Penambra and Gae. He said that their strength lay in their numbers and in their movements. He said that what one of them learned, they all then knew. He said this was clear when they left their northern Nests in the plains to join the assault on Gae.

"At first, he spoke of it only in terms of the maze—that we could not afford to let so much as a single Dark

One slip through its windings. But later, as cities and towns fell to the Dark and we found ourselve no nearer to an understanding of them that would enable our magic to work against them, he said that we must, at all costs, learn what their nature, their essence, was. He said that until one of us studied them by transformation, we could hold no hope for their defeat."

Ingold's face went white. "That was madness."

"So I told him," the Recorder said dryly. "But remember also that our backs were to the wall. There had been talk of going forth from Quo willy-nilly, to battle them without plan and ultimately without hope. Lohiro said that it would be madness for a weak man to take on a strong one, but he did not feel himself to be that much overmatched. He was proud, Ingold. Proud and desperate. You know he was ever one to throw his whole strength into a battle. Perhaps he thought that his own death was the worst that could befall.

"Then Gae fell. We watched it in Anamara's mirror; we saw you and Eldor and all the others cornered in the flaming Palace and we looked no more. It was deep night, close on to dawn. Lohiro left us sitting in the library, and my heart was so heavy I did not mark whether he went upstairs to his own study or down. I think it makes no difference.

"That day was bitter for us, Ingold. We sought you in the crystals throughout the daylight hours, Anamara and Hasrid and I, and we could find no sign of you. We mourned you for dead."

"I might as well have been dead." Ingold sighed. "I had passed the Void—I was in another universe entirely, I and Prince Tir. Did Lohiro seek me?"

Thoth shook his head. "That I do not know. None of us saw him that day. Toward evening, there was talk of going to Karst, where we saw the refugees gathering. We knew the Dark would strike there and that the only wizard within hundreds of miles was Bektis. We were still speaking of this when darkness fell."

The old Recorder fell silent again, his queer yellow eyes grown distant and pale. In the flickering witchlight, others had gathered around, silent, hardly breathing. Ingold's mouth was taut, his face drained of blood as if from

287

some internal wound. Through him, Rudy saw again the ruin of that small and peaceful city, smelled the autumn sweetness of the vines grown wild over colored stones, and heard the hushed rumbling of the sea.

"I do not know at what time that day Lohiro took the form of the Dark," Thoth went on quietly. "I only know that in the deeps of the night we were still gathered in the tower, talking of what was best to do. Then the walls shook with the echoes of a blast that sounded as if the foundations of the tower itself were ripping asunder, as if the earth beneath us were exploding. I think I rose, but no one else had time to move. The doors of the library were flung open, and I saw Lohiro framed in them, his eyes blank and empty, like blue-green glass; behind him lay such a storm of the Dark as I have never seen. He was the Archmage—he held the Master-Spells over us all." He shook his head. "And it was over.

"I think Anamara tried to fight him. I saw her face outlined for an instant in a burst of light against the darkness. But I knew there was no hope if Lohiro had taken into himself the essence of the Dark. So, as that terrible whirlwind of power fell upon the room, I turned myself into a grass snake, the lowliest and swiftest creature I could think of. My perceptions of what happened after that are not human perceptions. I knew only darkness and cries, fire and bursting lights. The tower crumbled around us. Lohiro faded into one of the Dark and whirled away into the night. From the rubble, I saw darkness covering the town and great columns of fire, smothered and sapped by blackness and magic. Hasrid was a dragon. Others took different forms to fight, but Lohiro's power and the Dark confounded them all. But none of that was important to me then. I was a serpent, with only a serpent's fears and hungers. I was cold and I hid in the rubble until dawn."

There was silence again. In the dim bluish shadows, Rudy could see several of the other mages in tears—for the Archmage, for the world whose fringes they had been on, and for the dream of that vanished city to which they had once all aspired. But Ingold's tears had been shed in the Seaward Mountains, and he looked only empty and exhausted, as he had looked in the desert.

Thoth's golden eyes returned to an awareness of the

present. "Have you ever spent time in another being, Ingold?"

Ingold nodded. No one else moved.

"Then you will understand that, after that, time meant very little to me. How long it took me to leave the Seaward Mountains, I do not know. The eaters of little insects do not count days. In part of my mind, I knew I was a man and a wizard, but there was very little in me that cared. Perhaps it was only mourning. I hid in the rocks and moved alone through wet grasses and rain. I was nothing . . . nothing. But I must have known I was a man, for I traveled slowly east, and I was far out in the desert when the yearning came to me to seek the Keep of Dare in Renweth at Sarda Pass. It was a man's yearning, far beyond what a snake could feel or accomplish. Yet such was its force that I knew that I could go there only as a man. So a man I became.

"I did not know," he finished quietly, "that the call came from you, my friend."

Ingold sighed. "Perhaps it were better had you kept your belly to the ground, serpentmage."

A single line, as fine as a pen-scratch in the corner of the long, wry mouth, briefly indicated a smile. "It is easier to live off the land so," Thoth replied, "but the company becomes boring. Nevertheless, I shall carry to my grave a horror of the road runner bird."

"Yes," Ingold agreed reminiscently. "I recall I had nightmares about dogs for many years."

"Eh?" a thin voice creaked. Nan the witchwife appeared suddenly in the circle, her pale eyes sparking with malice. "So, shall I get you some nice cricket soup, serpentmage? Or you some fat mice, Sir Tomcat? Or will you stand here talking until you fall down from hunger?"

"Mother!" Kara said, shocked. "That's—"

"I know who it is, girl," the old lady snapped sharply. "And I'm saying, let the poor men eat, before they go to trading war stories about how brave they all were." Her bent back forced her to twist her neck to look up at them, and Rudy found himself thinking that all she needed was a peaked black hat and a broomstick.

"Thank you," Ingold said gravely. "Your care for our comfort touches my heart."

"Huh!" she grumbled and bustled away toward the cubbyhole that Rudy guessed must be the communal kitchen. In the doorway she swung around again, shaking her wooden spoon at them, her thick cobwebs of grayish-white hair falling down over her bony shoulders and her eyes glittering in her haglike face. "Heart indeed!" she cackled. "Wizards have no heart. And I tell you true, for I'm one and I haven't any more heart than a shrike." With that she flounced out of sight.

"She's right," Ingold said mildly. Thoth looked shocked, but Kta laughed.

"Alwir subsidizes the Wizards' Corps, the same way he does the Guards," Gil explained as Kara, her mother, and a thin little red-haired girl served them oatbread and stew from a common pot. "Bektis still dines up at the high table—I suppose because the food's better—but I expect both he and Alwir will be along later." She grinned across the room at Alde, who sat cross-legged on a pile of bison and mammoth hides between Rudy and the sleeping Prince Tir, sharing the wizards' rough-and-ready feast. Fire flickered on the hearth, the room's only illumination, brightening over the assorted features of the very odd crew assembled there.

At Alde's side, Rudy felt that, with very little more provocation, he'd start purring like a cat. It was the first time in over two months that he'd faced the prospect of a night's sleep without four hours of guard duty first; he was bathed, shaved, and stationary, and the novelty of that was pleasant enough. He was with the woman he loved and among his own kind at last, after a journey he had never thought he'd survive. It would be odd, he mused, to sleep under a roof.

His hand sought Alde's under the furs. She glanced sideways at him and smiled.

Profiled against the dim light, Alde looked different, more sure of herself—*less pretty but more beautiful,* Rudy thought illogically. Gil had changed, too, he decided, glancing over at the thin girl sitting like some scrawny teen-age boy on the floor beside Ingold's chair. She was softer, somehow, though physically she was like a leather strap. Her eyes were gentler, but there was a firm line to her mouth that spoke of bitter experience and knowledge that she could never unknow.

Well, what the hell, he thought. *We've all changed. Even old Ingold.*

Maybe one day the old man would regain the amused serenity with which he had once viewed the world. Quo had broken something inside him that Rudy sensed was only partially healed. After his first flood of greetings and information, Ingold had relapsed into silence; throughout supper, he had spoken very little. This was not to say the room was quiet; once the initial chorus of chomping noises had died down, there had been news to exchange, stories to tell, and adventures to recount, most of these among Rudy, Gil, and Alde.

Now and then the old man's eyes traveled from face to face—not judging what this strange rabble was good for, though that would come. Now Ingold was only getting to know them—the goodywives and tea leaf readers, the two-and-thirty second-raters who had happened to miss the destruction of Quo, plus its single austere survivor, one wizened old hermit, and one punk airbrush-jockey who'd stumbled into the middle of his destiny by mistake. This was all the force Ingold would have to work with, all the magic left in the world for his command.

No wonder he looks like death warmed over, Rudy thought.

"Now," Ingold said finally, in the meal's comfortable afterglow, tightening his hand, which had come to rest easily on Gil's shoulder. "Show me these marvels you have found."

As if on cue, Gil and Alde leaped to their feet. "We've got them in the back here," Gil said, showing the way. "That door there leads into the room where we found the stairway down to the labs; we usually keep it bolted. We put our things in here . . ." Most of the other wizards had already seen their trawlings from the laboratories and storerooms and so remained in the common room. Some of them—Thoth, Kta, and Kara—followed Rudy, Ingold, and the girls through a dusty little cubbyhole scarcely wider than a hallway and into a kind of storeroom, where a plank table had been set up, laden with the mysteries from below. As they entered, a bluish drift of witchlight bloomed around them—the rooms of the Wizards' Corps were the only ones in the Keep to have decent lighting. Scattered across the table were vessels, boxes, chains of bubbled glass, apparatus of glass balls and gold rods, twining knots of metal tubes, sinuous pieces of meaningless sculpture, and slick, unexplainable polyhedrons, white and smoked.

"These were what blew us away the most," Gil said, picking up one of the white shapes and tossing it to Ingold. "They were everywhere—under the machinery in the pump rooms, in piles in the storerooms, and strung in nets over the tanks in the hydroponic gardens. So far, the only thing they're good for is that Tir likes to play with them."

"Indeed." Ingold turned the polyhedron in his fingers for a moment, as if testing its weight or proportions. Then, quite suddenly, it glowed to life in his hands, the soft, white radiance of it warming the angles of his wind-darkened face. He tossed it to Gil, who caught it ineptly on cringing palms. It was quite cool.

"Lamps," he said.

"Oh . . ." Gil breathed, entranced. "Oh, how beautiful! But how did the ancients turn them on and off? How do the things work?" She looked up at him, the light glowing brightly out of her cupped hands, illuminating her thin face.

"I should imagine they simply covered them when they wanted darkness," Ingold said. "The material itself is spelled to hold the light for a long time and can be kindled by a very simple means. Someone on the lowest echelons of wizardry, like a firebringer or a finder, could do it."

"Hmmm." Rudy picked up one of the white crystals on the table and studied the bottom facet. "You should have figured that out, Gil. It says 'one hundred watts' right here."

"Hit him for me, Alde. But I really should have figured it out, because I always did wonder about how the Keep was originally lighted. And there are hydroponic gardens down in the subvaults, room after room of them, with no light source at all—"

"You ever grow marijuana in a closet?" Rudy inquired, apropos of nothing.

292

"Hey, around my place the only things that grew in closets were mushrooms. But, Ingold, with this kind of light we could get the gardens going again. With hydroponics, we could grow carloads of stuff in almost no space; and down there it's warm enough to do it."

"You could draw off power from the pumps to heat the tanks," Rudy added. "And to heat water, for that matter."

"Yes, but we never did manage to find the main power source."

"It would have been magically hidden and sealed," Ingold said, interrupting a discussion that threatened to become increasingly technical. "At a guess, the pumps operate on the same principle as the lamps. The wizards of old times could probably alter the essence of materials and enable them to hold something—light, or some other force—for incredible periods of time."

Gil looked thoughtful. "You mean this whole Keep operates on the principle of a giant footwarmer?"

"Essentially."

"Fantastic," Rudy said, turning away from them to investigate the bits and pieces of glass and metalwork that strewed the table behind him. Alde reached tentatively around Gil's arm to remove the glowing polyhedron from her hands.

"Do you know what this really means?" she asked softly. "It means no more wandering around the corridors in the dark . . . or worry about setting the place on fire . . ."

"It means I won't have to go blind from reading those goddam books by the light of a spoonful of burning Crisco, is what it means." Gil was about to take another crystal polyhedron from the table when she froze, her movement arrested halfway. "What the hell . . . ?"

Rudy turned from the table, his face glowing with pride. Hefted in his hands were four or five of the miscellaneous objects Alde had brought up from the lab, now fitted together, ends and pieces mating to form something very similar to a huge and clumsy rifle.

"What is it?" Alde walked around the thing, passing in front of the muzzle with the unconcern of one who had never entertained the concept of a gun in her life. Rudy instinctively raised the muzzle to avoid pointing it at her.

293

"It's a—a—" There was no word for it in the Wathe. "It shoots things out of the hole at the end there."

"Shoots what?" Gil demanded, coming over to look. She touched the large glass bubble that fitted into the fluid curve of the stock. "What kind of firing chamber does it have?"

Rudy peered down the hoselike barrel. "I don't know," he said, "but I can guess." He set the gun upright at his side, like a rifleman on parade. "My guess is that it shoots fire. What other kind of gun would you use on the Dark?"

"It's a flame thrower." There were words in the Wathe for that.

"Yeah. And my guess is that it worked on magic."

"You mean," Alde broke in excitedly, "that this—flame thrower—could spurt fire out of the end?"

"With the barrel to channel it," Ingold mused, taking the gun and sighting awkwardly along the barrel, his hands competent on the smooth, triggerless stock. "The flame could go much farther than a wizard could throw it. But what would fuel such a flame?"

"I don't know," Rudy said eagerly, his voice rising with excitement, "but if there's a laboratory downstairs, I'm sure as hell gonna find out. Ingold, think about it! You've been telling me all along about a—a third echelon of the mageborn, about people who don't have but maybe one little bit of power. The firebringers and goodwords and finders, people who never developed their skill because the Church frowned on it and there were either trained wizards or just ordinary human civilization to cover for them. But it isn't like that anymore. I bet we could get up a flame thrower corps between the wizards we have here and the firebringers we could round up in the Keep! Ingold, this is it! We didn't have to trek out to Quo at all! The answer was right here all the time!"

"If this is the answer," Thoth said in his driest voice, "why was it not used upon the Dark three thousand years ago?"

Brought up short, Rudy looked uncertain and deflated.

The Recorder of Quo folded bony arms, his yellow eyes glittering in the gloom. "In all of our researches at Quo, I found no mention of such a thing being used against the Dark. It is my belief that you hold in your hands an experiment that failed."

"Or that was never performed," Alde said suddenly. "Because—well, Gil and I have found lots of places here, the labs downstairs especially, but the pump rooms, too, that look as if they were abandoned very quickly. They didn't get taken over by other things. They were just locked up and left."

"But why?" asked Kara, who had been standing quietly all this time, watching Kta pick through the smaller jewels in their boxes on the table.

"I don't know," Alde replied, "but I *think* something happened to the—the engineer-wizards who built the Keep. I think the Church had them exiled or killed. If it happened suddenly, they might have left the flame throwers downstairs and never returned to finish them."

"That's hardly intelligent," Kara protested.

"Neither was imprisoning me in the vaults beneath Karst on the eve of an attack by the Dark," Ingold pointed out acidly. "But we are dealing with fanatics . . . or with *a* fanatic, in this case."

There was an uncomfortable silence. Rudy cleared his throat. "Uh—how much chance would you say there is of that happening again?"

Ingold's eyes glinted with mischief. "Worried?"

"No—I mean, yes. I mean . . ."

"Don't be—yet. We have convinced Alwir that we have our uses, without which his invasion of the Nests must come to a standstill."

"What?" Rudy asked bluntly. "We're all the magic he's got and, present company excepted, it ain't much."

"Really, Rudy," Ingold said, and there was an echo of the old serenity, the old control, in the droop of his heavy eyelids. "What else would a Wizards' Corps be for? Military intelligence, of course."

"Holy hell," Rudy whispered.

"Ingold!" Dakis the Minstrel's voice called down the short passageway. Others joined it. "My lord Ingold?"

There was a quick flurry of skirts, and the red-haired witchchild appeared in the doorway, her dark eyes huge. "Me lord Alwir's here," she breathed. "Be askin' also for me lady Minalde."

Alde sighed, and Rudy thought she braced herself just slightly; a tiny fold of tiredness manifested at the corner of her eye.

He smiled wryly. "Sure is nice to be home." As he had hoped, it made her laugh.

"Catch," Ingold said. He lighted and threw a polyhedron of milky light to Rudy, ignited another and tossed it to Alde, then passed a third to the red-haired girl. A dazzling halo ringed them as they passed through the door, with Kara, Kta, and Thoth following, their shadows streaming long and black behind them. From beyond in the common room, a mingling of voices could be heard. Laughter blended with Nan's scolding and the light, dancing runs of Dakis' lute. Ingold went to the table, kindled a fourth lamp, and held it out to Gil.

"Thank you," he said softly. "You have done very well."

She took it, as she had once taken his glowing staff, and the soft brilliance of it poured out between the shadowed bones of her fingers. "Ingold?"

"Yes, child?"

"One thing I've always wanted to ask you."

"What is it?"

She started to speak, then stopped, confused and unable to go on, her pale, intolerant eyes unusually blue in the radiance of the lamp. What she did say might or might not have been her original intention. "Was there some reason you asked me to back you up, the night the Dark attacked the Keep? I know it was you who kept the light on the staff alive, but was there a reason you had me hold it?"

Ingold was silent for some time and did not meet her gaze. "Yes," he said finally, "and it was inexcusable of me to ask you to back me, for it was my doing in the first place that brought you here, and I had no right to place you in peril."

She shrugged. "It doesn't matter."

"No," he said bitterly. "God knows, I've done it often enough."

The bleak guilt in his voice and the self-hatred troubled and frightened her. She caught his hand in her free one, to draw his eyes to hers. "You do what you have to do," she told him gently. "You know I'd follow you anywhere."

296

"And that," Ingold said, his scratchy voice suddenly taut, "is precisely why I asked you." But the tension was caused by something in himself, and his tone softened again. "You were the only one I could trust, Gil, not to flee."

"That's a lot of trust," Gil said quietly, "for somebody you'd known only a month."

Ingold nodded. "But there are times, my dear, when I feel that I have known you all my life."

They stood thus for a moment longer, wizard and warrior, with Ingold holding Gil's fingers gently against the tips of his own. In his eyes she could read the tracks of the journey—pain and loneliness, and only the ghost of the old serenity which had once characterized him. A hint of another emotion was strange to her.

What he read in her eyes she did not know, but it made him look away quickly and drape his arm across her shoulders. He led her out through the maze to the voices and the lights.

About the Author

At various times in her life, Barbara Hambly has been a high-school teacher, a model, a waitress, a technical editor, a professional graduate student, an all-night clerk at a liquor store, and a karate instructor. Born in San Diego, she grew up in Southern California, with the exception of one high-school semester spent in New South Wales, Australia. Her interest in fantasy began with reading *The Wizard of Oz* at the age of six and graduated in natural stages through Burroughs, Tolkien, *Star Trek,* and Heinlein, and she has been writing fantasy almost as long as she has been reading it.

She attended the University of California, Riverside, specializing in medieval history. In connection with this, she spent a year at the University of Bordeaux in the south of France and worked as a teaching and research assistant at UC Riverside for two years, eventually earning a Master's Degree in the subject. At the university she also became involved in karate, making black belt in 1978 and going on to compete in several national-level tournaments.

Ms. Hambly currently resides in Riverside, California. In addition to writing and karate, her hobbies include sewing, painting, Regency dancing, and reading Tarot cards.